HAWK ISLAND

BOOK 1 *of The* HAWK ISLAND SERIES

MANUELA DACOSTA

ARCHWAY
PUBLISHING

Archway Publishing books may be ordered through booksellers or by contacting:

Archway Publishing
1663 Liberty Drive
Bloomington, IN 47403
www.archwaypublishing.com
1 (888) 242-5904

ISBN: 978-1-4808-5640-0 (sc)
ISBN: 978-1-4808-5641-7 (e)

Library of Congress Control Number: 2017919764

Print information available on the last page.

Archway Publishing rev. date: 02/14/2018

The spider jumped over the sea
From Brazil to Italy
From end to end, she roamed the earth
Hid her wares in limpets and firth
And counted the gold of a sunken ship
And left the grace of a given kiss
To weave a web on the darkened lip
Of a Hawk on a precipice

For my family and friends, who were my first readers:

Bob, Margarida, Sheila, Dalila, Janis, Julia, Claudia, Lara, Monica, Sandra, and Kerry

1

Hawk Island

Hawk Island stood in the middle of the Atlantic, small and defiant, like its people. No conqueror, no empire, no force of nature could bend this place of black lava and green pastures—and the sea, vigilant and vindictive, had tried.

Two Brooks, the most isolated village in Hawk Island, was perched on the highest elevation, surrounded by high cliffs and flanked at each end by a brook, hence its name. It was a village of tenacious people, hardened by isolation and punished by nature with crude winters and burning droughts. It was a place forsaken by God and men.

After Father Inácio died, the Bishop Dom Aurélio made many attempts to place a priest in Two Brooks, one who could withstand not only the village but also its people. Young priests succumbed to tuberculosis, melancholia, madness, and suicide; more mature priests died of heart attacks, gout, thrombosis, and indigestion.

While the bishop desperately tried to find a moral leader for Two Brooks, he imposed the village on the neighboring priests, who celebrated Mass and officiated funerals and christenings on the run, as if at any moment something unforeseen would happen.

Father Benedito, the priest for Little Branch village, was a benevolent man who had come straight from the seminary to Little Branch. He, too, believed that Two Brooks could turn a saint into a devil and a sane man into a lunatic. Any priest who came to stay had to be both in order to survive.

Monsignor Inocente came to Hawk Island many years ago from the mainland. Some say that he had a secret to bury or a sorrow to drown, but whatever brought him to Hawk Island also rooted him in Two Brooks. He vowed to turn Two Brooks into a beacon of virtue—if not by faith, at least by fear. And so the monsignor, tenacious and inflexible, loved all and punished all with the same sense of justice and creed. Two Brooks would be a God-fearing place, and God-fearing its inhabitants were, most of the time. Like a piece of beautiful wood, Two Brooks needed an artist to carve it into a remarkable village. Monsignor Inocente thought he was that artist. Just like everything else in life, it's not what is, but what we *think* it is that makes things true.

The monsignor started by demanding that every child have an education. Children would not leave school before they knew how to read, write, and do math. And if they wanted a higher education, the monsignor would provide for that as well. The monsignor was irascible, intolerant, and punitive, but he never lost sight of two things—the purity of the soul, and the belief that the human condition could only be improved through education. He demanded that children who left school without a completed diploma return if they were younger than fifteen years of age. Girls and boys who thought they were adults and saw themselves as ready for marriage found themselves sitting again at the same desks that they had left years before. Most cried with dismay and horror once again to face Dona Lidia, the teacher for Two Brooks, who had brutalized the children for more than thirty years. Between Dona Lidia's methods and the monsignor's dedication to education, Two Brooks became the most literate village in the whole archipelago.

But what could the monsignor do with so many literate people? They needed books to read, they needed to be challenged with creative ways, and they needed substance to entertain their minds. So he established a library in his house for everyone. Later he founded a public library, the only library in that part of the island.

The village also formed a theater group that became familiar with Molière and Shakespeare; they learned music and had a classically inclined philharmonic that perfected somber pieces in minor keys. If one wanted to listen to something beautiful and sad, they went to Two Brooks to listen to the philharmonic.

The Music Club House became the center for all functions in the village, and the monsignor became the head, the authority, the voice, the defender, and the advocate of all causes. It was known throughout the island that to offend one person from Two Brooks was to offend the monsignor.

Dom Aurélio, aware that Monsignor Inocente had to use unorthodox methods to keep Two Brooks in line, couldn't keep himself from intervening with suggestions and admonitions, forgetting that something could happen to the monsignor, as it had to so many others, and the villagers would be *priestless* again and left to their own devices of civil disobedience and moral defiance. Between the two men, there rose a wall of resentment; the monsignor resented the bishop for coming to him with tried and failed strategies of obedience, and the bishop resented the monsignor because he was turning into a rogue priest, constantly calling attention to the village, becoming more and more like one of the villagers.

Like all formidable men, the monsignor had foes, the bishop being only one. The other was far, far worse, and this foe he could not overcome—Night Justice.

The people in Two Brooks were so engrained in their right to punish those who they felt deserved punishment that no punishment or penance from the monsignor would dissuade them from their right to deliver justice as they saw fit. And once in a while there was a wave of Night Justice punishments that left the monsignor speechless.

The monsignor was again in the throes of a terrible suspicion—Dona Lidia's death. His first thought was that finally Night Justice had gotten to her. But then again, anyone could have. He himself had enough reasons to murder the woman.

What would he say to the coroner? Heart attack? Thrombosis? Poison? Fatal fall? Natural death or not?

Murder was a natural death for Dona Lidia, because so much hate could only result in murder. Never had he seen a person who was hated that much. Most of the villagers had started to hate Dona Lidia when they were children, and they held that hatred in their hearts into their adulthood. They grew into it as part of their nature. But he couldn't tell the coroner that hate was the cause of death. "Death by universal hate"—could he say that to the coroner?

Dona Lidia had been born in Two Brooks and was as old as time. When she had gone to the city to be educated, the very first thing she'd wanted to learn was sign language. After she had learned it, she had taught her mother, who no longer had to express herself with grunts and yelps of frustration.

Dona Lidia had become the teacher for the village before the monsignor had become their priest.

Father Inácio, who'd died with an attack of gout, was said to be Dona Lidia's father. This sin was never really proven because people were afraid of the teacher and of the priest.

Dona Lidia's mother, Adelaide—an inconsequential, forgotten, sad, and mute woman—was the natural victim for a predator. Some say that Father Inácio made a pact with her: She would never reveal that he was the father, and in turn, he would provide for her child.

And so he did.

Adelaide, like most of the villagers at that time, didn't know how to read and write, and being a mute, she was mostly disregarded. She served Father

Inácio as the cleaning woman and cook. When the village mute became pregnant, the church became empty. They all knew who the father was.

Father Inácio woke up one morning to find a bowl and knife at the door. This was the bowl and knife that the villagers used to bleed pigs after slaughter.

He called the whole village into church. Between gestures and screams, he put Adelaide in front of the congregation and pointed to her swollen belly. Adelaide pointed to the sea.

"This child is the product of a sin, a sailor from overseas who took advantage of Adelaide. I am a man of the cloth! I am an honorable man!" he screamed.

Adelaide continued to point to the sea when stared at, and her daughter was born incarnating all the rage and fury that Adelaide felt. Some say that, at a very early age, Dona Lidia wrote her mother's story and used it to control Father Inácio.

Two Brooks, like all villages, was a place of gossip and speculation, especially if it had to do with those in authority. So the fact that Adelaide's story was written and hidden somewhere could just be gossip. The reality was that Dona Lidia had free rein in the village, even over Father Inácio, and when he died, she cried copiously, as one does for a father.

Monsignor Inocente was praying, knees on the floor, in front of an altar decorated with wildflowers. The crucified Christ gleamed in His glory of pain. The women had taken down the cross and scrubbed Jesus and then applied a good wax that Jaime Nobre had brought from the American base. For a split second, the monsignor admired the results of the wax. Jesus had never shone so brightly.

The monsignor returned to the torments of his thoughts. He was feeling abandoned, forsaken by a God who seemed only peripherally interested in Two Brooks. At times, the monsignor's faith was tested to its last degree, and this was one of those times.

Dona Lidia and Mario were dead, and Mario had left behind a widow, Felicidade, and Ascendida, who was with child—Mario's love child. The Rocha family was swept to sea, leaving a little girl behind. Angela Gomes was being defiant, the Barcos family was under siege by Pedro Matias because of Madalena and Manuel, and Joaquim Machado was possessed by the devil, again. This type of demon, however, was the least of the monsignor's worries.

The most terrible of all things was the man from overseas who, like a demon, was spinning his own hell.

The monsignor raised his eyes again to Jesus. The wax had cleared the dirt so well that Jesus looked cross-eyed. His eyeballs were unnaturally large. Everyone was surprised when they realized that Jesus had his eyes open on the cross, now that the dirt was gone.

The Monsignor missed his nonstaring, dead Jesus.

Angela Gomes was looking at Jesus also, kneeling next to the monsignor.

"Those eyes …" she whispered.

"What do you want, child?" he asked.

"What do I want, always, from you?" she asked.

"I am not helping you this time. Your parents are right. You are too young, and you have your studies to finish."

"Please, Monsignor. I have to do this," she said.

The monsignor didn't answer her.

"Do you want me to live in sin?" she asked, placing her hands together in prayer and still looking at Jesus. *Dear Jesus*, she silently prayed, *he is going to slap me again. Make it painless.*

An exasperated monsignor pulled her up by the upper arm and forced her to look at him. The monsignor slapped her across the face, once, twice. Angela didn't say anything. She could feel the ringing in her ears and the echo in the empty church, like shots: *Someone is hunting rabbit*, she said to herself.

"I want to marry Lazarus," she insisted.

"You are too young!" he screamed.

"We've been sleeping together for years," she said, almost in a murmur.

"I don't believe you!" he screamed again. "You say that just to get your way."

"His father will kill him one of these days," she answered evenly.

"Angela," the monsignor said trying to sound reasonable, "you can't save the world; you can't change the fact that Pedro Matias is a brute."

"Please," she said, "please help us."

"Even if I agree and convince your parents, you still have Pedro to contend with."

"I'll deal with Pedro," she said.

And Angela told a dumfounded monsignor what she had done to Pedro Matias. The monsignor knew that it was just a matter of hours before the police and that brute Pedro would be looking for him. He sat with a thump on a pew.

The monsignor had never seen or met anyone like Angela. He had never loved a person like he loved her, as if she was his own daughter. He had fallen in love with that child the first time she'd looked at him with those stubborn, knowing eyes.

Once he had known someone with eyes like that …

"Go home child," he said tired and defeated.

Angela gave Jesus one last look. "He looks ridiculous," she said, pointing to the cross. "If one was being crucified, one's eyes wouldn't be open."

And she left after the pronouncement.

The winter came with rain and punitive winds that year, the year when the Rocha family died, all of them, from the baby to the grandfather, taken by the swollen brook and disappearing before a screaming village. Only Rosa had survived because she was in bed nursing a bad cold. Had she been on the small bridge over the Church Brook like her family, she would have been swept away by the angry, noisy, and dark water.

It was then, on that sad day, that Monsignor Inocente had given Aldo and Ascendida their first child—Rosa, the child so tragically orphaned. And Rosa, who was once gregarious, had become sullen and reserved. But love always finds a way out of darkness, and Rosa was loved by all, especially by Ascendida and Aldo, who hoped that Rosa would slowly forget about her brothers and sisters, about her parents and grandparents, lost in the deep sea. The future would allow Rosa to think that she had been born to Ascendida and Aldo. Only the nightmares would speak of her past, along with her fear of water, of the sea, and of the brook when it rained.

Ascendida was an only child. And being an only child, she swore to have many children to keep each other's company. Rosa was their first. Ascendida had been the one to go to the monsignor and ask to take Rosa in. At first, the monsignor was not sure if a young couple could deal with a nine-year-old recently orphaned. But Ascendida and Aldo had insisted, and so they had become parents just a few months after their wedding day.

Of course this was one story; the rumor was that the monsignor had given Ascendida a penance for being pregnant before getting married, and the penance was Rosa.

Ascendida remembered when she'd first loved Aldo. She was crying because Mario, the boy she had loved all her life, had gotten married. Mario had loved Ascendida and Felicidade at once and could not decide who to marry. But one day, he had decided. And later he had died, killed by a bull.

Aldo said, "Love me, Ascendida. Love me instead."

It was such a bewildering thing to say that she stopped crying and looked at him for the first time. She had gone to school with Aldo, they were neighbors, they'd played under the rain and under the sun, but she had never looked at him, not really, because Mario had taken everything she was. She'd had no room, not even for herself.

Ascendida and Aldo got married right after she finished school, getting her degree in nursing, just in time also for her condition. Now she was the village nurse, the one who brought the villagers back to health from cuts and bruises, colds and coughs, broken limbs, and infectious diseases.

Aldo didn't like school; he always thought it was a tedious place and a dangerous one if he had to face people like Dona Lidia. He worked the fields and sold his crops to the city market. He was a beautiful man with a penchant for drinking, was well liked, and had the soul of a lover, who lived in the shadow of his brother Mario. As soon as both brothers reached puberty, they wanted Ascendida. And when Aldo lost, he quietly cried, nursing a glass of moonshine.

Ascendida looked at the silent funerary carriage rolling somberly up the street, pulled by two men, as if they were horses. Not even a squeaky wheel denounced its passing. Mario's coffin, placed on the carriage, looked too small for a man like Mario. He'd had so much energy and love for life that it seemed impossible that he could fit in that box.

Felicidade, the widow, walking behind the carriage, with her eyes glued on the coffin, made terrible sounds, as if she was wounded, pierced, impaled on that cruel truth.

Everyone went to the funeral, except the very old and the postpartum. But they too could not distance themselves from that sorrow carried in Felicidade's voice. The villagers closed their eyes, squeezing out hot tears, keeping their eyes shut for a few seconds, to ward off that terrible procession.

Mario had been killed by a bull, in the middle of the village on the last day of the festivities, a bright November afternoon. He had been picked up by the bull, thrown high up and had fallen down on the stone-paved center of the village. His head had cracked open, and a puddle of blood had circled it like a halo.

Mario was buried, the funerary carriage was cleaned and put away, the gates of the cemetery were closed, and the flowers wilted on his grave. But they all knew that Mario was going to be around in their homes, in their beds, for Christmas and carnival, because his place was irremediably vacant, calling out their attention.

They all got home completely spent from that funeral. They were bewildered by their loss and by Felicidade being so publicly undone, screaming behind the coffin. Felicidade, always so composed, had screamed from one end of the village to the other end all of the things that should have been private.

But there was something else about Mario that only Aldo and Ascendida knew.

When Ascendida got home from Mario's funeral, she was saying his name between breaths of rage and disbelief, denouncing God as cruel and capricious.

Ophelia, Ascendida's mother, believed that Felicidade had won that battle of love and that Ascendida had accepted it and moved on. But now, looking at her daughter disintegrating with sorrow, she didn't know if she was right.

Ascendida cried just as hard as Felicidade, and Felicidade was Mario's wife.

Ophelia's hand, white and soft, caressed the tablecloth, and Ascendida thought that the last time she had washed that tablecloth Mario had been alive. The last time she had washed the kitchen floor, Mario had been alive. The bread in the cupboard was baked when Mario was alive. And everything for Ascendida was going to be between Mario being alive and Mario gone.

"Poor Felicidade!" Ophelia said, her big, gray eyes searching her daughter's face.

Ophelia was small and quiet and had an obsessive love for her daughter.

When Ascendida was a child, she carried her home from the church in her small arms. Ophelia huffed and puffed but never put her daughter down, assuming that Ascendida was saturated from the sermons and long masses and could not help but be tired and sleepy.

People would say, "Shame on you. Can't you see that you are too big to be carried? Get down! Can't you see that your poor mother can hardly walk?"

And it was the truth. Ophelia grunted and huffed at each irregularity on the road but would not put Ascendida down. While the other mothers dragged their kids after them, some soaked with urine and others crying, Ophelia carried Ascendida in her arms all the way home.

Ascendida's feet hit right below Ophelia's knees, and between that sweet rhythm of Ophelia's steps and the shame of being carried home in her mother's arms, Ascendida slept and only woke up the next morning in her soft bed made of new corn husk and fresh moss.

Ophelia, so small, so dedicated, so unassuming, wished she could absorb her daughter's pain. She wished she could strike a deal with God. She touched Ascendida's arm and murmured, "Give it time."

Poor Felicidade.

Life had always been so straight, her path evenly paved, the horizon clear. And suddenly, everything had changed, as if luck had repented.

Felicidade was the other side of Ascendida—in school, in the catechism classes, in the festivities of Our Lady of Lourdes, in the Milk Feasts, and bullfights. Everywhere Ascendida was, she was there in relation to where Felicidade was—like a compass.

Felicidade was beautiful, rich, smart, and assertive. Her beauty gave her the opportunity of a second look. No one could look at Felicidade just once. Her skin was white and clear, her blue eyes like the sky in spring, and her red hair impeccably braided. She dressed only in the best—shiny shoes, soft pastels, delicate fabrics, just like the Americans. She could be the ballerina on top of a music box.

Dona Lidia's voice softened when she talked to Felicidade, and if Felicidade made a mistake, Dona Lidia would say, "Try again, my dear. I know you know the answer." And when Felicidade finally got the answer right, the whole class let out a sigh of relief because the status quo was intact: Felicidade was so perfect that even Dona Lidia thought so.

Ophelia told Ascendida every day that she was beautiful, but Ascendida measured beauty by Felicidade's beauty. Ophelia told Ascendida that she was smart, but smart was the one who never got hit by Dona Lidia. In the catechism classes, Dona Teresa rested the stick on her shoulder when she heard Felicidade's prayers. Ascendida tried hard to say the prayers in the same way, but somehow, Dona Teresa thought that she said it too fast, too slow, too loud, or without conviction, and Dona Teresa hit her with the stick right on the middle of the head, leaving her dizzy.

One day, Ascendida decided not to live with Felicidade as her nightmare. She was going to give her a good beating, destroy that composure, and undo those braids. She was going to see Felicidade pulverized by life's cruelties, as Ascendida had been so many times. Felicidade was going to learn that life was not made of pastel colors.

That day, maybe because Ascendida was distracted with the preparations for the attack on Felicidade, Dona Lidia almost killed Ascendida with a spanking. Felicidade didn't even look; she had her head down, as if that tragedy had nothing to do with her.

Ascendida could see Dona Lidia's ruler up and down in the air, she could hear the noise it made on her body, but she was busy praying. Maybe God wanted to give her a lesson in humility, or He just didn't care at all about her pride, because Ascendida felt her body give up, and she urinated on herself.

Dona Lidia, perplexed, stopped with her hand up in the air, "Felicidade, go and call Mrs. Iracema," she ordered.

Mrs. Iracema, thin, inflexible, and judgmental, came in making sucking sounds against her teeth and shaking her head in disapproval.

Ascendida went home to change, and when her mother saw her beloved daughter with a broken lip and a torn earlobe, she cried. "That horse! I'm going to kill that horse!" She hugged and kissed Ascendida, inspecting every inch of her body to make sure that no injury went unkissed.

When Ascendida got back to school, there were dried figs on her desk. She looked distractedly at the figs, still plotting to beat happiness out of Felicidade. Feeling cowardly, she gave the figs to Rita for Rita to beat up Felicidade.

Rita was a menace and consequently had no problem creating mayhem. She could beat up the whole school without an incentive. She had, on a regular basis, beaten up Ascendida, Madalena, Nascimento, and Angela. Such choleric ways were attributed to the fact that she lived with her mother in a village close to the American base that serviced American military men; and that was no environment for a decent girl.

Rita's godmother, who lived in Two Brooks, came to her rescue many times and for reasons that people could only imagine. But Rita's mother—after months without a word—would turn up in Two Brooks to claim her daughter, who kicked and screamed but was taken away again to the village that serviced American military men.

At the end of the school day, Ascendida ran out in haste. She wanted to witness from afar Felicidade's beating. But what she saw, coming around the curb, were three people walking placidly, eating *her* figs and laughing about her.

"It was like she didn't pee for three days," Rita said calmly as if she was talking about the weather.

"Poor thing," Mario murmured.

"Poor thing my ass," Rita said. "That fool pisses herself for the most little thing!"

Ascendida felt a tremendous rage grab her by the throat, pulling her over the wall where she was hiding. With a long whip and her dog, she attacked Rita as if she was Sancho Panza destroying a windmill. While the dog ripped Rita's dress, Ascendida lifted the whip up in the air and let it whistle down on Rita's legs, shoulders, and back. Rita, terrorized by the attack, screamed. She ran down the street, pursued by Ascendida, while Mario grabbed Felicidade by the shoulders and watched in horror, their mouths hanging open and full of figs.

"Kill! Kill!" Ascendida screamed orders to the dog.

Rita, totally betrayed by such reversal of fate, ran away, pursued by Ascendida and the dog. The afternoon sun elongated their running shadows on the road until they disappeared down the hill.

Mario and Felicidade unglued themselves from the wall. They spit out the figs, and with small steps, they too disappeared down the hill, following Rita's screams, the dog's barks, and Ascendida's whip swirling up in the air and cracking down either on Rita or on the dusty road.

The following day, Rita showed up in school, flagellated. Dona Lidia looked at her for a few moments and asked dryly, "What happened to you?"

Ascendida blushed deeply, feeling Rita's stare bounce in her direction.

"She did," Rita said, pointing to Ascendida. "That cow almost killed me yesterday."

"Me?" asked Ascendida meekly. "Since when do I beat up Rita?"

Dona Lidia grabbed Rita by the arm and dragged her to Ascendida's desk. "Now ask for her forgiveness, you big liar!" she ordered Rita and slapped her across the face.

Rita stood there in front of Ascendida, trying to remember how to ask for forgiveness. "Fucking cow," she said.

Dona Lidia grabbed her by the hair and slapped her repeatedly. But all that Rita could say was, "Fucking cow!"

Ascendida had never looked into Rita's eyes before; they were opaque blue, like the dirty water left on the washing basin, almost as if she was blind. And as if the air had compressed in the room, Rita became small, alone, and inconsequential. She was no longer Rita the terrible; she was just poor Rita.

For Mario, that afternoon against the wall, as he'd grabbed Felicidade's shoulders and drooled figs all over his feet, Ascendida had been reinvented in his mind. She had become his friend and his fixation.

"We are just friends," she told her friends, who couldn't understand such tenacious love. "Felicidade is his girlfriend, but I am the friend who he can't live without."

When Ascendida could not be found, they knew that she was somewhere with Mario—catching frogs, reading books, exploring caves, or searching for hidden treasures in the brook.

And then elementary school was over, and they went to the city to study. Every day, they travelled to the city and back. In the bus, Mario sat next to Felicidade, and Ascendida felt a dull pain in her chest as if she was being betrayed. Mario never really liked school, just like Aldo, but continuing his education was the only way he could be with Felicidade and Ascendida.

If he had to choose between the two, he thought often, would he choose?

"I'm reading *Camelot*," she told him once. "I'm reading about love, betrayal, and forgiveness."

"Why must you be so sinister?" he asked with a stare.

She put down the book. She was looking at a man, not a boy. But only last year he had been a boy. She remembered that split moment when he'd stopped being a boy, when he was naked masturbating in a big pool in the brook.

"You always read the wrong thing," he said, trying to penetrate her thoughts.

"Why is *Camelot* the wrong book?" she asked.

"When you had your period, you thought you had burst, remember? You told me that you were going to die. Of all the things you've read you never read about a woman's period. When I first masturbated in front of you, what did you think? You thought that I was having an attack of epilepsy. You knew about epilepsy, but you didn't know about masturbation."

She made a disapproving sound and turned her head away from him.

"I'm going to marry Felicidade," he said after a long silence. "When we are finished with school, we will get married."

He sounded so sad, as if he was announcing a disaster. She buried her face in the book and said nothing.

"I love you," he said.

"You must choose," she answered, without raising her eyes to him.

"I did," he murmured. "She is better for me, but I love you more …"

2

The Treacherous Nature of Love

Mario and Ascendida met at the windmill, for the last time, on a moonless night. They ran into each other's arms, knowing that they were saying good-bye.

Mario undressed Ascendida without a word. They knew everything that was to know. Mario's circumcision was burning, not healing as it should, but he entered Ascendida in one swift movement. They both screamed at the same time and stopped at the same time. It was a silence of pain, and ecstasy. Mario was where he wanted to be—inside of that fool of a girl, who all his life had been his shadow and now was saying good-bye. He wanted to feel that pain inside of Ascendida. He wanted to remember. If he was going to lose Ascendida for good, he had only tonight.

A few weeks later, Mario and Felicidade got married. The island had never seen such a beautiful bride. Felicidade had saved a rare enchantment for that day. She had the demeanor of a queen slowly going down the road while Mario was throwing feverish looks and sweeping glances at the people gathered on the street watching them entering the church.

Where is Ascendida? he thought, while Felicidade smiled with little perfect teeth shining in the morning sun.

At night, when the entire wedding party left, Mario looked at his bride, beautiful and always so composed. She smiled again at him, this time a bit sadly, and she murmured, "You will forget her with time."

Mario embraced Felicidade, with her sweet smell and perfect skin. "When you circumcised me, I thought I was going to hate you forever," he said in a whisper. "My heart never does the right thing."

"Why don't you hate Ascendida? She plotted with me your circumcision. She witnessed your screams and your pleas, and she didn't assist you. Why hate me alone?"

"Maybe that's why. I can't hate her," he said, looking intensely at her. Then he smiled.

As he was undressing Felicidade, he remembered his forced circumcision a few months earlier. Ascendida had lured him into the windmill. The night breeze was bringing the soft sounds of the philharmonic rehearsing for the festivities; he was laughing, making comments, and biting her neck. "When I go to the military, I am going to take you with me in a little box … I'm going to take you. Felicidade will stay here waiting for me, imagining the first time we will make love, getting scared, red in the face, not knowing if I am going to devour or love her." He remembered so clearly that he felt clever and powerful saying that.

This was the Mario who Felicidade spoke of—one who could disconnect love from tenderness and one who had a recurring fantasy, like a dream, to take Felicidade against her will. "I want to fuck your perfect composure," he had said.

So young still and knowing how to hurt so dangerously.

He remembered getting an erection against Ascendida's leg while he was talking about devouring Felicidade.

He remembered getting to the windmill, and Felicidade was there waiting. She asked him to take off his clothes and allow her to tie him up. He laughed and asked if he could have his fantasy after she had hers. And she promised he could. He laughed again. And when he was tied spread-eagle, she pulled out a surgical knife.

He screamed at the sight of the knife, and when he looked into her eyes, he became afraid.

"Is it not what you want? To yank the clothes off my body and pin me to the ground while I scream? Is it not?" Felicidade's voice was cold. "When you fantasize with me, be tender, be loving!" she admonished.

"What are you going to do?" he asked, struggling to free himself.

"I'm going to circumcise you."

He started to scream, and she stuffed his shirt in his mouth.

"I learned this last week, I've read many books, and I've seen my father castrate pigs. So you see, I know what I am doing."

He said obscenities and verbalized vengeance into his shirt smelling of American cologne. He screamed muffled insults and fought his restraints without success. Then he cried Ascendida's name, his tears running down the side of his face.

"The more you struggle, the more it will hurt you," she said casually, disinfecting the surgical knife.

He stopped moving, looking at her with bulging eyes.

With the little surgical knife in her hand, Felicidade took his penis and slowly pushed the skin against his belly and forward again and painted it with iodine. He screamed but didn't move, afraid of causing himself more harm than Felicidade would. She took the little knife to him and performed the cut, swiftly going around his penis, leaving a streak of blood after the cut. With a pair of scissors, she snipped off the foreskin that was still hanging on by a thread and threw it on the floor.

Ascendida was speechless outside the door, never imagining how vindictive Felicidade could be. And Felicidade was thinking that she would have forgiven Mario if he didn't have sweet fantasies with Ascendida while his fantasies with her were crude and painful. This would be his punishment for wanting to crawl into a nice, soft, and warm bed with Ascendida, for wanting to make love with her with the brook running gently over their bodies or make love under a tree in a hot summer's day. Felicidade could forgive the violent fantasies he had with her, but she couldn't forgive the loving ones he had with Ascendida.

Felicidade cleaned him with soapy water, looking sternly at his face. "This is good for you; they were going to do it in the military anyway." She smiled and added, "Now, you can have your fantasy with me, and I will scream harder and louder than you."

Mario was no longer fighting the sword grass restraints on his limbs. Felicidade was dressing the wound with gauze, not paying attention to his sobs.

"Two months' time, and you will be brand new. Soak it in warm salty water and use clean clothes. By the time we get married, you will be more than ready," Felicidade said, hovering over him, her braids caressing his chest. And she ran out of the windmill, leaving him tied and all the candles ablaze.

Ascendida came in then. He looked like a sacrificial offering on top of two bales of hay. She took off his restraints and pulled the shirt from his mouth. Slowly, he moved out of the hay while Ascendida gathered his clothes and dressed him up.

"See what happens with stupid fantasies?" she said, kissing his hair and his face full of tears. "See? Dreaming never ends up well."

"Why did you let her do that to me?" he asked crying softly. "Why?"

Felicidade was now in Mario's arms, his bride, the girl who had so unceremoniously circumcised him two months ago. When he parted her legs to enter her, he saw a wave of panic in her eyes. There was no desire or love as he had seen in Ascendida. Felicidade was afraid, and he smiled. "Payback time," he said, searching her face.

"I will not scream like you did," she said.

"Won't you?" he asked coldly, driving himself very slowly into his wife.

And Felicidade knew that he was going to hurt her. She'd miscalculated his eagerness. She thought that he was going to drive himself into her body as if he was stabbing her. One sharp pain, maybe two, and it would be done. But no. Mario gave it some thought; he was entering her slowly, very slowly until all her muscles were tense with the pain, and then he withdrew. She let a heavy breath slip from her lungs and, as if getting ready to take a dive, filled her lungs with air again. And Mario repeated in slow motion the deflowering of his wife.

"I can do this all night long, you know," he said, caressing her clenched jaw.

"You want me to scream?" she asked.

He felt a wave of nausea remembering that night. He could see the surgical knife catching a glimpse of light and coming at him.

"I've done all the screaming for both of us in a lifetime," he said, pushing in again, very slowly. "I just want to punish you for your cruelty."

"We are even!"

"Not yet," he answered and drove himself into her with all his might.

Felicidade was prepared for more deliberate pain from Mario. She was not ready for him to end it, and she let out a scream, more in surprise than pain. The pain came seconds after under repeated thrusts, and she screamed again.

Mario laughed and rested his naked body on her. "Now we are even," he said.

Mario fell asleep thinking of Ascendida's softness; her body was round and dark. Her breasts were big and soft. Felicidade was thin and white as milk. He could feel her bones just by touching, and her breasts were small and hard. He drifted into sleep having erotic dreams of Ascendida. He woke up with the noise of his own voice. He was telling Ascendida that he wanted her to lie down on the grass, green and soft, and let him into her body, slowly and sweetly, without pain or tears, and stay there until he grew old.

Mario woke up sweating and breathing hard. For a split second, he didn't understand where he was. What house was this? Oh, this was his brand-new house, built for him and Felicidade. Everything was new and sparkling, like Felicidade. The furniture was new and beautiful, made by Lazarus Matias, the artist. The rocking chair gleamed under the moonlight coming through the window and hit the pillow embroidered by Felicidade's mother–Home Sweet Home.

Mario and Felicidade would go to the mainland to study at the university. He was going to be an agrarian engineer and Felicidade a doctor. Everything would be so clear and purposeful, if it weren't for his yearning. He wanted Ascendida.

Where was she? She hadn't gone to the wedding. Where was that fool? Could he go a day without seeing her?

He looked at his wife; Felicidade's hair looked like flames on the pillow.

The monsignor entered Ophelia's neat kitchen and sat down near the fire. It was a cold and rainy day, and what the monsignor had to say was even colder.

Ophelia's husband was older and somewhat sick with arthritis. He was a quiet man, never really interfering with the running of the house, but he cared about Ophelia and her daughter. The monsignor had asked him to marry Ophelia because she needed a husband and her child needed a father. He was happy being a bachelor, but he had accepted the challenge. And they lived peacefully, being kind to each other.

"Your daughter is going to get married next week," he said. "She is with child."

Ophelia put a hand to her chest and closed her eyes. João, her husband, shook his head.

"She is going to marry Aldo Costa," the monsignor added. "He is a good man."

"We know," João said quietly. Then he added, "He drinks."

"No one is perfect," the monsignor said. He vaguely thought about Mario and Aldo's parents. They had just buried one son; now they were going to lose the other in a fast, shotgun wedding.

"What do the Costas say about it?" Ophelia asked.

"They are in agreement. Felicidade left for the mainland, to study and to forget, I suppose. She left the house to Aldo for him to take care of it." The monsignor cleared his throat as if what he wanted to say was difficult to utter. "At least they have a house to live in…"

The first time Ascendida had entered that house, it had been a few days before Mario and Felicidade's wedding. Mario was in the kitchen, his back toward the fire in the chimney room, and he smiled.

"Felicidade doesn't bake bread you know … She will have someone do it for her. Do you want to bake my bread, Ascendida?" he said. "Her mother organized everything for her daughter—someone to clean the house, another one to do the washing, someone to bake her bread…" He let his voice trail and smiled again.

"Did she hire someone to fuck you?" Ascendida asked with a black, mean heart. "Since all Felicidade's duties have been assigned…"

He laughed and said softly, "That would have been you, my little Ass."

Ascendida was thinking about Mario's face, happy and mischievous. How would he look if she told him that she was pregnant? Would that smile be wiped right off his face? What would he say when, years later, she came back from Canada or Australia with a little boy who looked like him? Yes, she would leave; there was no room for her and her baby.

But she didn't say anything. If she had told him, he would be alive now. He was distracted during the bullfight. He was scanning the verandas for her; he was not paying attention. Pedro Matias swore that he had pulled the bull's rope, but Mario fell from the veranda right in front of the bull. Ascendida remembers when Mario's eyes finally found her behind a tree, and he let go of the veranda, to cross the street to come to her. One second, just one second later, and the bull would have been running past him. And then he would have crossed the street and asked her if it was true, if she was pregnant.

Just one second…

Nascimento, Madalena, and Angela were with Ascendida, preparing the house for her and Aldo. How strange life was, everything reminding her of Mario—even her new husband, being so identical to his brother, but no Mario. Ascendida sat down and cried. She would have one good last cry for Mario and just move on. How dare he love her and then die? How dare he?

Ascendida and Aldo got married, and a few weeks later, the monsignor brought them Rosa. He simply said, "Every child deserves a family. Be kind to each other."

Angela lived in a small place, up in the pastures, with no other house around. Joaquim Gomes, her father, was the beekeeper. He sold honey and made candles for the whole island. He had regular, well-paying customers, and he also worked for other men, when he had most of his own business done. Joaquim owned their house outright, and with Angela doing the books for some of the big landowners in the island, they wanted for nothing. They had everything they needed and even managed to save some money. Joaquim and his wife Maria were very proud of their daughter, who was smart and kind. She knew how to read and write at the age of four. By the age of ten, she knew English, French, and even calculus. The monsignor had taken special care with Angela, saying that one of God's gifts was intelligence; Angela had the gift. But Angela's gift went beyond intelligence. Intuitively, she knew how to fix bones, straighten limbs, and cure maladies. She also knew people's hearts, and some said that she could read people's minds. In medieval times, she would have been burnt at the stake as a witch.

Angela had loved Lazarus all her life. She was born already loving him, knowing that he was there waiting for her; they were predestined. To open the window in the middle of the night to welcome Lazarus to her bed was not only her right; it was a need demanding fulfillment—a need to be in his company, to caress him, and to feel his breath on her face.

Angela thought that, if she had a sibling, maybe she would not feel that naked desire to be with someone, to sleep feeling someone's body heat. She'd always missed a person next to her, sleeping with her, keeping her company, but she was the only child of a loving couple, as if God had forgotten something. And one day, her mother told her that she'd had a twin, who she'd miscarried. Angela knew it—she was never meant to be alone. And sometimes she carried the guilt that she had pushed the other sibling out and now was being punished by feeling that absence in such a tangible way. She had slept with her parents for many years, until one day the monsignor had shamed her into her own room. Then she had looked for Lazarus. Her intent and promise was to marry Lazarus and live in the house of her dreams. The house of her dreams was a sprawling property with pastures all around, a generous garden and patio, a vineyard, a windmill up on a hill overlooking the village, and the largest wheat-threshing circle in the island. But the house belonged to an American emigrant who was coming back after years of being in America. While he was away, the village had used his property, administered by Angela, who annually received an envelope with US money—nice, crisp and smelling like America.

Saul looked in the mirror. He examined his face with a critical eye. He had a scar above his eye, one that Dona Lidia had made when she'd hit him so hard that he'd fainted. He remembered the room spinning around before everything went black. His body was too big for the desk, and he fell like a mighty tree. He'd hit Maria Augusta with his elbow as he went down—Maria Augusta, big, fat, kind Maria Augusta, the only girl who smiled at him. All others ran away because he was too dark, too big, too quiet, too stupid. He was too everything, except in the eyes of Maria Augusta.

Saul fixed his thick, black hair. Should he do this? Should he accept Pedro Matias's proposal? He had come to the island when he was ten years old and lived with his family at the end of Two Brooks, next to Little Branch village but somewhat removed from the life of both villages. When he was fifteen years old, his father had gone to jail for murder, and he'd died there. Saul had become the man of the house, dealing with the business and making it grow. Many said that it was not Paulo Amora who had killed a man, but Saul, and that his father had taken the rap. Under that cloak of suspicion and gossip, the village shunned Carlota Amora and her son. Only the monsignor was kind to them.

Saul had loved Madalena from the first moment he saw her. Manuel Barcos, Madalena's boyfriend, was handsome, happy, and talented; he played guitar and clarinet and knew how to recite poetry. Sometimes at night, Saul listened to the music brought to him in the wind from the Barcos house. And what he wanted most was to be Manuel so he could have Madalena.

When Pedro Matias came to Saul's house, he said that Madalena needed to get married but not to Manuel Barcos. Would he be so kind as to ask for her hand in marriage? He was perplexed. "Why me?" he asked.

"For various reasons," Pedro said. "But the biggest one is that she is pregnant. The other reason is that the father is Manuel Barcos. You are rich, and he is not."

At that moment, he understood that the intention was for him to be the crown of her punishment; for getting pregnant by a poor man, she would be forced to marry the pariah. But he would not marry a woman if she didn't want to marry him. He knew who he was. He was self-sufficient and a good man. Whatever a mean-hearted village thought of him didn't change who he was.

"Only if Madalena tells me that she wants to marry me," he answered evenly.

Pedro laughed and shook his head. "Give me one day and one night. Madalena will be at your door by the end of the week."

This was the end of the week. Madalena would be knocking at his door at any minute. Maia, the woman who lived with them was in the kitchen with Saul's mother, Carlota Amora, preparing tea and cutting a cake.

Maia, some said, was someone who Saul's father had bought in Africa; some said that it was in Brazil.

Saul heard hesitant knocking, and he opened the door. In front of him stood Lazarus and his sister Madalena—two identical people beat up, with bruises on their faces. Madalena wore a yellow dress. He remembered her in that dress, in church, and he thought that she rivaled the sun. But now she was hurt; her lip was swollen, and both her eyes were black, one almost closed.

Lazarus was walking as if he had broken knees and every step was a struggle.

Saul stepped away from the door to let them enter at the same time Maia came into the parlor. She gave a shriek when she saw the two visitors and left under Saul's reproachful look.

Madalena thought that Saul was even bigger than she remembered; he was like a bull, enormous and full of muscle. His nostrils were large, and when she looked up, they looked like small caves on his face.

"Sit down," Saul said.

But Lazarus could not sit. His injuries didn't allow him to do anything other than stand. The only place in his body that was not hurt was the bottom of his feet. His whole body had been flogged by his father's belt.

Madalena stood in front of Saul and seemed to be lost for words.

Finally she asked, "Will you marry me, Saul?" She searched his face, looking for signs of rejection, praying to God that he would say yes before her father killed Manuel.

Manuel had told her that he could not afford her father's vengeance. Pedro had killed his dog, his cat, and his horse; now he was killing his cattle. Pedro had threatened to kill him one dark night with no witnesses. The village would wake up with Manuel drowned in the brook or gored by an enraged bull. Those things were so common.

The police were peripherally involved, but Pedro could buy many things, including the police.

Manuel could not hold on to such love, one that exerted such a high price.

"Yes," Saul said softly. "I will marry you, if that's what you want."

Madalena started to cry. She didn't know if it was relief or sadness. Her tears burned her injuries, and the crack on her lip opened up again and bled.

"When you heal, we will get married," he said, giving her a handkerchief. "And from this day on, no one will ever hurt you again."

She stared at Saul through blurred eyes. He sounded so sure. And something gentle settled in her heart—a sweet thing, like a promise.

Saul accompanied them home. They went silently up the road as if everything had been said.

When Saul came into the house, Amelia Matias was also hurt; some of the marks were recent some were healing. The four boys, younger than Lazarus, were sitting at the table. Pedro told them to leave, and they fled as if the devil had given them a reprieve.

Pedro laughed, looking at Madalena and Saul.

"Well, well," he said, delighted. "Is there going to be a wedding or a funeral?"

Saul fixed him with a stare. He felt the urge to grab the man by the neck and shake him until he lost consciousness. "We will get married when her injuries heal," Saul said. "I suspect that, in two weeks' time …the first week of spring …"

Pedro walked closer to Madalena, held her face in his hands, and looked her in the eyes. "Well, if she doesn't get another beating until then …"

"You will not hit her again," Saul said calmly, gently pulling Madalena away from her father.

"Won't I?" Pedro asked, amused.

"No, you won't, because now she is my fiancée."

Pedro doubled over laughing. "The prince and savior who looks like a horse!" he mocked.

Saul felt nauseous as he always did before he pummeled someone.

"Every day after work, I will come to court Madalena," Saul said, trying to contain the tremor in his voice.

"You know that she is a whore, don't you?" Pedro asked.

"No, she is not. Now she is my fiancée," he answered.

Pedro laughed raw, ugly guffaws. "If you don't keep her in line—"

Saul took a step closer to Pedro and interrupted him. "I mean it when I say that you will not touch Madalena again. Do you understand?" His voice was steady and low but held such threat that Pedro took a step back, his eyes widening a bit. "I will visit her every day, and I don't want to see her hurt."

"I can call this whole thing off, you know," Pedro said in a resentful tone.

"If she wants to marry me, you don't matter any longer. I will take her from your house and make her my wife. I'm not Manuel Barcos. Don't make that mistake," Saul answered evenly.

When Saul turned around to leave, Madalena followed him outside.

Saul touched her face lightly and said, "Don't be afraid. I will take care of you."

When Madalena and Lazarus told Angela about the impending marriage to Saul, Angela brought them in and made them sit in front of her. Madalena was very serious and simply said that she was going to marry Saul in the first week of spring.

There was no explanation, no reason given. "I'm getting married to Saul in the first week of spring," Madalena said.

Angela could not imagine Saul being married to beautiful Madalena. She thought of Saul—enormous, morose, and mean. He was mean; he was the slaughter man for the village. Cow, calf, pig, chicken, Saul would kill anything in a second.

"Saul, the killer?" Angela asked horrified.

Madalena was exhibiting her best stubborn look.

"Maria Augusta will kill you," Angela said. "She will sit her big fat ass on you and finish you off!"

"We have been so unkind, Angela," Madalena said quietly. "Poor Maria Augusta, she loves Saul … What is the crime?"

Maria Augusta was a rich, lonely girl, who sat at her window looking out at passersby. Everything in her was velvety—her skin, her clothes, and her voice. "Would you give me a kiss?" she used to ask people as they went by. No one ever crossed the street to kiss her. She looked so precious perched high up on her window, so plump, eating chocolates. She smiled like a little girl, making giggling sounds about nothing. The first day she went to school, a life of torment started and never stopped. She was teased about the kisses she had requested when she was three or four years old. Her braids were pulled and her chocolates stolen. And worst of all, Dona Lidia took a particular dislike of her. She was smart, diligent, and helpful to the less applied students, so everyone was shocked when Dona Lidia told her to lift her skirt up and pull her pants down to be punished for ten mistakes on the dictation lesson.

"But I didn't make any mistakes," she said feebly.

Dona Lidia pulled her up by the hair and forced her to take the punishment. They all saw her pink, big, fat buttocks turning into a mess of red welts as she cried silently, grabbing her dress up around her waist. Then it was Saul's turn; Dona Lidia told him to pull his trousers down. Saul's buttocks were something the class didn't expect—dark like his face, muscular, smaller than one would think. And the whip hit him ten times, leaving red welts. He stood with his back to Dona Lidia and with Maria Augusta one step away from him, sitting on her desk, tears running down her face, murmuring, "It will be okay, Saul. Don't cry." She kept repeating this mantra with every stroke of the whip. Maria Augusta's eyes were fastened on Saul's face, reassuring him, while the rest of the class followed the long and limp penis swaying from side to side, like the pendulum of a hypnotist.

And they grew older, linked by these humiliations.

The monsignor was again planted at the feet of Jesus Crucified.

Dona Lidia was dead, and the coroner was waiting for the monsignor to tell him what to put on the death certificate. He could say that it was a heart attack. Even that was ironic, because she had no heart. But how was he going to explain the bruise on her forehead? If a person fell from a heart attack, the bruise would have been on the back of the head if she was lying on her back, not on the forehead—a big, huge gash that almost split her head open. Someone had killed Dona Lidia and possibly with plenty of reason.

Monsignor Inocente was rarely confused or faced with problems of conscience. But this was one of those rare times when he was not sure what to do. Jesus was still looking at him cross-eyed. Was there a sign? Had Jesus opened his eyes to tell him that he was not being just?

Saul came up behind the monsignor and knelt at his side. The monsignor looked at him sideways. *The groom*, he thought, *what a fiasco*.

"Monsignor," Saul said with his head down, as if he was praying to a deity.

The monsignor looked at Jesus again. He concentrated on Jesus's knees—it was easier than the eyes. *Please, Lord*, he prayed silently, *please don't let this boy tell me something terrible*.

Saul hesitated for a moment, and then he spoke in a strangled voice. "I know that Madalena doesn't love me, but I couldn't resist having her. We are going to marry tomorrow, and I know she loves another."

The monsignor sighed, relieved. He had thought Saul was going to say something else.

"Well, my son, love is a dynamic thing; it changes. But, for your weakness, your penance is never to ask her for anything she doesn't want to give you out of her own free will."

"I can be patient," he said.

"Yes. And you can act in anger also. Be careful, Saul. You know that your demon is anger, and you don't know your own strength."

"I know," he said softly, his head bowed.

"Is there anything else that you want to confess?"

Saul looked at Jesus as if in mute consultation. "What's wrong with him?" he asked, pointing to Jesus, forgetting about his moral issues.

"He's been scrubbed, and we discovered that his eyes are open," the monsignor explained, a little out of temper.

"I'm not sure I like it," Saul said.

The monsignor had a soft spot for this boy. He looked at him and almost smiled. "Go home, my son. Tomorrow is a big day."

At the windmill, Manuel and Madalena were saying their final good-bye.

Saul waited, leaning on a high stone wall, hidden by its shadow, a dull pain growing in his chest when he saw Manuel running out as if the devil was in pursuit.

Madalena walked slowly home, looking at her feet. Those feet tomorrow would walk up the village, to the church, and to marry Saul Amora. And for the rest of her life, they would walk a person who had lost everything—her love, her life, and her dignity.

And there he was, Saul in front of her, quiet and questioning. Madalena stopped. She was surprised that he had just materialized out of thin air.

"Saul …" she whispered. And she knew that he had seen Manuel leave the windmill. "I was saying good-bye," she said.

His face got darker, his eyes narrowed a little, and his nostrils flared. He held her gaze. "We will respect each other." His voice was low and serene.

"I will remember that," Madalena said.

Saul was thinking about her beauty. He had never seen anyone so lovely. Now with the sun coming down behind the hills of Two Brooks, a golden light was cast on her face, and she looked translucent, her skin so pure that she didn't look real.

Madalena thought she saw doubt in his face, and she felt a wave of panic take hold. She couldn't go back home, and Manuel was not strong enough to fight for her.

"Do you want to call it off?" she asked.

"Only if you wish it," he said.

Madalena smiled sadly. "My wishes don't matter."

"What do you want to do? This is the time. Tell me, now." He reached for her hands and held them in his—such small hands.

There was strength and comfort in his touch.

"Marry me, Saul. I can't fight anymore. I'm tired. I have no place to go, and Manuel is a lost boy, without the courage to fight for me."

What a sad thing to say about a man, Saul thought.

He squeezed her hands a little and asked, "Are you afraid?"

Madalena looked at him in complete surprise. She was taking in his quiet demeanor. His hands were big but gentle, and there was a light of kindness in his eyes. "No. But I hardly know you," she said quietly.

"I will be a good husband to you."

When he let go of her hands, she felt oddly abandoned.

3

Madalena

Madalena woke up on the day of her wedding with her mother looking down at her. There was sadness about Amelia.

Why are you so weak? Madalena thought.

"The day I married your father was the happiest day of my life," Amelia said. "I was so in love with him!"

"Why are you telling me this?" Madalena asked.

"Because God owes me. You will be happy, although you are not happy now."

There was certainty in her voice, but Madalena could not see a happy ending to this. Yesterday when she had hugged and kissed Manuel for the last time, her heart had dissolved in tears. She no longer had a heart.

When Madalena entered the kitchen in her white bridal gown, her brothers and father were speechless for a few seconds.

"Let's get this show on the road," Pedro said.

And Lazarus started to cry. His father lifted a hand up in the air to hit him.

Madalena stepped between them. "Not today!" she said firmly. "Today no one gets hit."

Pedro looked perplexed at her, his hand still up in the air.

"Let's go," Madalena said. "I have a wedding to go to."

Madalena waited quietly at the door. The groom soon would come by, and they would walk up to the church, under the glare of the villagers. The procession of her wedding would be as quiet as a funeral—including the occasional sobbing.

When the wedding procession got on the road, one by one, the neighbors walked behind the bride as she went by their houses.

"Stop crying!" Angela told Lazarus. She was annoyed with him. All he did was cry since Madalena had agreed to marry Saul. "Your father will hit you again if you continue to cry."

When they got to the church, Saul looked back as if to make sure that his bride had followed. Carlota Amora stood by her son. Carlota was not a handsome woman, and the hat she was wearing didn't help. Everyone took a second look; they weren't sure if it was because of the hat or just because of Carlota …

Monsignor Inocente performed the ceremony, almost with haste. After all was said and done, the procession went to Pedro Matias's house, and a feast was provided for the village, with plenty of wine and food.

Angela kept an eye on Pedro, who was on his best behavior.

After a while, she walked up to him and said, "Soon it will be Lazarus and me."

Pedro laughed. "I don't think so. Maria Augusta appeals to me a lot better than you. She has money."

"So have I," Angela said without looking at him.

His head snapped around, and his eyes were like daggers. "That's not your money! You stole it from me!"

"Prove it," Angela said softly. She had gone to the police station to respond to an accusation of theft two days ago. They couldn't prove anything, and the monsignor had vouched for Angela. Pedro Matias's reputation was so terrible that Angela won without much fuss.

"Another thing," she said, "I will no longer do your books. You have to go to the city and pay an accountant. They are thieves, all of them, and you will pay them four times as much as you pay me."

"You are a thief too!" he snapped.

"Yes, but a smart one. I made your business grow by leaps and bounds. The accountants are not financial advisors like I am. You will be losing that too."

"I'll get even with you!"

"I'm sure you will try."

Pedro Matias gave her a long look. "You should have been my child, not those sissies that I have at home."

"I can be your daughter-in-law, and I would do your books for free."

He laughed. "Would you give me back my money also?"

"All of it."

He looked at her sideways, assessing her truthfulness. "How would I know that you are not lying?"

Angela got up and looked down at him. "If you don't kill Lazarus first, I will marry him. But if you kill him, I will find a way to kill you too. This is a promise."

Pedro was stunned. She looked like a sharpened knife at his throat. There was a tone in her voice and a light in her eyes that, for a split second, terrified him. It was as if he had glimpsed into a bit of hell.

Lazarus was talking to his sister, their heads together—identical heads, with copper brown hair and shiny curls. Madalena's hand, now with a wedding band, caressed his face. Saul was also observing. Then Saul got up and walked away, looking absently down the pastures. Angela walked up to him. He was surprised, almost annoyed, that she was intruding.

"I don't know what happened for Madalena to marry you, but something terrible is going on," she said.

Angela always intimidated him. She was this little, bitty thing, but she attacked Dona Lidia when no one else had the courage to do so. She brought the teacher down and kicked her in the teeth. There was something about Angela that disconcerted him.

"Leave us alone," he said.

"She is my friend, and friends don't quit!"

"She is my wife and my business now. Leave us alone."

Angela looked steadily at him. She had never looked that closely at Saul. Funny, that if she looked really hard, his face would change into a face that she never saw. His skin was dark, as if he spent all his days in the sun, but it had a soft look to it like satin. His mouth was large with thick, well-shaped lips; his eyes were black and fringed with long lashes like a girl's. She never saw him laugh or even smile. She hardly knew this man who had lived shoulder to shoulder with her in the same village.

"I know you don't like me. I don't really care, but I will be good to Madalena."

"How can you be good to someone who doesn't love you?" Angela asked.

What had the monsignor said yesterday about love? He thought for a few seconds. It had made sense yesterday, but today he could not remember. It was something that gave him hope, and he could not remember.

"Stay out of it. You don't know what hope can do," he said. "And I have hope."

This was not the answer of an ogre. Saul was nervously moving the wedding band around his finger. Was it true that those hands had strangled a man, and his father was now paying for it? Would this man hurt Madalena more than her own father did?

"I don't want you to come around," he said.

"Too bad," Angela snapped. "Unless Madalena asks me not to visit, I will."

Ascendida and Nascimento slowly walked toward Saul and Angela. He made a sound of frustration seeing the other women ganging up on him.

"She needs to forget Manuel, and you will not let her," he snapped. And he turned around and joined the wedding party.

Nascimento and Ascendida stared at Angela. "What was the ogre saying?" Nascimento asked.

"He doesn't want us around," Angela answered.

Nascimento closed her eyes and said, "One day, I looked into his window, and he was praying, on his knees, like a little boy. I think he was crying."

The others looked at Nascimento, the voyeur. She'd been one since she was a little girl. She claimed that she was a sleepwalker, just in case she was caught on the street at night. But she'd never been caught.

"When was that?" Ascendida asked.

"The day Dona Lidia died. If someone should be happy about her death, it should've been Saul. He was humiliated more often than anyone else."

"He is a brute," Angela said. "He kills animals."

"Everybody does, Angela. Animals are for us to eat," Ascendida said.

Not for Angela. Angela didn't eat animals. Rarely she would eat meat, and only if it came from the city. That's why she was small—bad nutrition—people said.

Angela was quietly looking at Madalena. She'd married an ogre who prayed and cried in his room at night when he thought he was alone, this being reported by their friend the voyeur. She sighed.

"I have to be careful," Nascimento said. "Deolindo Mendes is saying that there is a werewolf going around the village."

Angela had seen Deolindo's son, Elias, coming up the street one night when she met Lazarus. He was screaming about a ghost. She only had time to jump over the wall, the sheet covering her head flying as she jumped.

The party was over. Everyone went home. And Madalena and Saul left.

I can't believe that I am married to Saul Amora, Madalena said to herself. She felt a tremendous urge to cry, but she closed her eyes for a minute to collect herself.

"Are you all right?" Saul asked, looking at her eyes shut and rooted on the middle of the street.

Manuel's house was a few feet away. How could life be so wrong? Madalena felt that the ground was disappearing from under her feet, and she fainted.

When she opened her eyes, she saw two enormous faces looking down at her, one on each side of the bed. *Two horses*, she thought.

"Are you all right?" one asked.

Saul and his mother were both anxiously applying cold towels to her forehead. Maia, the woman who lived with them, was running in and out of the room, bringing new towels and fresh water.

Madalena looked around. Was this Saul's room? It was wide and spacious with an enormous bed in the middle. The heavy drapes on the tall windows gave the room a dusky gray tone. She felt that she was in the middle of a soft, warm island. She closed her eyes again, and when she opened them, only Saul was in the room, peering anxiously at her.

"I'm sorry," she said softly.

He smiled. Madalena's eyes widened. She had never seen Saul smile, never, not even when he was on the singing circles trying to fit in, or on the bullfights, looking up at the girls. His smile changed his whole face; he was almost good-looking.

"You have nothing to apologize for. Call me if you need anything. I'll be in the room next to yours."

Madalena felt a wave of relief come over her, and the smile that transformed his face was gone. He was looking intently at her.

"Sleep well, Madalena," he said.

She sat up in bed as he left the room. The door closed silently, and Madalena slept alone on her wedding night.

Nascimento was restless. Seeing Madalena and Saul walk down the road to a life of misery made her restless. She felt a tremendous urge to spy on Jaime Nobre. Of all the people who she looked in, Jaime Nobre was her favorite. He was good-looking, tall, and slim, always ready to laugh. Recently, he'd started working at the American base as a chauffeur for the American military. He worked different shifts, and sometimes she had the luxury of seeing him undress and lay in bed completely naked and spent. Last week, she had seen him masturbating. He had come out of the house, and she'd hardly had time to hide in the shadows. He was so close to her, moaning softly and splattering the ground.

Jaime Nobre lived alone with his mother. His father had died a few years ago, in the ocean, catching limpets. So many people falling into the ocean for those little dirty limpets.

Nascimento walked slowly to Jaime Nobre's house. There was no light in the kitchen, and only a faint glimmer of light was coming from his room. He was probably sleeping already and had forgotten the light on. The little stool that Jaime's mother used to sit outside was under the window. Nascimento stepped on it and looked into the room.

There he was, sleeping.

So handsome; even in his sleep, he seemed to be smiling.

She was mesmerized looking at him, and she fell off the stool. In the effort to steady herself, she hit the windowpane and broke it. Jaime got up in a flash and came running out the door. She had only two choices—run or fake that she was sleepwalking. If she ran, the dog would run after her, wagging his tail and thinking that he was playing. She walked down the road, slowly.

The night was clear, with a huge moon looking down at her disgrace. Jaime, wrapped in a sheet, caught her by the shoulders and shook her. His mother came right after him with a candle in hand and put the candle near her face.

She is going to burn my hair, Nascimento thought.

"That's Nascimento, Ana's daughter," Jaime's mother said in dismay.

"What is she doing here?" he asked.

"She sleepwalks. Everybody knows that she sleepwalks. Don't wake her up. It is dangerous if we do," his mother said.

"She broke the window," Jaime said.

Nascimento thought that it was time to wake up. She blinked a few times and let out a scream right in Jaime's ear as he was talking to his mother. Jaime screamed too.

"Where am I?" Nascimento asked.

"Come in, darling. Come in," his mother said, placing a shawl over her shoulders and walking her to the house.

Jaime was walking behind them, dragging the sheet on the ground. He disappeared into his room and came out fully dressed.

"I'll take you home," he offered, while Nascimento feigned confusion.

They walked slowly up to her house. At the gate she said, "Please don't tell anybody about this. I am very embarrassed by this condition."

He looked at her for a long while and smiled, "And what will be my reward?"

Nascimento was speechless. He was going to blackmail her.

"I have no money," she said.

He laughed. "I don't want money. I want you to go out with me. Allow me to call on you every afternoon and weekends, if I am not working."

She was amazed. "You want to be my boyfriend?"

"Thank you, I accept," he said.

"I …I thought you liked Lucia," she said surprised.

"Everybody likes Lucia," he said dismissively.

Lucia was almost as pretty as Madalena, and most men were infatuated with her, including Jaime.

"I think that you are very pretty, you are fun to be around, you make me laugh, and I want you to be my girl."

"What were you waiting for?" Nascimento asked rudely, "for me to break your window so you could ask me out?

He laughed. "Be my girl," he murmured and kissed her on the lips.

Angela tried to sleep, but when she closed her eyes, she saw Lazarus's face drenched with tears. She put a sheet over her head and ran barefoot as fast as she could toward his house while the sheet flapped softly in the wind.

Suddenly, something hit her thigh, and Viriato howled. She felt a sharp pain and a warm sensation down her leg. Blood gushed out of her thigh, and she tried to stop the flow. But she heard steps and voices. She left the sheet on the ground and ran to the barn behind Lazarus's house.

She ripped her nightgown and tried to stop the blood by applying pressure. Slowly she moved back in the direction of her house, while the voices continued down the road.

Angela got in the tank of water behind her house to wash off the blood. The fountain dripped slowly on her head while her leg throbbed.

What was that?

She heard a horse quietly come into the patio. Viriato growled, while a horseman, dark and silent, looked around. Viriato barked, and the horseman turned a beam of light on the dog. The horse was prancing as if ready to step on Viriato. Angela held her breath and waited under the water. When she came up for air, the horseman was gone.

During the night, Madalena woke up with a start. She'd had a dream that she was falling from a very high veranda, and on the ground, Manuel had his arms open to catch her. But at the last minute, he ran away, and she hit the ground.

She was wide awake, looking around the room, her heart beating rapidly.

Saul's house was big and quiet, like him.

She tried to fall asleep, but she had the same dream again and again. She screamed.

Saul came in, holding an oil lamp. Madalena was sitting in bed covered with sweat, taking shallow breaths.

"Are you all right?" he asked.

"I had a nightmare," she whispered.

Saul was leaning at the entrance of the room.

"I was falling …and I hit the ground," she explained with some embarrassment.

Saul placed the lamp on the side table and said quietly, "You will not hit the ground again. I will catch you."

She smiled with the irony, as if he knew that, in her dream, Manuel had run away.

"I will wait until you fall asleep again," he said. He sat on the edge of the bed, took her hand in his and gently stroked it with his thumb.

"I'm a very light sleeper by nature, I wake up with my own dreams, with the wind outside, with a thought …" she said.

Her hand in his felt so comforting. It was compared to a dream she had often—Jesus with his arms opened wide, and she, under one of his arms, where no one could harm her. She felt the same peace now.

"Go back to sleep," she said.

He pressed his lips together, almost a smile. "Go to sleep first, and then I'll go," he answered.

She looked up at him, and he was grinning—a full-blown grin that illuminated his eyes. She was perplexed. How different he looked when he smiled. She rested her head on the pillow and closed her eyes. "Good night, Saul," she said.

"Remember, if you fall again, I will catch you," he said.

"I will remember," she murmured as he took the lamp and left the room, closing the door quietly.

Madalena spent her days looking at time going by slowly, with nothing to look forward other than Saul coming home. Dear God, what had she done? How could she live beholden to a man who she didn't even like? Did she like Saul? She had never thought about it. He had been so unimportant to her that she had never thought about him. She vaguely remembered laughing with the others about his dark ass or when something was said about Maria Augusta. But other than unkindness, she had never thought of Saul. She was surprised by his gentleness since the first day she'd agreed to marry him. But the old habit of thinking about Saul as the big, fat fool crept in. It was as if she was thinking of a different person instead of changing her opinion of him.

Most days, he came home for lunch and asked her how she was. There was no smile, like the first night. He didn't smile in front of people, not even in front of his mother. They sat and ate as a family, but there was no talk, except by Maia, who engaged in long monologues.

There was a knock on the door. Madalena felt her stomach lurch. Saul was home. But it was not Saul. It was his mother, Carlota, who looked at her for a long while and said, "My son is the most precious thing on earth."

Madalena waited for more; surely that was just an opening statement for a longer conversation. But there was just that, so sincerely stated that it sounded like poetry. Was that a warning? A plea? Madalena thought of a poem she'd read: "My precious, will you ever know that you are my everything?"

Madalena had been married for one whole month. Life at Saul's house was unreal. She felt like a princess in a castle. Saul's house was big, spacious, beautiful, and wearily quiet. Even the radio played timidly. Saul came home for lunch and dinner most days, and according to Maia, this was something new that he'd adopted since he'd gotten married.

It was up to Maia to keep the family entertained and the conversation going. She talked about the weather and the village. Carlota and Saul never responded to her chatter, as if they were ignoring her. But they were paying attention. They were relieved that Maia was talking and entertaining Madalena. At first, Madalena felt uncomfortable for Maia. Even when she asked a question, they didn't answer. Then Madalena learned what were rhetorical questions and real questions for Maia. And to the real questions, Saul and Carlota answered with monosyllables.

Life at Saul's had a firm pattern: He left for work, Carlota returned to her embroidery, Maia went about administering the house, and Madalena was alone again.

She felt so alone that the height of her day was Saul coming home. And when he came home, they were quiet again, eating supper while Maia talked.

"Angela Gomes almost drowned at the Cat's Brook today," Maia said.

Madalena stopped in midbite. So did Saul and Carlota.

"What happened?" Madalena asked anxiously.

"Someone was drowning a cat, a little kitty, still with his eyes shut. And she jumped into a running brook after the bag where the cat was …"

"Is she all right?" Saul asked quietly, keeping an eye on Madalena.

"Yes, thanks to someone; no one knows who. People saw her being dragged down the water like the Rocha family, and she disappeared. People ran by the side of the brook, telling her to hang on to the blackberry bushes. But when she was about to disappear under the bridge, on that deep fall …someone fished her out. When she came out of the water, she was almost unconscious, but she didn't let go of the bag!" Maia said, shaking her head.

Madalena got up and went into the garden. High walls like a fortress surrounded Saul's house. The gate was unlocked, but there was something forbidding about opening it and getting out; yet today she walked out and up the road.

Saul followed her and held her by the arm, bringing her inside again. She looked at him irate and surprised.

"Sit," he said.

She sat on the edge of a bubbling fountain. A foolish-looking angel was blowing water out of a trumpet.

"I will find out how she is," he said.

"I am not a prisoner, Saul. If I decide to leave or go somewhere, I will!" she said, agitated.

"You are upset and I am concerned … You fainted in the past," he answered quietly.

Madalena lowered her eyes.

He had boots on. Those were the biggest boots she had ever seen. Every day, she discovered something new about Saul. Today it was boots. Usually men didn't wear boots. Either they put on sandals, sabots, or simply walked barefoot. She looked up at him and said, "I'm sorry. I never know what to expect … We hardly know each other, and I thought …" She fell silent.

He gazed at her, knowing the expectations she had of him—that he could turn unpleasant, make her do things she didn't want to do. She had known much violence, and she didn't expect much from men. His heart broke for that beautiful girl looking up at him, defiant and thinking that she had to fight, always.

"No harm will ever come to you," he said gently. "Come into the house."

Saul directed her to the bedroom. She sat down on the bed.

"You look tired. Are you all right?" he asked.

"I'm fine. But I'm worried about that fool, Angela."

Saul touched her cheek so gently that Madalena thought she had imagined it.

"Why don't you rest a while? I will find out how she is," he said.

That night, Saul didn't come home for supper. She wished he had. Even if he was quiet, his presence was soothing. She gazed at the walls surrounding the house, and she felt comforted.

Saul's house.

Would she ever think it was also her home? She had lived in her father's house, and now she lived in her husband's house; would she ever have a home of her own?

Ascendida answered the knock on the door. Saul was standing there, blocking the light from the afternoon sun.

"Saul?" she asked, as if she could be confusing him with someone else.

Saul looked at her almost bursting belly—Mario's baby. Everybody knew it was Mario's baby, as everyone would know that Madalena was having Manuel's baby. He felt a pang of sympathy for Aldo.

"I'm looking for Angela," he said. "Her mother told me that she was staying with you."

"Angela got hurt today. She is sleeping," Ascendida said. "Come in."

Saul came in and stood in the middle of the kitchen.

"What do you want with Angela?" she asked.

"I want to know if she is all right, so I can tell Madalena. She is worried."

"Why didn't she come?" Ascendida asked dryly.

"She needs to rest," he answered.

"You didn't let her come," she accused.

Saul thought about that. No, that was not the truth. He was about to answer when Lazarus came into the kitchen. Saul looked at the spitting image of his wife. There were no bruises on his face, and he was holding a thin, long kitten. It looked more like a skinny rat or a ferret than a cat.

"Saul wants to know about Angela," Ascendida said to a surprised Lazarus.

"She is sleeping. She is staying with Ascendida because of the baby, but she got hurt at the Cat's Brook, and she is resting," Lazarus said.

"Did she jump into the brook to save a cat?" Saul asked. There was no judgment in his voice. He just wanted the facts so he could tell Madalena, as he'd promised. He looked at the thing Lazarus was holding. It was making distressing sounds, looking for something with its eyes still shut.

"Yes, she did. This is Hercules, the cat she saved." And Lazarus stretched his arms toward Saul, who stepped back. He didn't like cats.

"Can I see Angela?" Saul asked.

Saul followed Lazarus down the corridor and entered a room sparsely furnished. Angela was asleep with the covers up to her neck. She looked so peaceful. Every time Saul interacted with Angela, she was agitated about something, but now she was so still.

"Where is she hurt?" he asked, lowering his voice.

"All over," Lazarus answered. "But the worst injury is on her thigh—a big hole, maybe from a rock or a branch as she went down the brook."

"Shouldn't she go to the city?" Saul asked.

"Ascendida took care of her."

Saul was looking at Angela, hoping that she would open her eyes.

"She will be sleeping for the rest of the day …due to the medication," Lazarus said quietly. After a long silence, he added, "I want to see Madalena."

"Why don't you?" Saul asked.

"Because you don't want people to visit," Lazarus said, almost annoyed.

Saul didn't answer. It was true. He didn't want people to visit and bring Madalena news of that foolish boy, Manuel. He wanted people to leave them alone, but not like that—not like as if she was all of a sudden abandoned by everyone.

"You can visit. She feels very alone I think. People must give us a chance … and stop talking about Manuel," he said, lowering his voice to a whisper.

Angela stirred, and Lazarus lay next to her, hugging her over the covers. That ugly thing was mewing while Lazarus made a little place for the cat, between Angela and him.

Saul turned around and left. He went by the kitchen and slightly bowed his head to Ascendida and walked out the door.

"That ogre," Ascendida murmured as he went up the road toward the church.

When Saul got to the church, the monsignor was yelling at someone in the sacristy, and Saul waited, hiding in the shadows.

"There is no such thing, you fool! There is no such thing as a werewolf!" the monsignor screamed.

"We saw it, Monsignor! We saw it jump over the wall, as if it had wings. And here is the proof; the end of my staff still has the blood it drew, when I threw it at him."

"What the hell was your dog doing that it didn't go after him?" the monsignor screamed again.

"Even the dog was afraid. Poor Nero ran toward that thing, but he came back wagging his tail."

"Out! Out of my sacristy, you imbeciles!"

Elias Mendes and his father came out running as if they'd been pushed violently as the door of the sacristy closed with a bang.

The monsignor came out and peered down the center aisle of the church to see if Elias and Deolindo had left. When he was assured that they were gone, he addressed Jesus, lifting his arms and gesticulating violently. "Why do you give me these fuckers to deal with?! Why are you so bent on making me suffer stupidity? Why? Is there no end to my punishment?"

A low, sinister-sounding laugh invaded the church. The monsignor was frozen, looking at Jesus, and Jesus stared back.

Saul felt that he should make himself small, because he could not witness something terrible—not again.

Slowly, the monsignor turned around. Saul thought he was looking at him. But the church was dark, and Saul was in the darkest corner, at the very back of the church.

A shadow walked up to the monsignor. It was a tall figure with a cape and a hat.

A hat in church! Saul thought in dismay.

"Take your hat off, you insolent bastard!" the monsignor said.

"I will, if you take off your surplice—or is it a dress?—you miserable louse." The man laughed again.

"What do you want now?" the monsignor asked, trembling with rage.

"Just to let you know that everything is all set. It is nice to know that at least this time you kept your promise."

The man turned around and walked out of the church. His cape swayed behind him, but the wide-brimmed hat hid his features.

Slowly, the monsignor turned around and left the church, and Saul did the same, forgetting his urgency to talk to the monsignor.

As Saul walked home, he was thinking about what to tell Madalena. He could talk about Angela and that ugly cat and even about Elias Mendes and the werewolf. But this encounter with the stranger and the monsignor … What was that?

4

Loving Saul

Madalena was at the open window looking into the night. She peered out more intently when she heard the latch on the gate.

Saul walked up to the window, rested his elbows on the sill, and looked up at her. He looked tired.

"I went to see Angela," he said.

"How is she?" she asked, full of concern.

"She was hurt, but Ascendida and Lazarus are taking care of her."

"You saw Lazarus?"

"Yes."

"How is he?"

"He looks good, very good."

He reached out and touched her face tenderly. "He sends you his love," he said and went inside of the room, through the window, in one easy jump.

Madalena let out a little yelp of surprise.

He laughed. It was a strange sound to hear him laugh.

"For a second, I thought you had wings," she said.

"Maybe I do," he answered.

He sat on the bed, and she walked up to him. Madalena felt an urge to kiss him. She wondered how it would be to kiss Saul.

"You look tired," she said. "You should go to bed. Tomorrow is Sunday, and you'll tell me all about Angela."

"I also saw Elias Mendes and his father, talking to the monsignor about a boogeyman they saw last night," Saul said, lowering his voice but sounding amused.

"You did not!" Madalena said.

"Did too," he said and walked toward the door. He turned around and grinned.

She looked up at him. "Really? What else?"

Saul got serious all of a sudden. He was thinking about the stranger and the fight with the monsignor.

Madalena pulled him gently into the room and they sat on the bench at the foot of the bed. "What happened?" she asked, sensing his mood change.

She slowly lifted her hand to his face and caressed him. He held his breath for a second. Then he pressed her hand to his mouth and kissed it gently on the open palm.

"Angela and Lazarus are fine," he said. "I went to talk to the monsignor, to let him know that we too are fine." He waited to see how she accepted this understanding of their relationship. "We are fine, Madalena, are we not?" he asked.

She was very quiet, and Saul, afraid that he had spooked her, attempted to distract her by telling her about the stranger in the church.

"Who in the world could talk to the monsignor that way?" she asked.

"Only the devil would dare." And he smiled.

"You should smile more often. You are very handsome when you do."

"Now you are pulling my leg," he said. "Handsome. I don't even know how to spell the word."

She thought about the stranger she had married and looked out the window into the beautiful June night.

"We could go out to the garden, if you are not afraid of the boogeyman," she said.

He got up and scooped her in his arms. She let out an exclamation of surprise.

"You are barefoot. You can't go into the garden barefoot," he said.

She laughed and threw her arms around his neck. They passed Maia and Carlota, looking on speechlessly.

"I don't remember the last time I heard him laugh," Maia said to Carlota.

"I do, and it was a long time ago," Carlota murmured. "This girl is good for him."

"We would kill her if she wasn't," Maia said with a grin.

In the garden, Saul and Madalena sat on a bench near the fountain. The moon was dancing fluidly in the water, and the crickets were singing. It was so peaceful that Madalena felt overwhelmed. She had never known peace before, not like this.

"Madalena," he said gently. "I've been trying to work up the courage to tell you something."

She was trying to make out his face in the shadows of the moonlight.

Then he said, "After you have the baby, you can leave."

Madalena didn't expect that. She felt a pang of terror invade her.

"Go where?" she asked bewildered.

"You tell me, and I will set you up. I can set you up in the city, here in Two Brooks, anyplace you want. And I will take care of you and the baby. No one will harm you." He said it so calmly, so businesslike.

She had been in his home for almost two months, and she couldn't see herself anyplace else. Where would she go with a baby?

"Is that what you want?" she asked softly.

"I want you to be happy. I don't want you to feel that you owe me anything …" He faltered. "I don't want you to feel lame. I have to do the right thing by you."

Tears ran down her face.

He wiped them with his fingers, tracing her cheeks and her lips. "Please don't cry," he said. "I will do anything you want, including letting you go."

"But I don't want to go. I want to be here, with you … I just need a little bit of time …" Madalena thought about Carlota and what she had said about her son being precious. But she wanted to be with Saul because she was selfish, not because he was precious. She was just thinking about herself. If she had someplace to go, would she leave?

"Time. Is that all you want?" he asked, his voice gentle and light with relief. He scooped her up again and walked back to the house.

Madalena put her hands around him and very intentionally nestled her face between his shoulder and neck. She felt his heart quicken and the beat of his pulse in her mouth as she lightly kissed his neck, before he placed her down.

The following day, Madalena had a visitor. It was her father.

Angela and the other friends had come over many times to see her, but they always received the same answer; she was not home.

Madalena's self-imposed exile was irking Pedro Matias. He wanted his daughter parading the streets with her new ogre of a husband and to show that bit of nothing, Manuel Barcos, that her belly was growing under another man. He was suspicious that she was meeting Manuel somewhere. Now the letters proved that Manuel had no intention of leaving her alone. And she was weak; she would fall.

"She is not home," Maia said to Pedro.

"I will go and look," he threatened.

"Leave my house!" Carlota said.

Madalena heard the commotion and came out. "Leave us alone!" she said, stepping in front of Carlota.

He advanced on Madalena, and Carlota's eyes widened in horror. Quickly she stepped between father and daughter. She knew that her son would kill this man if he so much as touched his wife.

"You are not my problem anymore, but I wanted to see if that cuckold man of yours had given you a good beating. Didn't he tell you about the letters?"

"What letters?" the women asked in unison.

Pedro let out a mean laugh. "Her boyfriend has been writing," he said.

Madalena paled, felt the room spin around, and grabbed the edge of a table before everything went dark.

When she woke up, Natividade, the midwife, was applying cold towels to her forehead.

"She needs rest or she will lose this baby," Natividade said sternly.

Carlota and Maia were looking down at Madalena, a frown of concern on their faces. Madalena opened her eyes and swept the room, looking for Saul.

"He will be here soon," Maia said, patting her hand.

Madalena felt reassured. Saul would come soon, and all would be well. And with this thought, she fell asleep.

When Saul came home, Carlota and Maia told him about Pedro's visit. Carlota kept an eye on her son. She knew his temper so well. She patted his hand gently and said, "Don't get angry. Don't make things worse for Madalena. She is sleeping now. We called Natividade just to make sure that all is well …"

"Madalena was asking for you," Maia said.

Maia had been ten years old when Saul was born. Mister Paulo had taken a wife, Carlota, and later brought them all to this island. She loved this little boy, who had never been little, not even when he was a baby.

Saul walked silently into Madalena's room and sat by her bed. The day was so bright that not even the drawn curtains could keep the light out. Madalena's hair was wet and curling around her face. He felt a surge of tenderness take hold of him. He had lusted over Madalena. He had imagined many things with Madalena. But he had never felt this thing tugging at his heart, this joy just to be looking at her.

She opened her eyes and looked around, startled.

"I'm here," he said quietly.

She let out a big sigh.

He sat on the edge of the bed and held her hand. "I'm going to have a talk with your father," he said evenly.

She looked at him suspiciously. She didn't want him to go near her father. She didn't want anything to do with her father and his poison. "No," she said.

"Yes, I am," he stated simply.

"Please, Saul," she said. "He is a terrible man. He harms people. Don't—"

"I know what I'm doing. Don't worry." And he smiled at her.

"He said that I've been corresponding with Manuel," she said.

Saul was quiet, and Madalena knew that something was going on. She frowned and waited for an explanation.

"He has been writing to you, and I intercepted the letters," he said.

"You …you read my correspondence before I did?" she asked.

"No. Just the letters without a sender—his," he answered quietly.

Madalena was not sure if she should be upset or if she should apologize.

"I didn't know he was sending me letters," she snapped.

"Well, now you know," he answered evenly.

"I had nothing to do with that!" she answered agitatedly.

He said tenderly, touching her face in a caress, "Don't get agitated. It doesn't matter … Think about the baby."

Madalena closed her eyes and let out a sigh. She was so still that she looked like a statue. Saul's gentle touch on her cheek was so soothing that she could fall asleep under such tenderness.

"I'm a bit frustrated with that silly boy …and with your father," he said.

"I'm more than what you bargained for," she answered.

"I didn't bargain. You asked me to marry you." He pressed his lips together to suppress a smile.

"You are making fun of me," she said, holding his hand in hers.

"Deservedly so," he murmured.

Angela ran limping all the way to Natividade's house. Viriato ran alongside Hercules, who never stopped mewing.

Ascendida was having the baby.

It was nightfall in the middle of July, and the threat of a drought loomed threateningly over the island. Two weeks without rain was a long time for a place that saw rain every day. Almost every year, the island was victim of a terrible drought, and any child born during a drought was considered an unlucky child. Ascendida was going to have her baby, Mario's baby, during a drought.

When Natividade arrived at Ascendida's, Angela already had the water boiled and towels prepared. Maria Gomes and Ophelia were with Ascendida, and the neighbors were waiting in the kitchen.

Aldo sat quietly outside the kitchen door while every conversation inside was about Mario and his baby. Aldo closed his eyes and thought of his brother; oh how he missed him!

And then they came, two baby boys. Francisco and Aurora Costa looked at the two babies, their grandsons, as they had years ago, with wonder and love. Life was repeating itself, like an amendment, a new chance.

Ascendida looked at the babies with curiosity. She didn't cry during labor because she saw Mario's laughing face egging her on. She could hear his voice in her ear, "Come on, little Ass, you can do it." And now she had two little Marios.

Angela limped out of Ascendida's house, feeling the throbbing on her leg. She wanted to tell Madalena that Ascendida had had the babies, and all was well. It was dark already, and Angela was thinking about those fools, Elias Mendes and his father, Deolindo, on the streets looking for the werewolf. Would they spear her again, thinking that she was the werewolf? It was almost a good thing that she had jumped into a running brook to rescue Hercules. How would she explain an injured leg like that if it had not been for the brook incident?

She heard a noise like thunder, but Viriato heard it first. He stopped and sat on the ground, growling softly. Hercules hissed, and Angela froze. A dark and tall shadow on horseback was coming up the road at a fast pace, going straight at her, deliberately seeking her. Angela was not one to be scared easily, but things that she didn't understand scared her most of all, and she didn't understand what was happening now. Viriato's fur stood up. Hercules hissed and ran away. Angela put her back against the wall. Should she scream? She could see Saul's house down the road, dark and big with a faint light shining over the wall. His gate was open. Would they hear her if she screamed?

An enormous black horse stopped next to her, moving impatiently as if ready to trample someone. The horseman laughed softly. He was wearing a cape and a wide-brimmed hat. He pointed a bright flashlight at her face.

Slowly, he moved the light down to her injured leg. "How is your leg?" he whispered.

Angela blinked and held Viriato by the scruff of the neck.

"Be careful, little girl," the horseman said. "Down the road, someone is hunting a werewolf." And he left at a high gallop, his cape flying behind him.

Angela turned around and went home. Her intention to visit Madalena suddenly lost its appeal. She ran all the way home, as fast as she could. And when she got there she sat, out of breath, outside of the house before going in. Her parents were asleep already, having no idea that their daughter was being chased through the village as the werewolf.

Hercules came around, peering into the dark.

"Coward!" Angela said picking up the kitten. She closed her eyes, rested her head against the stucco of the house, and concentrated.

What was it about that man on the horse that was familiar? She had never seen him, but his voice … She had heard it before.

Deolindo Mendes knocked at Angela's door in the middle of the night. Angela and her parents woke up, startled. Deolindo Mendes and his son came in as soon as the door opened. Elias was crying, holding his jaw in his hand with blood running through his fingers. His father was yelling something about the werewolf.

Finally, both men came down, and Elias looked at Angela's little hands coming at him to check the injury. He started to scream again, his jaw slanted and hanging to the side, as he drooled all over himself.

"Be quiet," Angela said softly. "I just need to see if it is broken or just out of place."

He tried to speak, full of tears and drool.

Elias was not a good-looking boy. He was tall and thin, with flaming red hair, freckled nose and cheeks, and a terrible case of myopia; the thick glasses sat on his nose like a crown of thorns. After his parents realized that their son was almost blind, not stupid, as Dona Lidia had said he was, he'd got eyeglasses. Elias was never tired of finding out things in the world—the saints in the church, the beauty of the girls, the teeth of his dog, the smile of his mother. It had been Elias who had seen the werewolf for the first time. Elias was so anxious to see the world that he could see things that no one ever did, like the werewolf. Everybody liked to laugh at Elias. Between what he thought life was and what life really was, usually there was a good laugh at Elias's expense. The Freitas brothers, the pranksters of the village, were always setting poor Elias up. They convinced Elias that the sound of applause during the theater shows was not clapping but the slapping of their own faces, just like during Lent, as a penitent gesture of self-punishment. And totally convinced that he had been told the truth, instead of clapping at the end of each song, Elias slapped his own face.

Angela looked at him. That boy had thrown a staff at her with a sharp nail at the end. He could have killed her. And now he was there, drooling all over her kitchen, where she was fixing his jaw.

"What happened?" Joaquim Gomes asked, getting closer with the lamp so Angela could see what she was doing.

"That goddamned boogeyman came at him on a horse and kicked him to the ground before he had a chance to stab him with the staff," Deolindo Mendes explained.

They had heard of boogeymen and werewolves before, and who knew if they were real or not, but a werewolf on horseback? They had never heard of that. But there he was, Elias, with his jaw out of place and a red, round mark on the side of his face, almost like a hoofprint.

Angela was touching Elias's face lightly, almost caressing it, and having a feel for the injury. Suddenly, Elias let out a terrible scream. And then through eyeglasses full of mucus and saliva, he fixed Angela with a look of wonder.

"It is not broken," she said. "It is just out of joint."

Angela never accepted payment for services, but the villagers always paid with wheat, corn, chickens, or eggs. Angela had cows, chickens, and everything she needed because she was showered with gifts—if not payment, at least gifts.

The following day, Elias brought her a duck. She put the young duck in the chicken coop. But the other chickens and the rooster immediately started on a terrible persecution, and the duck ended up featherless and bleeding. Angela decided to let the duck run free around the house. And the duck followed her everywhere—to church, to the store, to her friends' houses, to the fountain. Angela named the duck Dalia. Now she had a menagerie following her around the village——- a dog, a cat, and a duck.

The drought was getting its claws into the island.

Madalena sat in the garden, near the angel, but the angel and his trumpet were dry. She was hot and restless. She wanted news of Ascendida, and she was hoping that someone would have come by and let her know. But why should they? She didn't receive visitors and had refused to accept her friends' visits the many times they'd come to inquire about her. They would end up forgetting her, like a princess in a tower, guarded by a dragon—Saul.

Saul the dragon was not home. He had left early in the morning to go to the city, as he did almost every week. As always, she had her meals with Carlota and Maia, listening to Maia's news of the village.

"Ascendida had two boys, twins, like her husband and the dead brother," Maia had said earlier. "And Deolindo Mendes and his son saw the werewolf again. This time, the werewolf was on horseback and knocked Elias to the ground with a kick on the face. The poor boy went to Angela to fix his jaw."

Carlota had smiled. Madalena had looked at Maia to see if she was joking.

Now, sitting in the dark garden, Madalena was thinking about her friend fixing the damages caused by the werewolf. She heard the sound of a horse galloping down the road.

Saul.

The moon was bright and big, casting a blue light on everything when Saul came through the garden gate on his horse. He didn't expect to see her there, like a ghost, and pulled the reins back in surprise, and the horse almost threw him off. He dismounted and walked slowly to her.

"What are you doing here, little ghost?" he asked.

"I was waiting for you," she said, "I suspected that you are the werewolf ..."

"And if I am?" he asked.

She could tell that he was smiling. "Then you should do what werewolves do," she answered.

Saul suddenly lifted her off the ground. She let out a shriek and laughed when she found herself being carried home. She put her arms around his neck and hid her face under his chin. He smelled of sweat, of horse, and of soap. He carried her through the house to her room. She was still laughing softly as he put her down on the bed. When she looked up at him, he was smiling.

"That's what werewolves do," he said, kneeling at her bare feet, taking them in his hands and gently squeezing.

"What a pitiful werewolf you are ... Foot massages?"

Madalena felt again that warm tenderness spreading in her chest. She looked at his hands, so big and powerful, being so gentle and light.

Madalena put her arms around his neck, and Saul scooped her up and walked around the room with her hanging off his neck, his arms around her, his face buried in her shoulder.

She laughed.

His arms were so tightly wrapped around her waist that he could feel her hard belly pressing against him. Then he felt it—a small stirring in her belly. He was very serious, not really sure.

"Saul," she said, "I think you've been kicked."

He put her down on the bed and placed a hand on her belly. "I was, wasn't I?" he asked in wonder. And he did that rare thing; he laughed.

Carlota never slept until her son came home. She went to bed but stayed awake. She listened for the horse's hoofs on the patio or the door being opened and closed, and then she would go to sleep. Tonight, she heard other things; she heard laughter and amused voices. It was so rare to hear Saul laugh. He'd stopped laughing when his father had gone to jail, to Africa, on that terrible night. And since then, he had never again been the same. He had stopped being a child, a young boy, and had become the man of the house. And he'd carried since then that terrible burden—guilt.

That night before going to sleep, Madalena thought about love—the many faces of love. And her memory was betraying her love for Manuel. The way she felt about Manuel was so different from what she felt for Saul, and she thought that maybe it was not love that she felt for Saul. But what was it then? What was that warm joy when he came through the door? What was that complete and utter sense of peace when he was at home, even if they were not in the same room? What was that tenderness when she looked into his eyes?

Angela had told her that she was identifying with the ogre. It was a psychological phenomenon. Madalena smiled politely and said that he was not an ogre. And when Angela asked if she wanted to know how Manuel was doing, Madalena was surprised that Manuel didn't cross her mind.

"He wants to see you. He is thinking of leaving to Brazil."

Madalena felt nothing. She should be feeling something terrible. But she didn't.

I will see him and say good-bye—say good-bye for good; if he stays or if he goes, I will let go, Madalena thought. *I will let go of everything about Manuel.*

This was the last thing she remembered thinking before falling asleep.

That very same night, she woke up with a terrible pain in her belly, and she cried out. Saul ran into the room and found her in a pool of blood.

Carlota and Maia prepared Madalena in a hurry for a trip to the city while Saul was preparing the horse carriage. He wished he had his truck near the house, but it was with one of his managers in a different village. Like lightning, they got to the city hospital. But when they got there, it was too late.

Madalena had lost the baby, and everything about Manuel was truly gone.

The days that followed were a daze for Madalena. She remembered sleeping a lot and Saul sleeping on a chair next to her bed. She opened her eyes, and he was spilling out of a small chair, his legs spread apart, his head back, and his arms open as if he had been shot and fallen back. She wanted to call out to him, but she fell asleep again. At times, she looked at the chair, and it was empty. And sometimes Saul was there, as if dead. She tried to call out but couldn't find her voice.

And then he opened his eyes and saw her staring. He came out of his trance fast and disoriented and knelt next to the bed, his face almost touching hers. They looked at each other and said nothing; Saul was always lost for words, and Madalena didn't want to say the words stuck in her throat.

He kissed her cheek, the first time he ever kissed her, and she caressed his stubble chin. "I want to go home," she said, her nose touching his.

"Home?" he asked, as if confused about the meaning.

"Yes, with you, Carlota, and Maia … I want to go home."

And they went home. Saul picked her up and sat her in the backseat of a car that she had never seen—a black, shining Chevrolet, with beige leather seats, soft and warm from the sun.

"I should have bought a car a long time ago," he said, although she hadn't asked.

Saul was thinking that, if he'd had a car, maybe Madalena would have not lost the baby. The trip to the city would have been faster and smoother. He was frowning, lost in thought, and looked at Madalena through the rearview mirror.

Angela had gone again to talk with Lazarus. He was at the carpentry shop, completely absorbed with a piece of wood, as if he could see fascinating things in it. He was alone; most men stopped by after work or on weekends. Early in the morning, Lazarus was always alone in the carpentry shop.

"I came to ask you again," she said, "and this time you have to say yes."

Lazarus smiled at her. "I always say yes," he said.

"You have to go now with me to the monsignor and set a date. We are going to get married by Christmas."

He frowned. "Did you talk to my father again?"

"Yes."

"What did he say?"

"He said that he was going to talk to the monsignor."

"That was five months ago," Lazarus said, crestfallen.

"I talked to him today. He gave me a dead piglet, and he said that, if I made the piglet live, we could get married by Christmas."

Lazarus was fully aware that Angela was strange, but sometimes she pushed her luck. He crossed his arms and looked at her sideways. "As beautiful as you are, you don't make miracles," he said.

"You got it wrong, Lazarus. I am not beautiful, but I make miracles."

"The piglet rose from the dead?" he asked incredulously.

"He did."

Angela loved Lazarus with the single-mindedness of the undefeated. Everyone knew that, sooner or later, she would find a way to marry him, and it would not be with the tricks that Madalena had used hoping to marry Manuel. Angela was going to do it on the up-and-up, or almost.

That morning, before coming to talk to Lazarus, Angela had gone by Pedro Matias's house to talk to him about business. Pedro had finally relented and offered her more money so that she would continue to do the books for him. Angela refused, unless he agreed to let her marry Lazarus. Pedro was assisting the birth of piglets, and Angela was looking on, thinking that he was doing everything wrong with that poor mother pig. And after the birth, he discarded a small, black piglet with a white star on its back, dead, the runt of the litter. And that was when he said, "If you bring it to life, you can marry Lazarus or any of my boys before Christmas and consider the piglet your first wedding gift." He laughed, helping the other piglets get closer to the mother pig and throwing the poor lifeless thing out of the pigpen.

Angela took hold of the little pig, cleared his throat and gave him mouth-to-mouth resuscitation. She rubbed his skin for circulation, wrapped him in her apron, and cradled him against her chest. She waited. Suddenly, the little pig made a noise as if he had been stirred out of a deep slumber and immediately looked for nourishment.

"December 19," she said to Pedro, who had already forgotten the promise. "We will get married December 19." And she showed him the pig, oinking in her arms.

Lazarus was astonished to hear Angela's narrative. There was no defeating that heart of hers. He picked her up, and they both spun around the room laughing; the smell of cedar intensified with the stirring of the air.

Her beautiful and precious Lazarus would be her husband soon.

Together, they went to talk with the monsignor.

The newlyweds to be walked into the sacristy, where the monsignor was yelling at Antonio Dores, the deacon. Antonio had left the seminary under a cloud of suspicion, but he got a good education and consequently a good job at city hall, in the finance department. He had married Emilia, Nascimento's sister and had two little boys.

Emilia was once a fun loving, talented, and friendly girl. Poor Emilia …

As soon as the monsignor saw Angela and Lazarus, he let out an expletive of frustration. "What now?" he yelled.

And Antonio Dores bowed his head and left.

Angela and Lazarus told the monsignor about the wedding and about the resurrection of a pig. The monsignor sat and put his head down between his hands. "Angela, you are going to be the death of me," he said, as if Lazarus had nothing to do with it. "You wear people down; you are relentless."

"Please," she said, "please let us do this."

"And where are you going to live?" he asked.

"Don't know yet. But we would like to have a business, an inn. We would like to buy the Cardoso's house."

"How in the world are you going to do that?" the monsignor asked, "Pedro Matias will not give you a dime, and you don't have a dime to your name, and Joaquim Cardoso has no intention of selling his property. He is coming back from America to live there."

Everything the monsignor was saying was true, but she could try, couldn't she? She could ask Joaquim Cardoso if he wanted to sell. And if he said yes, she would find the money—a lot of it. Lazarus would have the carpentry shop. He made very good money there, and she could take more clients as a bookkeeper.

"How about your school?" the monsignor asked. "Weren't you going overseas to the university? Is it not what you said that you wanted to do?"

Angela thought about her dream to go overseas to school. She was going to be an economist, maybe a doctor, or even a lawyer … "We have many dreams," she said. "And sometimes they are incompatible with each other; this is one of those times."

"Child," he said, trying to sound patient, "you are too young. Go to the university first. Allow Lazarus to go to the military. Grow up, both of you, and then get married."

The monsignor was exasperated. He also knew that Angela had won. He looked at Lazarus. Why was he looking at Lazarus? It didn't matter what Lazarus wanted. Angela was the driving force for both of them.

And so, Angela and Lazarus were going to get married in December, in less than five months' time. Angela was sixteen years old, and Lazarus nineteen.

5

The Mysterious Horseman

After those initial victories, Angela was disheartened about the answer she got from America. Joaquim Cardoso didn't want to sell the house. He was coming back to show the village the rewards of his sacrifice—he was coming back as an American. He was going to fly the American flag during the village festivities, wear brand-new clothes and new boots, smoke cigars, and tell tall stories of faraway places. He was going to offer banquets during the Holy Ghost festivities and pay for the most expensive bullfights in the island.

Indeed, Joaquim Cardoso came back full of glitter and found himself a brand-new wife. His wife of thirty-three years died in the middle of the preparations to come back to the island. It was almost a self-fulfilling prophecy. When Joaquim made the decision to go back to the island, the poor woman said, "I would rather die than to go back to that hole of mud and lice." And so she did. She was buried in her beautiful America, the place that she loved more than any other. And Joaquim, with the deep but brief sorrow of a widower, found a wife half his age and settled in Angela's dream house.

Joaquim was a robust man of sixty. He was thick waisted, red faced and slightly bald. When he came back, he thought that he could have his pick of women because he was American. He addressed a few young girls, offered them marriage, stability, love … They looked at him and considered the sacrifice: If he went back to America, maybe. But to live in the island married to an old man, no. The sacrifice was not worth it.

He asked Ilda, one of five girls of a family of dreamers. Ilda's father was an artist and an inventor. He came up with great business ideas and ingenious concepts that only needed hard work behind them. But because he was an artist, the hard work didn't follow. His ideas would fall into someone else's lap, and he or she would make a go of it. And Miguel Duarte, Ilda's father, would say sadly, "You know, that idea was mine."

Ilda silently hated her father. If he only put hard work behind his ideas, they could be rich now. She wouldn't have to sacrifice her youth to escape the misery of the island. But by now, she knew that, if she didn't marry rich, she would never be anything but a poor islander. And she set out to find out if Joaquim Cardoso had money. She asked him right out, and Joaquim was taken aback by such abrasiveness. But he had a certain respect for the girl—she knew what she wanted.

"Money is not everything, my dear," he said with a half smile, trying to hide the bald spot on his head by moving his hair around with his hand.

"It is if the man who wants to marry you is old," she said straightaway. "A big house and flashy clothes are not good enough. If we go back to America, I'll marry you."

Joaquim looked for other young women, but any young woman willing to give him a thought was pretty much like Ilda. So he gave in and agreed to go back to America with his young wife.

Now the house was for sale, and Angela had her chance—just a chance, but no money. Joaquim Cardoso agreed to give her one month to finance the purchase, and Pedro Matias had already made an offer.

Angela thought about miracles. People had asked for miracles, and God had conceded them. Lazarus had asked for a wristwatch when he was a little boy, and he'd gotten it. This was a miracle. Little boys did not get wristwatches.

Everyone had left the church after the evening mass, but Angela stayed. She sat on a pew, her head bowed in prayer. She was doing more math than praying, thinking of the amount of money she needed for the transaction.

"What am I going to do?" she said, looking at Jesus Crucified.

She waited, as if Jesus was going to give her an answer. "Please, help me!" she finally said. "I'm sorry about your eyes … You look terrible."

"Angela!"

She jumped. She didn't expect anyone to be in the church at that hour, much less the monsignor.

"Go home child!" he said, infuriated. "Pray to God that He will provide you with wisdom!"

On the way home, Angela stopped at Ascendida's house. Aldo was sitting at the kitchen table, eating alone, as if he didn't belong. Poor Aldo, so in love with his wife, and Ascendida with a faraway look, stuck in her memories. The babies were crying, and Angela went in to help. Nascimento was already lullabying the babies.

Nascimento gave Angela a look of dismay. "My goodness! Where have you been, girl?"

"Trying to find money!"

"Any luck?" Nascimento asked.

"None."

"Why don't you ask Saul?" Nascimento said. "The only thing good about the man is that he is rich."

"Have you seen Madalena?" Angela asked.

"After she lost the baby, she went completely underground," Ascendida said. "I wrote her a letter. I said that we miss her and want to see her."

"Did she answer?" Angela asked interested.

"No. It is as if she died to the world."

"I wonder if she is given the letters," Nascimento said. "I could take a peek," she said, looking at her friends.

"You stop that!" Ascendida snapped. "The Mendes are hunting werewolves! If you are caught, it will not work out as well as it did with Jaime."

Angela was very quiet. The other two women looked at her suspiciously.

"This werewolf business is …strange," Angela said pensively. Angela knew that, on one of the instances, the werewolf was herself. But who was that macabre figure on a horse running through the village and breaking people's jaws? "I know every horse in this village, and no horse looks like that," Angela said.

The women were quiet, each one fascinated with the darkness of Angela's story and the mysterious things happening in the village.

Rosa sat silently near Angela. "I saw the man," Rosa said very softly.

After Rosa's family drowned in a running brook, she was terrified every time the brook engorged and ran noisily toward the sea. But she would look from afar into the turbulent waters and wait for her people to come out of it, like a miracle.

"Did you see him, Rosa?" Angela asked softly.

Rosa hid her face in the crook of her arm.

Ascendida said, "Did he see you?"

Rosa shook her head, no, he didn't.

"And what did he do, darling?" Ascendida asked, kissing the top of Rosa's head.

"He ran down the pastures and jumped into the brook and waited for the waters to bring Angela to him. He had one hand hanging onto the bushes, and with the other, he caught Angela." She extended a tiny arm to demonstrate.

Rosa looked sideways at Angela. "He …hit you," she said softly.

"How?"

"Turned you over and hit your back, and you threw up. He put his hat on …wet, dripping, and a cape …and left."

"Would you know him if you saw him?" Angela asked Rosa.

"No, I was far away … And I couldn't see well."

When the whole village was already crying for Angela, she had come up from the pastures, limping, all battered and wet but holding a kitten.

"The werewolf saved Angela." Nascimento laughed.

"What does the monsignor say about all of this?" Ascendida asked.

"He says that there are no werewolves, and he thinks that no one saved me from the brook; it was God wanting to spare me," Angela said quietly, as if in deep thought. She was going to talk with the monsignor about the stranger in the village. If there was a stranger, the monsignor would know … And she would tell the monsignor that God had a little help.

When Angela left Ascendida's house, she decided to pay Saul a visit and ask him for the money. The worst he could say was no. She walked down the village as the sun completely disappeared behind the hills of the Cat's Brook. She was followed by her menagerie, now with the addition of a pig called Nixon. Angela thought that it was a perfect name for a pig. Most people did not understand, but she liked it, thinking that Eisenhower was too long of a name, not practical at all for a pig.

Angela got to Saul's house. She stood outside the tall gate. His house was surrounded by tall stone walls, like a castle. And inside was Madalena—the enchanted princess. Angela turned the latch on the gate, half expecting it to be locked, as it had been before. But the gate opened with a soft mewing sound. Inside, everything was so quiet that Angela thought that no one was home. However, there was light inside. Angela felt her heart beat wildly. What the hell was she going to do? Ask Saul for money?

She knocked.

Saul came to the door, blocking the light from within, and stood silently staring down at her. He stepped aside to let her in. Carlota was embroidering, sitting by the window with an oil lamp perched on a nearby table. Maia was in the chimney room, washing dishes. No sign of Madalena. A radio played softly.

"I'll see if Madalena is available," he said quietly.

"I …came to talk to you," she said.

He frowned slightly. Carlota stopped her embroidering, and so did the clinking of the dishes in the kitchen.

"Can we talk in private?" she asked.

They stepped out into the garden. The moon was big and bright like an August moon should be.

"I know we are not friends," she said, "but we are going to be family. In a way, I am going to do for Lazarus what you did for Madalena."

There was an awkward silence. Then he asked, "What did I do for Madalena?"

"You saved her from her father."

"Is that why you are marrying Lazarus?" he asked.

"No. I love him, but I am also saving him from his father."

Saul was looking at her intently.

"I know in my heart that Pedro will kill Lazarus, sooner or later, if Lazarus doesn't leave," Angela said, her voice quivering with emotion.

Saul was very quiet, but the air around seemed to get heavier.

"When we get married, I am going to take Dona Amelia home with us and the boys also, if they want. I am going to leave that man alone with his own poison," Angela said. And after a pause, "And this is the reason I am here. I came to ask you for money. I need money to buy Joaquim Cardoso's house. I have less than a month to find the money, and Pedro already made an offer on the house."

He didn't say anything. He was looking at her with wonder. She had maligned him, protected Manuel, and here she was asking him for money, while Manuel was writing love songs and love letters to his wife.

The door opened, and Madalena came out. She had a white nightgown on. Her hair was longer than usual but still wavy and shiny. She looked like an angel.

"Angela?" she asked surprised. Then she smiled and ran to her friend and hugged her. "I've heard you won. You are going to marry Lazarus," Madalena said.

"Yes, in December," Angela said.

"Where will you be living?" Madalena asked.

Angela vacillated for a second and then said, "I'm still looking at possibilities …"

Saul was leaning against the wall, with arms crossed over his chest. He was looking at the two women with that look of his—lowered head and a veiled stare under the brow.

"Joaquim Cardoso's house is a good idea," Saul said. "You should make an offer soon."

Angela looked at him. He smiled. It was such a brief smile that Angela thought she had imagined it.

"Really?" Madalena asked delighted. "You always loved that house ... But do you have the money? My father will not give you a dime. Maia told me that his wedding gift was a dead pig ...and you—"

"Over there." Angela pointed to Nixon. The pig was sitting against the wall with the others. They looked like well-behaved children waiting for their mother. Nixon had a pink nose, and he looked up at them, with a smile.

Madalena started to laugh. She used to laugh like that, peals of laughter, throwing her head back and letting it out. Angela was laughing also and recounting the scene of Nixon's resurrection.

Saul had never heard Madalena laugh like that. She laughed a little here and there but never like she was doing now. He protected her, he loved her, but could he make her laugh like that?

The two friends forgot about Saul. They sat on a bench, talking and laughing, while he was still standing in the same spot, wondering.

Madalena looked in his direction and Angela saw something in her eyes, something good and peaceful.

"I should go," Angela said, standing up. "Are you all right?" she asked her friend.

"Yes. I am very well," Madalena answered.

"I will talk to you tomorrow," Saul said to Angela.

When Angela left, Saul sat next to Madalena on the garden bench.

The night was so peaceful, so light.

"You are barefoot again," he said.

Madalena put her hand inside his. He closed his fingers around her small fist.

"I am feeling so much better," she said, as if answering his thoughts.

He squeezed her hand in acknowledgment.

"Tonight you will sleep in your bed. You must be so tired," she said.

"I sleep better if I am with you," he said, getting up and, without a word, picking her up. It was becoming a habit. When Saul put Madalena down, she slid her arms from around his neck, but she held his face between her hands. And she looked at him for a long while. Saul was comfortable with silence, and he waited under her gaze.

"You are going to lend Angela and Lazarus the money, aren't you?" she asked.

"Yes," he said.

Madalena felt his breath on her face. "Thank you," she said and kissed him tenderly on the lips.

Saul closed his eyes and made a soft sound, as if he had been hurt.

Madalena was surprised at the softness of his mouth. Such a generous mouth, always so serious and quiet.

She pushed away and said, almost out of breath, "Good night, Saul."

"Wait," he said, holding her by the arm. "Wait," he said again.

He lowered his head and kissed her gently on the mouth, deepening his kisses as she responded. Madalena pulled away, and then she hugged him by the waist, a tight, full-body hug; turned around and went to her room, walking with haste as if something urgent was taking place and she needed to get there.

Angela was walking fast up the road, thinking about the werewolf. She was going home, and later Lazarus would jump through the window of her room and stay with her for the night. No more sleeping in the barn.

At this time of night, the men were at the Music Club House, at home, or at the carpentry shop. So when Angela heard the sound of a horse galloping up the road, she knew it was the werewolf again, as if he had been spying on her. She had heard the sound of the horse ever since leaving Saul's house, sometimes closer and sometimes farther away, but always behind her. Viriato had his hackles up and was growling. Hercules disappeared with Dalia. Nixon, small and smiling, was running ahead.

And in a flash, the horseman was cornering her against the public fountain. She held her breath. "Leave me alone!" she said.

"Something is happening up the road that you don't want to see," he said in a whisper.

"What?" she asked, between fear and surprise.

And then she heard sounds of screaming and crying. The horseman had the light focused on her face again.

"I'll take you home, by the forest road," he said. And in one swift movement, he leaned down and stretched his arms to her. As if bewitched, she grabbed on and flew up to him. He held her on the horse, encircling her by the waist. She let out a scream when she found herself tightly against a stranger, flying on a horse through the forest road.

"Be quiet," he said and grabbed her earlobe between his teeth.

Angela was hypersensitive about everything around her. The horseman smelled of soap, his grip was strong around her ribs, and his mouth was warm and soft on her earlobe. He was sweating, and Angela's back was getting damp from his chest. He gave one last suck and tug on her earlobe and then let go. They went around the village and came to her house by the opposite side, avoiding the area around Pedro Matias's house.

When they got to her gate, he dropped her down. "Night Justice is acting up. Be careful, little girl. Tonight was your turn, along with that poor boy."

Angela understood now when people said that they peed themselves with fear. She was not sure if she was afraid, but she wanted to pee herself, right there, looking at the horseman disappear up the forest road.

Maia came running in. The news she had from the village was more than news; this news was connected with them, especially with Madalena.

Carlota, who was preparing something for lunch, dropped everything and brought her into the chimney room.

"What is it?"

"The boy, poor boy; they almost killed him last night."

"Who?"

"Manuel Barcos. The Night Justice got him and gave him such a beating. He was found naked, his back full of lashings and with his ...his ...dove, I mean his penis, black, completely black with bruising!

Carlota put a hand over her mouth. My God. Madalena would immediately think that it had something to do with her. They had to keep quiet because she was just getting better ...

"And it is not all," Maia whispered. "He had a pencil up his ass—a pencil with a paper attached that said, 'I'm writing a love letter.' He went to the hospital. The monsignor is furious. He called the police, and the police will be here soon. And I'm sure that they will be coming by, because of Madalena."

Carlota was still speechless, with a hand on her chest, when her son came in. He looked at the women and asked, "What happened? Is it Madalena?"

Saul walked briskly to Madalena's room and opened the door without knocking.

Madalena frowned and waited for an explanation.

"I don't know what happened. I'm sorry I startled you," he said quietly.

"What happened?"

"I don't know. My mother and Maia looked anxious ..."

"And you thought it was because of me?" She felt her heart melt.

He let out a slow breath and caressed her face with the back of his hand as he sat down next to her.

She leaned toward him until she rested against his chest.

He closed his eyes. Then so softly that Madalena could hardly hear it, he said, "I love you."

She looked up and kissed his mouth. He responded kiss for kiss, gently, for a long time, without a word.

He felt her slim body under his relax and accept his insistence. "I love you," he said again.

There was a loud knock on the door, and they stood up in a hurry as if they were teenagers caught necking. They heard the slamming of car doors. Saul went to the window and frowned at the scene. Two police officers were walking up to the front door.

"Stay here," he said to Madalena.

But she came out after him and held his hand.

And then the cops told Madalena and Saul what Carlota and Maia already knew.

The interrogation started—about Saul's whereabouts, if he had witnesses, people to vouch for him. And of course he could have left during the night, so his mother and housemaid would not know. He could very well be Manuel Barcos's assailant.

"Saul didn't harm Manuel!" Madalena said.

The two cops looked at her. They knew her story. They knew that her father had made her marry Saul Amora and that she had been pregnant with Manuel Barcos's baby.

"He was with me," Madalena said.

And the two cops witnessed an unexpected glimpse of love. It was a second, if that. Saul placed his enormous hand on top of Madalena's head, and she looked up at him, and they smiled at each other.

This didn't agree with what the cops knew of these two people; there was no love in this marriage.

"We were told that Manuel Barcos had been sending letters to your wife. Is that true?" one of the cops asked. They waited for an answer, along with everybody else.

"Yes," Saul said.

"Did you threaten him?" the officer asked.

"I told him to stop bothering my wife," Saul answered calmly.

"Also, Pedro Matias said that you grabbed him by the neck a few weeks ago and threatened to kill him. Is that true?"

"Pedro Matias is my father-in-law as you know. He came into my house to intimidate my wife. I just gave him a warning."

"Did you threaten to kill him?" the officer insisted.

The three women looked crestfallen. Saul had assaulted Pedro Matias, and now Pedro was trying to create trouble for him.

"No. I told him to stay away from my family," Saul answered.

The cops were like statues, tense, glaring. "We will be back," one of them said.

When the police left, Carlota brought the soup and bread to the table, but no one wanted lunch.

"I didn't know you had a fight with my father," Madalena said quietly.

"We didn't have a fight. I told him to leave you alone. He said he wouldn't, and I gave him a taste of what he could expect," Saul answered calmly.

"Be careful, my son," Carlota said softly. "Pedro is not an honorable man."

Saul gave his mother a long look fueled with meaning, got up, and left the table. Madalena followed him into his room.

"Saul," she said, "don't get involved with my father. He does this on purpose, to provoke you."

Saul sat on the desk, and he was somewhat amused with her concern.

"I think I love you," Madalena blurted out.

He was very still; only his nostrils flared a little.

She said, "I never felt for anyone what I feel for you. But I'm not sure what it is. It may be just gratitude, for feeling safe and loved. And if I do love you, what happened to my love for Manuel? Was that love? And if it was, how could it be so easily forgotten?"

Saul pulled her into him and kissed her. Then he pulled away gently and said, "When you are sure, either way, let me know. I for one love you without a doubt."

Saul met with Angela about the house purchase, but he was distracted and concerned about what he heard at the Music Club House. The men were talking and joking about Manuel, but they were saying something about Angela. They were saying that Angela was going to be caught by the Night Justice. The rumor was that the Night Justice was going to give Angela a good lesson because of her disobedience to her parents and to the monsignor for insisting on getting married.

Saul, the man who hardly talked, was repeating a rumor to Angela.

Angela fixed him with a hard look. Was he the night horseman? No, he couldn't be. However, the night horseman always came from that end of the village. And yesterday, he had come right after she had talked to Saul.

No, she couldn't imagine Saul laughing like that and biting her earlobe.

"What's wrong?" he asked.

"You probably will think that I am crazy," she said, still looking at him.

He waited quietly for an explanation. He already thought she was crazy.

"There is someone very mysterious going around the village. He …he …" She stopped. She didn't know if she should continue. How could she tell Saul that a complete stranger had sucked her earlobe?

When Saul left, Angela felt cold, although it was August. The night horseman had saved her from the Night Justice. What would they have done to her if he hadn't taken her home? Manuel was still in the hospital with his genitalia swollen and bruised.

"The Night Justice did a job on Manuel …using their own cruel methods," Angela's father said shaking his head. "He could have died," he added.

Angela had heard about those methods, and she felt a perverted urge to laugh; she hid her face in the crook of her arm.

Her father looked at her. "What is the matter with you?" he asked, irritated.

Had he heard the rumors about the Night Justice wanting to get her? But if her father hadn't heard, Monsignor Inocente had, and he'd called her in to have a talk.

"I don't want you on the street at night!" he had said. "If you need to go somewhere, you go with company. And God forbid, if I learn that you are going out at night!" He was agitated and paced the length of the sacristy. "I swear to God that I will give you a beating!"

Angela had listened quietly before asking, "Who is the man with a hat and a cape?"

The monsignor stopped pacing and turned on her, "What the hell are you talking about?"

"He saved me from the brook, and yesterday he grabbed me and took me home on horseback. I was going to walk right into the Night Justice affair."

"Oh my God!" he had murmured. Then with fury, "How am I supposed to know that?"

Angela's father was still talking to her, but her mind was on the conversation she had had with the monsignor.

Yes, the monsignor knew who the stranger was. There was one thing that the monsignor didn't know how to do—he didn't know how to lie.

Saul had a gift for Madalena. He came into the room where she was reading and gave her a box. He didn't say anything; he just placed the box in front of her and smiled.

She took the box, smelled it, shook it, and listened to it. He laughed. Madalena could make him laugh with silly things. Or was it love that made people laugh so easily? He found himself smiling about nothing or staring at a bee, at a daisy, at the formation of the clouds ...

"I know what it is already," she said.

He lifted his eyebrows in disbelief.

"You bought me a pair of slippers."

He laughed again.

"That's a gift," she said, "your laughter."

"I would never buy you slippers," he said quietly. "I love your bare feet."

She caressed his face. The light of the day was dying out in orange hues, reflecting in his eyes, and Madalena knew that she was falling in love. She was so afraid of being happy and quietly denied that she could love this man, her husband, this kind, and gentle giant.

"Open the box," he said.

She did. "My own radio?" she exclaimed.

He was thinking that they could go to bed early and listen to the new radio in bed, her head resting on his chest. And he would kiss her hair, and they would fall asleep.

"I went to the city today with Angela," he said. "She now owns the house of her dreams. She bought it right from under your father's nose. He thought she would never find the money and relaxed. He should have known that one could never relax with Angela."

Madalena said pensively, "I only can imagine the vindictive ways he will try to get back at her ... She told me that, if she got the house, she would say a prayer every day for poor Ilda, who sacrificed her youth for America … She'd better pray for herself also."

"I also went to the police," he said.

Madalena's eyes widened, "Again?"

"They say it was the Night Justice who attacked Manuel."

Madalena knew it was her father. Maybe her father was part of the Night Justice, but it was her father. Maia had told her about the rumors going around the village and the danger that Angela was in, especially now that she had outfoxed Pedro with the Cardoso's house.

The joy about the radio was gone.

She looked at him for a long while. Sometimes she just looked into his eyes, and she knew what he was thinking. It was such a relief for Saul not to have to verbalize every thought.

"Manuel told them that he was not sure if I was part of the group that attacked him," he said.

Madalena was still, searching his face. Manuel was a romantic fool, but he was a good man, an honest man. He would not implicate Saul out of spite.

"Manuel told the police it was my father, didn't he?" she asked.

"Yes, but Lazarus vouched for your father."

Madalena was thinking about the things her father must have threatened Lazarus with to make him vouch for him.

Saul was still looking up at her. He wanted to ask her to stay with him tonight. He would leave the window open for the breeze to come in, and they would listen to the radio until they fell asleep.

Don't go into your room alone; please don't go, he thought.

But this time, Madalena didn't read his thoughts. She was worried about Manuel and Angela and angry with her father, who in a million ways never left her in peace.

6

Small Miracles and Other Blessings

The following day, Angela got up early to set up the chicken coop. She had ten hens and Narciso, the vain rooster, waiting for their new home. Narciso pranced around looking sideways at his chickens, and when he saw Angela, he walked up to her and stood in front of her with one leg up, making loving sounds.

Angela lifted her head in surprise when she saw Lazarus running toward her in complete distress.

"He took Nixon! He took Nixon to the market!" he said breathlessly.

Angela knew instinctively that he was talking about Pedro. She ran out to the street and saw Pedro's truck spinning dust on the forest road.

Angela had left her shoes somewhere between the chicken coop and the house. She only had time to mount Lazarus's horse and went after the truck, coaching the horse to go faster and faster.

Pedro Matias soon realized that someone was after him, and then he laughed ripe big guffaws when he saw Angela. Well, well, this little lesson was getting better than he had hoped. Not only was he going to give his son a good lesson on loyalty, but he was also going to have a bit of fun with Lazarus's soon to be wife.

When they entered the city, both the truck and the horse went side by side. Angela could see Nixon on the bed of the truck with a rope around his neck, making distressing sounds. Finally, they arrived at the wide square of the city market.

When Angela dismounted and went for the truck to get Nixon, Pedro grabbed her by the hair and started to yell that she was a thief trying to take his pig.

The police came, and people started to gather, fascinated with the commotion created by a wild girl fighting for a pig and a man between laughs and slaps, taking the pig away from her.

"Who wants to buy this pig?" Pedro Matias asked, full of laughter, looking to the people around them.

Some offered a sum, others offered more, and others were just laughing. But with all the commotion, the pig was getting quite expensive.

Angela screamed a higher offer every time someone offered a price.

Pedro looked at her and said, "Okay, you win; the pig is yours. Show me the money."

The people around applauded, and then they screamed with delight when Angela could not produce the money.

The auction started again. The cops were smirking, making sure that the public order was not totally disrupted. They just needed to keep an eye on the girl and let the man sell his pig.

And then someone bought the pig.

There was a hush in the crowd. Angela's eyes swelled up with tears. She looked at a tall and elegant man giving the money to Pedro, who laughed, "I could buy a cow with this amount!"

The spectators applauded. The man put the cord under his arm and walked out of the market with Nixon oinking sadly and pulling on the cord to get to Angela, who took the horse by the reins and followed the man outside the market square.

This tall stranger was looking at her, amused.

Nixon freed himself and ran to Angela's open arms. She kissed his snout, murmuring apologies, "I'm so sorry darling," she said to the pig. "One of these days, I'm going to kill that bastard."

The man cleared his throat. "You are kissing my pig."

Angela looked at the man. "I will buy the pig," she said.

"You don't have money. That's why I was able to buy the pig," he said evenly.

"I will get you the money. I live in Two Brooks," she said, wrapping Nixon's cord around her hand. "I'll give you …" She didn't have a thing to give him as a sign of good faith. She thought for a second. Then she unhooked the gold necklace, a gift from her parents when she'd graduated from school. "This is all I have. You keep it until I get you the money."

"I'll take the horse," the man said.

"No. This horse is not mine to give," she said firmly.

He extended his hand, palm up, to receive the necklace. The sun glinted on the gold before the stranger closed his fingers over it.

Angela became self-conscious when she realized that the man was taking stock. She was a mess—barefoot and probably with chicken shit on her clothes.

"Okay miss," he said. "I will find you and get my money. Then you will get your necklace back."

The stranger had the greenest eyes she had ever seen, and his skin was the color of his hair, a very light brown, as if he was tanned to perfection. When he smiled, two dimples appeared, one on each side of his mouth.

Angela slowly walked up to the man and kissed him on the cheek. He bent his head when he realized her intentions and laughed. He put his hands on her forearms and squeezed a little, looking down at her.

He said, "I will find you."

She was still trying to figure out the uneasy feeling in the pit of her stomach when someone stepped in front of the sun, casting a shadow.

"Saul, what are you doing here?" she asked.

"Lazarus asked me to come and bring you home," he said, getting out of the truck.

Angela let out a heavy sigh, and Saul waited for her to jump into the truck. He took the horse by the reins.

"I will go back with Wind. But you can take Nixon with you."

Saul was not sure if it was a good idea. When Lazarus had stormed the house looking for him, he had just gotten home, by chance. And both Madalena and Lazarus had told him to bring her back in the truck. Now this stubborn girl wanted to go back on horseback. What was he going to say to Madalena when he got home with a pig but no Angela?

"They want you to come with me," he said.

The stranger was observing the exchange. When Angela mounted the horse and the pig was put in the truck, he turned around and left. Angela was looking at his back, the sun shining on his wavy hair.

She frowned.

Something was off.

Lazarus was in the garden with his sister, both pacing nervously. "This is a warning," Lazarus said. "I told him that I was not going to cover for his deeds, and this was a warning. He knows that beating me up will not do anything, so he is using Angela to keep me in line. And he is getting revenge on Angela for getting the Cardoso's house."

"Is it true that Night Justice was waiting for Angela?" Madalena asked.

"I've ...I ...I think so. I asked father, and he laughed. He said something gross."

"He did it," she said softly. "He did that terrible thing to Manuel." Madalena narrowed her eyes. "Were you there?"

"I was waiting for Angela, hiding in her room. She came home and got in bed, without her usual exuberance. She kissed me good night without a word. When her father knocked at the door, I did my usual dive under the bed. She opened the door, and he asked if she had heard strange noises just before she came in. She said no. I knew she was lying, and she got in bed again, without locking the door. I was under the bed, still waiting for her to call me up. But she didn't. I was the one who locked the door. She was strange that night. I think she saw something."

Saul's truck entered the patio.

"She wanted to come with Wind," Saul said to two identical disappointed faces.

Nixon was looking around for Angela and making inquisitive sounds.

Soon, they heard the horse running down the road and into Saul's garden.

Angela dismounted Wind and ran to Nixon. She hugged and kissed the pig as if she hadn't seen him for weeks. Saul, Madalena, and Lazarus were watching, while Carlota and Maia were laughing behind the curtains.

"Is she going to kiss Lazarus with those lips?" Maia asked.

Carlota laughed. Much like her son, she didn't laugh much. But now she did, thinking of Lazarus being kissed as passionately as the pig had been.

"How did you get Nixon away from my father?" Madalena asked curiously.

"Dom Carlos," Angela answered.

"Who?" they asked in unison.

"A man who looks like Dom Carlos. He bought Nixon and then he sold him back to me. He will be coming for the money," Angela explained, frowning.

"How much did you pay?" Lazarus asked, worried.

"I paid as much as I would for a good horse," Angela said softly, as if in deep thought.

"That's not right!" Madalena said.

Nixon oinked, offended.

Angela turned around and faced three confused faces. "Do you believe in guardian angels?"

"Yes," Madalena and Lazarus answered at once. Madalena was thinking of Saul, and Lazarus was thinking of Angela.

Saul didn't know what to think.

From behind the curtains, Maia turned back to Carlota, "Do you, Carlota? Do you believe in guardian angels?" Maia's eyes were full of memories.

Carlota placed a hand on her shoulder and smiled sadly. She wished she believed in a celestial creature sent to earth by God to protect her, to ward off malice and hurt. But she didn't. She knew that this earth was her hell. If not, how could she believe that God was just? Where was the justice in what had happened to her Paulo? How could they deserve such sorrow?

"Do you, Carlota?" Maia insisted, looking at her.

"Yes," she lied.

Maia smiled. She was reassured that, above all, God was good. He had sent her Mister Paulo, Carlota, and Saul to take her away from a hopeless and bleak life.

Yes, there were angels, and she was surrounded by them.

The monsignor was desperately seeking a new teacher to take Dona Lidia's place. They were at the end of August, and there was no time to waste.

The monsignor told an ecstatic Angela that the new teacher should be her first lodger, and he was almost sure that they would have a teacher in a day or two.

Coming home from her conversation with the monsignor, Angela ran into Regina Sales.

"A man came by to talk to you today, but you were not home. He knocked and knocked and left. He came by car," Regina said, bursting with curiosity.

"Have you seen him before?" Angela asked.

"No. He must be the new teacher. He looked educated. He was a looker too."

Any man was a looker for Regina.

"He said he would return later today," Regina affirmed.

Angela was not prepared to receive the teacher yet, but she would accommodate him.

And later the man came with a traveling bag to Angela's home. When he knocked, the menagerie ran to the door as Angela swung it open.

"Dom Carlos!" she exclaimed, hardly containing her surprised.

He smiled. "You sound disappointed," he said. "And my name is not Carlos."

"I thought you were my new lodger," she explained.

"I am," he said. "I came to rent a room from you."

"Oh my Lord!" she said, completely taken aback. "You are the new teacher?"

"I'm sorry to disappoint you again, but no. I am not a teacher."

She was momentarily confused. "Did you talk to the monsignor?" she asked.

A brief darkness came over his face, almost imperceptibly, and he asked, "Do you need his permission to rent your rooms?"

"No!" she immediately said, not wanting to give this man the wrong impression. "Usually the monsignor is the first one to know a newcomer to the village ..."

"And he approves of them or not?" he asked with his head slightly to the side.

"Something like that," she said.

Angela was trying to decipher what was wrong with this man. She felt the urge to go up to him and smell him, like Viriato was doing.

"Well?" he asked, "do I have a room or not?"

"I expected you to come by to get your money, not to get a room," she said.

He took the necklace out of his shirt pocket and gave it to her, "I'll give you the necklace, and you rent me a room."

"I can't afford to give you a room for free," she said.

He grinned. "I paid a lot of money for that pig," he said.

"I'm running a business. I'll give you the money for Nixon and keep my right to rent my rooms at the rate I want."

"Fair enough," he said.

Angela had the feeling that this man was making fun of her.

"You keep the necklace, you don't have to pay for the pig, but you rent me a room, and I will pay the asking price," he said.

"Okay, I know a good deal when I see one. But I am not ready yet. I was ready for the teacher but not for anybody else," she said.

"I can have the room that you have prepared for the teacher, and you prepare another room, since the teacher is not here yet."

She had at least a few days to prepare for the teacher.

The man looked down at the smiling pig. "Hello, son," he said.

Angela laughed. He laughed too. And again she felt that she'd heard that laugh before.

Of course she had—at the market, when Pedro was selling Nixon.

The other animals were only mildly interested in the man. Dalia disappeared, Viriato was wagging his tail, and Hercules was smirking. Hercules smirked better than a person.

"I'm not renting you a room," she said suddenly.

"Why?" he asked, totally surprised.

"I know who you are."

Angela went up to him and, on her tiptoes, put her face to his and smelled him. The man was laughing and bent down obediently.

"I've never been sniffed by a person before," he said.

"At the market, I was too upset to recognize you, but I knew there was something about you. Now I know. You are the mysterious horseman. You smell like him, and you sound like him. Where is your horse?"

"I am not mysterious," he said. "And you saw me for the first time at the market."

"I can play with words too. I saw you for the first time at the market because I couldn't see you under a hat and a cape. And you bit my ear."

He threw his head back and laughed. Angela was dismayed with this man.

"I'm not renting you a room. You are up to something," she snapped.

He extended his opened hand to her, palm up, and said, "Give me back the necklace."

"No. I'll give you the money for Nixon, and I will do whatever I want with my rooms."

"You accepted the deal to keep the necklace, not pay for Nixon, and rent me a room. You did, just a few minutes ago," the man said firmly.

Angela was thinking.

The man looked up, as if expecting illumination from above. He fixed amused eyes on her again and said, "We can make a deal. Go to the monsignor and ask him if you should rent me a room. If he says you should, you will. And if he says no, you won't."

"And," she said, "you will tell me the truth about the mysterious horseman."

He laughed again and said, "Go to the monsignor first."

"Why?" she asked.

"Because."

"Because is not an answer," she snapped.

He was looking at her still, but he was not laughing now. He was looking at her as he had in the market, as if he was taking stock of her, evaluating her personhood. And again she thought of chicken shit and dirty feet.

"You will be sorry if you go around playing Zorro," she said, staring back at him.

"I'm not Zorro or mysterious or a horseman. I am a businessman with a car, not a horse."

"If I rent you a room, you have to come clean though," she said.

"Clean?" he asked mockingly. "I'm not dirty either; there is nothing to come clean about."

"Don't provoke me Mr. …whoever you are. If I rent you a room, you are going to fess up. I need to know who you are, what you want from me, and what the hell you are doing in Two Brooks."

"I'm sure you'll make me confess."

"Yes. If you want to rent from me, I need answers. And let me warn you that I detect a lie before it is uttered."

"Ah, yes … You are the little witch. I've heard about you."

"How?" she asked with curiosity. "Have you been talking to people about me?"

"At the market, when we were bargaining for the pig, someone told me that I was dealing with a witch."

"Good. Remember that then, if you are tempted to cross me. I can put a curse on you."

"I've been bewitched before, and I survived," he said, as if a curse was a common enough event. "I will be back tonight to learn of your answer," he told her dismissively.

"Not tonight," she said.

"Be here and don't go roaming about in the night," he said, as if guessing her thoughts. And he left.

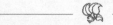

"I need to talk to the monsignor," Angela said to Catarina.

The monsignor came out of his study when he heard voices. He looked at both women and frowned ill humoredly. Catarina disappeared into the kitchen.

Angela asked, "A businessman wants to rent one of my rooms. Do you know him?"

"I know hundreds of businessmen. What's his name?" he answered impatiently.

She didn't know. "He is the same man who fished me out of the brook, saved me from Night Justice, and got my pig away from Pedro."

The monsignor let out a scream of frustration.

"What? What is the matter with this man?" she asked, spooked.

"He is a mainlander, a pain in the ass," he said, still screaming.

The monsignor didn't like outsiders.

"You know him then. You knew that this man was around, and you didn't tell me!" she accused.

"I was hoping that he would go away!" he said, still agitated. "He wants to mechanize agriculture. He is specialized in agrarian machinery. He wants to do it in Hawk Island on a big scale. He is an engineer, and I don't want him here!"

"What's wrong with that?" she asked perplexed. "What's wrong with progress?"

"Progress? What do you know about progress, child?"

"Monsignor, stop yelling at me. I'm getting a headache."

The monsignor sat down and got up again.

"I forbid you to rent to him!" he said.

"Why?" she asked, getting increasingly frustrated with the monsignor.

"Because!" he said.

"Really? Since when is *because* an answer?" she asked.

"Go home; I want you home before nightfall!"

"Is this man dangerous, Monsignor? Is he a bad man?" she asked, concerned.

The monsignor was quiet for a moment. Then he said in a calmer voice, "No, he is not dangerous like that. But he …he is an outsider with new ideas … and you know what I think of outsiders."

"You don't like him?" she asked.

"I don't like most people," the monsignor said after a long pause. "Go home, girl! It is getting dark, and I don't want you alone on the street!"

The village was winding down, performing the last tasks of the day, its inhabitants ready to close their gates, bring their animals down from the pastures, lock the chicken coop, bring the dogs and cats in, and finally sit for a restful supper. They looked reproachfully at Angela. It was almost nightfall, and she was on the street. They'd heard the rumor about what Night Justice wanted to do to her, but there she was on the street. Could this girl ever be tamed? She was not even afraid of the Night Justice.

Angela went by the carpentry shop. Pedro Matias was there too, and he smirked when he saw her.

"Be careful. I think the Night Justice is looking for you," Pedro said.

Lazarus approached her anxiously.

"I'm staying in the new house tonight," she said, "because we have our first lodger."

"The teacher is coming tonight? I thought it would be in a few days."

"Well, no and yes. We will talk later ..."

He walked her home. At the gate of the new house, he took her face in his hands and kissed her. He nibbled on her lips gently, as if tasting a delicacy.

"Kissing is overrated. Biting is much better," he said.

When Angela got inside the patio, the menagerie was patiently waiting, like a loyal army.

The house was large and generous, full of rooms and windows. Angela lit up all the lamps and locked the door. People never locked their doors, but with the Night Justice on the offensive, she didn't want to take chances. She locked the windows, sliding the top pane down to let the breeze in, along with the sweet smell of honeysuckle.

She was working the last details for the teacher's room when the horseman knocked. Through the window, she saw a confident man. She opened the door, and he came in carrying a few bags.

"I have more in the car," he said.

"I guess you already know that I am renting you a room," she said.

He smiled. "Did you talk to the monsignor?"

"Yes. And he forbade me to rent you a room."

He straightened up and frowned at her.

She laughed.

He let out a sigh, "You are joking, aren't you?"

"No, I'm not joking. He forbade me, but his reasons were not good enough."

"And what were his reasons?" There was coldness in his voice.

She took a second look to make sure she was getting the right nuance.

"The same as yours …*because*," she said. Then she added, "He doesn't like mainlanders and progress. You represent both."

They looked at each other for a while, measuring the impact of this decision."Come and see your room," she said, waving him up the stairs.

"You are going to defy the monsignor?" he asked.

"I don't do it often," she answered.

"And you are doing it for me?"

"No. I'm doing it for me. I'm starting a business, and I don't want the monsignor to get the idea that he has the right to interfere with my business decisions."

The room she showed him was spacious, with tall ceilings and gleaming hardwood floors. The furniture was simple but sturdy.

The man touched the rocking chair in the corner of the room and said, "Beautiful piece."

"Lazarus made it," she said, full of pride.

"Let's talk about business," the man said, standing in the middle of the room.

"Don't you want to go down to the kitchen and have something to drink?"

"Later," he said.

She waited, and he added after a pause, "I am a respectable businessman, to you and to everybody else. So I hope that there will be no talk about Zorro and other romantic notions."

She smiled smugly. "Only if you admit it to me now."

"Yes."

"Thank you," she said, reaching out and holding his hands. Thank you for saving my life, Dom Carlos."

He was looking at a most sincere and open smile. He smiled back. "My name is not Dom Carlos."

"What is it?"

"Antonio Manuel Saraiva Marques Castro da Silva e Nogueira."

"Are you serious?" she asked looking at him doubtfully.

"Yes. If there is one thing I know, it is my name."

"Wow! We are full of Antonios in this village—some good, some bad. Which will you be?" she asked.

"Dom Carlos it is then," he said.

There was a knock on the door.

"My mother is here. She is staying with us tonight, just in case."

"Just in case of what?" he asked.

"Oh …local stuff," she answered and went downstairs.

Dom Carlos was looking around the room when he heard a scream and a door slam. He quickly went down the stairs and into the kitchen, where a laughing man was advancing on Angela. She was on the other side of the table, putting distance between the two of them.

"What is it, my dear? I just want to see your brand-new house," Pedro said.

"Good evening," Dom Carlos broke in, slowly walking toward Pedro.

"Who the hell are you?" Pedro asked in dismay.

"I'm the new lodger, Dom Carlos."

"You are the guy from the market." He started to laugh. "Did she weave her charms on you too?" he asked, pointing at Angela.

"I suppose she did," Dom Carlos answered. "I thought I heard a scream. I didn't, did I?"

"What if you did?" Pedro asked with a smirk. "You know how women are—scaredy cats." He fixed Dom Carlos with a mean look. "You are not like these outsiders who think they can change things around here, are you?"

"God forbid," Dom Carlos answered evenly. "I just want to work in peace. If I hear that you are making Angela's life miserable, that inevitably will affect my peace. So …I will put your ass in jail."

Pedro Matias laughed, mean hardy guffaws. "Others have tried. It would not be a two-bit teacher who is going to do it." He opened his arms in a gesture of peace. "But why are we fighting? I just came here to say hi and to see the house. She is the one who got spooked for nothing. For goodness sake! She's my accountant, my financial advisor, and my little thief. This house was supposed to be mine; do you know that? But …we are all family now." Pedro Matias was laughing still.

Angela was spooked like a cornered animal.

"Do you want him to leave?" Dom Carlos asked.

"Yes, I want you to leave," she said, finding her voice and looking at Pedro.

"Wait a minute here," Pedro said, trying to sound polite. "This is my son's house also. You cannot throw me out."

Dom Carlos walked slowly toward him.

"Okay, I'm leaving. But I am telling Lazarus how I was received," Pedro said in an offended tone and left the house.

Angela waited to hear the gate close. "I'm sorry," she said. "He pushed the door in and then shut it with a bang. I was surprised and screamed."

"Is he always this charming?" Dom Carlos asked quietly.

"He is getting worse. He thinks he owns everybody. He thinks he owns the police; he thinks he is above the law. He is furious with me because of the wedding, and then I bought this house from under him. He thinks that everybody is laughing at him because he doesn't know the difference between a dead pig and a live one. He is dying to make me pay," she said somewhat aware that she was babbling.

"Well …it is true; he doesn't know the difference between a dead pig and a live one."

Angela shook her head as if to shake off a fly. "So you heard about Nixon, how I got him?"

Dom Carlos was leaning against the wall with his arms crossed over his chest. He lowered his head, maybe to hide the fact that he was smiling. "Yes, I've heard," he finally said. "I think the whole entire island heard that, somewhere, there is a girl who resurrects pigs, heals all kinds of ailments, and does magic."

Angela laughed, and he followed.

When Maria Gomes came to the door she heard laughter, and she waited a bit before knocking. It couldn't be Lazarus; he never laughed aloud.

It was late afternoon when a police car came to Pedro Matias's house. Two police officers asked for him. He was in the carpentry shop with his sons. And right there, he was arrested.

"What? What have I done? What are the charges?" he yelled. He knew very well that the police didn't have to have a reason. They could arrest anyone. And so they did.

Pedro spent half a day and one night in jail and had a conversation with the chief of police.

"You see," the chief said, "when a poor boy says that you did something to him, I tend not to listen, because there are no witnesses. I turn a blind eye. I know that you do other stuff, but again, no witnesses." The chief picked his teeth. "But," he continued and raised a pointing finger to Pedro, "when a dear friend of mine, and a very important businessman, tells me that you attacked a woman yesterday and that he had to defend her …well …life gets dicey for you."

"Me?" Pedro asked perplexed. "Me? I attacked a woman yesterday? Who was this woman?"

"Angela Gomes. Now I have a witness. I have a witness, Mr. Matias. I have a very dear friend and a very well regarded businessman telling me that he saw it with his own eyes."

"It is a lie! I didn't touch her! He is lying!" Pedro screamed.

"Well, it may be so. But he said he saw it, and I have to believe someone." Pedro looked at the chief in utter helplessness.

"We can agree on something," the chief said in a mild tone. "My friend will not tell me anything you've done to anyone he cares about, and you can go home. My friend comes here and tells me something unpleasant that you've done, and you are going to jail."

"But what if he lies again?" Pedro asked in complete terror.

"If he lies again ..." The chief pondered. "Well ...I will still believe him, even if I know that he is lying."

Pedro Matias left to Two Brooks with his reality adjusted and his confidence shaken, while the chief laughed heartily.

Antonio Nogueira, aka Dom Carlos, owed him big this time.

7

The Shoe on the Other Foot

The news spread like wildfire in Two Brooks. Finally, Pedro Matias had landed his ass in jail.

Angela was positive that it had to do with the new lodger. He had left early in the morning for the city, and in the afternoon, Pedro was in jail for assaulting a woman. That was even more embarrassing than not knowing the difference between a dead pig and a live one.

When Dom Carlos got home that day, Angela was waiting for him. It was dark already, and she was sitting in the garden surrounded by her menagerie.

"Dom Carlos," she called out from the bench.

He turned around and looked into the dark. "Aren't you afraid of the dark, little girl?" He walked toward the bench and sat next to her.

"Have you heard the news?" Angela asked.

"What news?" he asked.

"Pedro is in jail," she said.

"No kidding?" He tried to make out her face in the dark.

"Did you do that?" she asked.

"Well …" he said, "some have the power to resurrect pigs; others have the power to jail them."

"Indeed," she said. "Why did you do that?" she asked.

"I want to live in a place where there will be peace. I think that man was getting himself ready to give you and your future husband plenty of hell and, consequently, plenty of hell to me since I will be living here. I wanted to set the rules from the very beginning. As you see, it is all about me."

"I thought that your Zorro days were over," Angela said in a very low voice.

"Zorro never went to the police," he said with an equally low tone.

Angela smelled that fresh soap scent coming from him in the night breeze.

"What did you see when you went around in a cape and a hat?" Angela asked. She was wondering if he had seen Nascimento lurking around people's windows. "What did you see?" she insisted when he did not answer.

"Mostly you, being incorrigible," he said.

"That night when I got hurt, you came into my parents' yard looking for me. I was in the water tank, bleeding, in pain …and terrorized." *And naked*, she thought.

Angela could tell that he was looking at her. Dom Carlos was thinking that, if he had turned the flashlight on the water tank, instead of turning it on Viriato, he would have seen Angela in the water.

"Is this place as strange as I think it is?" he asked.

"I don't know. I never lived anywhere else," she answered.

They were quiet, thinking about small, mean worlds and listening to the noises of the night when Lazarus came into the garden. He came home always late.

Angela ran to him, jumped into his arms, and closed her legs around his hips. He walked to the house, receiving her attentions and singing softly in her ear.

Maria Gomes was already in the house waiting for Angela to go to bed, and Lazarus sighed deeply, knowing that he was going to sleep in one of the empty rooms, missing Angela.

Madalena held a letter by one corner, as if in risk of contamination.

"Another letter?" Maia asked.

Those letters had sent Manuel to the hospital and the police to their door. The police still came to the house with disturbing questions about Mister Paulo and the man he killed. Maia didn't want that kind of attention. So that letter was indeed a problem.

"Open it!" Maia said, sitting next to Madalena on the garden bench.

Madalena was thinking of Manuel. He was not so stupid as to write to her again. She had seen him once since he had come home from the hospital. He'd smiled at her in the way he used to when they were together. There was a promise in that smile. But since then, they hadn't talked.

When Madalena read the letter, she let out a soft moan and dropped it as if it was on fire.

Maia picked it up and read a neatly typed message, "I think of you day and night."

"He is crazy," Madalena murmured. "He must be crazy to persist in this madness."

The two women were quietly looking down at their feet when Saul came into the garden on his horse. He dismounted and walked in their direction. Maia went into the house. Saul touched Madalena's head in a caress and then sat by her side, looking at the letter on the ground. He picked it up and read it. Madalena could see his countenance darkening, and a muscle in his face tensed.

"Manuel?" he asked quietly.

"I don't know," she answered.

"Should I worry about someone else?" he asked in the same tone.

That sounded like an accusation. "I don't want Manuel to be hurt again!" she snapped.

She had seen Saul sad, hurt, worried, and even happy, but rarely angry.

"He has to leave you alone," he finally said in a measured tone.

"I'll talk to him. I'll ask him to stop this nonsense," Madalena said, losing her patience with that foolish boy.

"No," he answered flatly. "I will talk to him. I'm your husband, and he has to leave you alone." Saul took her face in his hands and brought his face so close to hers that she could feel his breath on her skin.

She tensed; her father used to do that right before he hit her.

"Do you still love him, Madalena?" he asked.

"I don't know. I know that I don't want you to hurt him," she said, holding his gaze.

Saul was so sad that, if sadness killed, he would be dead. He let go of her and went into the house.

Father Cruz, the saint and miracle maker, was coming to the island. Most importantly, he was coming to Two Brooks. Monsignor Inocente had been preparing the village for weeks. To have the saint visit such a far away and unimportant place as Two Brooks was a testament to the monsignor's influence with the bishop.

The end of August was always a beautiful time. August seemed to be the most forgiving month of the year. It ended droughts, it provided sun during the day and rain at night, the moon was big and closer to the earth, and people seemed mellowed; they sang more often and loved more generously during August. So it was fitting that the saint should come in August.

But the saint was only available in November. The village was utterly disappointed, as if miracles would be better during the month of August. This little snafu gave the village plenty of time to prepare for such an occasion. And prepare they did.

Antonio Dores was in charge of the choir. He was a very good musician, but he also had a narcissistic personality and, consequently, wanted to be the center of everything. He was the maestro, the singer, and the guitar player. And most terrible of all, he was the poet.

The village was beginning to understand that Antonio Dores was the worse poet around, maybe the worst in the whole island. Antonio could do many things well, but poetry was not one of them.

He also could do many things poorly, and being a husband and a father were his most flagrant failures.

When Antonio Dores left the seminary, he almost killed his family with grief. To have a priest in the family was having heaven guaranteed. His mother sacrificed his other siblings to support Antonio's studies and interests. Uncles, cousins, and friends in Canada and America all sent money to the future priest. Only his father didn't care if he finished his studies or not. If Antonio Dores didn't finish school, he would work in the fields, just like his younger brother. But his mother, quiet and loving Matilde, truly believed that her older son had the calling. And so she would accept the charity of the monsignor, relatives, and friends; she would sacrifice Antonio's sister, Olivia, and brother, Guilherme, to see Antonio ordained.

Everything was ready for Antonio to be a priest. The cow was fattened and ready for slaughter, the invitations were written, and the tablecloth for Antonio's ordination was embroidered by the most famous embroiderer on the island—Carlota Amora. But Antonio backed out at the last moment. The reason for his refusal was only too predictable; celibacy was something that Antonio couldn't live with. But he only found out about the pains of celibacy when he finished his studies and held a diploma in his hand.

Matilde was a sad and tormented woman. She'd married a brute of a husband who, on their first night, had slapped her across the face just to let her know that he could. Matilde, once beautiful and elegant, slowly became a shadow of what she used to be. And now she was watching her son, the light of her eyes, do the same thing to his wife, Emilia. She could accept the fact that Antonio would never be a priest; what she could not accept was the fact that Antonio was just like his father—violent and cruel to his family.

Antonio loved the church, and that was the simple truth. If priests could have wives, he would be a priest in a heartbeat. He was in his glory when he was around the church and its rituals. He loved the long ceremonies, the reverent ways people addressed the clergy, the golden vestments, the beautiful jewelry, and the gleaming pulpits.

The coming of a saint to the village was, for Antonio, one of the most exciting things in his life. He himself thought that he too could be a saint, someday, in the future. He imagined himself making miracles and people kissing his hands, crying out his name.

Antonio was also credited for getting Two Brooks the best choir in the island—better than the choir for the Cathedral—and it was said that the bishop chose Two Brooks for the saint's visit because of the choir. So the most obvious conclusion for Antonio was that the saint's visit was because of him, the maestro, and his choir.

Everyone was excited with the prospect of meeting a saint, but they were also concerned about the poems Antonio was writing for the occasion; even the monsignor was concerned. To sing in Latin was a great idea, but there were no more masses in Latin. Therefore, there shouldn't be singing in Latin, according to the bishop. Antonio was an accomplished composer, but the poems he came up with brought sighs of affliction and tormented comments, such as, "What a disaster!" Or those who were less tolerant might be heard saying, "I prefer to eat shit and die than to sing that."

> The saint is up the street
> Look how fast are his feet
> He comes to give us miracles
> And cut the devil's tentacles,
> Alleluia, Alleluia.

Nascimento was right behind Angela in the choir. One of Nascimento's amusements was to take liberty with Antonio's poems: "He comes to give us icicles to puncture the devil's testicles."

At the end of the choir rehearsals, the four friends always stopped by Ascendida's house to drink tea and talk about things or at least unburden their thoughts about Antonio's poems.

Today they were talking about miracles. If they were to ask for a miracle, what would that miracle be?

"For Antonio to write good poetry," Nascimento said.

The women laughed.

"I want Lazarus not go to war," Angela said. "I want him to be exempt from the military and just stay with me in our new house."

"I want to marry Jaime Nobre and have a large family," Nascimento said.

"That does not require a miracle," Ascendida snapped. "You are together and will be married soon. What is so miraculous about that?"

"I don't know," Nascimento answered dreamily. "Somehow I feel the need to ask for that miracle."

Her friends looked at her, waiting for more. But Nascimento hugged the tea mug in her hands and lowered her eyes.

"And you, Madalena, what is your miracle?" Angela asked quietly.

Madalena had a faint smile on her lips, as if she was having a private thought. "I need to know the difference," she said. "I need to know what a miracle is and what is not."

That was an odd thing to say. Her friends were in different stages of confusion.

Madalena looked at them and asked, "Unexpected blessings can be miracles, can't they?"

After a long silence, they looked at Ascendida, who was closing her eyes as if formulating a prayer.

"This is crazy," Ascendida said, "grown women praying for miracles as if we were children praying to baby Jesus during Christmas. Life plays a joke on us, and we think of miracles or tragedies. There is no such thing: miracles, There is only life being random! And a bitch!"

The women were quiet. Ascendida had, in the last year, gone through so much. She'd lost Mario, married his brother, given birth to twins, and been given the responsibility of an orphan child, traumatized and lost. Was she a sad woman? That line setting around her mouth, was that sadness?

Ascendida learned of her own story when she was small. Rita told her with a scream—"priest's fuck!" Having known all along that her father must have been someone else other than the father she knew, she asked her mother. But Ophelia, loving and protective, asked her, "Who told you such thing?" And Ascendida plagued with the fear of the truth sometimes sat across from her mother and silently asked her questions, hoping that her heart would tell her the things she craved to know and was afraid to ask. It was such a terrible thing to be a mother. It was a setup, so much love and so little power. The miracle of motherhood is not to give birth; it's to speak the truth, especially when it hurts. Ascendida found herself talking to her mother, in her heart, imagining that she could give her an answer.

Aldo sat at the kitchen table looking into his soup. He was almost invisible in the kitchen. The women talking in the chimney room knew he was there. But he didn't matter, except to Rosa, who came to him and touched his arm gingerly. Rosa, quiet and morose Rosa, was still living in her head with all her brothers and sisters, now at the bottom of the sea.

"Do you have a miracle, Rosa?" Aldo asked, caressing the child's head. She moved her head slowly—yes, she had a miracle. And Aldo knew what it was. It was the thing she prayed for at night, her little bonny knees on the floor and her head bowed to her chest. It was the thing she daydreamed with her dark brown eyes fixed on the wall as if she was hypnotized. How could so much sadness live in such a small body?

"I love you, Rosa," Aldo said, kissing the child on the head. And Rosa got him a glass of wine. She couldn't stand Aldo's sadness. Wine always made him feel better.

Aldo was thinking of his mother. She used to do the same. When he was sad, his mother brought him a glass of wine. Why was he thinking of his mother now? Aurora. What a beautiful name—the name of the birth of a day. If only he could tell his mother what was in his heart; maybe she would point him to a road less torturous. But would she know of one? Shouldn't mothers know these things? She should know how to appease his heart. He listened to the quiet murmur of the women in the chimney room. He could imagine Ascendida with her eyes closed and thinking about dark things—about her mother, about Mario, about the children and how capricious life was. Was she thinking about him? Was Ascendida hard and unforgiving?

Aldo got up and pushed the curtains aside. The women looked at him in surprise; all except Ascendida.

Her head was thrown back and, with her eyes closed, she thought of her mother.

Mother, where does love go when it dies? What remains in its place where it once burned like hell? What is between love and wisdom that they are at odds, always? Why Mother? Why are we born already divided or are divided as soon as we are born? Good, evil, wrong, right. Why don't you answer me, you full of answers and quiet like that? What is the force that pushes you to accept conditions? Am I your daughter, doing the same? I hear your silent submission. Do you remember the fire a few years ago at the teacher's house? Who set those flames? I think you did. You, quietly loving me, as if I were the world. What passion made it burn? I'm talking about passion, mother of mine. But you, quiet and sad, say nothing; you deny your own right to have joy. If I could, oh Mother, if I could help you in your sadness, I would die of love for you.

Ascendida opened her eyes. Aldo's intense stare burned her cheeks. The other women left quietly.

She asked, "Have you been drinking?

The wine warmed Aldo's limbs, and that sadness that had taken hold of him earlier was lifting off.

He smiled. "One glass of wine for supper will not destroy a man." He placed an arm around Ascendida's waist. "What were you daydreaming about? You were so deep in your head."

"I was thinking about my mother."

"I think of mine often. Mothers are like nature, implacable."

"Implacable?" she asked, surprised.

"Yes, they are brutal in the way they love their children to the exclusion of everything and everybody else."

"Men are so jealous of this utter and complete love," she mused.

Aldo was not jealous. He was thinking about mothers and their sons and how strange it was to come from a woman and be completely apart and unknowing.

Mother, what did you do with your dreams? Are they put away neatly just like your linen tablecloths that you take out only for days of celebration? How do you call that veil that you wear over your eyes? You clean our house as if you have been betrayed. Everything is organized chronologically, even your disappointments. "This was the year we got married," you said, showing me an old and yellowed calendar. "I had a bouquet of calla lilies, and there was mud on the road. My dress shrunk when I washed it. Everything changed. This is the year that you and Mario were born. It was winter, and the wood for the fire seemed to be cursed; it didn't burn. The house was cold and humid, and you couldn't sleep. I put your little bodies between your father and me to keep you warm. Your father was tormented with winter blisters on his toes and was scratching all night long, making our tiny bed rock. And you and your brother slept with the swaying of his agony." What happens to women like you, Mother? Why do you wear your courage as if it was an imperfection? Why do you harbor a weak man in your arms? When you open the window and look out into the night, what are you thinking of? Are you thinking about your mistakes? Where would you start making amends? Was I a mistake? Did I tag along with Mario without your permission? I wish I could understand the way a woman thinks. I wish I could see the soul behind her eyes. You are a fraud! Why don't you live with your heart? What is that force that fences you in, and there you stay as if betrayed? Why should we carry on our shoulders that perpetual accusation that we are born profaned? What is our original sin? Our presence and our absence have the same value in your eyes. Am I my father's son? Will Ascendida be like you? I can't understand your life as hard as I try. I look for signs. I read between the lines. But I feel that I lost the thread, that I took the wrong turn on the road, that I jumped a chapter in a book, and that's why I am lost. We never get it right, Mother. What can I do to make you happy? If I could change the blandness of your smile, I would die of love for you.

Ascendida's face was so close to his that, if she concentrated, she could see Mario's face. She kissed his mouth. "Do you have a miracle, Aldo?"

"Yes, but it is my secret," he said. "What will be your miracle?" he asked.

A veil of sadness fell over Ascendida's face. Her miracle was impossible. Not even God could give her this miracle lodged in her heart. She said, "I don't have a miracle, Aldo. You know that I don't believe in miracles."

Madalena came home after supper and found Maia and Carlota in the living room. As usual, Carlota was embroidering; Maia was listening to the radio and crocheting. Madalena was thinking about miracles as one thinks about secrets. What would be a miracle for Maia? Maia, so dedicated to Carlota and Saul. Did she have a miracle just for herself? And Carlota, what would be her miracle?

Both women looked up at Madalena, and for a split second, Madalena saw love in their eyes. Love had a certain look that could only be felt and just for a second.

"Where is Saul?" she asked.

"He must be asleep already," said Maia. "He went to bed about one hour ago."

Since their last exchange, Saul had avoided Madalena. He was not indifferent or unpleasant, but he didn't seek her company as before. Madalena felt bereaved. She had caused him deep hurt by telling him that she didn't know what she felt for Manuel. It was the truth, but nevertheless it was hurtful.

"Is he feeling well?" Madalena asked anxiously. Lately he had been tired and had gone to bed earlier than usual.

"No, he needs to rest," Carlota said. "He's been working long hours as you know; getting up at four in the morning because some of his managers are sick. Check in before you go to sleep," she suggested.

Madalena sat by Carlota and held a corner of the tablecloth she was working on.

"The saint is coming tomorrow, and everyone is thinking about miracles," Madalena said quietly.

Carlota smiled without lifting her eyes from the work. Maia lowered the radio to listen in. But with Carlota, just like with her son, the conversation was never long or even verbal. Carlota put down the work and held Madalena's hands.

"Do you believe in miracles Carlota?" Madalena asked, feeling the tenderness in Carlota's hands.

"Yes," she lied.

"Me too," Madalena answered. She was going to ask for her miracle tomorrow. And the saint would listen to her silent prayer and give it to her—one beautiful, possible, and gentle miracle.

"My miracle," Maia said, "is to have a man to love me and marry me and take me away to a magical place."

"Half of the women are asking for that Maia," Madalena said, and the three of them laughed.

Saul heard the laughter. He was barely awake in his bed, listening for the signs of Madalena getting home. He had been so tired lately and could hardly keep his eyes opened as soon as he hit the bed. Lately he had been careful with Madalena. He felt relieved when he got home and she was not there. They hadn't talked about love since Madalena had told him that she was confused. He didn't want to think that he had pushed her into a love confession that was not true after all. It would be a lot easier for Madalena to love him, but would it be true? He was wondering about the laughter in the living room. He rarely heard his mother laugh. It was a strange and soothing sound. Then he heard Madalena go to her room and open the window. Was she looking out into the night and dreaming about things that he was not part of?

Then his door opened noiselessly, and Madalena said, "Good night, Saul."

"Good night," he answered.

She pushed the door in a little and said, "Tomorrow the saint will come. Everybody will be asking for a miracle. Do you know that Maia wants a husband?" Madalena asked, amused.

"Shouldn't take a miracle. Maia is a beautiful woman," he said.

"Do you have a miracle that you pray for, Saul?"

"Yes, and you?"

"When your prayers are answered, is that a miracle?" she asked.

"I'm not an expert in miracles but I would say so." Madalena could hear that he was amused.

She closed the door and left.

He should have asked what she meant. What did she pray for?

He got up and knocked at her door, entering before she gave him permission.

"What do you pray for?" he asked, standing in the middle of the room.

"I pray for you," she said in a whisper.

He took her in his arms and said softly in her ear, "But you already have me."

Madalena was mesmerized with his gentleness as he undressed her.

"Tonight I just want to hold you," he said.

They nestled in each other's arms.

Madalena could hear Saul's heartbeat in her ear, loud and fast, and her heart swelled with tenderness. "Our time will come," she whispered.

She couldn't dare to ask God for more than she had in that moment.

He didn't have to ask God to have his wife in the way other men have wives, but then again, could other men claim such sweetness and tenderness as they were sharing that night?

And they fell asleep, warm and happy.

The new teacher had arrived a few weeks earlier. He was a tall young man, good-looking and sure of himself. He was like all youth, full of ideas about people and life. He made open fun of the ways of the village, was condescending to young and old, spoke disparagingly of his students and their parents, and had an opinion about everything, including the things he knew nothing about.

The villagers knew that it was just a matter of time before he was run out.

The monsignor tried to ignore the teacher's petulance, but finally he decided to have a talk with the young man.

"I've heard that you took upon yourself to explain miracles and religion to the village?" the monsignor said.

The young man frowned slightly, almost amused with the old priest. "I'm a teacher," he said. "My job is to elucidate whenever I encounter ignorance."

The monsignor knew this young man. He was a spoiled brat, full of privilege and disdainful of those who he perceived to be less than he was.

"André," the monsignor said, "I agreed to give you the job with the understanding that I could kick you out at any time. I told your father that you would not fit in, but he hoped. I want you to stick to the alphabet and mathematics and leave religion to me."

André also knew that his father was not going to give him an allowance unless he had a job, and it was damn embarrassing to have to earn a living when his father was rich and could give him an allowance. He was not cut out to be a laborer. He was twenty-seven years old and had never had a day of work in his life. And now he was stuck in this village of ignorant, gullible people, and he couldn't even tell them a few things. If he couldn't amuse himself with what he had around him, how could he survive this place?

He enjoyed the popularity with the girls, but his attention was stuck on a beautiful girl called Madalena. She was the perfect material for a paramour—beautiful, attached, and loveless.

André got his information about the village from Regina Sales, the village whore. At first he thought that Regina was beneath him, but her insistence convinced him that she was the perfect liaison; she told him stories about everyone in the village and did things to him that surpassed his imagination.

When Angela walked into the garden, she imagined that her mother and the lodgers were already in bed. At least she hoped that the teacher would be. But he wasn't. He was waiting for her, it seemed.

"The priest called me today for a scolding," he said with a tone of amusement.

"What priest?" Angela asked.

"The only one you have in this godforsaken place."

"Monsignor Inocente," Angela said coolly.

"Yes. I suppose he doesn't want me to talk about miracles."

"You shouldn't talk about things you don't know, Mr. Moniz."

He laughed.

Angela turned around and went into the house.

Dom Carlos and her mother were sitting at the kitchen table drinking tea.

"Prick!" Angela uttered, coming into the house.

Maria Gomes looked at her disapprovingly, and Dom Carlos said, "What have I done?

Maria Gomes took off up the stairs; she was tired and not in the mood for one of Angela's tirades.

Dom Carlos was still bewildered, looking at her, "What have I done?" he asked again.

"I'm not talking to you!" Angela said, annoyed.

"Well …" he said. "I was the only prick in the kitchen when you came in."

Angela sat and said, "I don't like that boy. He is so full of himself. I have a bad feeling about him."

Dom Carlos was drinking his tea and looking at her over the rim of the cup. "What has he done?" he asked.

"Nothing major. Nothing that you haven't done either—make fun of our ways, provoke the monsignor, get on my nerves—"

"Go to bed," he said. "I'll wait for him, and I'll lock the door. You give him too much credence. He knows that he annoys you, and he enjoys it. Take that power away from him; don't rise to the bait."

"He is making fun of our miracles," she said, feeling the scolding hurt more than it should.

Dom Carlos held her gaze. He was not smiling or doing anything, not even blinking. Angela was seeing him almost for the first time. What had changed?

"Do you have a miracle, Dom Carlos?" she asked, breaking an odd silence.

"No. I don't believe in miracles. Do you?"

"Yes."

"What is it?"

"I don't want Lazarus to go to the military and consequently to the war."

"I hope your prayer is answered."

"Me too … If that prick doesn't come in the next five minutes, lock the door," she said, leaving the kitchen and going upstairs.

Dom Carlos waited for the teacher, and when he didn't come in, Dom Carlos said into the dark garden, "If you are not in the house in five minutes, I am going to lock the door. You can always wait for Lazarus, who will be home around midnight."

A smirking André emerged from the garden, "Are you the man of the house? I thought it was Lazarus."

Dom Carlos didn't answer; trying to follow is own advice, he locked the door and went up to his room. "Yes, the boy is a prick," he murmured.

When Lazarus came home, Angela woke up. Her mother was peacefully sleeping next to her, breathing softly. Slowly, she walked out of the room and went down the stairs to see Lazarus, who was in a small room next to the kitchen. She stood at the door looking at him undressing, with his back turned to her and she saw again the deep grooves on his back left by his father's lashings.

"Your back," she said with a sob.

"Oh, they don't hurt," he said, turning to her.

"They hurt me every time I see them."

8

The Miracle Maker

The following morning, the whole village woke up with renewed faith—miracles were going to happen. Every house got ready with the lighthearted enthusiasm of a child who was going to receive a precious gift, and they put on silk dresses, starched skirts, shirts and petticoats; the hats had new bows, and the gloves were whitened to a tone of blue. They were going to stand in front of a saint and ask for a miracle.

And so they went up the street like a shining procession of laughing angels, all the way up to the church door.

The church door, for the first time in their lives, was locked.

They gathered outside, asking one another why the church was locked. But no one knew.

Slowly, the church door opened, and the bishop and his entourage came out—seminarians, priests, and monsignors from all over the island and even from the mainland. And in the midst of these shining vestments, the saint—small and unassuming, wearing a black cassock and a black hat—looked like a black stain in an otherwise sea of splendor.

The monsignor explained to the village that the church was too small to accommodate everyone. So he asked his parishioners to stand at the bottom of the steps while only the choir would be allowed in the church entrance, so they could hear the organist, exiled behind the large instrument.

The parishioners did not object to standing outside under the brilliant morning sun, since church events were almost always torturous—long, full of ceremony and strange rituals, with singing at every turn and the constant sitting down, getting up, sitting down …altogether tiresome. If the church was too small for the day of miracles, they were only too happy to stand outside.

Antonio Dores was strategically standing sideways at the church door, half in half out, so the organist could see him also. With a wave of his golden wand, he gave the signal for the choir to start.

The glory of the day is clear
Father Cruz the saint is here
He will teach my happy heart
Not to doubt and fall apart

Nascimento, who always tried to distract herself from the atrocities of
Antonio's lyrics, promised herself that, today, looking at a saint, she would not
be irreverent. But the devil being shameless also came to the event, and when
Nascimento opened her mouth, she sang, "He will teach my gassy heart not
to doubt that it can fart."

No one really heard it. She was careful with "pianissimos" when needed.
But she was dismayed with her impulsiveness. She could not resist certain
things, such as being irreverent and ...a voyeur. And this was truly the miracle
she needed—to stop being a voyeur.

Finally, the saint came to the front of the steps. The congregation let
out a whoosh of pent-up breath. The saint looked at them with eyes full of
compassion. Maybe the saint was thinking about the lyrics, and thinking
that, if they were subjected to such poetry day in and day out, they were saints
already.

"My brothers and sisters," said the saint. "I am here today to pray with you
for miracles. I don't make miracles. I ask God to grant them to all of us. But
the greatest miracle of all is the love in your heart. Be generous to each other,
be kind, and be forgiving and tolerant. Your faith is the way to your miracles.
If you believe it, it will be granted. Pray, pray, and you shall receive—that's the
miracle. Pray, my friends. May God be with you."

That was it. No more sermonizing, no more torturing. *That's a sermon!*
This was what sermons should be, thought the parishioners. There were no fires
of hell or the glory of heaven hanging over their heads; it was short and to the
point.

Maybe it was why he was a saint; he knew the human heart.

The parishioners were asked to stay put in the churchyard, the choir was
asked to join the masses at the bottom of the steps. The saint would answer
the parishioners' requests, wholesale, all at once, with one wave of the bishop's
hand.

The monsignor explained, "Since there are too many of you wanting
miracles, each one of you will formulate the wish in your heart, and Father
Cruz will bless you all at once. When you see our Eminence Bishop Dom
Aurelio move his right hand, ask for your miracle."

There was a murmur of disappointment. They felt cheated, and they were not sure if God would pay attention to collective miracle making. They had envisioned the saint with his hand over their heads and praying to God for their individual miracle, looking into the saint's eyes. This wholesale miracle delivery was wrong.

People were murmuring to themselves and to each other, trying to absorb the news.

The saint came to the edge of the steps with his arms opened wide and waited for the bishop to move his hand.

But before the bishop had a chance to move his jeweled hand, the village saw a green hat and white crocheted gloves move from the crowd.

It was Ascendida.

Rarely did she put on a hat, so it took a few seconds to identify the woman underneath it. But this day was special and she wanted God to know how special it was, so a hat and crocheted gloves up to her elbows were a manifestation of her intent.

She couldn't lump her miracle in with everybody else's. No. She needed God's full attention for this one miracle.

She pushed people out of the way and ran up the steps with her hands up in the air, already opening her mouth to tell the saint what she most desperately needed.

Father Cruz looked at that young woman full of energy running up the steps, defying the rules of the session.

For a split second, they made eye contact, and Ascendida was certain that God was already listening. But the monsignor got in between the saint and Ascendida, and the miracle was interrupted.

Ascendida, in her despair, pushed the monsignor aside to have access to the saint. The villagers screamed in horror as they saw the monsignor tumble down the steps, feet up, cassock over his head, and face down at the bottom.

In a sea of screams, the bishop's entourage whisked away the saint into the sacristy and into a car, and they left to the city like a monarch running away from a lynching mob.

The bishop was terrified of mobs. More than thirty people for him were a mob, and today this village full of strange people was not only a mob, it was a dangerous one.

Angela and Nascimento took Ascendida away while Antonio Dores scraped the monsignor off the ground. The monsignor was hurt; his head was bleeding, and he was holding his arm close to him, as if it was broken.

"Dear God, Ascendida is fucked," Nascimento prayed. "Please be merciful with her; otherwise the monsignor will finish her off."

The villagers, who had the whole day dedicated to the session on miracles, didn't know what to do with themselves now—without the saint, the bishop, and his entourage and without the banquet that was going to be served right after the miracles.

And they started to walk home slowly, talking about Ascendida.

"The girl is a cow," some said, "daughter of a priest, poor thing, never really felt the guidance of a father who cared."

"Not fair," others said. "João Matos has been a very good father to the girl. It is her mother's fault; she always spoiled her."

But they were all curious about Ascendida's miracle. What in the world did she want from God that she had done that to the monsignor?

At Angela's house, Ascendida, surrounded by her friends, was crying copiously. Her friends could only look at each other and make soothing sounds. They were having tea now, with plenty of sugar to appease the shock or dizziness that they were feeling.

"I just needed to touch him," Ascendida said between sobs, "and ask him for my miracle."

"But I thought you didn't believe in miracles," Nascimento said. "You said that that life is a bitch, and that's it."

Madalena was caressing Ascendida's hair, black, straight, and shining, like the wing of a hawk, like Saul's hair. Saul. She didn't even ask God about her miracle, so disoriented she was with Ascendida. And where was he? He hadn't shown up for the miracles. Did he have a miracle?

The teacher came in. He looked at the women around the "*sinner*," and he smiled. Of course, when Angela looked up and saw him she didn't see a smile; she saw a smirking, condescending, vain man.

The women could see the teacher with the same fate as the monsignor. Angela was dying to inflict pain on someone; she was rigid, cold, her eyes narrowed, her lips thinned—and her friends looked at her in alarm.

"This is somewhat a private moment. I'll keep you company. Please come with me," Madalena said to the teacher and hurried him out the door.

If André had thought of a plot to have Madalena all to himself, he would never be as lucky as he was at this moment. Here he was, sitting on a bench in a garden with Madalena.

He talked and talked, mostly about himself, giddy with joy to be in her company. Madalena was only half listening. Her attention was in the kitchen with Ascendida and the others.

"Maybe we could go to the city together sometime … I could really use a friend since I feel so isolated in this village. Your friendship would mean a lot to me."

Madalena turned her attention to him. "I thought you had plenty of friends in the city. Weren't you born there?"

He made a dismissive gesture by waving his hand, "They all got married or went away, have children, and so on. I was away for many years. So when I got back, my friends were elsewhere occupied." He gave her a self-deprecating smile.

"I'm sorry to hear that," Madalena said.

"I need help with my job. The monsignor can't imagine how damaged these kids are. They don't understand anything else other than violence, and I refuse to hit them. But they are disobedient. They don't do what I tell them. They don't do their homework … It has been very hard."

Madalena looked at a very handsome young man full of sadness. "I'm so sorry, André … Maybe I can help."

"How?" he said, full of hope.

"Maybe I can help you in the classroom. I always wanted to be a teacher, but I didn't finish my studies. I will talk to the monsignor and see if I can assist you with the kids … I don't have much to do in Saul's house."

"Saul's house?" he asked interested. "Isn't it also your house?"

"Yes, of course. Everything is so new; I sometimes forget that my house is now somewhere else …" Oh, how she wished she hadn't said that. She could see a gleam of misunderstanding in his eyes, and she became worried.

André thanked her for her generosity and friendship.

Life was so easy, he thought, and women were so gullible. He laughed as he entered his room and lay on his bed, thinking of Madalena and the things he could do with that beautiful girl. He was getting an erection just by thinking of her. With a grunt, he sat at his desk and caressed his typewriter.

When Madalena got home, Saul was in the kitchen looking at the flames in the fireplace. He lifted his head when she came in.

Something warm filled her heart to see him there, quietly looking into the fire, waiting for her.

"Have you heard about the day of miracles?" she asked.

"Yes, I have," he said. "Did you have a chance to ask for your miracle?" he asked.

"No. And how do you know that I have a miracle waiting to happen?" Madalena sat on her heals facing him.

He leaned forward and rested his elbows on his knees. His face was just inches away from hers. "I imagine that everyone must have one."

"I think I have it already," she said.

"What is it?" he insisted.

She knelt in front of him, and he pulled her into his arms.

"You," she said softly, her mouth close to his ear.

She felt his body tense.

He looked at her. His face was so close to hers, and she wanted to kiss his mouth. "I have never been as happy as I am here in your house, with you, Maia, and your mother …"

Madalena felt it again—that tug inside her belly—and she felt her heart beating all over her body. She was falling in love with her husband. And to think of life without that gentle man made her so sad that she couldn't stand it. But she should be careful. And above all, she should be sure.

"Of all the things I thought I was, a miracle never crossed my mind," he said, caressing her cheek.

Madalena looked intently at his features—so gentle and quiet.

"Stay with me tonight," he said.

"I was hoping that you would ask," she said.

The next morning, when Saul left, Madalena went to see the monsignor. She had much to talk to him about. She was feeling happy and confused all at once.

When she got to the church, she heard voices in the sacristy. The monsignor was not screaming, but his voice was loud. She quietly sat on a pew behind Saint Anthony. Between the saint and the lamb he was holding, she could see the door of the sacristy. She didn't mean to overhear, but she did. The monsignor was now speaking loudly, and the person who was with him could barely be heard.

"Remember, my boy, your demons! You cannot let yourself be caught again by rage. Let it go! Let it go!"

And again the murmur of the voice talking to the monsignor reached Madalena.

Finally the monsignor answered, "If you could have a civil conversation about that, I would say it is the right thing to do. But I fear that you will not!"

There were more murmuring sounds, and then the monsignor yelled, "I will talk to him! Let me talk to him first! And then if she receives more letters, you talk to him!"

Madalena felt a stab in her heart. It was Saul talking to the monsignor about Manuel's letters. She took in a sharp breath and hid behind a column until she saw Saul leave the church.

The monsignor was still bristling from the conversation he had with Saul when Madalena knocked at the door.

"What is it now?" he asked, thinking it was Saul again.

"I need to talk to you," Madalena said.

The monsignor raised one arm up in the air and addressed the ceiling of the sacristy as if God was peering down at him. "Do I really deserve this?" he sat down and asked. "Did you hear anything?"

"Yes, Saul wants to talk to Manuel about the letters," she said.

"You shouldn't be listening to confessions!" he yelled at her.

"You shouldn't yell so much," she said. "I couldn't hear what he said. I just heard you and figured out what he was saying."

"What is it?" he asked impatiently.

"I think I am in love with Saul."

The monsignor looked at her for a long while. Then he said, "It's about time! You've been married for seven months! Have you told him?"

"Well …I told him I was confused. I wanted to talk to you first. I feel that I must be sure. I was so in love with Manuel, and now I am not. Is this normal? Am I confused and forcing something on myself just because it is easier?"

The monsignor was now pacing the floor. He stopped in front of her and said, "Only you, child, can answer that question, only you."

"But what if I don't know the answer?" she said. "I think I need to see Manuel, to talk to him and tell him not to write to me anymore. If I look at his face and tell him that, if I can say it, then I know I don't love him anymore. I have to see him. I have to know."

"I can't believe that you are asking me to bless an encounter between you and Manuel!" he yelled. "I can't do that."

"You have to help me, Monsignor. I don't want Saul to be hurt. He is the kindest man … And he loves me."

"Yes, he does."

"Then help me. Ask Manuel to come to you, and I will come too."

"I have so many demons placed at my door every day, Madalena. Don't ask me to do this. If you want to see Manuel and talk to him, do so. But I cannot be a part of that. Ask Angela to help you. She is such a romantic fool."

When Madalena left, the monsignor started to pray, right there in the sacristy. "Listen, Jesus," he said in complete frustration. "Give me a hand, will you?"

"My hands are tied," he heard.

The monsignor turned around and faced the voice coming from the church. "Damn it, Dom Carlos!" he said with fury.

Ascendida knew that she was in deep trouble with the monsignor, so there was no point in putting it off. She came up to the church, and Jesus Crucified followed her with a big warning look.

A bruised monsignor, with an arm in a sling, was waiting for her.

She said, "I'm sorry you got hurt, Monsignor. I didn't mean for that to happen."

"What did you mean then, by being disobedient?" he yelled.

"I wanted my miracle," she said. "I just wanted my miracle." Her voice was low and contrite.

But the monsignor now had the person in front of him who had foiled one of the most important days of his life—the coming of a saint to the village.

Then Ascendida said, "It wasn't right to keep him from us. He came to see us."

And that did it. The monsignor, with his good hand, slapped Ascendida across the face. It was a loud slap that vibrated throughout the church.

"How dare you to question my decisions? How dare you?" He shook with ire.

Ascendida was prepared for the slap and did not go stumbling across the room with the impact, as it had happened before. She lowered her head and thought that this time he was going to hear it. After all, he had slapped her already, and the only thing he could do was to slap her some more.

"The saint came to see us, and you had him with the bishop and priests and seminarians, as if they were better than us. He came to see us! I'm sorry that you got hurt, but I am not sorry that I disobeyed you."

One slap and then another and another. Ascendida's head was going from side to side with the impact.

The monsignor walked away from her. He was shaking with rage, but above all, he was disconcerted with the vehemence of this stubborn girl. What miracle did she want that she would provoke his ire?

"To expiate your sin of disobedience, you will take care of José Eremita. As you know, he has no one, and he is in a wheelchair."

Ascendida thought she hadn't heard him correctly. In less than one year, she had lost Mario, had two babies, had taken on a traumatized adoptive daughter, and had a husband who was a drunk. And now, just because her wish for a miracle had backfired, she had to care for a paraplegic. What more God wanted of her?

"Do you hear me, Ascendida? This is your penance. You are a defiant woman! This poor man needs care, and you need to atone for your sins."

And so this was the way Ascendida took José Eremita to her home—as a penance.

The monsignor felt that he was in a losing battle at times. There was a time when people had seemed to listen and follow his guidance. But now he could see more and more people doing their own thing and making decisions that directly impacted and challenged his authority. His greatest concern was the four women—the Sacristy, as they were called by the villagers, due to the fact that they were summoned almost every month, by the monsignor, to receive penances and reprimands. These women had the power to instigate with such conviction that he was powerless. It wasn't that they were immoral or acted with malice. But they acted independently from the village norm—the norm that he had defined as proper behavior. Angela, Ascendida, Madalena, and Nascimento—the Sacristy—were his most challenging demons, even more so than Joaquim Machado, who was possessed by the devil. The monsignor had fasted forty days and forty nights to exorcise the devil from Joaquim's body. If only he could do the same to exorcise the demons the Sacristy had unleashed on his authority. The Sacristy was a cross. He knew how to deal with the devil, but he didn't know how to deal with those four women.

Angela was going to get married at sixteen to a boy of nineteen—two children who had plotted and persevered in this terrible mistake. Neither of them knew what love was. And then Angela told him that she'd been sleeping with Lazarus since she was twelve. Dear God, what was he going to do with that? What penance could he give her other than her promise that they would not have sex? And Angela had promised she would not, and so had Lazarus.

And now Madalena with her doubts about love. She wanted to be sure that she loved her husband. That child had never loved in peace. Her idea of love was so distorted by violence and fear that she could not see love staring her in the face, especially if it was kind and giving love.

And Saul. Always Saul. The village had never forgotten that Saul and his family had come from afar and, consequently, were always outsiders. Carlota, Paulo, Maia, and Saul had come from Brazil with enormous wealth. They'd bought half the island, but were completely isolated. Some of it was self-imposed exile, but the other half was the village never accepting them as part of the whole. When Paulo Amora killed that man and was sent to Africa, the village redoubled the isolation for Carlota, Maia, and Saul. It was like they were also condemned. Saul was only eight or nine when he came to the village and twelve when his father was sent away. The monsignor was the only father he had now, and he loved that sad and quiet boy.

The death of Dona Lidia was his most staggering dilemma. The woman was killed, he now had no doubt. And he'd said that she'd died of a natural death, when he knew what had happened. Nothing in that woman was natural, not even her death. And to top it all, the Night Justice was acting up again, in a very bad way. It was not just small warnings, petty humiliations; it was cruel acts of hatred and vengeance.

But the one who could really destroy the village was Antonio Nogueira, so-called Dom Carlos. He could destroy all his work and the faith of this people who had grown so much under his guidance.

The monsignor sat, holding his hurting, battered arm. His head was throbbing, and he couldn't stop thinking about his village, once peaceful and obedient, now erratic, difficult, and violent.

The one who at this time was of least concern was Nascimento. Voyeurism—in the scheme of things—was quite innocuous.

The monsignor wiped his face with a tremulous hand.

There was a noise at the door. He looked. "Oh no! God, you are not going to do this to me today!" he exclaimed.

Dom Carlos laughed softly, came in, and closed the door, "Do you still have any influence with God?" he asked mockingly.

"What do you want?" the monsignor snapped.

"I just wanted to let you know that I am upholding my side of the bargain ...for now. Everything is going according to plan."

"Then leave me alone! Go away!"

"I don't know if you know that the teacher you found for the children is a complete disaster," he said with relish.

"And what business is that of yours? Why are you meddling in the village's affairs?"

Dom Carlos put a hand over his heart as if wounded. "But I am living here now. Their business is my business. I love to live with Angela and Lazarus."

"You listen to me you. If you so much as—"

"Calm down, Monsignor. I like those kids," he interrupted.

"What do you want?" the monsignor asked again.

"Angela has concerns about the teacher," he answered evenly. "You failed those children, again. First you allowed that vicious woman to brutalize them, and now you get this incompetent, lazy, womanizing boy as the teacher. Your mistakes are too costly, Monsignor."

"Angela didn't say anything to me."

"No, because she knows that he is the son of a friend of yours. I don't know why people are so concerned with your feelings. You are a tyrant."

"I love them, and they know it."

"Love …" He laughed.

The monsignor was looking at a very cool and collected Dom Carlos.

Dom Carlos said, "I heard Madalena and Angela talk about the teacher last night. Madalena would like to be an assistant to the teacher. She is hoping to give some structure to the classroom."

"Madalena is a married woman. She should be taking care of her husband at home," the monsignor snapped.

"Shouldn't that be her decision?" Dom Carlos asked. "If she wants to do something with her life, why can't she?" Dom Carlos turned around toward the door. "Well, she will be here asking your permission. You'd better have a good answer because, the way I see it, these young educated people tend to not follow you blindly anymore. Furthermore …André Moniz is infatuated with her. I thought you should know. You don't want your favorite son to kill again, do you?"

He left, amused with the jolt of irritation he had just delivered to the monsignor.

Madalena was about to tell Angela that she was getting too skinny, looked tired, and had dark circles under her eyes; and that didn't look good in a bride.

But André came into the kitchen, uninvited, and sat next to Madalena. He smiled broadly at both women and poured himself a cup of tea from the teapot in front of them.

"Wow, two days in a row, what a treat," he said.

"Well, we were talking about me being your assistant and talking with the monsignor about it," Madalena said.

"You haven't talked to him yet?" he asked

"Not yet," Madalena answered.

And the teacher winked at Angela, almost defiantly. He was going to have an assistant, and it was going to be the girl he wanted.

"Carmelina completed her studies and is at home also taking care of her husband. Maybe she would welcome the opportunity. She went to school to be a teacher," Angela said.

André gave her a murderous look. Carmelina was a short, fat woman, married to a short, fat man who drove a motorcycle as a means of transportation. He was so dumb that his wife fell off the motorcycle, and he only noticed when he got home, four villages later. André wanted Madalena, not Carmelina! Madalena!

He had to be careful with Angela, or she would mess up his plan.

"Yes," he said, "Carmelina is also a good choice. But Madalena asked first so …"

Angela was looking at him as if reading between the lines. The man was lying. "I can talk to Carmelina for you," Angela said, "and then talk to the monsignor about it."

André waived a hand in dismissal. "Oh I will talk to Carmelina and her husband, and then I will talk to the monsignor. Thank you though," he said and got up fast, as if he had something important to do.

The women were quiet for a moment.

"What is it?" Madalena asked.

"He is up to something," Angela answered.

Madalena was very quiet. She was not thinking about the teacher but about her plan to see Manuel again and how she was going to ask Angela to help her.

When Madalena finally broached the issue, Angela was full of concern.

"I need to see him. It is important," Madalena said quietly as an explanation.

They agreed that Angela would talk to Ascendida and Nascimento and set up the meeting.

It was almost nighttime when Madalena got home. Much to her surprise,

Saul was also home, washing up for supper. She felt the same familiar joy of having him, without a word, caress her head and kiss her mouth softly and slowly. When he did that, the world spun in slow motion.

They had been sleeping together for a few weeks now. Tonight, Saul would do the same ritual; he would come into her room, slip her nightgown off over her shoulders, and embrace her. The radio would play softly, and the night breeze with its sounds would come through the window.

How strange it is to love this man, Madalena thought. And her heart was full of love, gratitude, and joy.

When André saw his little plan foiled by Carmelina's name, he went to the monsignor with a proposal. The monsignor, aware of the debacle, was prepared for Madalena but not for André. He tried to pay heed to Dom Carlos' warning, since it was so easy to decipher the young man's intentions.

"You know that Madalena is married, don't you?" the monsignor asked.

"Of course I know. It is one of the reasons I want her as my assistant. No romantic fantasies. You know single girls …can be difficult …"

The monsignor was staring at him. No one could stare like the monsignor— he didn't blink—and that meant that he didn't believe you.

André laid down his plan. "Of course my first thought was Carmelina. But when I talked to her husband—I thought I should give him the courtesy—he said no, almost immediately. I explained the benefits of the experience, but he didn't care. He told me not to call again with the offer."

And some of it was true. When André had called on Juliano Batata, or Juliano Potato Head, as he was known, he was received with the utmost attention. Carmelina cut a cake and laid out tea in their most precious china set. Throughout the conversation, André was very attentive to Carmelina (not many people had bothered with her). Mostly, she was forgotten, along with a heart full of dreams just like any pretty woman. At night, she closed her eyes and imagined a kind, caring man cupping her face in his hands gently, saying, "Carmelina, you are the love of my life." So the attention of a gorgeous, young, educated man was truly welcome. Carmelina smiled broadly and didn't allow his cup of tea to go empty.

By the time André left Carmelina's house, he was stuffed with tea and cake, Carmelina was swooning with his attentions, and Juliano Potato Head was telling himself that he would never allow his wife to work for such a philanderer.

Although Carmelina would not be allowed to have the job, André's visit left a useful fear in Juliano's heart; his wife was desired by other men. She was desired by young and good-looking men. He'd better be careful.

That night, he made love to his wife as he had never done before, and he whispered in her ear, "Carmelina, you are mine and mine alone."

André was waiting for the monsignor's response. The young man had a self-assured look; he had covered all bases.

"Maria Augusta could be your assistant," the monsignor said, blinking repeatedly.

André's self-assurance dimmed a degree or two. He was not going to be stuck with that pink cow. "I'm sorry to bring this up, Monsignor. But unfortunately, Maria Augusta is infatuated with me. That would not be fair to the girl, don't you think?"

The monsignor had seen Maria Augusta's little squeals of pleasure when she was in André's presence. But Maria Augusta was going to get married to a Canadian emigrant. She had finally found someone who liked that Rubenesque soft flesh and white skin.

"Well …if Saul doesn't mind, we will see," the monsignor said.

The King of Leon

That night, Madalena told Saul about the letter. She was under the covers, feeling his warm skin on her back and his arms around her waist.

"What does it say?" he asked quietly.

"I don't know," she answered as she reached for it on the night table.

He got up, lit up a lamp, and read it. Then he got in bed again.

"What does it say?" she asked.

"I think of you day and night," he answered evenly.

Madalena turned to him. Their faces were touching.

"Please don't do anything to Manuel," she said. "And it is not because of him alone; it is because of you too. I don't want you to get in trouble."

She was remembering the monsignor's warning about his rage.

"Sleep!" he said, and put an open hand on her face like a mask.

"Why would that silly man type the letters? Where would he get a typewriter?" she asked as if speaking to herself.

"I don't know … There is one in the library," he said. He pulled her closer and added, "I want it to be Manuel. Please tell me that you don't have another man after you."

He hid his face on her neck. She felt his mouth right on her pulse.

She laughed, and he bit her neck slowly.

"Vampire," she murmured, wondering if he was leaving a mark.

The following day, Angela told Madalena that Manuel was going to meet her at the windmill in the afternoon.

Angela was feeling remorseful. Saul had been very good to her, and here she was helping his wife keep illicit assignations.

When Madalena faced Manuel in that rainy afternoon, he let out a soft cry, like a suppressed sorrow and embraced her as he used to do. She felt a pang of familiarity, something bruised and hurting—so different from what she felt with Saul.

"Manuel," Madalena said, "it has been so long."

Manuel's embrace, tight and desperate, did not carry the magic it once had. It felt foreign and frantic.

She closed her eyes to give her heart time to adjust to this truth.

"I love you, Madalena. Forgive me. I never stopped loving you. I was weak," he said, holding her hands and looking into her eyes.

She smiled sadly and established distance between the two of them by stepping back a pace.

"Manuel, forget about me. Please don't write anymore. I don't want something terrible to happen to you again," she said with kindness in her voice.

Manuel was not prepared for this. He was prepared for accusations and tears but not for a good-bye shrouded in kindness.

"But I love you. What can I do with all this love?" he asked.

"Love somebody else, Manuel. It is possible to love again," she said.

"It's you I love!" he answered feverishly.

He was looped in the pain of loving her, in the drama and anguish it generated. The despair and love victimized by cruel fate was only too familiar to both. He didn't know that love needed peace and kindness to survive, because he had never experienced it. But she had.

"You are going to be hurt if you insist on something that can never happen. I'm making a life with my husband."

She turned around and left, running all the way home.

Her friends who were keeping guard saw Madalena run home and then Manuel coming out, calling after her. That scene was so familiar that they just shook their heads.

When Madalena got home, she went into her room, claiming that she had a headache. Her heart was throbbing as if it wanted to jump out of her chest. She didn't love Manuel anymore. When she had seen him, a wave of pain had come over her. Everything associated with Manuel reminded her of suffering. Even their lovemaking was shrouded in pain. All the violence and mistreatments to both of them had come at her in one breath from Manuel. When she had run out of the windmill, she had left all that pain behind.

She was now in her home where the only thing she knew was love.

The late afternoon light came through the window, promising more rain. The wind was blowing around the leaves, and Madalena listened for the sound of the horse's hooves clapping on the stone courtyard.

But Saul didn't come home for supper. It was very late when he got home and quietly went into his room, not to hers as he had done in the past few weeks.

The following morning, Saul got up before the sun and before the roosters started their morning songs all over the village.

Madalena woke up with a start, as if she had missed something important by a second of neglect—just like her dream.

"Where is Saul?" she asked Carlota and Maia.

They were quiet. They also thought it was strange for Saul to come home so late and leave so early. Lately, he couldn't wait to come home, and at times, he came home during the day.

They felt that something was wrong, and they hoped that Madalena would know what it was.

The three women sat in the kitchen looking at the fire. The smell of boiled milk and fresh bread was so comforting, but they were anxious.

They heard noise outside, and the three women ran to the window. But it was not Saul. It was the policeman who, a few months ago, had interviewed them about Manuel's assault.

The policeman also wanted to know where Saul was. The women could not tell, since Saul had many responsibilities all over the island dealing with his business.

When Madalena asked the officer why he wanted to talk to Saul, the policeman said, matter of fact, that Manuel Barcos had placed a complaint.

The policeman was keeping a close eye on the women.

"Do you know anything about that, Mrs. Amora?" he asked Madalena.

"No, I thought that Manuel had said it was not Saul who attacked him, and he was with me all night long."

"Who was with you, Mrs. Amora?" the man asked.

Madalena colored deeply.

"You said *he*. Who? Saul or Manuel?" the man insisted.

"Detective Lourenço," Maia intervened, "would you please come in and have some tea or a bowl of soup while we talk?"

The man came in and smiled at Maia. He was medium height, and his hair was graying at the temples. Deep lines at the sides of his mouth indicated that he laughed easily. Detective Lourenço looked at Maia and Carlota. His eyes were deep gray, almost dark blue.

"Do you know where he is?" he asked again.

"May I ask why you want to talk to him again?" Madalena asked.

"Last night, he assaulted Manuel Barcos," he stated simply.

Madalena let out a short scream, as if she'd been poked on the ribs, and sat with a thump on a chair.

Detective Lourenço was looking at her with interest. "You were not with your husband last night?" he asked.

"I …was asleep when he came home."

"At what time did he come home?"

"I don't know. I was asleep," Madalena answered softly. "How is Manuel?"

"Bruised. It is not really a fair fight, is it?" the detective answered.

"What do you mean?" Carlota asked. "There was a fight?"

"Yes, there was a fight. Manuel hit Saul a few times, and Saul hit him once. Manuel went flying across the street, toppled over a wall, and fell down a ravine."

The women moaned softly, imagining what could have happened to Manuel and, consequently, to Saul.

"I understand that your son has a problem with containing his rage," the detective said to Carlota.

"Not rage, Detective. He does not know his own strength. You said that Manuel hit him first and more than once." Carlota was almost pleading for understanding.

"Well, I need to talk to him," the man said, getting up.

Maia got up too. She said, "Have a bowl of soup first before you go. Tomorrow, I promise that Saul will go to the city to meet with you."

The man looked at her for a while and then smiled. "Will he?"

"Yes. Saul is a good man. Come into the kitchen with me. I baked bread yesterday, and we have fresh blackberry preserve that I made from the berries that I picked."

Carlota and Madalena were observing Maia enticing the detective. Later, they heard Maia and the detective laugh in the kitchen. Carlota and Madalena looked at each other disconsolately.

Where is he? they asked without saying the words.

"I need to talk with the monsignor," Madalena said as soon as the detective left.

When Madalena got to Angela's house, she was soaked to the bone. Her shoes were muddy, and her coat and hair were completely drenched. On the way up to Angela's, she passed by Manuel's house. There was light inside of his room. She imagined Manuel battered and bruised in bed, being tended by his sisters and mother.

What happened? Why did Saul hit you? And where is Saul?

When she got to Angela's, she started to wipe herself down with a towel. Dom Carlos was sitting at the kitchen table reading by the lamplight. He lifted his head as if bothered by the commotion.

"Do you need me to leave?" he asked Angela.

"Get me a blanket," Angela ordered.

When Dom Carlos came down, Madalena and Angela were in the chimney room with the curtain closed. He stuck an arm in with the blanket.

Madalena came out of the chimney room wrapped in the blanket and damp hair curling around her face.

When André came in the kitchen, he was delighted to see Madalena curled in front of the fire. He was thinking that, between his eyes and Madalena, there was only a blanket. He smiled.

"Would you mind? This is a private conversation." Angela addressed the teacher coolly.

André looked offended. Why was Dom Carlos part of the conversation and he couldn't be? Actually he had more rights than Dom Carlos because Madalena was going to be his assistant.

Angela was narrowing her eyes at André, which wasn't a good sign.

"Hey," Dom Carlos said to André. "Be a gentleman for once and leave the women alone."

André left, and Madalena silently got up and picked up the clothes Angela had found for her. "I'll change in the bathroom and then go on my way," she said to Angela, who was still ready to pulverize the teacher.

Angela sat down on a chair and hugged herself as if she was cold.

Dom Carlos crouched in front of her. "You are too tired, irritable. And although André is a petulant snob, you don't have to fight with him every time. Lately, you've been picking fights with everyone."

"Oh …I feel tired, and I feel …that if I could kill …Pedro, I would release this tension," she said, rubbing her eyes and sounding despondent.

Dom Carlos looked at that face, so young and yet so wise. He had never met a person like her. There was rawness about her beauty, although common understanding of beauty would say that she was far from it. Her mouth was too large, her skin too dark, her eyes too big, and she had a lump on the bridge of her nose, as if she had broken it. And that long and straight hair of hers fell on her shoulders like a black shawl. She was small and bony, but strong in a funny way.

"What? Why are you looking at me like that?" she asked, puzzled.

He got up and said, "Nothing. Don't let other people consume you."

When Madalena got to the monsignor's house, the rain stopped. She was wearing clothes left behind by Ilda before she left for America. The monsignor was quietly surprised with her frumpiness. Much to Madalena's surprise, he didn't scream at her. He simply listened to her concerns and then said, "Saul needed to be away for a few days."

Madalena sighed with relief. "I met with Manuel and asked him to leave me alone. But I don't think he listened …"

"Did you tell him that you love your husband?" the monsignor asked.

"I didn't have the heart … He was crying. But I said good-bye."

"Saul found out about your encounter with Manuel," the monsignor said.

Madalena looked horrified. "How? Who told him?"

"I don't know, and I didn't ask. But I told him that I knew of your meeting with Manuel …that you'd talked to me beforehand …"

Madalena sighed deeply. "Was he angry with me?"

"He was sad. I think he doesn't understand your confusion about love. Not he, who is so sure of his own. And he was furious with Manuel for not leaving you alone."

Madalena got home and told Carlota and Maia what the monsignor had said about Saul's whereabouts. Carlota put a hand on her chest as if suddenly she could breathe. Her heaving sigh seemed like a gust of wind.

"He does that when he is upset. He disappears," Carlota said. "He's done that since his father …since he was a young boy."

Maia said, "I don't know what to do with the detective then. I promised that Saul would go and see him."

Carlota said with hope, "You go and talk to the detective. Tell him that Saul will see him as soon as he comes home."

Carlota was afraid that her son was going to be arrested in the city—if he was in the city. There were not many people who looked like him, and the police had had an eye on Saul ever since Night Justice had assaulted Manuel and Pedro Matias was grabbed by the neck.

Maia felt like Egas Moniz, a revered historical figure, who had made a promise to the king of Leon about the actions of his king. And now Maia was going to offer herself for punishment and to expiate for someone else's deeds, as Egas Moniz had done.

"He likes you Maia," Carlota said. "He may be more inclined to listen to you."

"He likes my bread and my soup. I don't know if he likes me," she said, worried.

"Bring him some sweet bread then. He would appreciate that," Carlota said.

Maia thought that, to bribe a policeman with sweet bread, was the lamest thing that she had ever done. But for Saul, she would do anything. And she resigned herself to go to the city with a loaf of sweet bread under her arm and meet with Detective Jorge Lourenço.

Maia was tall and thin, with a delicate bone structure. If she was not Maia, Maia Maria Sampaia as she was called since she had come to the island, she could even be handsome. Her eyes were light brown, almost the color of honey, kind and melancholic, as if they'd cried many sorrows. Her mouth was large, with thick lips and a permanent smile; it was her natural countenance. Her hair was dark, curly, and shiny, softly framing her face.

Madalena had known Maia all her life and had never given her a second glance. She could be pretty. Why had the village made her a pariah? Because they thought she was Paulo Amora's illegitimate daughter, because she came from Brazil, because she was an outsider. How unkind people could be. The village was happy with the stories they imagined about the Amora family, giving themselves permission to make them castaways.

And the islanders resented the Amoras because they had bought the most fertile land of Two Brooks and the most inaccessible coast in the island, where ships from afar could get close to the island without being seen by the authorities. And there was also the gold from the slaves Paulo Amora's family sold and bought in Brazil and the contraband the Amoras were involved in and the treasure they had hidden in their land, or in the caves on the cliffs.

There was a reason why, of all places, Two Brooks was the place where the Amoras landed.

There was a reason why Paulo Amora killed a man on the cliffs.

And with these stories, the village was familiar and comfortable.

And now Madalena was part of them. She was part of that strange family that sang the words as they talked, like Brazilian people do, making simple words sound like poetry.

Maia looked at her hands, rough and cracked from work. "I'll go," she said. "I'll go and talk to the detective. I need to do something with my hair. I look like a sheep."

Madalena and Carlota were preparing Maia's meeting with the detective. They applied cream on her curls to tame the hair, gave her a manicure, and applied lipstick that she kept on licking. They laughed and immediately sobered; they shouldn't laugh without knowing where Saul was and how he was.

Madalena took a few dresses out for Maia. Although Maia was taller, Madalena's clothes fit her well, if not a little short; even that worked in Maia's favor, showing her well-shaped legs. The dress was swaying gently, hitting Maia right above the knees.

"How old are you, Maia?" Madalena asked.

"I'm thirty three years old, just like Jesus when he was crucified."

They laughed again. "You are going to be fine. Just be yourself. You can't go wrong being yourself," Madalena said.

Madalena waited for the bus with Maia. She kissed her on the cheek before Maia boarded the bus, holding the loaf of sweet bread under her arm. She had carefully wrapped it on a tea towel that she had embroidered. And all the way to the city, Maia prayed and rehearsed what she was going to say to the detective.

Maia Maia Maria Sampaia, she thought, *what the hell are you doing trying to bribe the police with a loaf of sweet bread?*

When she got off the bus, she went straight to the police station and waited in the wide hall. A well-groomed secretary gave her a cold look and pointed to a chair. Maia wished she had the demeanor of the secretary, who walked to her desk making click-clack sounds with her high heels on the stone floor.

It didn't take more than a minute for the secretary to ask her to go into another huge room with high ceilings and wide windows overlooking the public garden. She could smell freshly brewed coffee, and she wished she could have a cup at that moment. She felt as if she was naked, exposed in the middle of the room, her dress too short for her to feel comfortable.

If Master Paulo were alive, he would know what to do; he wouldn't let her be here looking like a fool.

A door opened behind her, and she turned to see Detective Lourenço. He gestured for her to sit as he sat across from her.

He looked around and asked, "Where's Saul Amora?" He kept a sharp stare on Maia. Like all detectives, he was with all his antennas up to catch a lie. He could see the woman in front of him tremble with nervousness and waited for her to speak. He was not even blinking.

While in the bus, she had rehearsed countless times the opening statement, but when she opened her mouth she said, "I'm Egas Moniz, I'm afraid."

The detective was taken aback. He was not often surprised with what people did and said, but he was today. He smiled broadly and tried to stifle a laugh.

"Then I must be the king of Leon?" And now he laughed; he couldn't help it.

Maia was disconcerted. She placed the sweet bread on the table and didn't know if she should laugh with him or wait for what he had to say next.

"What's that?" he asked pointing to the parcel on the table.

"Sweet bread, for you." She felt lame and sounded even worse.

Detective Lourenço had his head slightly tilted to his shoulder as if trying to get a different perspective on her. "Thank you," he said. "What happened to Saul?"

"We don't know. He didn't come home. He does that when he gets upset."

"Does he get upset often?" he asked.

"No, not since he ... his father ...was sentenced and went to Africa."

The detective was just staring at her. Maia felt that she was blushing, looking stupid and guilty. She had nothing to feel guilty about.

She got up picked up the bread and turned around to leave. "I'm sorry," she said. "I'm sorry I took your time ..."

"Maia!" he called after her. "Sit down!" He went after her and took her by the elbow back to the chair again. "I'm sorry. I was not making fun of you. I was caught by surprise."

"It makes two of us then," Maia said and placed the bread on the table.

"I'm very happy that you came to see me. However you shouldn't make promises for other people. But you came to explain, and I really appreciate that."

Maia was thinking that, if he had said that in the beginning, he would have saved her a whole lot of affliction. "Saul doesn't know that you are looking for him. If he knew, he would be here."

"Are you making promises again?" he asked quietly.

"I know Saul. He is kind, good, and honorable." Her tone was stern.

"What are you to him?"

Maia looked down at her hands. She was afraid of this question. But she was going to tell him, if it helped Saul.

"I was given to Mister Paulo, by my father, when I was ten years old, as payment of a debt."

"In Brazil?"

"Yes. But I hardly remember anything. My memories are so faint ..."

"You know that slavery has been abolished?" he said with an even tone.

"I'm not a slave," she said defensively. "And I have never been one."

"No? You were given to the Amoras and you work for them, as a housemaid. Do they pay you?"

"Pay me? I don't need anything. They give me everything I ask for. I'm family."

He smiled. To Maia, it looked like a kind smile, but she was not sure.

"And what do you ask for?"

Maia thought for a moment. Her eyes were lowered, and Detective Lourenço could see her long lashes shadowing her cheeks.

"What was the last thing you asked of anybody?" he insisted quietly.

"The last thing I asked was of you, to believe that Saul is good and honorable." She looked up at him, and he noticed again how beautiful her honey-colored eyes were.

"I believe you, and I'll wait for Saul to come and talk to me," he said.

"Thank you, Detective," she said with a brief smile and a sigh.

"With one condition," he interjected.

Maia tensed, and her smile disappeared. She waited.

Detective Lourenço looked at her for a long while and said, "Have dinner with me."

Maia was speechless. She was trying to make out words to explain why she couldn't, but the words were not coming up. She wanted to say that she had to take the bus home, that she really couldn't be out at night with a stranger, even a policeman. "I ...I ...can't," she said. "The bus ... I must take the bus ... home."

"I'll take you home."

She made a face, a sad grimace, and then said, "You could have dinner with me, and I could cook for you, in Two Brooks, next time you come to the village ..." She waited anxiously for his answer.

At home, she could control the situation. This man, with a kind smile, could be just another man who could harm her.

He said, "But Maia, I want to treat you. No cooking, cleaning, and serving other people."

"I don't mind. I love to cook." She felt relieved with the compromise.

"When?" he asked.

"Whenever you want," she answered.

"Tonight?" he asked.

"Tonight?" she asked taken aback. She was thinking about how shocked Carlota and Madalena would be if she came home with the detective, without giving them time to prepare. And how about Saul? She couldn't bring the enemy home.

"Yes, tonight. I can take you up; you don't have to take the bus. And tonight we will not talk about Saul. It is my condition, as the King of Leon."

A smile warmed her face.

"Wait for me outside. I will not take long," he said getting up.

Maia got up too and pushed the sweet bread toward him. "This is not a bribe."

When Maia sat again near the cool secretary she wished she could look that pretty and that confident. The secretary felt Maia's gaze and lifted her head. And then this cool, well-mannered woman, with clickety-clack shoes, smiled at her.

This is a sign, Maia thought. *This is a sign that all will be well with Saul and the detective.*

Madalena was looking out into the garden. She was praying for Saul to come into the patio on his horse, smile at her, and kiss her the way he did when he got home—a long, sweet kiss.

It was raining again, and the wind picked up, making everything colder and grayer.

And there he was, exactly as she'd imagined, on his horse coming into the patio and dismounting. She ran out of the house, barefooted and with no coat.

Carlota ran out too and looked lovingly at her son scooping Madalena into his arms and kissing her under the rain.

Carlota closed the door after Saul and Madalena as they went into the bedroom. They removed the wet clothes and got under the covers, both shivering.

"Saul," Madalena said, with her head on his pillow and her nose touching his, "I love you. I love you. Forgive me for being so suspicious of my feelings, but it was too good to be true."

He caressed her face while thinking of miracles. "I knew our time would come," he said kissing her face, tasting the moment that he had dreamt about more times than he could count.

He felt her body under his open up, her arms tightened around his neck, and her legs encircled his hips as he sunk into her with a soft cry.

Sometimes dreams come true, and when they do, we question ourselves as to whether it is really happening. And the fear of it not being real doesn't allow us to be completely happy. This was what Saul and Madalena were feeling.

Saul's long life's dream was to be in bed with Madalena as his wife and look into her eyes while he entered her body, slowly and tenderly and whispered her name, as he was doing now, kissing her mouth as she moaned with pleasure.

Madalena's dream was to be loved by someone who would not allow harm to touch her, someone strong and good like Saul, someone who could only remind her of love every time she looked at him.

And there they were in each other's embrace, making love, living the dream they had always wanted to live and being afraid of it, because it was too precious.

Angela and Lazarus were setting up the woodshop in the garden. She stacked the fabric for the lining of the coffins.

Lazarus pointed to a finished coffin. "That's for Isaac Lima."

"He died?" Angela asked.

"No, not yet. But when he does, it is ready. He's been dying for years."

"When I die, I want a place in paradise just like our new house," she said dreamingly.

"You are my paradise," he said. "When I die, I want to go into you."

Dom Carlos had been at the door for a while before they realized he was there. He said, "You should shut the door at least, especially if you are talking about paradise."

"And you should have said something," Angela retorted.

"I did, but you didn't hear …" he replied.

Lazarus put an arm over his shoulders. "My best man," he told Angela.

"No!" Angela said.

"Why? Don't you think I can be his best man?" Dom Carlos asked, surprised.

"I wanted you to be my matron of honor." She laughed.

Lazarus was smiling. He rarely laughed aloud, but his smile was broad and sweet. Angela gazed at him; there were no bruises, no storms brewing, no Pedro Matias to torture him, and all because Pedro was afraid of Dom Carlos.

Angela walked up to Dom Carlos and kissed him on the cheek. "Thank you," she said in his ear.

"What is she telling you?" Lazarus asked.

Dom Carlos didn't say anything but gave her a quick hug.

"I guess you've been approved as the best man," Lazarus said.

"Your wedding dress arrived," Dom Carlos said. "Hercules sat on it. I thought you should know."

When Angela got in the house, Hercules was sitting on the dress as Dom Carlos had said. She screamed, and the cat looked at her disdainfully.

In a matter of months, the thin and scrawny kitten had turned into a mean and huge cat that bit people and did other misdeeds, but Angela loved that cat as if he was a person.

The dress was wrapped in a white sheet. Angela looked at it with amazement—her wedding dress. She was going to marry her beautiful man— Lazarus. She put the dress in front of her; the dirty sabots peeked from under the skirt. She smiled up at Dom Carlos and said, "I think it is beautiful. I've never seen such a beautiful thing, don't you agree?"

"Yes, it is beautiful," he said.

The teacher came into the living room. He looked at the dress and said, "The wedding dress I assume … But it looks like a first communion dress … and on you, so small and skinny, you will look like a first communion kid instead of a bride." He laughed.

"One of these days I'm going to hurt you," Angela said dismissively.

He laughed even more.

In two quick steps, Dom Carlos crossed the room, grabbed him by the arm, and walked him out.

"No one asked for your opinion," Dom Carlos said after they reached the kitchen.

André sat down on a chair laughing. "Come on, Dom Carlos! Are you telling me that you don't think that dress is plain? I was kind saying it looked like a communion dress because in truth it looks like a night shirt."

Dom Carlos said in a quiet voice, "If you so much as make a comment about anything that has to do with the wedding I will hurt you, boy."

André laughed even harder. "Okay, Daddy!" he said, feigning fear. André was so entertained with his own wit that he didn't see Hercules come in, but

Dom Carlos did and left the kitchen. A few seconds later, André was screaming and running up the stairs.

Lazarus came in at the sound of screams and laughter. He looked at Angela's dress and said, "Oh, my angel, you are going to be the most beautiful creature on earth."

Angela yelled, "Lazarus, you can't see the dress before the wedding!"

"Why not?" he asked, looking back as she pushed him out of the room.

"Bad luck!" she exclaimed.

She came back to the living room and wrapped up the dress again.

"Two days, Dom Carlos, two days, and I will be with Lazarus for good," she said, looking up at him with the happiest of smiles.

Dom Carlos touched her cheek lightly. "Are you happy?" he asked quietly.

"Oh, Dom Carlos, if I was any happier than this, I would burst!" she said, whirling around the room with her dress as if she was dancing.

10

Maia, Maia, Maria Sampaia

Maia came home in the middle of the afternoon in the company of the detective. When Carlota saw them at the door, she stepped back speechless. Maia gave her a warning look.

"Detective," Carlota said in a contained tone.

"Mrs. Amora, Maia asked me to have dinner with her, and I accepted," he said with a charming smile.

Carlota knew that something else had to have happened for Maia to bring the police officer to the house. She said, "We are honored."

Carlota took the detective to the living room and offered him tea while Maia went to the kitchen to prepare dinner and gather her wits.

The detective said in a gracious tone, "I can help Maia with dinner, Mrs. Amora. Please don't trouble yourself."

Carlota was anxious and her hands were trembling a bit. "Detective," she said in a whisper, "Saul came home while Maia was in the city. He is with his wife. Please let them be, just for tonight."

"I told Maia that this evening it is not about Saul. We are just going to have dinner." He smiled at a relieved Carlota.

The detective got up and went to the kitchen where Maia was nervously peeling potatoes.

"I will do that," he said, "and you do something else. I am a good potato peeler." He extended his hand to receive the knife.

"Here," she said. "Put on this apron or you will get dirty." And she tied the apron around his waist. He laughed and lifted his arms for her to tie the apron around his waist. There was a second of intimacy; they both could smell each other and felt the gentle heat of proximity.

Carlota was pacing in the living room. She didn't know if she should go into the kitchen to help or knock at Saul's door and tell him that the detective was going to have dinner with them. She stood in the middle of the house, and she could hear laughter in stereo, Saul and Madalena from one end of the house and, from the other end, the detective and Maia. Only Carlota was not feeling humorous.

When Carlota knocked at the bedroom door and told her son the news about the detective, Madalena whimpered. The world was intruding already.

"It will be okay," Saul promised.

Detective Lourenço was cutting fresh parsley into small bits to crown the codfish. And in their conversation, Maia learned that Detective Lourenço had a wife who was in the asylum. She'd been there for many years.

He said, "I've gotten used to be alone. I have a cat who greets me every day with enthusiasm, until I feed him, and then he ignores me until he is hungry again."

"Will she ever leave?" Maia asked.

"No. Her mother was like that and her grandmother also. They both committed suicide, and I don't want Isabel to have the same fate."

"Is she …happy … Is she aware?" Maia wanted to know where one went in such a world.

"When I visit her, she seems to be upset that I interrupt her routine. She needs everything to be predictable—her meals, her walks, her games, going to bed, and taking her medication. Because I am not part of the everyday routine, she gets very anxious when I visit."

They were quiet, caught in the awful reality that life could be so capricious. After a while, the detective told Maia about the time he had found his wife with her wrists cut, in the middle of their kitchen, bleeding and screaming because she was afraid of the blood.

For Maia, it was difficult to understand why a man like him had chosen such a frail creature for a wife. What attracted men to women who couldn't pull their own weight or even their own happiness? Did she give out that vibe?

"What do you think of me, Detective?" Maia asked.

Detective Lourenço was slicing bread, and he stopped, surprised with the question. He could guess her line of thought; her lack of confidence was showing in her countenance.

"I think you are dedicated, loyal, strong, and with a straightforward streak."

"Do you?" she asked, almost toneless.

"I also think that you are very pretty," he said quietly, looking at her with tenderness.

Carlota came into the kitchen to announce that the table was set, and the magic was broken.

When Saul entered the room, he nodded slightly to the detective to acknowledge his presence. Maia, after a moment of hesitation, fell into Saul's arms. He hugged her and lifted her from the floor and whispered in her ear something that sounded like a love poem. Maia laughed and whispered back.

Then they all sat down and bowed their heads in prayer. There was no talk at the table. Detective Lourenço was almost sure that such deep silence was his doing. He was feeling increasingly intrigued with the awkward ways of the Amoras and, at the same time, the deep love and commitment they had for each other. He felt like an intruder.

"Detective Lourenço," Madalena said and cleared her throat before adding, "usually Maia and I entertain the family. But today we are a bit …constrained with your presence. Forgive us and please believe that we are not inhospitable people."

"I understand," he said.

Saul looked up and asked, "When should we talk?"

"Whenever you have a moment," the detective said. Then he grinned and asked Maia, "What would you be talking about if I was not here?"

"We would be talking about you," Maia said. "I would be saying that you had invited yourself for dinner and rejected my sweet bread and that you made fun of me when I said I was Egas Moniz."

Madalena started to laugh and then everyone followed, except Saul, who smiled at his wife and continued to eat in silence.

"I didn't make fun of you. I asked if you thought I was the King of Leon."

The ice was broken. After that, they talked about the rain and the winter and the wedding of the year in two days. The detective told stories about pirates and contraband on the coast of the island and silly stories about his job, about the jail always empty and without a key.

Saul was thinking that all the talk about jail probably was not innocent talk, but Madalena was laughing. Carlota and Maia seemed tense with the talk of jail and contraband. There was a false sense of gentleness on the island, with its empty jails. Saul's father had gone to Africa to jail. Why hadn't the authorities kept him here in the island in their empty cells?

After dinner, while the women cleared the table, Saul and the detective sat alone in front of the fire.

"I hit Manuel," Saul said.

"I know that much," Detective Lourenço answered.

"In self-defense; he hit me first," Saul added. "He doesn't leave my wife alone. I told him to leave her alone."

"And he hit you?"

"He accused me of being in cahoots with Madalena's father, doing all that mayhem to his crops and cattle ... And then he punched me."

"Were you in cahoots with Pedro Matias?"

"No. I'm sure you already know this, but Pedro came to me to offer his daughter in marriage. I never really had many dealings with the man."

"You don't like him, do you?"

"I challenge you to find a person who does," Saul answered evenly.

"Witnesses say that you hit Manuel when he said something about you ... killing a man."

"I hit him because he was disrespectful to my father, and he hit me first."

"What did he say?"

"He said that my father was a pirate, a contrabandist on the coast of the island, and that I was just like him, taking what was not mine. Then he said I killed a man, and my father took the wrap."

"Did you?" Detective Lourenço asked quietly.

"This is not about Manuel after all, Detective. Is it?" Saul asked, his voice taking a colder tone.

Detective Lourenço didn't say anything. The light from the fire illuminated a slice of the room, but Saul was standing in the shadow.

"Do you hate Manuel?" the detective asked.

"I can't stand the man. He is a coward."

"Coward. How so?" the detective asked.

"He made promises and made decisions and didn't have the strength to stand behind them," Saul answered.

There was a long silence, and neither man moved. Finally Detective Lourenço said, "I'll tell Manuel that he has no case against you; it was self-defense …although that is almost a joke—Manuel could never hurt you, could he?"

"He hurts me every day," Saul said evenly.

When the women came into the room, the men were sitting in front of the fire in complete silence. Carlota and Madalena looked at Saul inquisitively.

"I should be going," the detective said, getting up.

Maia followed him to the door.

"What was it that Saul called you when you saw him?" The detective asked.

"Maia, Maia, Maria Sampaia." Maia laughed. "That's how the village calls me."

Jorge Lourenço narrowed his eyes at her. She was laughing about something that hurt her deeply. He felt a surge of revolt against that ignorant village. "What fresh little poets you have in this village," he said.

"Often, when we are alone, Saul and I repeat those hurtful names, until they lose their power to hurt us," she explained.

He felt the need to caress her curls and say that nothing would hurt her again. But he was going to hurt her most certainly, in the near future, pursuing the investigation about the activity in the coast of the island and the connection with this elusive, cunning village.

Maia, if he was free … But he was not free, and he hardly knew this woman.

He thought about the wife he hardly knew. She was so much younger than he was, but she was quiet and beautiful, almost mysterious. And he had married her. And then he had never been able to make her feel safe or happy; that was her mystery, her inability to be happy. She only wanted to be touched as if she was a child—kissed and hugged. He had married a sick woman and he hadn't even noticed because she was always so quiet, and their courtship had been brief and superficial.

When Isabel went to the asylum, the only thing she asked for was chocolates with a pink wrapper and books with pink butterflies. He knew so little about her world.

Was he about to commit the same error?

When he found his loneliness to be insufferable Jorge frequented the brothel at Green Street in the city, and he asked for his favorite girl. Maia looked like that girl. She had the same singsong way of talking, and her hips had the same gentle sway.

He composed his thoughts and said to Maia, "I should be leaving. I didn't feed the cat."

"Drive safely," she said. "Be careful with the werewolf."

Detective Lourenço touched her hand gently. He would give anything to be able to lower his head and kiss her lips. But he simply said good night and left.

He went straight to Green Street and asked for Susana.

He took a good look at the woman smiling warmly at him.

"What do you dream of, Susana?" he asked, surprised at himself for never having wondered before.

She was surprised too and thought about it for a moment. She was thinking about whether she should say what he wanted to hear or what was in her heart. She gauged his mood.

"I dream of a kind man falling asleep in my arms and staying with me all night long without sex."

"Let me be that dream tonight," he said, gathering her in his arms.

They fell asleep like old lovers who don't need to do anything else other than being together.

At home, Maia was thinking about the detective. He wanted something from her, but she was not sure what. All that talk about pirates and jail was disturbing – he wanted something. Oh yes he did, and she would find out what it was.

She could fall for a man like him—good-looking and kind, with good, easy conversation and a good sense of humor. She was wondering how it would feel to kiss the cleft on his chin. Would he seek her mouth? Maia felt a wave of warmth. She had to stop thinking about stupid things that would never happen. She would never be involved with a married man, much less a detective trying to put Saul in jail.

The last time a man had paid her such attentions, he had almost killed her.

It was so long ago … Why was she thinking of Ivo?

Ivo was a farmer who rented fields from Saul. His wife had died with tuberculosis soon after their marriage. No one wanted to be associated with that awful sickness or anyone who had been close to it. But even worse than to be a widower of tuberculosis was to be the son of a man who was possessed. That association with tuberculosis and the devil gave people some pause.

Ivo came to Saul's house often to talk about business, and he took an interest in Maia. One day, he asked her to be his girlfriend, and she said yes because she was falling in love. And soon the courtship began.

Carlota and Saul were apprehensive because Ivo was wild. He liked to drink and fight, but he was also a hardworking man, and that meant a lot to Carlota and Saul.

Maia thought that Ivo was two different men: When he drank, he turned crass, put his hand up her skirt or squeezed her breasts. When he was sober, he was polite and refrained, even charming. But he drank more often than not. Maia would admonish him gently when he was sober, and he would apologize profusely. Nevertheless, he would do it again, and Maia ended the relationship, tired of the same vicious cycle.

One day, Maia went to the orchard as she did so often, and Ivo followed her. Maia was surprised to hear footsteps behind her, and then she saw him.

"You scared me," she said, trying to assess whether he was drunk.

"I'm the boogeyman," he said and laughed.

Maia looked into his wild eyes and she saw that light she'd seen so often. He had been drinking again.

"Don't say crazy things, Ivo," she said dismissively and stepped back.

He grabbed her by the arm and kissed her hard on the mouth, bruising her. She screamed and tried to get away, but he pulled her to the ground and pulled her skirt up.

"Shut up!" he said. "You have been teasing me for months, and now you are going to get it! I'm going to give you what you want."

He held her arms behind her back, and with the other hand, he pulled down her pants and stuffed her mouth with them to muffle her screams. He pried her legs apart with one knee and pushed himself into her repeatedly like stabs. He grunted obscenities while she was struggling.

Maia looked at that face that she still loved, that mouth that she kissed so tenderly, calling her names, killing the sweet memories of what love could have been. She felt the green grass under her being crushed and staining her back. She looked up and saw the blue sky. A bird flew over her head and butterflies rested on wildflowers, indifferent to her on the ground being raped.

Suddenly, he stopped. Tears ran down Maia's face, and her screams were so muffled that she stopped screaming; she only cried.

"Turn around," he ordered.

Maia tried to run away, but he hit her on the back of the knees, and she fell down. Ivo forced her on her hands and knees and sodomized her. "Maia Maia Maria Sampaia, being fucked in Atalaia," he said going in, and out of her body using the rhythm of his words. "You are not even a virgin, you slut!" he laughed. "I'm not taking anything from you. You gave it to somebody else!" Before withdrawing from her, he said," If you tell Saul, he will come after me and kill me, and then he will go to jail like his father. You've been begging for it. You are a fucking Brazilian tease!"

Ivo pulled up his pants, stumbled around and vomited something dark and foul.

Maia got up and ran down the pastures, leaving behind her pants with little lilac flowers.

She came into the garden like a blind creature, not knowing where to go. She couldn't go into the house with blood running down her legs. She couldn't tell Saul because he would kill Ivo for sure.

But her plans to keep it from Saul were foiled because he was on the patio and saw her come in.

He held her in his arms while she cried deep sobs of humiliation and shame. She didn't have to say anything; Saul knew.

Saul found Ivo in the carpentry shop, laughing with Pedro Matias.

He went in, grabbed Ivo by the collar of his shirt, and brought him out into the street. The men in the carpentry shop were saying things to Saul, but he didn't hear it. He pummeled Ivo with such ferocity that Ivo didn't do anything else other than scream. With each punch, there was a scream; and Saul thought of Maia's screams and how no one had come to save her. The men from the carpentry shop came out after them and tried to get Ivo off Saul's hands, but it was almost impossible. Finally, Saul let Ivo fall unconscious on the street.

The men picked Ivo up and took him to the monsignor, not really sure if it was to be patched up or for last rights. If Ivo was not dead, he was in bad shape; he was unrecognizable.

The monsignor couldn't fix that mess, and Ivo had to go to the hospital.

The hospital called the police, and the police came again to the Amoras. But the monsignor, having a soft spot for Saul and knowing about Ivo's drunken ways, was able to deflect the importance of the incident. He told the police that Ivo was a violent drunk and that he had attacked Maia. The monsignor vouched for this statement, and the police went away, though they made mental notes about Saul.

As for Maia, the monsignor and everybody else knew that the law would not care. She was from Brazil and spoke seductively, with a soft tone, so different from the rest of the women. The man was her boyfriend ...or had been; maybe she'd asked for it. That was what the police would say.

And very secretly, the monsignor was happy with Saul—he only prayed that Ivo didn't die.

Maia became even more of a recluse after the attack. Saul and Carlota became her world. The people who helped around the house were summarily let go. They sent the laundry to be done in the city, and only once in a while they would hire a girl from a neighboring village to help during harvest. They became each other's jailers.

Ivo became a pariah for some and a hero to others. When he was sober, he would think of Maia, sweet and gracious, feeding him hot soup and sweet bread. And when he was drunk, he would think of her on her hands and knees, crying in pain, with blood running down her legs.

When Detective Lourenço showed interest in Maia, all these concerns rose up with Saul and Carlota. A detective could be just as corrupt as a drunken farmer. And they had a nagging feeling that the detective could hurt them even more; he wanted something from the past.

No bride should have a matron of honor as beautiful as Madalena. It was simply not fair. One, instead of looking at the bride, was looking at the matron of honor. These were the thoughts going through Nascimento's head while Angela was getting ready.

Dom Carlos came out of his room, in a beautiful suit and with perfectly coifed hair.

Angela stood on the landing looking at him. "You look very handsome," she said.

"And you look beautiful," he said, placing his hands on her shoulders.

"Do I?" she asked, feeling hopeful.

"Today, you are the most beautiful woman in this village," he said.

"Wait till you see Madalena." Angela said in a self-deprecating tone.

"I've seen Madalena. You are beautiful."

Angela smiled at him. "I will be a married woman soon."

"So you will," he said. And he bent down and kissed her on the forehead.

André opened the door of his room and said, looking at Angela, "Wow, here comes the bride …" He laughed. "I'm sorry. I'm not laughing at you." He pointed at Angela. "I was thinking about the lyrics Antonio Dores wrote for you."

André was in a state of permanent mirth when it came to Two Brooks, but today, his most derisive chuckles were at Antonio Dores' songs. In a theatrical manner, he put a hand on his chest and sang in exaggerated falsetto:

> Here comes the bride
> All happy inside
> She looks like a flower
> Coming down from her tower
> Where love was absent
> And now is heaven-sent

"Let's go," Maria Gomes urged from downstairs. "Lazarus is coming through the gate."

And finally, everyone went to church to be the witnesses of the purest love they knew and then went back to the newlyweds' house to celebrate.

Throughout the celebration, Saul caressed Madalena's soft, shining curls, his big brown hands contrasting with her fairness.

Could that be? Nascimento thought. *Could it be that Madalena loved Saul? No, how could she? Look at those nostrils!*

Aldo was getting drunk by the minute. Ascendida took the glass from him. "Enough," she said with a clenched jaw. "Tonight you are not going to be drunk."

Ascendida looked at him with such sadness that Aldo froze.

Pedro Matias pranced around as if he was the king of the event. He went to Angela and placed an arm over her shoulders, his face close to hers. "We are family now," he said aloud. And in a softer tone that only Angela could hear, "I can slap you around like I do with the others."

Nascimento heard Pedro's whisper and Angela's response, and she looked at her friend, petrified by her quiet rage; and she was not sure if she was more afraid of Pedro or of Angela.

There was something so raw about Angela.

"You so much as raise your hand to any of us, and I'll find a way to kill you," Angela whispered to Pedro.

Pedro's smile died on his lips. "I'm not afraid of you," he said.

But Pedro only had to look at Angela and at those two black holes on her face; her pupils were so dilated that she looked like the devil incarnate.

Nascimento slowly walked away and stood next to Dom Carlos, who was surrounded by giggling girls. She pulled at his shirtsleeve.

"I think you should intervene over there," she pointed at Angela and Pedro. "They are going to create a scene."

Dom Carlos slowly walked around the tables full of food and drink. He stopped in front of Angela and her father-in-law.

"You look very intense. If this were not a day of celebration, I would say that the two of you were fighting. You are not, are you?" he asked, his tone matter-of-fact.

There were tables full of people and food in three different rooms around the house and patio. December 19, as if ordered by the gods, was warm, sunny, and with minimal wind. Everyone was laughing and drinking, and no one was paying much attention to this threesome looking intensely at each other.

"Well, well," Pedro said. "Here comes daddy. Is it just daddy or something else?"

Dom Carlos felt something that he rarely felt—anger. He felt many things that were not good, such as disdain, pity, sadness, annoyance, or discomfort, but anger was something that he didn't feel often.

Dom Carlos said in a low voice, "If you so much as open your mouth to say anything that isn't pleasant, you will have the police at your door in less than two hours. I will lie. I will say things that you wouldn't believe. But the chief of police will."

Pedro turned around and left the party.

"Are you all right?" Dom Carlos asked Angela.

"Yes," she snapped. "That man is a menace. One of these days …I'm going to … I don't even know what I am going to do, but I am going to do something."

Dom Carlos held her trembling hands in his. "Don't let him spoil this day for you." And he vaguely thought about Maria Gomes telling him that Angela had bitten Pedro on the leg—just like a dog—when she was about four or five. It would be disastrous if the bride—

"I've waited all my life for this day, and everything was just perfect," she said interrupting his thoughts.

Lazarus came around, and Angela nestled in his arms. He lowered his lips to her ear and sang softly: "She was my beautiful boat ..."

Nascimento went home alone, walking slowly down the road. Jaime was doing double shifts, and she was not going to see him for a few days. The night was very dark, perfect for snooping ... But she shouldn't.

Just for a few minutes, she lied to herself.

And she looked at the lights coming from the windows of her neighbors.

Regina's house ...always so interesting ... Just a peak ...one look, and if nothing was happening, she would go straight home.

But something was happening, as invariably did at Regina's house: André, tied, facedown was moaning with anticipation.

Nascimento winced when Regina slapped his buttocks with all her strength. She couldn't move her eyes from André, with his face buried in the pillow while Regina talked to him. And when he answered, she hit him again, his buttocks turning pink. André's screams were high and vibrating, sounding like his falsetto rendition earlier in church.

She laughed, and both Regina and André stopped to listen.

Nascimento moved on silently with the firm purpose of going home. But then she saw light on Geniveva's window ... She should have not seen it, but now that she had...

Geniveva was an older woman who had moved to Two Brooks from another island. Like any outsider, she was immediately put aside. This silent neglect from the village suited Geniveva well. She was quiet, minded her own business, paid her debts, and went to Mass. But no one visited her house, and she visited no one.

When Nascimento looked into her house, she expected to see a quiet woman maybe mending clothes or reading the Bible. She didn't expect to see Elias naked pushing himself into Geniveva and pushing the glasses up on his nose with the same diligence.

Nascimento covered her mouth to stifle an exclamation of disbelief. Elias's skinny body rippled with delight while his love expletives sounded like a call for help. Elias with a penis? A wave of remorse took hold of her. Poor Elias; how could a person who was born and raised next to her be so irrelevant? She didn't even think of him as a man, with a penis …with needs and wants. He was just …poor, dumb, blind Elias.

Suddenly she felt tired by the surprises of those alluring windows with beckoning light. She sighed and turned around to go home.

Before she turned the corner, she saw a glimpse of light coming from the pastures near the coast. Again, the light … Vaguely she thought about pirates and the stories she'd heard all her life. And like a moth, she went down the pastures in the direction of the flickers of light. On and off the light went, and Nascimento now identified the place—the barn by the sea. She was now on Pedro Matias's property, walking in the direction of the barn. His dog, a mean, scrawny thing called Ferocious had a few friends, and Nascimento was one of them, because she fed him. Every time Nascimento left at night, she always brought with her something for the dogs. And the dogs knew her and loved her.

The windows were too high up, and the walls too thick for Nascimento to see anything. But she could hear the voices of various men talking about what had happened with Manuel. She recognized Pedro Matias's voice.

There was laughter, and some of the men howled like dogs.

"Who is next?" someone asked.

Someone said something, and there were sounds of agreement. There was laughter.

And Nascimento heard names—André, Geniveva, Miguel Valentino, Manuel, Angela …

Is this Night Justice? she thought, feeling dizzy.

She would wait for the men to go home, and then she could see who they were. She had to know who they were. She had to!

She was freezing. It started to rain. The men talked about their next victims and the things they were going to do to them. Geniveva was going to be first and then the teacher, and after the teacher, someone who was putting his fingers up Maria Augusta. Why would they care if Maria Augusta were being fingered? Why the teacher? He was a nuisance but nothing else. Of course, thought Nascimento, one of the guys must be Maria Augusta's father, and the other one was Sérgio Leal. André was making pretty eyes at Sérgio's wife because André had heard that Sérgio was impotent.

Finally the men got up to go home. Nascimento waited behind a broken wall, peering from an opening between the rocks. Pedro Matias was holding a Petromax lamp, and everyone was around him getting their last cigarettes lit. Ferocious came around wagging his tail, gave her a lick, and left again to join the men. She felt faint and peed herself. Not only was she looking at Night

Justice but also Ferocious was going to give her away. The warm urine spilling down her legs felt oddly comforting. But the men were too engrossed in their own conversation and didn't look at Ferocious.

Slowly, after the silence told her that no one was around, she crept up the pastures.

Witness of Love and Malice

Madalena opened the letter and read it, "I think of you day and night." It was the same consistent message. She made an exasperated sound.

"Whatever you do don't show it to Saul," Carlota said.

"I can't keep these things from him. He gets hurt if I do."

"He may hurt Manuel if you don't," Carlota said, somewhat frustrated.

And that night, Madalena told Saul about the letter. He listened in his brooding manner.

If Saul was difficult to read at times, he was impenetrable now. "He has no shame," he said in a low, rumbling voice.

"I doubt he is the one writing me these letters," she said. "I was talking to Angela, and she said that she thinks the teacher is the one."

"André Moniz?" he asked, surprised.

"Yes, the only teacher we have," she snapped.

"And you want to work with him?" he asked with a frown.

"Not anymore if my suspicions are true," she said. "I will take care of this. Angela will help me."

"I'm sick of it!" Saul said and got up abruptly, leaving Madalena facing an empty chair.

"Saul!" she called after him.

He turned around to face her.

"I've done nothing for this silly man to be interested in me. I hope you know that."

"I do," he said walking back to her. "I'm frustrated. That's all."

All that she needed now was his sweet, shy smile.

And as if reading her mind, he smiled.

The following day was Christmas Eve. Much to Angela's chagrin, the family was going to have supper at the home of Pedro Matias. He had insisted in having the whole family, especially the new members, over to celebrate. Angela had declined and immediately reconsidered because of Lazarus; he missed his mother and worried about her.

Angela had a premonition about that night. She had a nervous alertness and was reading signs everywhere and on everyone; everything seemed a bit out of kilter. Even Dom Carlos looked subdued.

Dom Carlos was quietly staring at his coffee.

Angela put an arm around his shoulders. "Why are you so pensive?" she asked.

He looked up at her. "Christmas makes me feel this way, very … melancholic."

"Memories?" she asked.

He didn't say anything. He was staring up at her as if he was reading something on her face. "And you? What is eating you?"

"The dinner tonight; he is up to something."

"It will be over before you know it," he said.

"I would prefer to spend it with you and my parents. We could drink hot chocolate and sing Christmas songs sitting by the fire. Then we would open our gifts and wish each other Merry Christmas," Angela said dreamily.

"That sounds so lovely," he said in the same tone.

"My first Christmas with Lazarus should be as I dreamt it, don't you think?"

"But you are going to his parents' because of him …because of his mother."

"Yes, I'll do anything for him. He is my everything." It was just a whisper, but Dom Carlos heard it.

"It is quite a responsibility—to be someone's everything …" Dom Carlos murmured.

Angela thought about that comment. How strange Dom Carlos was tonight—moody, sad, and mysterious.

"André has a crush on Madalena," she blurted out, hoping to sting him out of that strange mood.

"I know," he said almost absentmindedly.

They listened to the fire crackling on the iron grate.

Angela sighed. "When I went to clean André's room, he had a crumpled piece of paper in the trash bin. I usually don't look at people's trash, but somehow I wanted to see that. It said, 'I thinj of.' That's all it said."

"Thinj? What's thinj?"

"He probably wanted to write I think …but made a mistake and threw it in the trash."

Dom Carlos laughed.

"I saved it. And Madalena showed me another letter she received."

Angela took the piece of paper from the pocket of her dress and showed it to Dom Carlos. Then she took out the letter Madalena had received. "Look at the *n*, how it is nicked on the bottom of the second leg. Then I typed on his typewriter the same message, and it is identical. Unless someone comes here to type love notes for Madalena, he is doing it himself. And he was too insistent for Madalena to be his assistant."

She walked away from Dom Carlos. Then she turned back and said, "I told you that he was a prick."

He said, "Don't get into trouble tonight. Don't pick a fight either with Pedro or André. Remember it is Christmas." He got up and kissed her cheek.

"You make it sound like I am picking fights with everybody," she retorted, offended.

"Well," he said, "you rise up to the bait too often and too easily. You don't have to save the world."

It was such a quiet scolding on Christmas Eve.

"You don't understand. If we let our guard down, we will be crushed. Look at most women in this place. They've been beaten down every second of their lives. I made a decision to fight back—that's all."

Dom Carlos was very pensive, his eyes fastened on her face. "Tonight, be peaceful if you can, little girl." He placed a hand on her shoulder and squeezed it slightly.

Angela was surprised by the sadness in his voice. "I'm not a little girl," she snapped. "I've never been a little girl; only you have called me that. I was born old, and I'll die ancient. Everyone knows that, except you."

"See? You are picking a fight with me, me who loves you," he said.

When Angela and Lazarus walked to Pedro Matias's house, the whole village was festive. There were candles on the windows, and people sang Christmas songs inside their homes, the sound spilling out to the streets.

> Blessed you are, my sweet Jesus
> I am yours to follow your light

Angela sang as she hugged Lazarus by the waist, her baby Jesus. They laughed quietly and kissed as they went down the road.

As soon as they got into the house, Lazarus's smile disappeared, and a look of anxiety took hold of him. Saul, Madalena, and André were there already. Madalena was helping her mother, and Saul was just sitting as if he was ready to spring up and leave.

Pedro Matias opened his arms to Lazarus and Angela. "The newlyweds!" he exclaimed with false joy.

During the meal, the other four boys were so quiet that one forgot that they were there. They were sullen boys, never laughing and never talking. They had learned how to make themselves invisible.

Dona Amelia was very happy to see her family together and especially to see her son Lazarus. How she missed that boy—her Lazarus. André Moniz was trying to make conversation with Madalena, but she was quiet and looking at her mother.

Her sweet, loving mother had a fresh bruise on her cheek.

Angela looked at Lazarus and Madalena. Dom Carlos's words came at her: *Don't pick a fight tonight.*

"What's that bruise on your face Dona Amelia?" she asked, placing everything on the table and putting both hands on her lap.

Dona Amelia colored violently and said demurely, "Oh, that's nothing."

"What is the matter, Angela? Have you never seen a bruise? I can give you a few if you don't behave," Pedro said and laughed.

Angela felt and heard the blood go around in her head—*swoon, swoon, swoon.* This was a bad sign, especially when that sound came along with bright red behind her eyelids.

"Let's not do this tonight," Lazarus said.

"Do what? In my house I can do what I want," Pedro said belligerently.

"We don't have to be in your house," Lazarus said. "We can leave right now."

Pedro looked at his son as if he had two heads. "Do you think that I will not slap you because you are married?" he asked irately.

He got up and went to Lazarus, who was sitting on the opposite end of the table.

"You will not do this today," Madalena said calmly, standing between her father and her brother.

"Who do you think you are?" he screamed. "I am still the boss; what I say goes!" He lifted his hand to hit Madalena.

But Saul grabbed his wrist and pulled his arm behind his back. "No one will ever hit Madalena again. If you ever lift a hand to her, I will break you in two," he said, his voice so low that only Pedro heard him fully.

Pedro screamed as Saul's hold increased. "Get out of my house! You big fat, ugly cuckold bastard!"

Saul let go of him with a push, and Pedro fell against the wall.

"Mother," Lazarus said, "come with us. And you too," he said, looking at his younger brothers. "Come with us. You don't have to be here."

André got up and took off like a shot ahead of everybody else. All his mirth had dissipated into a mask of fear.

Madalena and Saul were waiting at the door, not knowing what to do. They looked at Angela.

This was too much for Pedro. His children were creating mayhem in his own home. He turned to Lazarus and said, "Listen here, boy. Sit down and tell your wife to behave, or I'll make her and slap that girly face of yours."

The sound in Angela's head increased, the red in her eyelids turned brighter, and all of her focus ran into her closed fist as she punched Pedro's mouth. *Be peaceful tonight*, she thought as she saw her hand fly in slow motion to Pedro's face.

He fell back, utterly bewildered—assaulted twice in a few minutes in his own home.

"If you ever so much as touch or threaten my family, I will kill you!" Angela's voice had an unreal tone—low but clear. Her eyes were like two black pools, and like a demon, she was ready to take him under.

There was complete silence.

"Come with us," Angela said to Dona Amelia.

But Dona Amelia was too scared and confused with the events. They shouldn't have provoked Pedro. Now it was going to be worse.

Saul said from the door, "Dona Amelia will not be hurt tonight. If she is, I will come back for you."

They all left. Dona Amelia shook her head in disbelief while, in a corner of the kitchen, Pedro was spitting out codfish and teeth.

Dona Amelia cleared the table; it was something to do to establish normalcy. Pedro got up and went out to the garden.

"Boys," she whispered, "get some of your things together."

The four kids looked at her in complete terror.

"Go on," she said hurriedly.

She went out holding a knife under her sweater and addressed the area where a cigarette was burning. "I have a knife in my hand," she said, shaking with fear. "If you hit me, I will stab you. I will kill you because you are drunk and weak. We are leaving tonight. The kids are getting ready."

She turned around and left to pack some of her things, and the five of them walked up the road and knocked at Angela's door.

Pedro Matias was speechless. His wife of twenty years had just left him and taken his boys with her. He would be the laughing stock of the village. He couldn't let that happen. He had to convince her to come back to him; he had to! He would even promise not to hurt her again. He could very well do that. He didn't have to hit her; it was just a habit. He looked at his dining room with the dishes unfinished and the brilliance of the night gone. He had done that. Why had he done that?

He went to bed but was not able to sleep, so he drank all night and woke up Christmas Day sitting in his own vomit.

Dom Carlos opened the door. He saw five anxious faces looking up at him. Each had a little bag in hand. They came in, and Dona Amelia looked around for Angela and Lazarus.

"They are in the bathroom," he said. "Lazarus is throwing up."

Dona Amelia sat down with a sigh. The boys looked at her anxiously.

"Come," Maria Gomes said to Dona Amelia. "Angela prepared a room for you. The boys can stay in the attic. Angela has everything ready."

When Dona Amelia found herself alone, she sighed. Where had her life gone? Only yesterday, she was the prettiest girl in the village. She was happy and loved by her parents, her parents who died within six months of each other, as if life without the other was not worth living. They had left her alone. She'd had no place to go, no arms to hold her.

Angela and Lazarus came out of the bathroom, both looking yellowish and tired.

Lazarus hugged Dom Carlos. It was a long hug as if tonight something profound had been revealed. Then he went up to see his mother.

Angela's parents left. They'd had a wonderful meal with Dom Carlos and were about to sing some songs when that procession of disgrace had come through the house. André come in first, but this time, he was wise enough to walk right up to his room without commentary. Madalena and Saul had gone straight home to celebrate with Carlota and Maia.

Angela was now in the kitchen looking around as if dazed. Dom Carlos was also sitting quietly. She walked up to him and fell in his arms, crying.

"I'm sorry. I picked a fight," she said between sobs.

Dom Carlos cradled her in his arms, holding her head against his chest. He murmured in her ear, "Everything will be fine. Don't cry, little girl."

"I thought of you when I punched his face," she said sobbing.

"I beg your pardon?"

"I thought you would say that I picked a fight," she said, looking up, her face full of tears. "I did pick a fight," she admitted quietly. "I wanted to punch him, you know. I wanted to let him know that things were going to be different from now on, and I picked Christmas Eve." She started to cry again, letting the tears and the mucus ran freely down her face. "You see, he wanted us there to let us know that he was the boss, and I picked a fight for the same reason."

"I know," he said, a bit amused. "The way you were feeling, I knew that Pedro was in for a surprise."

"Why didn't you tell me then, if you knew?" she snapped, pushing him away.

"I did," he answered gently. "I asked you not to pick a fight. Pedro is a mean, cowardly bastard. The less you entangle yourself with him, the better. All I have to do is call my friend, the chief of police, and Pedro goes to jail. You don't have to fight him."

"How? He is part of my family now. Unless he dies or I kill him," she said, starting anew with deep sobs. "When you leave, there will be no police protection. The police will do it for you, not for us. All we have is ourselves!"

"You are such a mess," he said, repressing a grin. "Look what you've done to my shirt."

He held her head against his chest. His heartbeat was gently drumming in her ear, and she felt peaceful and safe.

Christmas day was sunny and cold. Angela got up early to prepare breakfast. She had a house full of people, including André, who'd decided not to go to the city: People in Two Brooks kept him continuously entertained, so he stayed for the show. Angela's parents came to spend the day and brought gifts and food.

Dona Amelia and the boys were very quiet. Lazarus sat at the head of the table and looked at his family. All of them were now his responsibility.

And then there was a loud knock on the door. Dom Carlos looked at Lazarus, and Lazarus got up. They knew who it was. Dona Amelia and the boys, who were prepared to have a peaceful day, suddenly crumpled before the impending doom.

Pedro Matias came through the door of the dining room. He looked terrible. His lip was split, and his two front teeth were broken in half. But his demeanor was different. He was subdued, ceremonial, holding his hat in his hand.

"I came to talk to Amelia," he said quietly.

"No. You are not going to talk to her today or any other day," Lazarus said. His voice was shaking. He almost preferred to get a beating than to face his father with a defiant move.

"Please, son. I know you don't have any reason to listen to me, but I need to talk with your mother."

Please. He said please, Lazarus thought. Lazarus summoned all the courage he had left and said, "Not today. Today is Christmas, and we had enough commotion yesterday."

Pedro looked at his wife. Dona Amelia lowered her head as if in prayer, and the boys stared at their father with wide, expectant eyes.

"Boys?" Pedro Matias said.

"They are not going with you either," Lazarus said.

"I want my family back," Pedro answered, his voice rising a bit.

Angela could see Lazarus shake. She knew how much this valiant effort was going to cost him. She got up and walked up to Pedro Matias. "We want you to leave. You are not welcome in this house. Tomorrow, Dona Amelia will talk to you in the church. The monsignor will be there …with Lazarus and me. Now, leave."

"When? At what time?" he asked anxiously.

"We don't know yet. I'll send word," Angela answered coolly.

Pedro looked again at his family.

Angela's menagerie sniffed the air with morbid interest. Nixon and Viriato made low sounds in their throats, Hercules smirked, and Dalia snapped her bill. They knew something was going to happen.

When Pedro turned around to leave, Hercules bit him on the ankle, but

Pedro didn't scream. In the scheme of things, it didn't even hurt. He made a mental note that he should kill that cat, although his previous attempts had failed miserably. For Hercules, this lack of theater was anticlimactic, quite disappointing, and the cat followed Pedro to the gate to pounce on him again.

There was a sigh of relief when Pedro left. Lazarus went straight to the bathroom to throw up again.

After the meal, they went to the Christmas Day Mass, and Angela told the monsignor what had happened while he quietly and slowly folded his vestments.

"That poor woman ..." he murmured. "She should leave him to his misery ...that bastard!"

"Monsignor," Angela said, "Pedro promised Lazarus the carpentry shop. But after he married me, he reneged on his promise. I want him to give Lazarus the carpentry shop, and we can use this situation with Dona Amelia to make him."

"Angela!" the monsignor exclaimed. "You cannot blackmail people, even if it is someone like Pedro. It is not right!"

"It is right for Pedro. He is a despicable human being, and Lazarus deserves the carpentry shop," Angela refuted, raising her voice also.

Lazarus was pale, looking from one to the other, not sure who was going to win.

"I will not propose such a thing!" the monsignor said. "Come to me at two o'clock tomorrow for us to talk about Amelia and Pedro but not about that. I will not do that!"

Angela had that stubborn look on her face. "You don't have to," she said. "Just don't knock it if it shows up in the conversation."

"Angela, what are you plotting?" he yelled again.

When Angela got home. she told Dona Amelia about the meeting on the following day. "You are going to give him a chance to talk, but you don't have to do anything," Angela said. "Even if you go back, our house is always open to you and to the boys."

Dona Amelia said in a soft voice, "I will miss my house and my things, but I will not live like that again."

Angela looked at Dona Amelia, once so beautiful and now so sad and battered. What one person can do to a life! What horrible power we have over others. And Angela thought about the power of kindness—to rescue and provide, to protect, and to love—and about power without kindness and the destruction it caused. She couldn't think about anything more destructive than the power to break a spirit. And she was surrounded by broken spirits—by the deeds of one man. With sadness, she realized that she would never forgive this man who had caused so much hurt. She knew that she was pushing joy out of her heart to make room to hate him. She needed to hate him. If she found a path to forgiveness, she would not take it. She wanted to hate Pedro till the end of her days and have in her heart a place that belonged only to him—a dark and cold place.

Everybody from the family wanted to witness the talk between the monsignor, Pedro, and Dona Amelia. Even Saul and Carlota, who were so private in their affairs and in the affairs of others, got ready for the event. Maria and Joaquim Gomes where sitting next to Carlota.

When the monsignor saw the entire family, he asked, "What is this, a public trial?"

But Angela explained that Pedro needed to see all the support given to Dona Amelia and the boys. "All abusers need isolation," she said, full of conviction. "He needs to see that she is not alone, and he can't abuse at will because we will step in."

When Pedro got to the sacristy, he was taken aback by the audience. "What is this, a public lynching?" he asked, ill humored.

"That remains to be seen," the monsignor snapped. "Sit down, man, and think carefully about every word you say."

Pedro looked intensely at his wife. She was quietly sitting next to Lazarus but held his gaze.

"This is the deal," the monsignor said in a businesslike tone. "You abused your family for years, and now they left you. Look around you, man. Every person in this room will take your wife and boys into their homes. They don't need you for anything, and they should have left you a long time ago."

"Yes, Monsignor. You are right," Pedro said clearly but with a bowed head.

"Why should they do such a stupid thing? Go back with you?" the monsignor asked. "Go back to a tyrant when they can live peacefully with Lazarus?"

"Yes, Monsignor. You are right," Pedro said again. His speech was a bit impaired by the broken teeth, and the monsignor could not put his finger on what was different about the man. Of course, no one offered any information.

"What is the matter with you, man? Did you swallow a recorder? What happened to your face?" the monsignor asked, mildly curious.

Everybody wiggled in discomfort in his or her chair. Angela colored deeply.

Pedro looked at Angela and then at the monsignor. "I drank a bit too much yesterday and hurt myself."

"Well," said the monsignor, "I advised your family to stay where they are—with Lazarus. Madalena and Saul also offered their home to them. So did Joaquim and Maria Gomes. I'm sure that half the village would offer them shelter, not just because of them but to stick it to you."

Pedro looked down at his hands.

"We will go back," Dona Amelia said, "with a few conditions."

Everybody looked at her in surprise, including Pedro, because he thought he had lost this round.

Dona Amelia said, "You will give the carpentry shop to Lazarus as you had promised."

Lazarus looked perplexed at his mother and said, "No! I can start my own carpentry shop if I need to—"

"I agree. Lazarus will get the carpentry shop free and clear," Pedro interrupted.

"Then, when that's done, we will go home and not before. And you will not hit anyone, not even the dog," Dona Amelia said.

The monsignor looked accusingly at Angela. *That little manipulator. I am going to skin her alive*, he thought.

That afternoon, the papers were drawn. The following day, Lazarus and Dom Carlos went to the city and made everything legal. And Dona Amelia and the boys went home.

"From now on, I will sleep in Madalena's room. Alone," Dona Amelia said and turned her back on Pedro.

Nascimento was having problems of conscience. She wanted to tell her friends about the things she had learned on her night escapades, but she didn't want them to find out that she had lied. Every week, she gave a report on her anti-voyeurism efforts, and she had been lying. Not only had she lied to her friends, she had also fallen into the disgrace of looking into their homes. Just the other day, she had looked into Madalena's room, and Saul was naked kneeling on the bed, his back shining with sweat from loving Madalena. His buttocks muscular and tight moved rhythmically in his lovemaking, erasing the image of when Dona Lidia had hit him and he'd swayed in pain with each stroke of the whip.

She had gone as far as climbing up to Angela's terrace, taking down the potted geranium perched on a pillar of the veranda, and looking in at Angela and Lazarus. If she'd fallen, she would have broken her neck. And she had seen Angela massaging Lazarus's legs, completely oblivious to his erection. He was moaning softly, his eyes closed. Then Angela dropped oil on his penis. He opened his eyes and looked at the window. Nascimento wanted to run away, but she couldn't move her eyes from Angela's fingers going up and down on Lazarus.

Her voyeurism had gotten worse since she'd set the date to get married, but she had told her friends the opposite. They would know that she had been fudging her reports to gain their approbation. They would know that she still could not resist the soft sounds of sleep and the darkness of the night turning the moon into an enchantress and her into a shameful voyeur.

It was a curse.

After Christmas vacation, André was sure that Madalena was going to start work as his assistant. Much to his surprise, Madalena stopped by the house and told him that she would not be able to work with him.

"Why?" he asked, his voice almost in falsetto. He was not used to being surprised at his own games.

"I thought better of it," she said coolly.

André didn't know what to say and stood looking at Madalena's back as she walked away.

Angela smirked.

Nascimento said, in a matter-of-fact way, "Be careful, man! Or you might get a typewriter up your ass. Then you would sing in falsetto."

"What in the world do you mean?" André asked, highly offended by the comment.

"Well, ask Manuel," Nascimento said.

André went up the stairs, leaving the women in the kitchen laughing. He was furious with his failed plan to seduce Madalena and with the mockery that was ensuing. He couldn't stand the job of teaching those kids. He let them play outside for hours while he plotted one thing or another. Now he was plotting about finding someone to do the work for him. He had no patience to teach those little savages with runny noses. Carmelina was out of the question because of her husband. His only solution was Maria Augusta. She probably would accept. He would much prefer Lucia or Elvira, but they didn't have teaching degrees.

So André went to the monsignor and told him that Maria Augusta would do.

Maria Augusta, as the monsignor had known she would be, was a kind and loving teacher. Kindness begets kindness, and in turn, the kids did almost anything Maria Augusta asked of them; she was gentle and wanted them to enjoy learning.

The kids went from being beaten every day to being completely neglected to being cared for.

André avoided Saul at any cost. The letters stopped, but his determination to seduce Madalena didn't. He found other ways to make sure she knew of his interest. He smiled at her in public places; stared at her in church; and waited for her on the street, making believe it was a chance encounter.

And one day, André wrote her another letter. This time it said:

> I love you and you know it. Meet me at the windmill tomorrow night. Wear your red dress this afternoon in church if you've read this letter. I will be there anxiously waiting. Meet me at seven.

Much to Madalena's surprise, Saul said that he was going to church that afternoon with her. Even more surprising, he asked her to put on a red dress, since he loved to see her in red.

She looked at him suspiciously. He held her gaze and smiled.

"I didn't think you cared about fashion," she said, surprised.

"I don't," he answered, "but I like you in red."

The draconian rule that the monsignor instituted in church was firmly observed: The men sat at the back of the church, and the women at the front pews. When some misguided emigrant sat with his wife in church, the monsignor screamed, "In this church, I want skirts up and pants down!"

Madalena went to church in her red dress accompanied by her husband, who rarely went to church or cared about fashion. She sat at the front pew, making sure to keep an eye on Saul, who in turn sat in the back of the church directly behind André, who had his eyes glued on Madalena. Every time Madalena looked back in Saul's direction, André smiled smugly, completely unaware that Saul was behind him, smiling at his wife.

12

Night Justice

The following day was the day of assignation, according to André's plans. She had worn the red dress and had smiled at him in church. He was overjoyed, singing around the house with a conspirator's smile. Not even Hercules bothered him. Nothing would ever bother him again; he was going to have that pretty thing tonight!

Saul left the house as soon as it was dark enough. He got in the windmill very quietly and waited behind a wall of bales of hay. He checked the butcher's knife, from Maia's collection. Soon he heard someone at the door. Then the door opened, and a candle was lit. Saul was telling himself that he was not going to hurt the teacher. He was just going to give him a good scare. He kept on repeating that promise to himself as other thoughts assaulted him. He peeked from behind the bales of hay at André, who was whistling gaily and placing a bottle of wine over a blanket.

André looked at his watch—seven o'clock; he walked a little around the room. And Saul, very quietly, came around too and locked the door with a wood contraption.

At the sound of the door being locked, André turned around and faced Saul with a butcher's knife in his hand.

André said, "Ahhhh." He put his hand up to his heart and said, "Ahhh, ohhh, please, please …"

Saul walked slowly to him, pointing the knife; André rolled his eyes and fainted. As he fell down, he hit his head on the stone floor. Saul peered closely at the teacher and realized that he had a gash on the back of his head. He picked the teacher up, slung him over his shoulder, and went down the pastures, praying that no one would see him coming down from the windmill with the unconscious teacher. Slowly he felt a warm feeling spreading over his torso, and he realized with a grunt of frustration that the teacher had urinated himself.

The closest house to the windmill was Angela's. But afraid that someone would be home Saul dumped the teacher in the woodshop and went into the house to call Angela.

When she saw the teacher with a bloody head she let out a shriek of horror. Saul had done something stupid. But after Saul explained what he had done, Angela started to laugh—first a small, quiet laugh and then roaring laughter.

Saul was smiling, looking at Angela.

André woke up to Angela's mirth. He looked around and saw Saul's big face looking down at him and screamed.

Saul took the knife off his belt and said, "I will cut your prick off if you so much look in Madalena's direction again."

He left, convulsed with laughter. He had never laughed like that in his entire life. It was a strange and cathartic thing.

When he got home, he took a long bath. He stayed in the bathtub a lot longer than usual.

Madalena came to check on him. "Where have you been? And what are you smiling about?" she asked, between peeved and curious.

"I was settling an account," he said, closing his eyes and sinking deep into the tub.

At Angela's, André was also taking a bath and then having his head checked. It was just a small cut. Angela was still laughing when he came out of the bathroom.

"I'm going to report that ogre!" he said.

"Report him for what? He didn't touch you. You fainted on your own, like a little girl afraid of ghosts." She laughed again.

"He came at me with a knife!" he said, still shaking.

"No. I didn't see any knife."

"You mean to say that you would not be my witness?" he asked incredulously.

"Witness of what?" Angela asked innocently. "All I can do for you is to tell the police that you've been trying to seduce Madalena and that Saul warned you to stay away. I can be a witness to that."

"He has a record. It will be easy to convince the authorities that he assaulted me."

"I will deny it," she said simply.

"We'll see. It's your word against mine," he said defiantly.

And true enough, the following day, André went to the city and reported Saul, citing Angela as a witness.

Detective Lourenço welcomed the excuse to go to Saul's house again. He could see Maia. But when she opened the door, she didn't show pleasure upon seeing him. A frown of worry marred her face and she let him in without a word.

Detective Lourenço was in the same kitchen where they had prepared food together a few weeks ago, and now they were looking at each other as if they had just met.

"I need to talk to Saul," he simply said.

"He is not home. He went to the city with Madalena."

"When will he be back?"

"Much later. When he takes Madalena, sometimes they stay overnight. May I know why you want to see him again?"

Detective Lourenço hesitated for a second. "We received a complaint of assault."

Maia was totally taken aback. "Manuel?" she asked, placing a tremulous hand on her chest.

"No. André Moniz."

"The teacher?" she asked, totally surprised.

"Yes. He said that Saul assaulted him. He threatened him with a knife, a butcher's knife, and then hit him. He fell and hurt his head."

"No. Why would Saul hit him? They have absolutely no connection," Maia said, still flabbergasted.

"Maia," he said in a conciliatory tone, "I'm not saying that he did this. I just have to talk to him."

Maia smiled weakly. "I will tell him when he gets home."

Detective Lourenço was in the middle of the kitchen. He could smell the food that was being prepared and hear the soft sound of the wood burning on the iron range. Those domestic little nothings were so dear to him. It reminded him of when he was home with his parents and siblings—that complete assurance that he belonged and that he would be taken care of. He wanted very much to be part of that with Maia. It was becoming his most ardent wish.

And as if Maia could read his thoughts, she said, "I just prepared a nice chicken stew. Are you hungry?"

That night, when Saul and Madalena had come back from the city, the Night Justice had been victimizing Geniveva, Elias's lover. Madalena was thinking about the complete disconnection between human beings and their pain. As they were driving by Geniveva's house, five or six men, in the name of justice, were raping her.

And they hadn't known that the noise they'd heard or the light from a Petromax lamp could be anything other than Geniveva having company at odd hours. Shouldn't the pain of that woman somehow have crossed the distance between her house and Madalena's car and touched her? Shouldn't the air have been so charged with pain and humiliation that she would breathe it and know? Madalena lowered her head in complete shame for being part of this island, of these people who could be so cruel to each other. And then she fixed her eyes on her wedding ring and thought about love and kindness.

The monsignor was beside himself with rage. The Night Justice was crossing a most definite line. This was not justice; this was terrorism.

When the police came by and took poor Geniveva to the hospital, the monsignor didn't want to talk to mere officers; he wanted the chief. And he left that morning for the city. But in the city, the chief couldn't do much with the information he had. Five or six men had gone into the woman's house and thrown out a naked Elias and then, one by one, raped the poor woman. They had tied her up on the kitchen table and used her like a latrine, and then they had shaved off her nipples. These were the monsignor's parishioners, the people he cared for; he heard their confessions and absolved their sins.

The chief of police, in a very patient tone, said to the monsignor, "Monsignor, do you know who these people are? Don't give me the bullshit about the sanctity of confession, blah, blah, blah."

"Shame on you, Chief!" the monsignor said, vibrating with anger. "You know that, if I don't uphold the sanctity of confession, I will be just a police informant. How dare you!"

The chief tilted his head and looked at the monsignor. "You are in a predicament, Monsignor. I am tired of dispatching my officers to your village and having them come back empty-handed. I have even jailed the whole entire village last year, and nothing. You know who is doing this, and you give me that bullshit of sanctity of confession."

"If your officers are not competent enough to do their work, it is not my fault!" the monsignor snapped.

The chief smiled complacently. "How long have we been friends? Thirty some odd years? So I know that you know that confession was invented in the Middle Ages to inform those in power of what people were doing. This is a good example, Monsignor! What the hell is happening with your people?" he yelled.

Outside the heavy, wooden doors the officers on duty were exchanging looks. The chief and the monsignor from Two Brooks were fighting again.

Nascimento crossed the road, running toward Angela's house to meet with her friends.

"If you only knew what I know, you would die," Nascimento said, out of breath.

The others looked at her expectantly.

"What have you done?" Angela asked.

"Well …" she said. "I think I know who the Night Justice people are."

Her friends were silent.

"Didn't I say you would die?" Nascimento said.

"Who?" they asked in unison.

"I knew Geniveva was going to be attacked. I've heard them talk about it."

The women were stunned. "Who?" they yelled.

Nascimento though for a second and then asked, "Who is fingering Maria Augusta?"

The others were perplexed.

"Well, I couldn't hear very well, but I think someone is doing something to Maria Augusta and since Saul …" Nascimento stopped and looked at Madalena.

"They were kids," Madalena said. "This damn village never forgets anything. Poor girl! Just because Saul put his hands between her legs, that now seems to be the only thing people know about her …that she is being fingered by everybody."

"Well, we will know who is doing it to Maria Augusta because he is the second victim of the Night Justice," Nascimento said.

"Do you know who they are?" Ascendida asked, lowering her voice.

Nascimento made a movement with her head; yes, she knew.

They were quiet. This was too much for them to absorb. The elusive Night Justice had its cover blown. They wanted to ask, but they were afraid.

"And then it will be André," Nascimento said quietly.

"The teacher?" they asked.

"Do you know another André?" Nascimento asked.

"But why André?" Angela asked. "Not that he doesn't deserve a good lesson, but to be the target of Night Justice is quite harsh."

"He's done something to Sérgio Leal's wife ...or Sérgio Leal thinks so ..."

"Sérgio Leal is part of Night Justice?" Angela asked.

"Yes," Nascimento said.

"Who else?" Angela finally asked.

Nascimento looked sadly at Madalena and then said, "Your father, Ivo Machado, Raimundo Pereira, Deolindo Mendes, and Fernando Cardoso."

"Oh my God!" Madalena murmured. "Oh my God!"

Fernando Cardoso raped a beggar girl from some other village and tried to hurt Luciana, and he was out there dishing out justice.

"Those fucking bastards," Angela said softly. "Not that we didn't suspect some of them, but ...my God. Deolindo Mendes? I didn't think he had the balls ..."

"And you were lucky; they were going to do something to you before you married Lazarus," Nascimento said.

Angela was very quiet remembering Dom Carlos's rescue and the bite on her ear. Finally she said, "It will not do any good to go to the police. If we do, we have to say how we found out, and Nascimento would be truly fucked."

"There is nothing we can do," Madalena said.

"Let's be sure first. And then I have an idea," Angela offered.

The following weeks were quiet. Other than a visit from Detective Lourenço because of André's complaint, nothing really happened. Saul told the detective about André's letters to Madalena, and Angela was his witness, stating that André had wet himself with fear just because Saul had addressed him.

Detective Lourenço was only too willing to forget about that incident, especially if it endeared him to Maia. And Maia fed him again her marvelous food, and they sat by the fire listening to the radio.

Detective Lourenço looked at Maia; the flames on the fireplace illuminated her features. "I am in love with you, Maia," he said quietly.

She looked at him with sadness. "You are married."

He closed his eyes, as if trying to forget that truth. "I am still a man who loves you."

"What can I do with that, Jorge?" she asked.

"I don't know," he said. "We could live together …is the only thing I can offer you, and much love for the rest of your life."

How sweet that sounded—much love. But how would other people perceive her? Would she be considered a pariah like Geniveva? Would she be hurting the family?

"Are you asking me to live with you?" she asked.

"Yes. There is nothing in this world that I would want more than you."

"Not even to catch the pirates on the coast of the island?" she asked, bemused.

"Not even that."

"Not even to catch the Night Justice, who have been eluding you for years?"

"No, not even that."

He leaned in and kissed her on the lips. It was a soft, small kiss with all the sweetness of a first kiss.

"Would you leave Saul alone?" she asked.

"I will," he said. "Saul didn't do anything anyway."

"You don't believe he is a pirate?"

He looked at her and smiled, "I don't care if he is a pirate."

"Jorge," she said, "sweet Jorge. They are going to say that Two Brooks bewitched the police again …if you don't put someone in jail before you go off with me."

"And they would be right. I'm totally bewitched, and I have no one to take to jail."

Maia laughed and hid her face in her hands to stifle the sound.

He got up from the chair and hugged her. He had never been this happy, never.

"I'll talk to the family. But for now let's keep it just between us for now," she said. "I'm almost afraid to be happy, just like Madalena—afraid of happiness."

Detective Lourenço looked at her for a long time. "Who hurt you, Maia?" he asked quietly.

"It was a long time ago, king of Leon," she said sadly.

He closed his eyes, and she kissed him gently, as only someone like Maia could.

The rains of March were abundant, and so was the mud on everyone's feet. But village life was quiet. And most importantly, there were no more Night Justice incidents.

Maria Augusta became André's assistant, right after Christmas. She was doing a good job and finding out that André was nothing more than a narcissistic, self-centered, lazy womanizer. At first, she was delighted to be in his presence, but his lack of work ethic and responsibility started to bother her. As she distanced herself from him emotionally, he became aware that her adulation was waning. This bothered him to no end. If Maria Augusta could just dismiss him, then anything could happen.

The turning point was when the kids went home, and André asked Maria Augusta to stay over to review the lessons for the next quarter. She accepted his offer in her giggling, smiling way. As soon as they were alone, he told her about a fantasy he had with her. She was speechless at such revelation but did what she knew how to do best—she giggled.

"Tell me, where was your desk when you were in school?" he asked.

She pointed to the front desk right behind him.

"My fantasy," he said, "is to lift your dress up, pull your panties down, and spank your naked butt with a ruler."

He waited for her to giggle, but Maria Augusta paled.

André saw no harm in that little game. It was a lot less complicated than if he asked her to let him put his hands inside her pants; that would be his second request.

Maria Augusta had had a brief romance with Miguel Valente, before her Canadian came along, and he'd also talked about the same fantasy. He'd asked her to pull her pants down and let him spank her. But he didn't even have a ruler; he had cleaned a small tree branch for the occasion. Maria Augusta had been so disoriented with embarrassment that she had run inside of the house and never again wanted to see him. So he had started to spread the rumor that she liked the finger. Would she ever be free of that awful destiny that any man who looked at her wanted to beat her naked ass? Would her Canadian ask her the same thing? Maria Augusta wanted to die.

This man was having fantasies that involved her humiliation. She turned pale, and André misread the signs. She could only be pleased that he was fantasizing about her; hence, she had gone pale. But Maria Augusta picked up her sweater and ran away.

That cow! That cow ran away from me! How dare she? André thought, looking at Maria Augusta's white plump legs and her skirt flying around her knees.

At home, dissolving in tears, Maria Augusta told her father what the teacher had said.

Raimundo Pereira hugged his plump daughter. "Don't worry," he said. "He will not be around for long."

With the end of March came torrential rains, the kind that engorged brooks, destroyed bridges, and left everyone nestled safely at home in front of the fire. Rosa was fearful of those rains.

Lazarus was in the carpentry shop. Dom Carlos, Angela, and a new lodger, Mr. Leitão—a distributor of sewing machines—were in front of the fire drinking tea.

The teacher came down and said with a smile, "I have an assignation. Au revoir."

Dom Carlos looked at Angela and raised his eyebrows. "Must be a woman," he said.

"And married," she added, looking at André's back going out the door.

"Or Regina Sales must have a steak for him," Dom Carlos said with a smile.

"Have you been eating steaks lately?" Angela asked.

"Not since your last rescue," he said.

The lodger smiled; he had eaten a few delicious steaks at Regina's. Everyone knew, even Mr. Leitão, what Regina did to men if they ate her steak.

Dom Carlos had been one of them. He was interested in buying a parcel of land from her, and before he knew it, he was tied to a chair and Regina was doing things to him that his fertile imagination couldn't match. He had thought that he could charm his way through the conversation, but Regina was not a woman to be charmed. She was a woman to have or to be had; and she was having Dom Carlos.

But then, Angela had knocked at the door and Dom Carlos was untied and let go. He was stained with almond oil and had bitten his own lip, or Regina had.

When they got home, Angela quietly prepared him a hot bath and said, "I told you that Regina always wins." Angela fixed him a good look before he got into the bathroom and asked, "What did she do to you?"

"I'm not telling you," he mumbled.

Angela laughed softly. "Shame on you, Zorro, caught with your pants down."

Angela's thoughts were drifting to the time Dom Carlos had come to the island and how he had inserted himself expertly in their lives, even Regina's. He had become such a natural part of their existence. She and Lazarus had become partners in the Cooperative, an endeavor brought to the island by Dom Carlos to mechanize most of the field tasks and the pasteurization of the milk. In a few months, Two Brooks had a company that served every farmer, more efficiently and cheaper than if they had to pay labor. Now they were working on the rest of the island.

The monsignor, who was suspicious of Dom Carlos and of progress, called Angela and Lazarus to place veiled warnings about strangers, mainlanders, and progress, without ever saying anything against Dom Carlos.

As for Dom Carlos, he never tried to put the monsignor's doubts to rest; it was as if he enjoyed seeing the monsignor display his fears in front of him so he could mock or dismiss him. The last time they'd had that conversation was in the sacristy—late at night, at the monsignor's summon.

"Come on, Monsignor," Dom Carlos had said, half amused. "I will not harm your little girl. I am giving her the opportunity of a lifetime … Besides, she has a husband. Shouldn't he be the one throwing me admonitions?"

"If you are using her and Lazarus to get to me—"

"You think too much of yourself," Dom Carlos had responded. "Just don't forget, keep your side of the bargain." There was a cold edge in his voice.

Both men had looked at each other for a second, and then Dom Carlos had left.

Dom Carlos and Angela lifted their heads to the sound in the wind. It was a howling, whistling sound that made one shiver. Lazarus was still in the carpentry shop, and it was almost midnight. André was not home yet, and Angela started to feel anxious.

"What is it?" Dom Carlos asked.

Angela was looking at the door as if, at any moment, someone would be coming through.

"Something is off tonight," she said.

Dom Carlos thought about the rumors that she was a witch. "Lazarus?" he asked.

"No … more like Madalena," she said, frowning.

"Madalena?" he asked surprised. "She has a husband who would not let a flea touch her."

"I need to check," she said.

"You are not going out in this weather just to check if Madalena is all right."

"I am."

"I'm not letting you," he said.

"Sure. As if you can stop me," she said, getting up and putting a heavy coat on.

"I'll drive you, damn it!" he snapped.

They sat quietly in the car until they stopped at Madalena's house. The gate was locked, and inside of the walls, the house was in complete quietness, other than the howling of the wind and rain.

"Help me climb the wall," Angela said to an astonished Dom Carlos.

"Angela!" he uttered with a frustrated grunt. But nevertheless he lifted her up to the top of the wall, and then she disappeared on the other side.

"This girl is impossible!" he muttered, getting in the car.

When Angela knocked at the door, she felt self-conscious. What was she going to say when they opened the door?

And there was Saul in front of her, sleepy and frowning, looking down at her.

"Is Madalena all right?" she asked.

"Yes, she is sleeping …was sleeping …" Saul said at the same time his wife came to stand at the door looking at Angela.

"I'm sorry," Angela said, "I had one of those feelings …that Madalena was in trouble."

Saul looked at Angela as if she was crazy, but Madalena smiled.

"You came out in this weather at this time of night because you thought I was in trouble?" Madalena asked.

"Dom Carlos drove me. He is outside in the car," she said. But Dom Carlos had jumped the wall also and was now behind her.

The wind and the rain were blowing into the house, and Saul ushered them in. Everybody was wet and embarrassed. Madalena chuckled and placed a hand over her mouth to stifle her hilarity.

"Let's go home, Angela. Lazarus will be worried if he doesn't find you there," Dom Carlos said.

And they left after the proper apologies. Angela was relieved that she was wrong, although still worried about her premonition.

Lazarus had just gotten home when he saw Angela and Dom Carlos drive in. He smiled at Dom Carlos when they explained the trip in the middle of the night, and his eyes said, *She's crazy like that.*

When Lazarus was lying in bed, he said to Angela, "My father asked me to vouch for him tonight. But he was not in the carpentry shop. Most men left around eleven, and he wants me to say that he was with me until close."

Angela tensed. "You are not going to cover for him anymore."

"Remember Nixon?" he asked with worry.

"I don't care. He is not going to use you for his misdeeds," she answered angrily.

"I don't know if it is a misdeed … It may be for something else."

Angela was thinking about Nascimento's discovery of the Night Justice, and she was positive that tonight they were hurting someone.

"Lazarus, the night Dona Lidia died, your father also asked you to cover for him, didn't he?"

Lazarus didn't answer.

"I think she had found out who the Night Justice was. She'd been throwing hints and taunts around. One week before her death, she said at the grocery store that she knew who was doing 'mayhem' and that she had a surprise for them," Angela said.

Lazarus sighed. He still remembered his father coming into the carpentry shop, drunk and saying, "It was an accident!"

Angela had suspected all along that Night Justice had killed Dona Lidia. She had blackmailed Father Inácio—her own father. She had thought she was going to do the same to Night Justice. Dona Lidia was a mean, foolish, arrogant woman. Angela's heart jumped when she thought of Nascimento. If they knew that she knew, she could be hurt or killed. They must be careful and very strategic to deal with people like Pedro Matias.

He must be paid in kind, but very carefully.

A few weeks before her death, Dona Lidia had come to visit Dona Amelia. Dona Amelia was intrigued and asked what she wanted, but Dona Lidia, with a malevolent smile—she couldn't smile any other way—said that it was business; she wanted to talk to Pedro. And soon after, Dona Amelia was instructed by her husband to bake bread for Dona Lidia, to send eggs, chickens, legumes, fruit, and anything that the teacher asked for.

It didn't take long to put all the elements together. Dona Lidia was a blackmailer, and the village was serving her because she held their secrets. Dona Lidia was probably the first werewolf of the village, the first voyeur. She must have been the first person who Elias had encountered and had thought was a werewolf. She sniffed around, full of malice, and used the information to her own ends.

Dona Lidia's house had always been freshly painted, her gardens always well tended to. She'd always had meat and plenty of food. And when she needed to go to the city, Raimundo Pereira would drop everything and take her to the city. Antonio Dores was also part of this petrified group of servants; Dona Lidia had something on him, as well as she had had something on Angela. The teacher saw Lazarus jumping out of Angela's window at night. The teacher would keep her silence, if Angela accepted the task of correcting schoolwork for Dona Lidia's students.

The only person she had not been able to blackmail was Regina. When she'd tried, Regina had given her such a severe beating that Raimundo had had to take the teacher to the city hospital. The police had come to arrest Regina, and the whole village had denied such assault; Dona Lidia had fallen down the stairs of the church.

When Dona Lidia was found dead in her kitchen, there was a sigh of relief from the village. Someone had slain the dragon. Even the monsignor had blessed himself as if to ward off her spirit. And then he had written the death certificate—heart attack. What better justice than your own heart attacking you?

Now with the Night Justice acting up again, the death of Dona Lidia loomed large. The police had always been suspicious about the so-called accident. And with the escalation on the of Night Justice tyranny, the police could very well start making connections.

Two Brooks, once again, was poised for disaster.

The following morning, the whole village was up in arms. The Night Justice had attacked the teacher, André Moniz. He was found in the schoolroom tied to a desk, with his pants down and his buttocks so terribly whipped that he was bleeding. Ms. Iracema, the lunch lady, who opened the school early in the morning found him there with a rag stuffed in his mouth. She came out screaming with her hands up in the air as soon as she was faced with that spectacle.

The teacher had been strategically tied on top of two desks for his penis to be soaking in an inkwell. His buttocks had been severely beaten with a ruler, and he had a pencil up his anus.

André, who was spent from screaming into the rag, started again. But only weak moans could be heard. Because Ms. Iracema was screaming, the people on the street ran into the schoolroom and André had an audience. No one felt the compulsion to do anything. What should they do? Shouldn't they call the police first, or the monsignor? Should they at least take the pencil out? And what would they do with it? Was that evidence?

In this turmoil of hesitance, Natividade, the midwife, decided to act. She asked people to leave, and Victor Costa, the village administrator, and Natividade attended to André. The pencil was thrown in the trash, and his much-flagellated buttocks were anointed with cream.

Natividade looked thoughtfully at André's inked penis; there was nothing she could do about that. "Maybe soak it in vinegar," Natividade recommended. "Wash it with warm milk …maybe … But the ink will take a long time to wear off; vinegar would work faster …"

A note sat on the desk: "I'm writing love letters with my dove." *Well*, Natividade said to herself, *this evidence is much better than the pencil*. She folded the paper and gave it to Victor Costa.

André went straight to his parents in the city, and from there, he accused Saul of the attack. That had been Saul's second attack on him because of Saul's wife.

When the police came to arrest Saul, Madalena was not a credible alibi. But Angela and Dom Carlos were. At that very same time when André was being attacked, Angela and Dom Carlos were jumping over the wall and knocking at Saul's door.

13

A Turning Tide

After the police left, Dom Carlos said, looking sideways at Angela, "You are impossible. Do you know that?"

"What have I done now?" she asked.

"Your premonition," he answered.

Angela sighed with relief. Madalena was fine because Saul was exempt of guilt in André's attack. Her premonition—as strange as it was—had saved Saul from a nasty accusation. Nevertheless, the poor monsignor was without a teacher.

Two Brooks had such a bad reputation that the rest of the island avoided them like the plague, and most of the teaching candidates put down on their applications that they could teach anywhere, except in Two Brooks.

"Poor monsignor," Angela murmured.

"Save your compassion for Lazarus. He looked mighty worried," Dom Carlos retorted.

Angela gave him a long look. "If you see sadness or worry in Lazarus, you will know, always, that it has to do with his father."

Dom Carlos placed an open hand on Angela's head, "I'm so sorry," he said.

Angela was looking at that tall, elegant man caressing her head. "You are the father he never had, and for that, I will always love you."

"Always?" he asked.

"Till the end of time," she promised.

Everyone was hoping for spring. They were tired of the winter that had been windy, rainy, dark, humid, and cold; and like a crown of thorns, the people of Two Brooks had been cruder and meaner than usual.

Another Night Justice incident had happened, a few weeks after the attack on André Moniz. This time it was Miguel Valente, Maria Augusta's former boyfriend, and the village moaned with disgust and fear.

He was tied to a bale of hay, in his own barn, with a stick up his anus. His father found him in the morning. The police were called again. Detective Lourenço talked to the victim and with some other people, but he had absolutely no hope of getting anywhere.

Detective Lourenço came again to the village.

"This is a place with an anal fixation," he said to Maia. "What do you know about these brutes?" he asked.

"You can't prove it, but Madalena's father is the ring leader. Everyone knows, but no one wants to say it because he is vindictive and buys everyone."

"Why do you accept this kind of thing?" he asked.

"These are strange people, Jorge. This island is strange and this village is even more so. When the monsignor came here, they were a bunch of savages. It got better with the monsignor, believe it or not."

"Would you like to leave? Go to the mainland and leave these strange creatures to their ways?"

She had a dreamy look in her eyes. "Yes, I would like to leave. I've never been part of them anyway."

"I can ask for a transfer to the mainland. We can live as husband and wife, and no one would have to know anything different."

There was so much joy in his voice.

"Would you Jorge?" she asked, full of hope.

The monsignor was beside himself with the new incident of Night Justice. The village was terrorized, not knowing who was going to be next. Everybody was itemizing his or her sins and mistakes and measuring his or her worth. No one knew what the rationale was for the Night Justice anymore; they just knew that it happened to those who transgressed against someone. Geniveva's case was a departure from what they knew Night Justice should be. She was not bothering anybody; Elias wanted to be with her, and he was not married. Why had she been punished? If immorality was the reason, then Regina should have been punished a long time ago.

And this was the source of the fear—Night Justice seemed increasingly capricious and mean.

Lazarus lost that brief happiness that had come after he'd gotten married. He was sure that his father was the head of that terrorist group. If the Night Justice were really just, his father would be a victim, as well as Ivo Machado and Fernando Cardoso, those bastards who raped and hurt women. But what worried Lazarus most of all was the impending threat that Angela could be hurt at any moment if he didn't cover for his father.

Love, for Lazarus, was not joyous; it was a terrible thing that left him petrified of losing it. If anything happened to Angela, he would forever lose the capacity to be happy.

Love, after all, was limiting; it kept people in emotional bondage.

One night, while he was in his woodshop, Dom Carlos stopped by. Lazarus didn't mean to say anything to Dom Carlos, but Dom Carlos was a compassionate listener.

"When I go to the military or to the African war, which will be a sure thing, will you keep an eye on Angela?" Lazarus asked.

"Who knows? You may be one of the lucky ones; you may not go."

"But if I do, will you keep an eye on her? She is fierce, and she provokes my father all the time."

"I will. But you will be here to do it yourself."

They walked home, like father and son.

When they reached the kitchen, Angela jumped up to meet them. She kissed Lazarus. "Where have you been?" she asked, ill humored. "I was worried about you!"

Since the teacher had left, the three of them were like a family; they had all meals together and sat by the fire afterward, reading or listening to the radio. They had plenty of lodgers coming and going and paying well. Even American emigrants who came to visit stayed at Angela's Inn, especially if the house of their relatives was not big enough for their glitter. But these visitors, as much as they were welcome and well treated, were not able to infiltrate the trinity.

If Two Brooks had been terrified before, nothing would compare to the fear they were about to experience.

The Sacristy gathered at Ascendida's house after the choir rehearsal. Aldo wheeled José Eremita to the Music Club House, the babies were sleeping, and Rosa was now working at Angela's Inn. Small and sullen, Rosa refused to go to school; she couldn't go by that brook every day.

The four women sat in Ascendida's kitchen, quietly drinking tea. Madalena was thinking about her second anniversary, Ascendida was thinking about her new pregnancy, Nascimento was thinking about lighted windows, and Angela was thinking about vengeance.

As the others talked, they noticed that Angela was unusually quiet.

"What is it?" Ascendida asked.

"A plan," Angela answered.

They waited. The air was charged, as if they were going to be struck by a thunderbolt.

"From now on, we will be the Night Justice," Angela said.

The others were speechless.

"You are not serious," Nascimento said.

"I've never been as serious as I am now. It is the only way to stop those men—turning the tables."

"I can't do that!" Madalena said.

"Of course you can! Remember when you used to fight your father? Now we will be with you when he gets his …punishment."

"How do you propose to do that?" Ascendida asked, bewildered.

"We plan it, we study it, and we do it. We know who they are. Every move will be totally predicted. First we choose the person, let's say, Raimundo Pereira or Deolindo Mendes. We plan what we want to do to him. We study his comings and goings, his behaviors and his quirks. And then we act. Pedro Matias will be the last one. We want him to sweat it out; we want him to wonder when his turn will come up. Remember that only these men know that they are the Night Justice, and they will know that their group is being targeted. We want them to be afraid for a change; we want them to wonder and die of fear."

The others looked at Angela as if she was something dangerous. Lately everything had been so terrible. They were tired of terrible, and they wanted peace. And now Angela was going to declare war on war. This couldn't be good.

Leave it to Angela to do something like that.

"Are you telling me that you don't want those bastards to get a taste of their own medicine?" Angela asked belligerently.

Nascimento was horrified. She had the guts to snoop at night, stick her nose into the most private moments of people's lives. but to put her hands on people and do harm was not her thing.

"Nascimento?" Ascendida asked.

"My God! I can't believe that we are thinking about this. We could all go to jail!"

"We are smarter that those fools, and they never went to jail. We will be better prepared, and we are standing on moral ground," Angela said. 'Besides, no one will suspect us."

Moral ground. Could justice ever be immoral? Morality was so subjective—sometimes hard to explain but clear in one's heart. Not everything legal was moral and vice versa. It would be a lot more immoral not to act.

"I would like to start with Ivo," Madalena said. "Do to him what they've done to Manuel. Have him suffer like he made poor Maia suffer."

They agreed that they would get together a few more times and talk it over.

Nascimento was hoping to talk them out of it and even made promises to the Virgin Maria. If her friends decided not to go through with Angela's terrible plan, she would stop snooping. But the Virgin Maria was not listening, or knew that Nascimento would not hold up her end of the bargain.

The next time the women met, it was to plan the deed. Nascimento, being the consummate snoop, was assigned to note Ivo's routine, as well as that of the other men, for one whole month and then provide the Sacristy with a detailed account of their comings and goings.

Nascimento did her job to perfection; now she had a higher purpose other than to snoop. She had the schedules of these men down to the minute detail—even how many times they went to the latrine.

And the day of reckoning for Ivo arrived.

They decided on a night of full moon, when the other men were at the Music Club House playing cards and Ivo was going to visit Regina. In the last month, he had visited Regina every Thursday.

He was heading up the street whistling softly, already feeling an erection coming on, when he felt something hit him on the head. He fell to the ground losing consciousness. When he came to, he had something stuffed in his mouth and a bag over his head. He struggled but he was tied spread-eagle to something hard, scratchy, and uncomfortable.

And then someone started to beat him with stinging nettle all over his body, burning him with a terrible rash. He struggled but to no avail. But the worst was yet to come. He felt someone hold his penis and cut it. The pain was such that he fainted, but most of all he fainted with the fear that his penis was being cut off. When he came to, everything was quiet, and he didn't know if he was lying there with or without a penis. He cried and struggled again but nothing happened. He fell in and out of sleep. His penis was throbbing with pain, and he wished he could touch it to see what was left.

The following morning was beautiful and bright. Rosa came running through the door, spoiling the peace. "The Night Justice is doing it again," she said.

And she told a perplexed Dom Carlos what she had heard. Maria Gomes was also in the kitchen. And so was Lazarus. But Rosa was only addressing Dom Carlos.

"They cut his thing off, and he is in the hospital."

There was a murmur of horror. This time the Night Justice had gone too far!

"Cut it off? Who …?" Maria Gomes asked with a weak voice.

"Yes, off," Rosa said, making a gesture of decapitation.

And so the news spread all over the village.

The police came and talked to Joaquim Machado, the father of the victim, and to Regina Sales, the woman he was going to visit, and his friends Pedro Matias and the others. Everyone was a bit pale and stumped, but Pedro Matias and his friends were truly preoccupied.

"Who in the world did that?" Pedro asked, stupefied.

"Night Justice," Detective Lourenço said.

"No it wasn't!" Pedro said vehemently.

Detective Lourenço looked at him sharply. "No? How do you know, Mr. Matias?"

Pedro colored deeply. "Well, I don't know …"

And Saul was interviewed again. Saul had almost killed the man before because of Maia. But Saul was in the carpentry shop with Lazarus all night. He had come home with his wife, who was visiting her friend Ascendida Costa.

"The man had a mock circumcision. His penis was not cut off, but the foreskin was cut all around, although not removed. Later it was removed in the hospital …a mess," Detective Lourenço explained to a terrorized group of men who had gathered in the carpentry shop. "And the men who did this to him said that next time it would be his balls."

The audience let out a shriek of terror.

Detective Lourenço put his pen and pad in his pocket and got in his car. He wanted to tell Maia that someone finally had given Ivo what he deserved. He wished he knew who had done it—and he wished he could give the perpetrator a medal.

Lazarus came home late, hoping for Angela to be asleep. But she wasn't. There was another case of Night Justice. And this time it was simply terrible, according to Lazarus.

Lazarus got into bed and told his wife about the new incident with Night Justice.

"Did your father ask you to cover for him?" Angela asked.

"No, he did not! He even told me that the Night Justice didn't do it," Lazarus answered, confused.

"How does he know?" she asked.

Lazarus was quiet.

Angela was smiling. She was hoping that Pedro Matias was not only confused but also terrified. "Was he …scared?" she asked.

Lazarus touched her face in the dark. Was she smiling?

"He is …confused, I think," Lazarus said.

"Not scared?" she insisted.

"I think he was scared …or not in control. As you know, he must be always in control."

"But not this time, I think," Angela said. "How about the others?"

"What others?" he asked.

Angela bit her lip. "The other men …in the carpentry shop, what did they say?"

"The Freitas brothers were making jokes as always. Most of the men were taking it seriously though. Sérgio Leal and Raimundo Pereira were really concerned. Fernando Cardoso was laughing … He was still boasting about what he did to Piedade, the beggar girl."

"Poor girl," Angela murmured.

"He was saying that he was going to the orphanage they took her to and do the same to her and the nuns."

"He should be next," Angela said softly.

"What did you say?" Lazarus asked, surprised.

"Nothing of importance," she said and breathed in his smell of cedar and sweat.

All that Angela needed was life full of moments like this—Lazarus slowly relaxing, turning around, and moving on top of her, humming, "She was my beautiful boat …"

Fernando Cardoso was not hard to track. He had a construction company, mostly with business in the city and other villages. He commissioned Lazarus for custom work and was always free with information about his whereabouts. He was going to go to Regina Sales's this Friday and celebrate a new and profitable contract.

Friday was a perfect opportunity because everyone was busy with something else, and the women could move around without risking suspicion. The person most concerning for Angela was Dom Carlos, but he had gone to the city and was planning to stay there.

When Fernando Cardoso left Regina's, it was almost ten o'clock.

The Sacristy had agreed that he should be nabbed at the same place as Ivo. His other friends were in the carpentry shop, still talking about Ivo, who was home recuperating from a forced circumcision.

Nascimento, Ascendida, and Madalena would nab Fernando Cardoso, and Angela would wait at home for the signal. Angela's job was to prepare hot oil, as hot as possible, without boiling.

As soon as she heard the signal—a faint whistle, like an owl—she crossed the street with the pot of hot oil.

Fernando Cardoso was lying in the same spot where Ivo had been just a week ago. He was spread-eagle, with his mouth stuffed with a rag and a bag over his head. He looked strangely vulnerable, with a small and crooked penis, almost hidden in pubic hair.

And then they let the hot oil fall on his genitalia. He screamed and struggled but to no avail. When Angela emptied the iron pot of hot oil on Fernando Cardoso he had fainted already. Nascimento emptied a jug of water on his head, and he gained consciousness. And then he heard the whisper: "Next time we will cut your balls off." And he fainted again.

When Dom Carlos arrived from the city, Angela and her friends were sitting in front of the fire in the kitchen, drinking moonshine. They were startled when he came in.

"I thought you were going to stay in the city tonight," Angela said, almost accusingly.

Dom Carlos looked intently at the women. "I decided to come home," he said, still looking from one to the other. "Moonshine, hmm? What is going on?"

"Nothing is going on. Nascimento is getting cold feet," Angela said.

Nascimento gave Angela a wounded look. Whores, her friends were whores …

"Moonshine won't help," he said.

"That's what you think," Nascimento mumbled and emptied the glass.

"You smell like a brewery," Dom Carlos commented, addressing the women.

"I spilled some," Nascimento said. "Let's go home, people."

When they left, Dom Carlos took a good look at Angela. "You look nervous. What's wrong?" he asked.

"Nothing is wrong!" she snapped, leaving the kitchen and going into the bathroom where their clothes full of moonshine were soaking in the bathtub. She only hoped that Dom Carlos didn't decide to take a bath. He was not supposed to be home today. She took the clothes out of the bathtub and drained the water. When she came out of the bathroom, he was still sitting on a chair as if waiting for her.

"Good night," she said.

"Hey," he said, holding her by the arm, "you are strange today."

"I'm always strange. Do you want to take a bath? I will heat up water."

Dom Carlos still had her wrist in his hand, and he was looking up at her. "I didn't know you liked moonshine."

"There are many things you don't know about me."

"I don't think so."

"Goodnight, Zorro," she said hurriedly and left.

Angela waited in bed for Lazarus. She needed Lazarus to kiss away the dark edges of her mind. And when he came home, she heard him in the kitchen laughing with Dom Carlos.

The laughing sounds of those two men who looked out for her and loved her made her cry with gratitude.

Madalena entered the house still with her nostrils full of moonshine, and she wondered if Saul would smell it on her. She hadn't stopped shaking since Ivo Machado's incident. She didn't have Angela's courage and her cool demeanor about justice. She needed to take a bath, she needed to be in Saul's arms and feel his quiet lovemaking, and she needed to feel his hand caress her head. She wanted the quiet life Saul offered her. These adventures were not for her.

As silently as possible, she lighted the fire, heated the water, and carried it to the tub. She was so absorbed by her task that she didn't notice Saul entering the kitchen. He was leaning on the door frame looking at her. Madalena felt his presence, turned around, and smiled.

"I was splashed with moonshine tonight," she said.

He didn't say a word; slowly he undressed her and gently helped her into the tub. He washed her hair, scrubbed her skin, and caressed every inch of her.

"My precious," Madalena said, "will you ever know that you are my everything?"

Saul wrapped her in a towel, picked her up and walked to the bedroom. This was their favorite ritual.

That night, before going home, Nascimento looked into Jaime's window. He was asleep, sprawled all over the bed. Tomorrow she would start the wedding plans and stop with voyeurism and stupid adventures of vengeance. Her precious Jaime deserved a better woman, and she would be that woman, she said to herself as she lifted the window up and crawled inside. And she stood there, looking at love personified. His mouth was slightly open as he slept deeply, not making a sound. Maybe it was guilt or love or a tremendous sense of having wronged this wonderful man that made Nascimento do what she did next. She lay down beside him and put is limp penis in her mouth. He stirred a bit but didn't wake up. She smiled when she felt his penis grow larger. And then he woke up bewildered, and she let go.

"Man!" he said. "What are you doing here? Are you awake?"

Nascimento laughed softly. "I am awake, but you are not. You are having a dream. I'm not here."

Jaime became extremely still. Nascimento could see his eyes darting back and forth to her face and to his penis.

"What will you do in your dream?" she asked in a whisper.

She kissed him, and said, "I love you. You are everything love should be."
And she left, going out the window before a speechless Jaime.

Ascendida looked in the room where Rosa was with the babies. José Eremita
and Aldo were coming down the street singing. They were both drunk; Aldo
was pushing José Eremita's wheelchair, and they were singing:

> The American car
> Has only one wheel.
> Jump girls on that car
> From here to Brazil.

Ascendida put her head down on the kitchen table. Where was God? What
in heaven was He doing that He couldn't let her have a breather? She had three
children and was pregnant again, maybe with two more; her husband was a
drunk, and so was the paraplegic man she cared for.

The two men got to the door and lowered their voices. Ascendida waited
for them to come in. It was almost midnight.

José looked back at Aldo and said, "She is up and awake. She is going to
kill you."

Aldo drove the chair to José's room. There was laughter and noise, and
finally Aldo closed the door on the old man and looked at Ascendida.

"My little Ass, why are you angry?" he asked with such tenderness that
Ascendida smiled.

"I'm not angry, Aldo. I am sad because you are drunk again."

"I'm not drunk; I'm happy," he said and lifted one foot off the floor.

Ascendida looked at him perfectly still, standing only on one foot as if he
was a ballerina.

"I thought you were drunk," she said softly.

"You are a dark woman, my little Ass. You confuse joy with a vice."

Ascendida walked to Aldo and embraced him. He laughed softly and
whirled her around the kitchen. "I love you, my little Ass. I love you to the
point of madness."

But it was never madness what Ascendida felt every time Aldo looked
at her; it was pure love, with a bruised softness caused by sorrow. Ascendida
touched his face, so beautiful, so kind.

"How many times have I told you that I love you, Aldo?"

"You've never told me that you love me," he said. It was not a reprimand, but it was a firm and clear statement.

"I love you," Ascendida said.

Everyone in Angela's house heard the screams, and they ran out the door in the direction of the noise. Regina Sales was screaming at the top of her lungs.

Other neighbors were already running in the direction of the barn, and they brought out Fernando Cardoso, semiconscious and with fried genitalia.

Fernando's wife pounced on Regina. This was her doing. But then the monsignor came and dispatched Fernando to the hospital and the women home.

The monsignor sat at Regina's table and looked around the kitchen. It was a pleasant room with colorful curtains and generous space. She had wild flowers on the table and potted plants on the windowsills. He suddenly remembered Regina as a little girl. Her parents had died when she was young and a godmother who died when she was only twelve raised her. He remembered sitting in this kitchen then, when Regina was a child. One day, Regina stopped coming to confession and sat in the back of the church with the men. What happened to that dark young girl? Where had he been when she had gotten lost?

The police came and interviewed the monsignor and Regina regarding Fernando's attack.

The village was pulsating with terror.

The Night Justice was out of control, and the monsignor could not contain that devil. It wasn't that Fernando Cardoso didn't deserve the treatment—he was a rapist and a pig. But frying a man's parts—to the point that he probably would never be able to use his …his … It was …well …it was something that they couldn't find a word for.

"I wonder if he thought about the girl he raped while he was being … fried," Angela said while serving coffee to Dom Carlos.

"I hope he did," Dom Carlos said. "I heard that he was brutal with that girl."

"Every rape is brutal," Angela said accusingly. "But he almost killed her."

"And he didn't go to jail," Dom Carlos said, feeling dazed.

"Justice is a relative thing on this island," Angela said. "The Night Justice raped Geniveva and cut off her nipples with a pocket knife. Talk about brutal. And you wonder why I am combative."

Lazarus put his hands up to his own nipples. "How terrible," he murmured.

Angela sat across from Dom Carlos and Lazarus. "Who do you think did that to him?" she asked.

"The Night Justice, of course," Lazarus said, still massaging his chest.

Dom Carlos was quiet for a moment, and then he said, "I don't particularly feel sorry for the man, but this Night Justice thing is really worrisome."

The four women—the Sacristy—sat in Ascendida's kitchen. She was baking bread. Aldo and José Eremita were playing with the children in the garden.

"The next one must be less severe," Madalena said. "Otherwise I am going to have a heart attack."

"What did you say to Saul when you got home last week?" Nascimento wanted to know.

"I took a bath and went to bed. He didn't say anything," Madalena answered. She was right about that. Saul hadn't said a word while he loved her tenderly for hours.

"I think we should go after Sérgio Leal. He is a little pig, that one," Nascimento said. "Remember the fig tree?"

The women remembered, feeling sorry for the poor woman from Little Branch, whose husband owed money to Sérgio. When she'd asked for a reprieve, his request had been for her to climb the fig tree naked and bring him the figs. And she did, crying all the way up and all the way down with a basket full of figs, while he was on the ground with a Petromax lamp lighting her humiliation.

Madalena chuckled and covered her mouth, embarrassed; as much as she felt for the woman, that story always made her laugh. The other women looked at her reproachfully.

"It is not funny! Abusing a poor woman like that. She had no money to feed her family, and he knew it," Ascendida barked.

"She should have thrown the basket and the figs right down at his face and broken his teeth, along with the Petromax lamp," Nascimento said, experiencing again the revulsion she felt every time she heard that story.

Two days later, Sérgio Leal was taken down from his own fig tree. He was covered with insects and insect bites and had to go to the hospital.

The Night Justice had stripped him naked and covered him with honey. It was high noon when the mailman discovered Sérgio. It was a sad commentary to think that his wife didn't look for him when he didn't show up at home.

When she was asked, she said that he liked to stay out sometimes, and she hid a smile.

14

It Was a Dark, Dark Cloud

The police refused to go to the village. The chief asked Dom Carlos about the incidents, and Dom Carlos made a dismissive gesture.

"Those men are despicable, according to what I hear," he added.

That was good enough for the chief.

A few weeks went by without any incidents from the Night Justice, and people started to relax a bit: Regina Sales started to receive her men almost with regularity, Antonio Dores bruised Emilia's face, and even Pedro Matias was almost his insolent self.

But Raimundo Pereira spoiled that brief peace.

"He was found tied to a tree trunk and covered with olive oil," his wife said. "And the neighborhood dogs were licking him all over," she added amid shrieks of horror from the neighbors.

The monsignor was beside himself again. This was a provocation to his authority, and he was going to bring someone from the mainland to discover this horrible group of men. The chief of police had given up on Two Brooks, so it was up to the monsignor to put a stop to it.

The sermon on that Sunday was brutal.

When Angela and her lodgers sat at the dining room table for lunch, Dom Carlos looked at the salesman sitting across from him. The poor man looked terrified.

"I'm leaving this place before someone puts something up my ass," the man said.

He was selling hats. He couldn't think of anything offensive he had done or said, other than stick a few ugly hats on a few people. But to be on the safe side, he left that afternoon, and Two Brooks was not only terrified about Night Justice but it was also hatless for that season.

Deolindo Mendes was so terrified about Night Justice that he became ill and took to bed. His wife, Maria, and son, Elias, consulted the monsignor. But there was no cure for fear; Deolindo came down with a nervous attack and cried night and day. Maria called Ascendida because she was a nurse by training, and Ascendida looked at that excuse of a man lying in bed with the covers up to his neck on a beautiful spring day.

"Why are you so afraid?" she asked.

"Because ..." And he started to cry. "My boy was attacked last year, and I thought it was the boogeyman. But now I think it was the Night Justice after us ... They almost killed my boy. They ...kicked him in the face ... And they are going to kill me too."

"I don't think they will kill you," Ascendida said softly. "I think that maybe they will do to you what they've done to poor Manuel, but they won't kill you."

"I should go to the police for protection," he said between sobs.

"Yes, you should, and they will ask you why you are this afraid. Why are you more afraid than the other men? You and Pedro Matias—the two of you are terrified. Why?"

"You think they will ask me that?" he asked incredulously, momentarily stopping his sobs.

"I'm sure they will ... I would."

Ascendida took his temperature and blood pressure. Seeing that the blood pressure was only a little high she said, "Who knows? It could be Dona Lidia's spirit looking for revenge ..."

Deolindo doubled over in panic, and Ascendida left.

When the women gathered in Ascendida's kitchen, they agreed that they were going to bring the Night Justice to a stop. They were going to get to Deolindo Mendes and wait a long while to get to Pedro. Pedro should wait in fear, never knowing when his day would come.

When Deolindo got his piece of justice, he had recuperated feebly. He was skinny and yellow and coughed incessantly. Elias followed him about with cough syrup and handkerchiefs.

"What can we do with that spectacle?" Ascendida asked, looking at Deolindo coughing all the way up the street.

"Just a few lashes," Nascimento said, looking almost remorseful.

And they waited for him, but he was never alone.

One day, the Sacristy found out that Elias and his mother were going to the city, and Deolindo would stay home alone, in bed, no doubt.

They came into the house quietly. He was sitting at the kitchen table eating milk soup, slurping the milk and smacking his lips together.

They didn't even have to hit him over the head. When he turned around and saw the Night Justice with masks on their faces and sheets over their clothes, he fainted. Without much enthusiasm, they stripped him naked and beat him up with stinging nettle. When he woke up, he was tied to the bed with his own sheets.

"Next time, it will be your balls," they whispered, and he fainted again.

Before leaving the house, they took off the masks and the sheets and walked out silently. The nearest house to the Mendes's was Angela's parents'. The four women sat quietly in Maria Gomes's kitchen and waited for Elias and his mother to get home.

"What a poor excuse for a man," Nascimento said softly. "I was almost sorry for him, that poor thing. Did you see his penis? What was that?"

"That was not a penis," Madalena said. "You have never seen a penis."

The others looked at her, interested. "What do you mean?" Ascendida asked, almost in an offended tone.

"Nothing," Madalena said.

But Nascimento knew. She'd seen what a penis was when she had looked into Saul's room. And she smiled.

"Now we must go to the monsignor and confess what we've done," Angela said.

"No way!" Nascimento objected. "He will kill us."

"We must. He already called a detective from the mainland. If we confess, he cannot reveal our deeds to the detective or help him find out."

"There are benefits to confession ..." Ascendida added with a long sigh.

"And we will not do this again unless some bastard really deserves it. I'm hoping that the Night Justice is over in this village, at least for now," Angela said.

"I still think we should do Pedro Matias. Or Antonio Dores—he hits my sister and their kids," Nascimento said.

Angela said softly. "Let's wait and see. Maybe Pedro Matias will be more decent in the future. As for Antonio Dores, the monsignor is working on him ...although he should get it up his ass just for the poetry ..."

They were drinking moonshine when Maria Gomes got home from church. Maria Gomes liked moonshine more than tea and happily sat sipping her glass when terrible screams erupted up the road. She dropped the glass, spilling the contents on herself and started to scream.

The Sacristy and Maria Gomes were the first on the scene. They called the monsignor to the Mendes house, and the same terror took hold of everybody all over again.

The following day, the four women got together at Ascendida's orchard.

"Tomorrow we must go to confession," Angela said.

"I think I'll ask Lazarus to make me a wooden mask," Nascimento said. "The monsignor is going to slap the hell out of us."

"Oh yes he will. And if he leaves a mark, Saul will kill him," Madalena said.

"Saul loves the monsignor," Angela countered. "He will not harm him."

"But he loves me more," Madalena said with a gentle smile.

The others stopped their leisurely walk and looked at Madalena. She never talked about Saul.

"Saul is a gentle and kind man. Things are not always what they appear to be," Madalena said and walked down the pastures in the direction of her house.

Nascimento gestured, without words, in the middle of the dry brook. Then she said, "Didn't she put that candle up Raimundo's ass because of Manuel? What is this *gentle* and *kind* crap?"

Manuel continued to be terrified of the Night Justice. However, it didn't stop him from trying to see Madalena. He created all kinds of opportunities to see her, to talk to her, or just to look at her.

For Madalena, it was over but not for Manuel; he was a romantic young man attracted to Shakespearean outcomes but without the courage to live them through. He was an artist fascinated by drama in the theatre but not able to live it in his own skin.

Madalena started to avoid the places where she could find Manuel, and he became even more desperate. He feverishly scanned village gatherings and crowds searching for Madalena. When he found her he kept his eyes in her direction.

The village knew where Madalena was just by looking at Manuel.

Saul knew it too, and he would scowl and keep Madalena company, although he didn't like public events. He much preferred to stay home or go to the city alone with his wife. There, they would go to a restaurant or to a movie and sometimes stay in the hotel, like honeymooners. They would talk, laugh, and love each other without people glowering and thinking about Manuel's love.

With Saul and Madalena, there was always Manuel like a shadow, a comparison, a story to be told, something to comment about. Sometimes Saul felt the need to pulverize that boy, make him nonexistent.

And this, more than anything else, worried Madalena.

At the Holy Ghost rosary, Maia and Carlota surprised everybody. Carlota never went anywhere other than church, and Maia was Madalena's chaperone. But here they were without Madalena. This readjustment of their understanding was a bit disconcerting.

Maia looked very pretty and different somehow. There was something about her that peaked people's curiosity. The attention she received went almost unnoticed because she was thinking about her detective; soon she would leave the island and go far away from Two Brooks. The knowledge that she was loved, respected, and wanted was like a light from within that she could not dim.

Ivo Machado, brooding in a corner of the room, sent her looks of despair. She would not even acknowledge his presence. To Maia, he was nonexistent. Maybe she couldn't destroy evil, but she would not acknowledge it either.

Ivo approached Maia on the street a few days after the rosary. He said to a stupefied Maia that bygones were bygones, and he wanted her back. Maia looked around; the houses on the street had the windows open, and she heard people talking and radios playing. All she had to do was scream. They would come to her aid, wouldn't they?

"You are a rapist and a drunk. Only in this godforsaken place would someone like you roam around free. If you so much as look in my direction, I will make sure that you are arrested."

His face darkened, and he moved closer to her. He stunk of alcohol as he spoke, "I made a mistake and paid for it. Saul almost killed me; it is over. I want you back."

"A mistake is when you don't look where you are going and step on bullshit. That's a mistake. What you did to me was a crime."

"Maia, I want to marry you!" he said, grabbing her arm.

Maia felt something tighten in her throat. A wave of heat came up from the bottom of her belly, and she punched his face, right in the nose. He fell back, sprawled like a cockroach, waving his arms and legs. She kicked him in the groin until he seemed motionless and curled in a fetus position.

"Don't you ever talk to me again!" she said to a groaning Ivo.

She walked down the street feeling light, so light that even her sinuses cleared.

That night, Detective Lourenço came to visit and talk to Maia's family. They were going to the mainland. Detective Lourenço had asked for a transfer and had gotten it. He loved Maia and wanted to spend the rest of his days with her. As for his wife, she was in a world of pink rooms and fake butterflies. His visits were upsetting to her, according to the nurses; she wouldn't miss him. Detective Lourenço could have had his marriage annulled because it had not been consummated, but he couldn't get it annulled because Isabel was mentally ill; that was the law of the concordat, an agreement between church and state.

Maia and Detective Lourenço left Hawk Island at the end of spring.

After Maia left, Madalena, Carlota and Saul looked around the house. There was sadness in everything. Even the pots and pans, neatly cradled in their shelves, looked strangely still.

Everything was too quiet and less bright.

Saul walked to Maia's room. It was neatly put together, as if she was about to walk in. He sat at her table, where she kept a vase of wildflowers and a book.

She forgot her book, he thought, looking at the bookmark sticking out. *The Black Mule*, he read.

Maia. Saul didn't remember life without Maia. She had always been there for him, always, since he was born. But here it was—life without Maia. It was his fault that she was gone. It was because of him that Detective Lourenço had come into her life, because of him. And now here they were missing Maia as one misses a limb.

He didn't even realize that he was crying, but his face was wet, and the tears were dropping onto his chest and spreading on his freshly ironed cotton shirt. Madalena walked into the room and held Saul's head against her breast. He let go of his silent pain and moaned with sadness, a deep, mournful wailing. Though muffled by Madalena's embrace, his lamentation still could be heard at the other end of the house.

Carlota was in the kitchen looking at everything the way Maia had left it. She heard her son cry. The last time he had cried like that was when his father had left. Then he'd had Maia to cry with him, and now he had Madalena.

Love was always near if one paid attention.

The day for the confession finally came. The Sacristy went together, one after the other. And the only thing they confessed was the Night Justice deeds. There was no point throwing other sins in the mix. The monsignor would not pay attention to those.

Nascimento even thought about confessing that she kissed Jaime's dove while he was sleeping. *I took that beautiful thing and kissed its head.* But how could she say that to the monsignor? She could say, *I kissed his head,* and let the monsignor decide which head she was talking about. No. She'd better not provoke fate.

And they went to confession.

"Just wait for me in the sacristy," the monsignor said after he confessed each one of them. No penance as of yet; that would be coming soon with a hail of slaps.

The women sat in the pew in the sacristy.

They were quietly waiting for the monsignor when the door opened and Dom Carlos came in. He smiled at the women.

"Hello, little sinners," he said.

"What are you doing here?" Angela asked, surprised. "I didn't think you went to confession?"

"I don't," he said, sitting next to Angela and squeezing her hand resting on her lap.

"Oh, I don't think you want to be here when he comes in," Nascimento said in a warning tone.

"Why?" he asked.

"Because we are here for a penance. And as you said, we are sinners," Nascimento warned.

"Why doesn't he give you a penance at the confessional like everybody else?" he asked and bent forward to look at Nascimento, sitting at the other end of the pew.

"Because we are not common sinners," Nascimento answered.

Dom Carlos was slightly bent forward, looking at Nascimento. Angela felt like tracing his perfect profile—the nose, the lips, and the chiseled chin. She moved her head forward, just a little, and her lips touched the side of his face. "Stay," she whispered. "Maybe he won't slap us if you are here."

The other women were astonished, looking at Angela with her mouth touching Dom Carlos' face, and then they realized that she was whispering in his ear.

Dom Carlos sat back in the pew and turned his head to Angela. "Why do you allow him to hit you? If you were mine, I would never allow that to happen."

If you were mine ... Angela thought. The others were already discussing other things, but Angela was stuck on what Dom Carlos had said.

"I am yours," she said quietly. "I am your friend and your landlady, and you saved my life. I am yours in a way. Stay."

He laughed softly. The other women looked at him reproachfully.

The monsignor came through the door almost flying in his rage. "How dare you damn—" he yelled. Then he stopped when he saw Dom Carlos sitting next to Angela.

"What do you want?" he screamed at Dom Carlos.

"Temper, temper," Dom Carlos said, getting up and walking toward the monsignor.

"I have business with these girls. Go away!" the monsignor yelled again.

"I will be waiting outside to walk these lovely ladies home," Dom Carlos said. He went out into the church, leaving the door of the sacristy opened wide.

The monsignor sat down, completely deflated. He didn't know where to start. "I can't believe you girls," he said in a very calm voice. "How could you do that to those men? It is not only criminal but also immoral! How could you?" And this last question was a scream.

The women jumped, startled. Nascimento was the one near him, and she was thinking about that wooden mask she wanted Lazarus to carve for her; every time she talked to the monsignor, she would have the mask on, just in case. She could feel a slap coming soon, and she tensed her face.

He zeroed in on her and *bam*!

The others let out a shriek.

Dom Carlos came through the door. "Are you going to take long?" he asked nonchalantly.

"Go away!" the monsignor screamed.

"Not without them," he answered evenly, without moving from the door.

"Just one more minute," the monsignor said, pushing him out and closing the door.

"The only thing I'm going to ask of you is your promise that you'll desist of this insanity of justice! Do you hear me?" the monsignor tried to scream silently. He wanted to scream at them, but he didn't want Dom Carlos to hear. It looked like a bad comedy, and Nascimento didn't resist and started to laugh sitting on the pew with tears running down her face. He could kill her if he wanted, but she couldn't stop laughing. The others stepped in front of that laughing fool, and in a hurry, they promised the monsignor not to hurt those men again. With heads hanging low, they left the sacristy.

They found Dom Carlos and Jesus Crucified staring at each other, and as if choreographed, the five of them left the church at a fast pace.

"Too late for me, Engineer. Too late for me!" Nascimento accused.

"Oh, was that you?" he asked. "I'm so sorry."

Angela put her arm in his and felt comforted by his company. They went by the carpentry shop and looked in from the dark night. They slowed the pace to take a look at the men with Lazarus. He was in the company of the same group that had been punished by the Night Justice and other men, less harmful. Lazarus was smiling at something that had been said.

Angela murmured softly, "I love you." And Lazarus looked out into the dark as if he had heard.

They went by the Music Club House full of people; the sounds of the philharmonic rehearsing followed them down the street. The village was illuminated now, the light filtering from under the doors and cracks on the curtains. Radios were playing, and children laughed. Walking arm in arm, making a human chain across the street, they listened to the sounds of the night, of their village getting ready to go to sleep.

The women were thinking about their sins and atonement. They were going home with a promise for a penance and one slap. No doubt they had been very lucky.

"Was it a collective sin this time?" Dom Carlos asked, dying to know what it was.

"We are not telling," Ascendida said.

"And you? What did you want with the monsignor that couldn't wait?" Angela asked.

"Nothing. Rosa told me that you were worried about going to confession because he was going to hit you, so I went to the sacristy and foiled his plans."

"You were too late for me!" Nascimento accused, and then she started to laugh, remembering the monsignor screaming silently.

"Sorry, Nascimento," he said, leaning over to look at her again. "Somewhat successfully," he amended.

The night was warm and serene with crickets singing and the brook gurgling gently. This could have been a perfect night, Nascimento thought, if it was not for the slap.

"I have a poem for the occasion," she said before opening the gate of her house.

The four of them waited for Nascimento to recite the poem. Her friends were rolling their eyes, and Dom Carlos was already laughing into his hands.

> Lazarus will have the task
> To carve for us a wooden mask
> For when we go to confession.
> Imagine now the procession
> Of wooden masks with fangs
> To bite the monsignor's hands
> To teach him about aggression.

Nascimento had always some poem or some rendition of someone's poem to make fun of situations. She couldn't resist. She dealt with turmoil by making fun of life. And with this poem, she turned around and went into the house.

One by one, the women were dropped off at their homes. Angela and Dom Carlos were standing in the middle of the road absorbing the sweetness of the moon and the sounds of crickets and running water and still laughing about the poem.

"What a strange place this is," Dom Carlos said.

"Not as mysterious as you," Angela added.

"I'm not mysterious," he said.

"Every person with a secret is mysterious, and you have a secret," she concluded.

"Why do you say that?" he asked.

"I know it. You've been told that I am a witch."

"Yes, but I don't see a sorceress. I see a warrior, a kid, a pain in the ass," he said.

When they got home, the new lodger was already in bed. He was a round, fat man who didn't want to be confused with a gipsy. He was very animated in his conversations and whistled all the time. He was selling impermeable fabric, and the dark green material was a success, so he needed a few more days to unload this product. Dom Carlos didn't like to have lodgers, so he was not very pleased with the extended stay of the whistling gipsy.

"You don't like lodgers," Angela stated.

Dom Carlos didn't answer.

"Will you need anything before I go to bed?" she asked.

"You can't give me what I need," he said.

"You would be surprised at what a sorceress can conjure up," she said. "But no, I will not turn away lodgers because you are secretive." She held his gaze. "Good night, Zorro," she said.

When Madalena got home, Saul was waiting for her. He looked at her face for vestiges of a slap.

"He didn't slap you, did he?" he asked.

He had asked the monsignor not to slap his wife. He could slap him if the monsignor needed to slap someone, but not Madalena. The monsignor was furious with such suggestion and asked him if he knew the story of the prince and the pauper and the whipping boy. No, Saul didn't know anything about that; he just didn't want Madalena to be hit.

"Please, Monsignor. She's been slapped enough. Why don't you slap Angela? She is the troublemaker …"

"Get out of my sacristy!" the monsignor had said, full of rage.

When Madalena got home without being slapped, Saul let out a sigh of relief. "This beautiful face can only be kissed," he said.

"Nascimento was not as lucky. He slapped her," Madalena said.

"What did she do to be slapped?"

Madalena thought of that peripheral sin that Nascimento was going to throw in to distract the monsignor.

"She jumped through Jaime's window and kissed his *dove* while he was fast asleep."

Saul laughed with his head thrown back. Madalena knelt at his feet and opened his fly. He stopped laughing and looked down at her crown of curls.

He held his breath in surprise and slowly let out a deep sigh, caressing her head while receiving her attentions.

After the confession, the village experienced a period of peace. One whole year went by without Night Justice incidents, because the Night Justice was afraid of the Night Justice, and everyone was on his or her best behavior.

The summer came lazy and hot. The Americans and the Canadians were visiting, and Angela's Inn was in high demand for rooms. The families of the emigrants had houses too small and too full of children to accommodate the visitors with all those hats, boots, and handbags. This was a time when young, unattached people were wishing for an American, a Canadian, or even an occasional Brazilian to marry, so they could leave the island for kinder worlds. The islanders who left, skinny, burned by the sun, with cracked hands and feet, came back robust and white skinned. They looked different, as if this world beyond the edge of the horizon had transforming magic.

There was nothing like an emigrant to speak of transformation.

The emigrants always coveted Lucia, the second prettiest girl in the village. She had many proposals and some of them very tempting. But she was in love with Samuel Barcos and was waiting for his proposal.

Samuel Barcos, on the other hand, was sure of his charms and would only get married if a girl proposed to him. Well, Lucia would never propose to a man, and the man she loved would never propose to a girl. This was indeed a difficult impasse, but they persisted in their platonic relationship—even when Samuel received proposals by many emigrant girls. He was waiting for Lucia.

According to the village, Samuel had the looks of an Adonis and the manners of a gentleman. He was everything a man should be, except rich. He was from a good family, he was a hardworking man, he was well educated and well read, and he was loyal to his friends and family and compassionate to others. His brothers were more or less like him, but Samuel had the strength of character that Manuel and Francisco lacked. Samuel would never have abandoned Madalena and then cried for her all over the island as Manuel was doing. Samuel would have taken Pedro Matias, like a bull, to the slaughterhouse.

Angela's Inn was housing two cousins from Canada, and the parents were next door. Mia and Nina were well padded, slightly soft, and full of bubble gum and chocolate. They were immediately smitten with Dom Carlos. Their mission on this trip was to find a husband, a good man to work hard and be successful. Dom Carlos was already successful; so half their task was done. But they needed Dom Carlos to take notice. And he didn't.

One day, Nina decided to be bold and cornered Dom Carlos on the patio. Hercules was observing with a smirk. After many attempts of engagement, Nina sat near him and asked point-blank if he would like to go to Canada. He said no; he had been in many places, and he didn't care much to go to Canada. Nina didn't expect this response. Everybody liked to go to Canada. She got closer to Dom Carlos. He looked at her plump, wet mouth when she said, "You are dying to kiss me." And she got closer and closer.

"You are just a kid. Be careful in this place ... Someone can take you up on your offer and make you very sorry." He was somewhat annoyed with the girl and with his thoughts about a soft, pink mouth and a soft, tender body ...

Bam! She slapped him and turned around, walking away, her short skirt allowing the view of nicely shaped legs.

Angela was looking precisely at the moment he was being slapped, and she let out a scream. Lazarus gazed in the same direction, and Hercules guffawed.

"Oh my God!" Angela said, running toward Dom Carlos.

"She hit me!" he said, bewildered. He had never been hit before, and he looked up at Angela with a frown on his face as if she could explain to him that unfortunate event.

"What happened?" Angela asked, looking at the red mark on his face.

"She hit me," he said again, as if he was mortally wounded.

"I know, but what happened for her to hit you?" she asked impatiently.

"I ..." he stopped.

Lazarus and Angela were still waiting. Hercules sat at his feet and sneezed.

"Hercules is laughing," Lazarus said, trying to contain his mirth.

"Damn cat!" Dom Carlos said demurely.

Angela lifted her hand and caressed the red spot on Dom Carlos's face.

"You are dying to laugh, aren't you?" he accused.

Lazarus was laughing softly behind Angela, and she was trying to keep a serious face. But she couldn't. She turned around, falling in Lazarus's arms and hiding her face in his chest.

Dom Carlos waited. Lazarus and Angela were in each other's arms laughing their heads off at his expense.

"She's been after you since she got here," Lazarus said. "I can get you a chastity belt, made of aromatic cedar ..." And they laughed again and reminded Dom Carlos of Judite, the American emigrant still in love with him.

Judite was an older woman who had come from America to find a husband. She could have almost any man she wanted, but she wanted Dom Carlos. While Mia and Nina found nice boyfriends who were more than happy to kiss them, Dom Carlos was forever teased about that slap, and about Judite's big hands grabbing him under the table. Judite rested her large, white, manicured hand on his lap, while pontificating about virtue. It was Nixon that came to his rescue, when he oinked on Judite's hand, and she removed it as fast as she could from the pig.

15

Shining, Clean, Pretty People

Francisco Barcos was one of the lucky ones who got engaged with a Canadian girl, or so he thought. This Canadian girl, Evelyn, was petite and blond and looked like an American from the military base. He was at first smitten with the idea of immigrating to Canada. But then he fell for that small girl who spoke a strange language that he didn't understand. Somehow the fact that they didn't speak the same language didn't bother anybody.

"Je vais aller a la fenetre!" she told her mother, and Francisco fell in love without really knowing what she was saying. Samuel, his brother, knew French. But Francisco never really liked school. Now he had a girlfriend saying things to him whose meaning he had no idea of.

Samuel taught him a few things that would help Francisco to converse. There were only so many times one could say, "Mon amour."

Francisco tried something new that Samuel had taught him: "Je t'aime mois non-plus," he said.

Evelyn suddenly became very serious and closed the window in his face.

Francisco was bewildered and furious with his brother. What the hell had he said to Evelyn? He went to the library and looked in all the dictionaries he could find, and according to his research, he said to Evelyn that he loved her so much that he had no room for more love. But much to his chagrin, that was not what he said. According to Angela, he had told Evelyn that he didn't love her anymore. And he lost Evelyn, his petite French Canadian, who looked like an American from the military base.

For the rest of the summer, when Evelyn told her mother that she wanted to go to the window, it was not to talk to Francisco; it was to talk with João Godinho, who went to school and knew French.

For the rest of the summer, Francisco's sisters and brothers sang softly:

> Je t'aime mois
> mois non plus
> hoooh hoooh hoooh

Francisco couldn't believe that Evelyn, that angelic girl, who had allowed him to squirt milk straight from the udder of the cow into her mouth, was not even looking in his direction. He thought about her little mouth trying to catch the milk flying at her, while the cow mooed softly and looked sideways at the fanfare.

And that summer full of love and shining people, Francisco and Manuel moped around the island parading their broken hearts.

The islanders were exhausted with Americans and Canadians looking for love and marriage. They were afraid of the emigrants because emigrants had much to offer, and they simply took other people's boyfriends and girlfriends, leaving the rest of the islanders rooted in resentment and misery.

This was Saul's most secret wish—for someone to come from somewhere and take Manuel. How wonderful it would be if some shining, pretty girl would take away that sick puppy, who wouldn't leave him and Madalena in peace. But Manuel was so desperately focused on his love for Madalena and the wrong that had been done to him that he had no interest in anybody.

One day, Saul waited for him after a bullfight and held him by the arm. Manuel looked at Saul feverishly and said, "What the fuck do you want?"

"I want you to leave Madalena in peace," Saul said.

"Or what? Are you going to kill me this time? Are you?"

"Leave us alone, or I will skin you alive," Saul said evenly.

"I don't care. You already took everything from me!" he yelled.

People were staring at David and Goliath. Francisco rescued Manuel, giving Saul a sour look. And Manuel started to talk about leaving. He wanted to go to Canada, to America, to Australia, or to Brazil, but he would go alone. He was not going to marry any silly emigrant girl who could hardly speak his language. He was going alone, and he would come back rich and powerful, and he would buy off the whole island and kick the Amoras out all the way to Brazil.

Manuel's family, as well as the whole village, thought it was a good idea. He needed to leave the island and be away from Saul and Madalena.

The monsignor was having doubts about Manuel's health. He looked gaunt and nervous, found no joy in anything, and was smoking too much and eating very little. The monsignor was seriously thinking that the poor boy was losing his sanity. Manuel also kept on changing his mind. Sometimes he wanted to go to Canada, other times to Brazil. He didn't like the idea of having to work in the fields or in a factory. But at times he didn't care if he lived or died; he was confused and in pain. But one day, he finally made a decision; he started to make plans and save money for his voyage to Brazil.

The monsignor seized this opportunity with both hands and helped Manuel with money and the necessary connections. Everybody, including his own family, let out a sigh of relief. Manuel had always been pampered because of a heart condition; he worked less than his brothers and stayed in bed later than any member of the family. Now he would have to succeed in a totally different place, without help and protection from anyone.

But he had to leave because there was no other solution.

For the remainder of the summer, Manuel walked around the village with the demeanor of a sacrificial saint. He was going to leave this place forever, and then they would see how much they would miss him.

He started to think that Madalena could go with him. Being Manuel, enthralled in his drama and self-fulfilling prophecy of unhappiness, he sent her a letter.

Madalena read the letter in her garden, with the autumn leaves turning colors and swirling around in the afternoon cold.

> My beloved Madalena,
>
> You probably heard already that I will be leaving the island to places unknown. I just can't leave without trying one more time to undo the terrible harm I've caused us. I was a coward because I ran away afraid of your father, and I lost you. But it doesn't have to be forever. Come with me, Madalena, and we will live the love that had always been ours. Please think about it and write me back. Place the letter in the church under the dress of Our Lady of Lourdes, right under her broken toe.
>
> I love you forever,
> Manuel

Madalena felt faint. That misguided young man was going to get himself in trouble. And far worse, he was going to provoke Saul and get him in trouble. Now they didn't have Detective Lourenço to turn a blind eye and write innocuous reports, and Saul was losing his patience with Manuel.

"You can't tell me where to look, you beast!" Manuel yelled at Saul the last time they had exchanged words.

"That boy needs another lesson!" Pedro Matias had said in the carpentry shop.

Lazarus had told Madalena that Manuel's lovelorn antics were being talked about all over the village. She was worried, although she knew that her father would not be so quick to put the Night Justice in working order. His friends were terrified of being punished again, and Pedro was more than suspicious about his turn coming up soon. He didn't want to provoke fate.

The following day, Madalena went to Angela and showed her the letter. Madalena looked so sad and worried that Angela took out the moonshine.

"I don't want to get home smelling of moonshine again," Madalena said.

"Who cares if we smell of moonshine? We need it to write a letter to this fool."

When Dom Carlos entered the kitchen, the two women had their heads together over a piece of paper.

"What are you doing?" Dom Carlos asked, looking curiously at the paper.

"What are you doing home?" Angela asked, almost annoyed "I thought you were going to stay in the city."

"I know, but I ended my meetings earlier than I thought. And I always prefer to come home," he said, smiling at both women. "What? You are not happy to see me?" he asked, feigning offense. But he left, giving another look toward the paper and at the moonshine.

Dear Manuel,

Please don't write anymore because it causes all kinds of problems. I am glad that you are thinking about your future. I want you to be happy, but I cannot go with you. My future is here with my husband. I will see you before you go away to say good-bye.

Be well,
Madalena

"Yes, this will be palatable to Manuel. If you sent a letter dismissing him, he would be knocking at your door demanding his love back. He is losing his mind," Angela said.

"He loves drama," Madalena said. "He always did."

Before going home for supper, Madalena went to church and knelt at the feet of Our Lady of Lourdes. She looked up at her beatific face. Madalena had never really looked at Our Lady of Lourdes's face until now. She looked like Felicidade, Mario's wife, with her creamy skin, and red hair. Maria, mother of Jesus, was from the Middle East; she shouldn't look like Felicidade.

Slowly, Madalena lifted the dress a little and looked at Our Lady's feet. She was barefooted and had a chipped toe. And right above the ankles, there were two pieces of wood—two-by-fours—for legs.

Madalena put the note under the broken toe, lowered the dress, and left.

Saul was looking at Madalena from inside the confessional. He had intercepted the letter, opened it, read it, and given it back to the little boy who had delivered it to Madalena. The other letters delivered by the mailman simply confessed Manuel's love for Madalena and asked her for a response. Madalena had never responded because she had never gotten the letters. But this letter was different; this letter promised action. Manuel was going to leave, and Saul needed to know if Madalena would answer.

And she did.

When Madalena left the church, Saul went straight to Our Lady of Lourdes and lifted her skirt.

"Damn it, Saul! Did you lose all sense of decorum?" the monsignor said from the back of the church.

"Monsignor!" Saul said, completely taken aback. Then more calmly, he added, "I need to see what Madalena put under that skirt."

The monsignor went to the statue and lifted her dress, revealing the two-by-fours. Saul looked under her feet, and there it was—the piece of paper. Saul took the paper and said to the monsignor, "This is what I was looking for."

The monsignor snagged it out of his hands and read it. Then he lowered his head and said, "Dear Lord, give me strength. Give me strength!"

Saul was standing up in front of him without knowing what the letter said. He stretched his hand to the monsignor, and the monsignor gave him the letter.

"Monsignor, that boy is getting on my nerves," Saul said calmly.

"And your wife is getting on mine!" the monsignor yelled.

The monsignor sat in the nearest pew and pulled Saul to sit next to him. "Listen here, my boy," he said, fighting to calm his voice. "You are not going to do anything. You are not going to say or do anything to Manuel. Do you hear me?"

"Monsignor, he has to leave us alone. It has been more than two years since I married Madalena. He is getting worse."

"I know, I know, but he is leaving. I am getting the money ready for him to leave. By next summer, he will be gone," the monsignor said in a low, conciliatory tone.

"I'll give you the money. Just tell me how much you need, and I will give you the money," Saul said, full of hope.

The monsignor looked at him for a few seconds. "Are you sure? This will be part of your confession. No one will know, and Manuel can leave this Christmas."

"Tomorrow I will bring you the money, and you can buy him a trip to the end of the world—whatever it costs, I'll pay."

"He wants to go to Brazil."

"Brazil it is then," Saul said, relieved.

When Saul got home, he looked around for Madalena. He was so happy with the prospect of getting rid of Manuel that he felt like letting out a howl.

Madalena was out, and Saul waited for her in the garden. He sat for a while, feeling the cold get into his bones. Then Madalena came through the garden, unaware of his presence. When she realized that he was sitting waiting for her, she ran to him.

"What's wrong?" she asked, scanning his face.

Saul lifted her up from the ground and kissed her tenderly, "Everything is right," he said. "And tonight I am going to give you a bath, take you to bed, and make love to you while we listen to the radio."

And so they did.

Saul savored the heat of Madalena's skin against his body. She intertwined her legs in his and hummed a song playing on the radio, "Tombe la neige ..."

So this was happiness. They had finally met that elusive phantom.

The winter promised to be dark and cold in so many different ways, and that winter, the sun refused to shine on Two Brooks. There was a deeper sting on the wind, the salty air was heavy and humid, and the rain fell determined to drown everything. The villagers hurried to and fro as if running away from a villain.

Lazarus tried to get home earlier since he got married, but there were times that he couldn't. Tonight was one of those times. He could have sent everyone home and closed shop, but the conversation was far too intriguing. The men were talking about a dark figure roaming the village. He was on horseback and was mainly around the cliffs, near the Amoras land, which was almost all of the land edging the cliffs. João Lionel, holding a flashlight, had approached this horseman, but he'd taken off. He hasn't said anything or done anything. He'd simply taken off and disappeared up the pastures, galloping in the dark as if the horse had hoofs of lightning. They were thinking about the Night Justice. This horseman could be the head of Night Justice. It made perfect sense for Pedro Matias, who knew all about the Night Justice and again knew nothing. Or this horseman could be that boogeyman that Elias and his father saw last year. Whatever this horseman was, he had to be bad news. But what was there on the cliffs that one mysterious horseman was keeping watch over? Those pastures were believed to have a buried treasure, and the village believed that it was why the Amoras had bought all that land. But according to the monsignor, the buried treasure was the land itself and the richness of the soil.

The monsignor got upset with the villagers when they indulged in thoughts of this kind—boogeymen, werewolves, vampires, pirates, buried treasures, and sunken ships. Usually when the villagers were confused or upset, the monsignor always clarified and educated. He would do so screaming all the way, no doubt, but he did help put things into perspective. However, they would not talk about this boogeyman or vampire or whatever this thing was, because the monsignor did not believe in those things.

One thing that João Lionel saw was that the horse was big and all black, at least the legs, because its body was covered by a cape.

"If the devil had a horse, it would look like that," João said.

"Well," said Ivo. "My father has been a little strange lately. I think he is fighting again the devil trying to possess his body. The devil is out and about, I think."

"There are things that we don't understand," João Lionel said. "The monsignor believes in a person being possessed by the devil …but doesn't believe in boogeymen or vampires. Tell me, what's the difference? A vampire or a boogeyman … It sounds just as real …and evil."

"I've seen the devil inside my father's skin," Ivo said. "At first I thought it was contagious—that being closer to my father would make the devil enter my skin also. But what the devil wants is for you to be afraid of him. And I am. I'm not like the monsignor or my mother, may God have mercy on her soul. My mother was not afraid of the devil either. One time, she took the crucifix up

to my father's face and said, 'Look at it. Look at it!' And my father closed his
eyes and howled like a dog. My mother hit him on the chest with the crucifix,
and my father fainted. Then the devil was gone for a very long time."

The men were pensive. There were too many things going on, and they had
no understanding or control over any of them. Lazarus was thinking that the
devil had been in Ivo's skin when he'd raped Maia a few years ago. Sometimes
Lazarus could feel the darkness around his father and people like Ivo.

To Pedro Matias, it was very upsetting to be involved with things that he
could not understand or control, the devil being one of them. He thought he
was the head of everything in the village, and now all seemed to be running
out of his grasp, with the devil complicating matters.

"Someone is vandalizing the construction of the new Cooperative," João
Lionel said.

Lazarus paid close attention to the men. This was important to him
because he and Angela were Dom Carlos's partners in the Cooperative. They
were investing in a new, modernized building. Every time there was something
done during the day, someone vandalized it at night, costing a fortune in time
and money and putting the whole project behind schedule.

Lazarus looked at everyone's face.

"Maybe it's the devil," Pedro said with a smirk. And Ivo laughed.

"Night Justice, the devil …these things take a darker meaning on a cold
and windy night such as this," João said.

The men in the carpentry shop started to go home slowly, but none went
alone. They waited for each other, for someone to go in the same direction, but
they didn't go alone. And if they found themselves alone, they sprinted, got
inside of their gates, and closed the door of their homes with a sigh of relief.

Lazarus walked home with his father. They were both quiet and looked
around when the wind blew leaves in their direction. Pedro had a Petromax
lamp in his hand, casting a bluish light that lengthened their shadows over the
walls and houses of the quiet village.

Pedro left Lazarus at home and walked briskly down the road in the
direction of his house. He could see the light on in the window of his kitchen.
His wife had left the light on until he came home. He felt a sense of comfort
just by looking at his house in the dark, announcing his sanctum with that
small feeble light flickering in the window.

Suddenly he heard the sound of hooves, as if a thousand horses were
running toward him. And like a flash, a huge, tall shadow came upon him and
knocked the Petromax lamp out of his hand, and a horsewhip wrapped around

his legs with a castigating swoosh and pulled him up. He felt his feet lift from the ground and his back hit the road, knocking the air out of his lungs.

And then it was over. The phantom disappeared with the same speed it had appeared. If the Petromax lamp was not shattered to pieces and if Pedro's legs and back were not stinging, he would have said that he'd imagined the whole thing, spooked by the stories at the carpentry shop.

He looked for the light on in the window, and like a curse, the light was gone. Terror took hold of him, leaving an acid taste in his mouth, and he ran home like a child runs away from the boogeyman.

When he opened the door of his home, everything was dark and silent. Amelia had stopped leaving the light on for him a long time ago. The light he had seen in the window was not for him.

He felt like a pirate who had mindlessly plundered a treasure. He had destroyed the love and alliance of a good woman. The woman he married was long gone, and he knew that she was there only for the boys. Soon he would be alone.

And his sadness was greater than anything he had felt in a very long time.

Lazarus opened the door quietly in order not to disturb Angela. She always left the hot water on the range, but tonight, she was up and carried the pans of water to the tub, wanting to be with him, to wash him, to dry his beloved body, and to comb his silky hair. She felt a tightening in her throat with the realization that Lazarus was precious and the world was cruel.

"Go to bed, my angel," he said. "I'll be with you in a minute."

"No. I want to wash you and groom you today," she said with vehemence.

"Why?" he asked, perplexed

"I don't know, just need to."

Angela knelt at his feet and kissed his naked belly. Lazarus laughed softly. She slipped the wristwatch off his arm, and he got into the hot water.

Angela wanted to memorize that moment, everything about it—Lazarus naked in the water, smiling, and inviting her hands to go to fun places; his closed eyes; the sound of his soft moaning as he bit his lip at her touch.

"Did you have a bad dream?" he asked softly, relaxed in the hot, soapy water.

"No," she said. "I just missed you."

"I saw you for lunch."

"That was hours ago."

"Why are you spooked, my angel?" he asked.

"I don't know. But tonight I felt a terrible longing for you, as if life wanted to tell me how it would feel if I lost you."

"You will never lose me."

"No, never. I would die."

That night in bed, Lazarus held Angela and loved her with slow caresses, as if she needed time to memorize every tender touch.

Angela was thinking about the vandalism to the new project and the talk about the boogeyman and the devil and that Lazarus suspected it to be his father and Ivo Machado vandalizing the new building.

She felt that familiar grip on the base of her throat—anger. She knew it was Pedro; she just couldn't prove it. She had a talk with Dom Carlos regarding the measures that should be taken. One could have a guard twenty-four hours, but if Pedro were bent on damage, he would find other ways.

Angela, quiet and safe in Lazarus's embrace, was thinking about hurt. She wanted to wait for Pedro at night and break his legs. She also remembered Dom Carlos glaring into nothingness, his eyes taking a brighter tone of green when she told him that she suspected Pedro.

When Dom Carlos asked Angela if she was sure about Pedro vandalizing the project, Angela hesitated a second—not because of Pedro but because of Dom Carlos. She was protective of her family, and Dom Carlos was family to her.

"Don't get into trouble," she had said. "That man is lethal."

Dom Carlos looked at her for a long while, and then he said, "So am I."

Angela laughed. She couldn't imagine Dom Carlos being lethal. But now, thinking about the whole conversation, something had crossed her mind, for a split second.

She knew very little about Dom Carlos.

Saul went to the monsignor's house with three times the money needed for a voyage to Brazil.

"Are you intending to send the whole village away?" asked the monsignor.

Saul left the money necessary for Manuel's journey and left, feeling happy.

He rarely felt that sense of complete happiness, but today he did because Manuel was going away. Saul knew that Madalena would always love Manuel. He could make a case for justice; he could beat Manuel up every week, and no one would blame him. But even if he made a case for justice, there was always Madalena's heart that could be won only with love and kindness.

He would not tell Madalena that he had funded Manuel's voyage to Brazil. His money would be his secret weapon to protect the tender love that had flourished between the two of them. And he was hoping that Madalena would not meet Manuel to say good-bye.

He was more than hoping; he was praying.

As the village was preparing for Christmas, Manuel was preparing to leave; his days on the island were numbered, and he became even more dramatic and lovelorn. He wanted to convey to the whole village that he was leaving because he could not live without Madalena. He sat on his patio in the afternoon and sang beautiful love songs accompanied by a crying guitar, while people went by, slowly shaking their heads because of the relentless love of that poor boy.

To get to his own home, Saul had to go by Manuel's house and endure the singing and the guitar moaning love songs to his wife. At times, Saul felt like crossing the street, grabbing the guitar and the guitarist by the neck, and breaking both in half.

But now Saul had hope; Manuel was going to leave in a few days. There would be no cloud in his sky after that.

Saul got home wet and cold. The evening was windy, and the rain was hitting the windows and the roof, as if it too were in a hurry to get into the house. He changed his wet clothes while Madalena was getting ready to go to the Christmas rehearsal.

She looked beautiful and happy.

Saul sat near the fire, hoping she would stay with him by the fire, listening to the radio. The light of the fire was playing different colors on her skin, and Saul felt an urge to hang on to that moment.

"Stay with me tonight," he said.

The request was so unusual and was uttered with a quiet longing that startled them both. Madalena knelt at his feet, her back to the fire.

"What's wrong?" she asked, placing her hands on his thighs.

"Nothing," he said. "I was just thinking aloud."

Madalena smiled. "Angela is waiting for me."

"I will tell her that you can't go," Carlota said. "I have an order to be delivered tomorrow, and Dom Carlos offered to take it to the city."

Probably Carlota was lying, but she left, closing the door against a howling wind.

Saul caressed Madalena's hair and looked at her as if searing her in his mind.

"What is it?" she asked. "You look a bit strange. Did something happen?

"No," he said, still caressing her.

They sat quietly by the fire, listening to the radio.

"I want to have children," Madalena said, "so I can teach them that silly poem that you taught me about a spider."

Saul's heart skipped a beat. He said, "It's a riddle."

> The spider jumped over the sea
> From Brazil to Italy
> From end to end, she roamed the earth
> Hid her wares with limpets and firth
> And counted the gold of a sunken ship
> And left the grace of a given kiss
> To weave a web on the darkened lip
> Of a Hawk on a precipice

"Do you know what it means?" she asked.

"Not yet," he answered.

My beloved,

I am leaving to Brazil in a few days. I want to see you. Please give me this last wish. I will be waiting for you at the windmill Saturday night right after the Mass.

With love,
Manuel

Saul read the note and put it back under the foot of Our Lady of Lourdes. Madalena would be checking for a message.

As his love for Madalena intensified, Saul's dislike for Manuel grew by the same proportions; he had an urge to hurt the man.

He had confessed this fantasy to the monsignor, who had become silent with worry.

Saul hid inside a confessional and waited for Madalena.

She came in looking around. Her eyes rested on the confessional as if she could see him. She approached Our Lady, lifted the dress up, took the note, and read it. Then she wrote something on a piece of paper and put it under Our Lady's foot and left.

Saul waited for a long time, as if afraid he would be caught. Finally, he came out like a prowling cat and took the note.

> Manuel,
>
> I will go and say goodbye to you at the windmill because I care for you. But my caring for you is simply as a friend and as someone who suffered along with me during a time in my life. I want you to go away and be happy, because I am happy here with Saul. I love him. We are going to start a family. And for the first time in my life, I am truly happy. I'm sorry if this hurts you, but you need to know that I will never be a reason for your stay or your return.
>
> Be well,
> Madalena

Saul put the note back and went home, where he found Madalena helping Carlota with supper. The two women were talking about Maia and letters that spoke of Maia's happiness with her detective. Saul loved to sit by the fire and just listen to his mother read aloud Maia's letters. He found so much comfort in the chatter of women, especially his women.

That night, before going to sleep, Madalena said, "I love you more than I can say."

"Tell me why," he said.

"Some people love without a reason. I love you because I have one. You are the kindest, the gentlest of men."

With this sweet prelude, he told her about his childhood full of gentle people—his father, Maia, his mother, and his grandparents in Brazil. He talked about his horses and dogs and the beautiful house on acres of land. He talked about his servants' children, bathing in the river and playing in the fields. He was remembering a magical life of light, love, and wonder.

Saul never talked so much. He was giving her his most precious gift—a glimpse into his past.

"Why did you leave Brazil?"

"I don't know. My parents never really wanted to talk about it."

"Do you want to return?"

"Someday …"

There was so much she didn't know about her husband. He had a past painted with brilliant colors, but he was here in this small and unforgiving place.

The monsignor was thinking about justice and Saul. That young man had been wronged so many times by so many people. And now that he'd found happiness with the woman of his dreams, Manuel Barcos was throwing mud at it.

The monsignor himself felt the urge to break some of Manuel's bones. The boy was trying everyone's patience, and not a day too soon, he would be leaving. But somehow, the monsignor was anxious about this whole affair. It seemed that Manuel, knowing that he was going to leave, was even bolder in his provocation of Madalena and Saul. The monsignor sensed that plenty of crying was coming down the road.

Yes, plenty of crying—more than the monsignor could ever imagine.

16

The Devil is Out and About

Dom Carlos was sitting at the kitchen table looking into numbers and proposals for the Cooperative. He was frowning. Angela refilled his teacup, and he looked up at her.

"If the vandals continue in this fashion, we will go bankrupt before the building is up," he said.

"How many vandals are we talking about?" Angela asked.

"About two," he answered.

"Do you know who they are?"

"Yes. I had a pretty good idea before, but now I am sure."

"How?" Angela asked, sitting down opposite him and placing her elbows on the table.

If Angela was sitting and looking at him like that, she would not leave him alone until he gave her a satisfactory answer.

He laughed softly. "You are a bully."

Dom Carlos had met many people in the world but none like Angela. She was always sure about everything and went about life doing what she thought should be done. She was a terror—a loving, loyal, strange terror. She loved in a relentless way—people, animals, and causes.

"What? Do I have dirt on my face?" she asked.

"I know who the vandals are," he said. "I had a suspicion based on a conversation I had with Lazarus and you. Lazarus heard things at the carpentry shop. Then Lazarus helped me get that proof."

Angela asked bewildered, "My Lazarus?"

"Yes. I don't have a Lazarus." He smiled.

They were quiet for a moment.

"Why are you so surprise that Lazarus would help me?" Dom Carlos asked.

"Because I think one of the vandals is his father, and he would never do anything against his father."

Dom Carlos lowered his eyes to the page full of numbers in front of him.

"He helped because he wanted to prove that his father would not vandalize his son's business," Dom Carlos said evenly.

A shadow of sadness came over Angela's features. "Poor Lazarus; he is always dreaming that his father can be a decent man."

They were silent again for a long time. Angela broke the silence by asking, "Does Lazarus know that it is really his father?"

"I don't know. I haven't talked about it with him yet."

"What did you do?"

"I used a product, sulfur based, on the construction site, after the construction men left. If anyone went to the construction site, that product would be transferred to their shoes, clothes, and hands; and they would glow in the dark. There were two men glowing in the dark two nights ago, Pedro Matias and Ivo Machado."

Angela was looking attentively at Dom Carlos, and he continued.

"I went to the carpentry shop with an excuse that I needed to get this book, and Lazarus had it in the back room. The two men were in the carpentry shop. Lazarus took the Petromax lamp into the back room, leaving the front room in the dark. It was a setup."

Angela turned pale. Pedro was in bed with a case of back pain and maybe a concussion, according to Ascendida, from falling off a horse. And Ivo Machado had gone to the hospital because he had fallen off his horse and broken a few ribs, all in the same night. "Please tell me that Zorro has nothing to do with this," she said, almost in a supplicant tone.

Dom Carlos stared at her for a while. "The construction resumed, and there has been no vandalism," he finally said.

Angela looked up at the ceiling as if God was hiding in the rafters. "Oh, God, help me with this man!" she said, exasperated. She turned to Dom Carlos. "You have to promise me that you will not fool around with those men. They are dangerous."

"They think it is the boogeyman or the devil that afflicts Joaquim Machado."

"They are ignorant, but they are not stupid. And above all they are mean, malicious men," Angela said with conviction. "Promise me that you will not play Zorro anymore."

He laughed and placed a finger in front of his lips, asking for silence. "No one knows I am Zorro, only you. Be quiet. Rosa may hear you."

Angela was looking at him with alarm.

Dom Carlos said, "I didn't go after those two men. I went after the men who were destroying my hard work. They know what they've done, so they know why they were attacked."

"Don't you think that they will know it is you? Who else is interested in the Cooperative other than you, me, and Lazarus?"

"They also think that I am a city slicker. They don't know that I ride horses and …" He smiled. "And roam at night as Zorro. This boogeyman has been going around long before I came to the village—or at least long before they knew I was in the village."

"You are so smug. Smug people get hurt; do you know that?" she said with fury.

Dom Carlos gave her a hug. "Are you worried about me?" he asked, amused.

"Yes. No. I just don't want to lose my best paying lodger," Angela said in response to his gentle laughter.

She added as if speaking to herself, "We are the holy trinity; you are the father, Lazarus is the son, and I am the Holy Ghost. Don't do anything to upset this balance."

Dom Carlos felt rooted, arrested by a second of complete well-being. He felt a wave of tenderness hold his heart.

The boogeyman was out again hurting people. The men in the carpentry shop were talking about the injuries they'd suffered by way of this cunning horseman, boogeyman, or werewolf. Elias caressed his jaw while Pedro and Ivo retold their story.

Pedro Matias was thinking that the horseman could be Dom Carlos. But it made no sense: The attacks had started long before Dom Carlos had come to the village, he didn't own a horse, and Pedro doubted that Dom Carlos knew how to ride a horse like that; Dom Carlos was a city sissy. The horse was big and black. There was no such horse in the village. The only horse that was that big was the new horse that Lazarus had bought from the chief of police in the city. However, that horse had his front legs marked with snowy white stripes, and he was certainly smaller. The boogeyman's horse was all black, legs and all, and it was a huge animal; Pedro had had a chance to look before he was knocked out on his ass. Ivo said the same thing. It could not be Dom Carlos. He would never have the nerve to mount a horse that wild.

When Lazarus came home for lunch, he found Angela sitting at the kitchen table with a cake and a candle.

"Happy anniversary, darling," she said.

They'd been married for two years. To Lazarus, it seemed like they'd always been married. However, Angela liked to celebrate everything. She remembered the first time they kissed on the lips, the first time he said I love you, the first time he bit her nose, the first time he sang to her.

The lodgers, including Dom Carlos, were already sitting around the table marveled by the lunch before them—steak. Everyone was always hungry for meat. At Angela's, meat was so rare that the lodgers dreamed about eating steak. So when they went to the city, they would go to their favorite restaurants and just say, "Bring it on."

During lunch, they talked about the boogeyman.

Lazarus looked at Dom Carlos and said, "The men were talking about you, Dom Carlos—saying that you could be the boogeyman. But they concluded that the boogeyman was attacking people way before you came around. They also don't believe that you are that courageous or that you know how to ride a horse like that."

Lazarus was grinning, and Angela was assessing how much Lazarus knew about the whole thing.

"They said this horseman flew with the horse ... The pair galloped with the speed of lightning. Do you know how to fly a horse, Dom Carlos?" Lazarus asked, amused.

"No," he said, "I don't know how to fly a horse ... I don't even know how to fly a kite," Dom Carlos said, matching Lazarus' amusement.

Angela gave Dom Carlos a reproachful stare, and he lowered his eyes to the steak.

"The good thing about this boogeyman business is that construction for the Cooperative is taking shape. The old building was really getting too small for the business we are receiving," Lazarus said.

When Lazarus left, Angela asked Dom Carlos, "What does he know?"

"He only knows that I suspected some of the men in the carpentry shop that night when he took the lamp into the back room. I didn't tell him who, but he knew I suspected his father."

"I think he knows in his heart."

"Angela, you can't protect him as if he is a child. He is a man, and there are things that you will not be able to protect him from—such as his father's malice."

"Yes I can," she said stubbornly. "That's why we got married so soon. I should have gone to the university in the mainland and then gotten married when I was finished. But I knew in my heart that Pedro would kill Lazarus or hurt him so much that he would never be whole again …"

"You too," he said sadly. "You too, as courageous as you are, have fallen victim to that man."

"Dreams can be adjusted," she answered quietly. "And Lazarus was not called to go to the military. My miracle was answered. See? Dreams can be adjusted, and miracles do happen."

Dom Carlos was restless. He walked around the kitchen, scratched Nixon's head, and sat down again.

Angela was immersed in her task of washing dishes. She frowned. "Do you want to have children?" she asked.

Dom Carlos was surprised by the question. "Whatever made you ask that?"

"Sometimes I think that you see me and Lazarus as your children."

He held her gaze. What could he say to this intense creature? He finally answered, "I don't know if I think of you as my children … I don't think so." He was very serious, and then he added, "I love you. I don't know if it is like a father because I've never been a father. But I love you."

"We love you too," she said quietly.

Angela walked over and sat next to him. She took his hand in hers and said, "If anything happens to me, if I die, if …I don't know, if …lightning strikes me or something …" She paused, searching for a more adequate thought.

Dom Carlos frowned at her.

"You will never leave Lazarus at the mercy of his father …" she said hoarsely. "Promise me."

Dom Carlos squeezed her hand and asked, "What the hell are you talking about?"

"I guess I am asking you to take care of Lazarus," she said very quietly, looking at him with such intensity that he felt overwhelmed.

"Where are you going?" he asked, trying to dissipate the somber mood.

"Just promise me," she said impatiently.

"I promise," he said. Then he laughed.

"I'm serious!" she said accusingly.

"I know you are. But Lazarus made me promise that I would take care of you if anything happened to him."

"He did?" Angela asked, touched by Lazarus' concern. "And what did you say?"

"I promised I would."

A smile spread over Angela's face. "And you will take care of me? How? You can't even deal with Hercules …"

"You are two morbid little creeps. That's for sure. As for Hercules, I would've finished that cat off if only I could forget that you almost drowned to save him, and I to save you," Dom Carlos said.

Manuel was going to leave, finally. The only thing he asked of his village was to let him go and to let him say good-bye to Madalena. He didn't want to say good-bye to anyone—not even his family. And so, given that Manuel was leaving and taking with him his broken heart and overplayed theatrics, the village became coconspirator, and the villagers arranged for Madalena to meet him at the windmill, for the very last time.

When Manuel opened the door to the windmill, Madalena was there, standing up, waiting, with her arms crossed over her chest.

Manuel ran to her and hugged her. Madalena didn't uncross her arms. A feverish Manuel, saying all kinds of things in a gibberish fashion, was hugging her. He talked about his love for her and about the baby, about Saul, about her betrayal for loving Saul.

Madalena gently pushed him away and said, "Go in peace, Manuel. Go. There is nothing here for you."

"I love you!" he said with tears in his eyes.

"It is too late for us," she said quietly.

"You love me too. You'll always love me, Madalena! Always!"

"I will always care for you, yes, but not the way you want. I am in love with Saul, my husband. I am happy, Manuel, happy! Do you remember us ever being happy?" She searched his face for understanding.

But he cried, covering his face. "I hate him, that ogre, that thief!"

Madalena was looking at a very different man. Manuel was not right. There was something crazy in his eyes.

"Please," she said. "Please accept that it is over. It is over. I don't love you any longer." And she turned around and ran out of the windmill.

She heard Manuel's screams carried in the wind, and finally she was too far away to hear anything else. She ran all the way home, under the castigating, cold wind.

When she got home, Saul was sitting in front of the fire. He was pensive. He didn't even look back when the door opened, and she came in with a gust of wind.

Madalena knelt in front of him, as she usually did, and looked up. He was so sad. "What is wrong?" she asked.

"You tell me," he answered.

"Nothing. From now on, there is nothing wrong."

"What do you mean?" he asked.

"Just believe me. Believe me when I tell you that, from now on, there will be nothing wrong with us," she said, cupping his face in her hands and kissing him gently on the mouth.

Saul started to undress her right there in front of the fire, vaguely aware that his mother was out only for a few hours, but he had never been so intent on loving Madalena as he was at that moment, and she abandoned herself to that sweet gift. He loved her so tenderly, as if it was the last time he would ever make love to her.

Saul pulled a blanket over them, and they looked at the fire die on the iron grate.

Madalena fell asleep, and Saul took her to bed.

He kissed her gently, put on his clothes, and went out.

Angela wanted to wait for Lazarus, and she fought the drowsiness taking hold of her. All week long, she had felt uneasy about Lazarus, as if he was in danger. But he would come home, humming his love song about a boat, and they would fall asleep. Today she waited again, but Lazarus took a long time to come home and Angela fell asleep.

Dom Carlos was in the city, and there were no lodgers in the house. Even the menagerie was quiet.

When Lazarus came home, it was late, very late, and he was covered with sweat. He lay down with his back toward her, and she touched his shoulder. He winced.

Saul got home after one in the morning. Madalena was not sure if she heard him talk to his mother or if she dreamed it. She was a very light sleeper, but lately, she had slept so heavily that, in the morning, she was amazed at the blankness of her mind. But she remembered vaguely that there was something different about Saul that night. He was less inhibited and made love to her until the wee hours of the morning. He murmured her name more times during that night than he had during the entire time they'd been married.

When the weak rays of the morning sun came through the shudders, Saul said, "Rest, my love. I'm going now. I love you."

In the back of Madalena's mind, there was a warning, an alarm going off. But Saul was there, propped on his elbow looking down at her and smiling, albeit, a sad smile.

"Do you know that I love you very much?" he asked.

Had she answered? She couldn't remember.

"I will be back for you," he said.

"Where are you going?" she remembered asking.

He had said something about the city …

Madalena remembered Saul looking back at her before closing the door, and there was something in his eyes that she didn't understand—was it pain or betrayal?

During the day, Madalena could not find Carlota. Finally she found a note on the kitchen table saying that Carlota had gone to Little Branch to deliver her embroidery. When Carlota got back, it was late and dark, and Madalena was not home.

The Sacristy was at Ascendida's house; the children were sleeping, and her men were out.

"Manuel left yesterday," Madalena said. "I am relieved. Now Saul and I can live without Manuel making a drama everywhere we go." There was a note of worry in Madalena's voice.

"What is it?" Nascimento asked.

"I had a dream about Saul—that he was leaving to the city and ... I don't know ... It was so strange ... He was sad."

"Lazarus was strange last night also," Angela said. "He was strange this morning, thinking of it. Your father must be doing something to torment them."

"My father ..." Madalena said pensively. "Everything bad has to do with him."

Suddenly, Madalena said, "I need to go home. I need to check something. I don't know why, but something is not right."

"What?" the others yelled.

But Madalena was already running down the street with people wondering about such haste. When she got home, she stopped breathless in front of Carlota, who was sitting and crying, her face buried in the tablecloth she was embroidering.

"He left," she whispered, hugging Madalena. "He left, to a very faraway place."

"Why?" Madalena asked softly, not able to absorb the truth.

But Carlota only said, "I don't know. He only said that he had to leave."

"Was it because of me?" she asked, tears running down her face.

"I don't know. But I know he will be back for us."

"When?" she asked timidly. Life, fate, God, whatever forces she had no control over could not be doing this to them, not now.

Carlota was not planning to tell Madalena the conversation she'd had with her son. But now facing Madalena, Carlota was vacillating; she was feeling remorseful for not being able to assuage Madalena's heart.

Carlota kept on repeating, "I don't know. I don't know. He didn't say why ... It may be because of his father ... But please, darling, don't say this to anyone."

"His father? He died, didn't he?" Madalena cried. "Are you telling me that he is alive and Saul is looking for him?"

"No. I don't know. Please don't say it. People will think it is true," Carlota said, flustered with her own admission.

It was her fault. Saul had found out about Manuel, about their silly correspondence, and about their meeting to say good-bye, and he felt betrayed. But he had to come back. He had to. He always went away when he was upset, and he always came back.

But this time he didn't.

The next few days passed for Madalena as if she was in a trance. She didn't eat, sleep, or leave the house. Finally, Carlota called the monsignor, and he came to visit.

"My child," he said, resting a hand on her head, "I also don't know why he left. He didn't even tell me in confession. I don't know."

Madalena had no more tears to cry. She had no more voice to curse God, life, and luck. She had done it all in a vicious cycle of despair.

She looked up at the monsignor. Her face was gaunt. There was no light in her eyes. "It was my fault, Monsignor," she said softly. "I betrayed him with Manuel. I met with Manuel, more than once. I just wanted to ask him to leave me alone, and the last time was to say good-bye."

The monsignor said, "Well …there's no harm in that …although Saul was very insecure about Manuel and you. There is no point in you punishing yourself with that thought. Let's hope that he will write and let you know what he is thinking and when he will come back."

"Do you think his father has anything to do with this?" Madalena asked in a whisper.

The monsignor became visibly nervous. "No, child, the man is dead. People keep spreading rumors, but Saul knows that they are not true."

At least Manuel was gone, and that was a good thing. However the monsignor was having a nagging thought: Manuel and Saul leaving at the same time—how odd. Manuel was supposed to come and see him before going to the city, and he hadn't. The monsignor had money for him. Manuel had also wanted to go to confession one last time. And he had simply left, just like that. Something was not right—Saul and Manuel disappearing at the same time. Manuel yes, but Saul? Why? What had happened for Saul to leave?

Pedro Matias was saying that Saul had left because Madalena had betrayed him with Manuel. The whole village believed that, and Madalena was cloistered in her pain and shame. Carlota had heard the same rumors, and she knew they were not true. She knew that her son had not been betrayed by Madalena but had left because of her. And even though she loved that girl, the only person who made her son happy, she also knew that, because of Madalena, her son was gone.

Angela could not understand Lazarus's sadness. At first, she thought it was the connection with his sister that was making him sad and lifeless; twins usually felt each other's deepest sorrows and joys. But something else was happening with him. He was withdrawing from everybody, even from her.

At night when they went to bed, he cried in her arms but never said a word. Angela knew that Pedro Matias was also involved, because he was looking stranger and meaner than usual. He was pale and morose instead of loud and boisterous, as he usually was.

Dom Carlos tried to talk to Lazarus, but all he could get from him was silence or the reiteration of his promise to look after Angela if something happened to him. Dom Carlos was really at a loss. Manuel and Saul had left the island, maybe in the same ship, and Lazarus was falling apart.

That week, there were two ships in port—one to Brazil (Manuel's ship) and another one to somewhere in Africa. Did Saul go to Africa to look for his father? Maybe Saul's disappearance had nothing to do with Madalena and all to do with the secrets of the Amora family. What if something had happened in Africa that had made Saul go and look for his father? But Paulo Amora was believed to be dead. And Carlota, quiet, mysterious Carlota, was more silent than before. There was a sadness about her that made people swallow their curious questions.

Dom Carlos talked to Angela about all kinds of possibilities. But even Angela was stuck on the idea that whatever was going on with Madalena and Saul had to do with Pedro and that he had ensnarled Lazarus in one of his schemes.

After the initial shock, Angela and Lazarus visited Madalena to give her comfort. They were not even approaching the topic of conversation when Pedro Matias came in, almost out of breath, and sat with them at the table.

Carlota was in a different room, purposely avoiding the visitors. Angela looked at Lazarus and then at his father. Lazarus lowered his eyes.

"We don't want you here," Angela said, taking the lead.

Madalena and Lazarus seemed to regress to their submissive ways with their father. They looked timidly at him, and then they looked away into nothing.

"You have no say in this house," Pedro said in a contained voice.

"I don't know what happened, but I am sure that you are in the middle of it, as you always are when there is strife and confusion," Angela said, getting closer to him, as if she was going to pounce.

"I came to talk to Lazarus," Pedro said, getting up and slowly backing away from Angela. "And if Saul left, it was all Madalena's fault. A married woman meeting with her old boyfriend! He didn't believe me that she needed a slap once in a while, so there you have it!"

Lazarus got in between his father and his wife. "Please, let's go home," he said in a deflated tone.

But Angela stayed with Madalena, and Lazarus left with Pedro. She looked out the window at Lazarus following his father, his head bent, and Pedro closing the gate behind them.

Angela had never felt so powerless, so impaled by the sadness around her.

That night, Lazarus came home early. Angela was coming home from the garden, and she gave him an inquisitive look.

"I have a few things to fix in the backyard. I'll do that since the weather has been tolerant. Call me when dinner is ready." And he walked down the garden, looking at the winter shrubs and winter daises, resilient and wild. He walked all the way back to the garden, to the wall that had fallen with the last tremor. Angela had been pestering him to fix that wall for months.

During dinner, everyone was uncharacteristically somber. There was no small talk, no banter. All they could hear was the silverware clinking on the plates. Viriato whimpered, and Hercules sniffed Dom Carlos's leg; but not even Hercules was interested in a few juicy ankles. Angela was thinking about her home and how happy it had been just a few weeks ago. And now here they were, soaked with sadness.

When Angela talked to the monsignor about Pedro, the monsignor said, "Hate is harmful child. It is more harmful to those who hate than to those who are hated. Get it out of your heart."

"I can't. It is as if I need it to protect Lazarus. I always thought that Pedro would end up harming Lazarus, and now I think that Pedro has found a way to do harm. Look at what is happening with Madalena and Saul. I think my father-in-law has a hand in it."

The monsignor was quiet. He too believed that Pedro was doing his own special brand of evil.

"Lazarus has been under his father's influence in this last week. It seems like he is ten years old all over again," Angela said with disgust.

"I've noticed it," the monsignor said.

"And he told me that he is going to catch limpets with his father this evening. Lazarus hates limpets."

The monsignor was quiet for a long while. "Pedro used to force Lazarus to go and catch limpets," the monsignor said.

"That's what I mean, Monsignor, when he was ten or thirteen. But now he is a married man. He doesn't have to do what his father wants him to do."

The monsignor breathed heavily and got up from the chair. "It is very hard to get out from under oppression, Angela. The door may be open for Lazarus to escape, but his spirit may be blind from years of abuse."

Angela left with a heavy heart. When she got home, Lazarus was already there. It was not like Lazarus to come home early like that, and he had done it almost every day that week.

"I'm going to make you the other sabot," he said to Angela.

Lazarus had made a pair of sabots for her a few days ago and lost one. Angela felt that Lazarus was doing odds and ends as if he was going away.

Her imagination sometimes ran away from her, and this was one of those times. Her skin lately was prickled with goose bumps, as if tiny antennae were capturing nuances in the air—something that she should be aware of, but it was escaping her.

During that week, Lazarus came home early. And right after supper, he wanted to go to bed and make love. It was not his free spirit and laughing sessions of lovemaking; it was lovemaking, quiet and intense, without words or silly songs.

He held onto her with a grip of a drowning man and whispered, "I love you, and I will love you even when I'm dead."

Angela didn't know what to do to bring his joy back. She held him tightly against her breast and kissed him incessantly, murmuring all the things she knew he liked to hear.

At eleven o'clock, he got up to meet his father at the cliffs. Angela saw him get dressed with heavy clothes, as if the weather was colder than it really was.

"Be safe, Lazarus. I wish you didn't have to go," she said as the hair on her scalp rose with alarm and cold sweat coated her skin.

"Me too," he said. He kissed her again and left.

And that was the last time she saw Lazarus.

17

Losing Lazarus

Angela woke up with a start. It was as if someone wanted to knock the door down. She ran downstairs, and in front of her, all wet and disheveled, Pedro Matias was screaming, "Lazarus fell into the sea! He fell into the sea, and I couldn't help him!"

Angela lit up a lamp and pushed Pedro into the house, near the light so she could look at him. Maybe this was a dream. She would wake up soon. Lazarus would shake her, and tell her that she was making weird noises.

Pedro was crying and holding in his hand Lazarus's wristwatch.

"This is the only thing I saw on the rocks. Lazarus is gone," he said. And he sobbed uncontrollably.

Dom Carlos came down the stairs, following the noise. He heard what Pedro had said and looked at Angela. She was as if made of white stone—pale, rigid, and very quiet. Slowly, she closed her eyes and fainted.

When Angela woke up, she was in her bed. *So this was a bad dream*, she thought. She turned her head to the side; Lazarus would be there, sleeping peacefully.

But Lazarus was not there. Dom Carlos was sitting on a chair looking at her, while downstairs, people cried.

"Dom Carlos," she said weakly, "this is a dream."

Dom Carlos got up knocking the chair down and held her in his arms. "I'm sorry," he said. "I'm so sorry."

Is he saying that Lazarus died? Angela looked at him to be reassured that everything was a mistake. Lazarus was downstairs after all.

She looked at Dom Carlos, and then realization sunk in.

She let out cries, as if she was being stabbed to death. People came running up the stairs and crammed the room, adding their cries to Angela's. Then the room was full of wailing and praying. Someone was screaming, and she vaguely recognized the agonizing sound of Dona Amelia's despair. Then it was the monsignor yelling, "Get out!" as if they were all in a sinking ship.

"Wake me up," Angela sobbed, hanging onto Dom Carlos' shoulders, not allowing him to leave her with that awful reality.

Dom Carlos rocked her back and forth gently in his arms, tears falling on her head.

"Where is my father?" she sobbed.

"At the cliffs with the other men …" He couldn't say the rest.

"To save Lazarus?" she asked, her voice replete with hope.

"No … They are hoping to …recover his body," he whispered.

The men were at the cliffs, in vigil by the sea. Sooner or later the sea would return the lifeless bodies of those it killed. Sometimes, they would wash ashore at a different village. But sometimes they never came up; these were the eternally gone.

"He is alive, I feel it. He can't be gone …" She keened, falling to the floor on her knees and placing her hands high up in a pyramid of prayer.

"Please, please, bring him back. Bring him back!"

For the next few days, the house was full of people—Angela's parents, her friends, Lazarus's family, the neighbors, and the monsignor.

The sea had kept Lazarus. By now, there was no hope the sea would return him. There would be nothing of him, between the sharks and the rocks. And with this knowledge, the villagers slowly retreated into their homes, praying for Lazarus's soul and Angela's sanity. And although the village knew that he would not come back, Angela kept on asking; it was the first thing she asked coming out of her heavily induced slumber. "Did you find him?"

Small, sullen Rosa whispered to Dom Carlos, "Tell her that they never come back, never, even when we pray to God. The sea is stronger than God."

"I will," he answered and looked at Angela sleeping.

Angela had taken tonics from the monsignor, from Ascendida, and from Natividade and medication from the city doctor who had come at Dom Carlos's request. She could hardly keep awake, and she remembered vaguely that, if she died, she would catch up to Lazarus in his journey to heaven. She dreamed of running after Lazarus, walking toward a bright light, calling out, "Wait for me, baby Jesus!" He stopped and looked back at her, waved, and then disappeared. There was no more light. Angela was standing alone on a cobblestoned street that she had never seen, and she didn't know how to get home. She looked around at the freshly painted stucco houses, their windows open letting the curtains gently sway in and out with the breeze. It was such a beautiful place. She called out, but no one answered.

After the second week, the monsignor talked with the authorities about a death certificate. There would be a Mass for Lazarus. The monsignor was afraid that, if Angela didn't have a ritual to make her accept that Lazarus was dead, she would lose her mind.

And so they had the Mass, the condolences, and the last good-byes to Lazarus.

Angela couldn't feel her feet on the ground as she walked to church and back. The church was full of people praying and crying, but they sounded so distant. Around her, there was a silence that she had never experienced; it made a buzzing sound inside of her head. She squeezed Lazarus's wristwatch, the only thing that felt real, in her hand.

Her friends and family stayed with her at night, cajoling her to sleep and rest. Maria Gomes sat terrified in the corner of the room as Angela prayed, her eyes burning, her voice cracking with sorrow, kneeling on the floor, bending over, heaving with sobs, screaming at God, praying, and falling spent on the floor.

"I died and went to hell because I hurt someone. I am expiating now for that sin, something I've done in a life that I don't remember, something terrible. Forgive me, forgive me. Forgive me if I caused someone to suffer. This is the only explanation for my sorrow and the only way I can forgive You for taking away my Lazarus. I chose this path for the enhancement of my soul; this is my redemption. If not, then I cannot love You, a mean-hearted God who allows his children to hurt this much. I cannot live in a world that delivers such random suffering. I've been good. I've been good. I've tried to be the best that I could, and You took my Lazarus!" Angela accused, her voice faltering from her ire.

When Angela fell asleep, sometimes on the floor, her father placed her on the bed and kept vigil. They took turns. Only the very close were allowed to stay with Angela, cloistered in her room. Madalena and Ascendida were terrible reminders of loss, and every time Angela looked at them, she went into despair. "You, you know what I'm feeling, don't you?" she cried.

The village got together and divided the chores around the house so Angela's parents could keep her company. Nascimento came every morning, while Maria and Joaquim were working. She sat reading to her, but Angela slept. Sometimes they asked Dom Carlos to take over so they could take a reprieve. The lodgers kept coming—some because they needed a place to stay, others because they were curious about the young girl losing her mind with grief. Maria Gomes and her husband ran the house as Angela would. They never turned out a lodger; they never explained or apologized for the crying in one of the rooms. As much as Dom Carlos wanted to stop them from taking lodgers while Angela was mourning, her parents never listened.

"This is what she expects of us—life as usual," they said.

Christmas had come and gone. Angela became aware of time when she heard a child on the street yell out a game. "January thirty-first; you're it!" Her mother was sitting next to her, embroidering a tablecloth. Angela was just sitting, looking into nothing, once in a while letting out a wail as if the whole tragic event was just happening, and she was too tired to pray.

The doctor said that Angela was suffering from melancholia—a very natural process of grief. She should be allowed to be sad. The trick was to move through her sadness and not be stuck in it. She needed her family and friends to keep her company and slowly regain normalcy.

She was doing well, even if it didn't seem so.

Neighbors and friends slowly left, only visiting occasionally to offer food and other services. Angela started to refuse the medication, looking suspiciously at it. Those were the pills that made her sleep and forget, and then she woke up, and it was like walking on clouds, her head heavy with a buzzing silence that made her cry.

When she asked her mother to go home, Maria did, a ray of hope in her heart. The doctor said that it would be good news when Angela started to want to do things. It was a good time too; there were no lodgers. Angela could slowly get used to the house again. Maria Gomes warned Dom Carlos that he should be alert that Angela probably would scream in the middle of the night and run all over the room looking for Lazarus.

But there was no screaming in the middle of the night. The house was as quiet as a sepulcher. Dom Carlos spent the night sitting on a chair in his room, forcing himself not to go to sleep so he could hear everything that was going on.

A week went by, punctuated by a weird silence and false sense of normalcy.

And one night, he woke up with the door opening and closing softly. He ran down the stairs and out into the garden following a light. Angela was holding a Petromax lamp in one hand, and with the other, she was holding a cape over her head. The menagerie was following her, one after the other like a rehearsed procession.

"Angela!" he called out.

She stopped and looked back. The lamp was casting a weary, ghostly light.

"Where are you going?" he asked, catching up and taking the lamp from her.

"To the cliffs," she said. "I need to see where he fell."

Dom Carlos was speechless. "What did you say?" he asked after a brief silence.

"I just need to sit by the cliffs and look at the sea. That's all."

"Can't you wait for the morning?" he asked.

"No. It was night when he fell into the ocean. I want to see how."

"I'll go with you," he said.

And they walked down the pastures, followed by the menagerie. Dom Carlos had his arm around Angela's shoulders, for support and for warmth.

She was so thin. She had always been thin, but her bones were now sticking out under his hand.

"You are too thin," he murmured.

"I will get better with time," she answered quietly.

To Dom Carlos, this sounded like a promise, and he felt joy. Angela was on her way up if she was making plans to be better.

When they got to the cliffs, Dom Carlos illuminated the narrow path to the rocks where the village caught limpets. It was a narrow, treacherous path, and at the bottom of it, there was a very small, rocky beach. In low tide, no more than three of four people could stand on such a small beach; at high tide, the beach completely disappeared. As they descended, Dom Carlos was ahead of Angela to illuminate the path. He turned back to look at her, and a mile away, he saw light on the cliffs farther north on the island, behind Pedro Matias's barn.

They stood on the small beach, the wind fustigating their bodies.

"Where did he fall?" she asked, looking up at Dom Carlos.

There were so many points of danger on that narrow path. If one lost one's footing, he would topple sideways right into the sea.

"Over there." he pointed to the rock where Pedro Matias had stood as he'd explained how Lazarus had fallen.

Angela was looking at the ragged edge of the cliff, imagining Lazarus falling over with a scream.

"He must have called me when he fell, and I didn't wake up," she said quietly.

Dom Carlos placed the lamp on the ground and embraced her.

"Oh, Angela, don't torment yourself with *ifs*; it doesn't change anything."

"But I can't understand how I was so oblivious to his terror; I should have known! I should have awoken!" she wailed.

Dom Carlos said, trying to protect her from the wind, "Promise me that you'll never come here without me. I'm not asking you not to come. I just don't want you to come alone."

She looked out into the dark sea. Was Lazarus there, in that water? She couldn't feel it. If he was there, she should be able to feel it.

"He is not here, Dom Carlos," she said softly.

"What do you mean?"

"He is not here, in this sea. I can't feel it," she said, again looking up at him.

Denial, he thought and sighed. "Let's go home before the tide gets us."

Angela was walking up the incline ahead of him. They were soaking wet from the angry waves battering the rocks. Dom Carlos held the Petromax lamp high up so she could see, and then the Petromax light went out. He saw again the same light on the north cliffs. People were on the cliffs for reasons other than limpets, and he tensed.

When they got home, it was almost dawn.

Dom Carlos took the cape from her shoulders and placed it open on two chairs to dry.

"Go and change and come down. I need to talk to you," he said.

He too changed, and when Angela came down to the kitchen, the fire was burning, and Dom Carlos was drinking moonshine. Angela had never seen Dom Carlos drink moonshine. She stopped in front of him, looking at the empty glass. He poured a glass for her and another for himself.

This village was going to be his undoing.

They sat down in front of the iron stove in the kitchen. They were quiet, making faces and drying up moonshine tears.

Dom Carlos turned to her and smoothed her hair. There was such sadness in her eyes that he too wanted to cry.

"Angela," he said with a strangled voice, "I promised Lazarus that, if anything happened to him, I would take care of you." He stopped because the words were choking him as he looked at her crying, silent tears that fell on her hands.

"I know that you can take care of yourself. You are like this island, small and tough. But please let me keep my promise to Lazarus," Dom Carlos said, letting the tears and sobs pour out of him. His trembling hands picked up another glass of moonshine. "You have to promise me that you will not go to the cliffs alone."

"I promise," she said quietly. "I am like Hawk Island—tough. From now on, you can call me Hawk."

And they fell into each other's arms, sobbing.

They stood like that, crying and hugging each other, until she fell asleep, her head heavy on his chest from moonshine and crying. He took her into her room. She feebly opened her eyes, looked at him, and fell back to sleep. He took her shoes off and pulled the covers up to her chin. He gently caressed her face and went out to call Maria Gomes, to direct the running of the house.

When Maria Gomes got to the house, Rosa had just arrived. She looked up the stairs, waiting to see Angela.

"Is …Lazarus with my family?" Rosa asked quietly.

"Yes, darling," Maria said. "They are in heaven."

Rosa was not thinking of heaven. She was thinking about the deep and dark waters of the sea. She was thinking about that brilliant blue in the summer and the dark gray of the winter and Lazarus and her entire family at the bottom of that sea, resting in a bed of sand, with their eyes closed and arms stretched out, as if waiting to be rescued. She almost could see her mother's black hair swaying with the water and her baby brother's beautiful curls getting undone. Esperança, her sister, was wearing her brand-new shoes before she had gone out to see the angry brook. Did she still have her new shoes on? Did Lazarus fall softly among her family? Or did he end up somewhere else, alone?

"What is it, darling?" Maria asked, placing a hand on Rosa's shoulder.

"If they are at the bottom of the sea, how can they be in heaven?" Rosa asked with big, inquisitive eyes.

"The soul, honey, the soul goes to God when we die."

"I wish their bodies were also with God," Rosa added sadly.

Rosa was thinking about the power of God. He could do anything, and He decided to separate the body and the soul at the end. That didn't feel right at all. She had never seen anyone's soul. She only remembered loving the body. Why would a loving God think that the body could be discarded? *Maybe God never looked closely at my baby brother, how beautiful he was*, Rosa thought. If He had, maybe he would have changed His mind.

Dom Carlos came down quietly and sat at the table waiting for breakfast. He heard Rosa's simple wish. At times, he felt jealous of other people's faith.

They were never alone if they believed that God was there with a higher plan and that, in the end, all would be revealed. That surrender to a higher power must be so liberating. Just to believe in that was comforting.

But not for Dom Carlos; there was no comfort for him, because he had no use for a capricious God.

After that night, Angela didn't go to the cliffs. Either she wanted to spare Dom Carlos from the treacherous trip, or she didn't feel it helped her understanding. But she couldn't sleep. Slowly she stopped the sleeping potions, and now she couldn't sleep. She never had slept well, especially if she was alone; and now she was alone.

Angela came down the stairs trying not to make noise so Dom Carlos would not jump out of his skin. She sat on a kitchen bench, her back resting on the cold stucco. The menagerie came slowly to her, sniffing, licking her hands, and making soft sounds.

But Dom Carlos was in tune with the noises of the house and heard Angela's footsteps on the stairs. He came down running.

"Where are you going?" he asked.

"I couldn't sleep," she said, sitting down at the table.

Dom Carlos sat next to her. "Do you want tea?" he asked.

"No. I wish I could sleep. I haven't slept for days. I heard my parents talk to the monsignor about having me …hospitalized. They thing I'm going crazy."

Dom Carlos frowned and added. "You will sleep … Give it time. You don't need to be hospitalized … They are just worried."

She stared at the wall. "I can't sleep alone," she said. "Those stories that you've heard about me sleeping with Lazarus since I was twelve are true."

He had heard those stories, and he'd wondered.

"I will die if they stick me in the hospital … They will pump me full of drugs so I will not feel anything. Don't let them do that …if I'm not strong enough to fight them; don't let them do that to me. I must find my way. I must find my fisherman," she said.

"Your fisherman?" he asked puzzled.

"Every night, since I can remember, before going to sleep, I closed my eyes and saw a fisherman with a net over his shoulder going by the gate. I look after him, barefoot, straight back, his pant legs rolled up to his knees. He wears a black beret and a green and white, gingham shirt. After he goes by. I fall asleep. But one night, I closed my eyes, and the fisherman didn't come, and I couldn't sleep."

"And this temperamental fisherman, how often does he come by?" Dom Carlos asked.

"He is a fair-weather friend. He only comes by when I am happy. When I am sad, he doesn't, unless I am with Lazarus," she said. "I slept with my parents until I was ten, and then the monsignor found out and shamed me into my own bed."

"No wonder you don't have other siblings," Dom Carlos said.

Angela smiled sadly. "Yes, no wonder."

And she thought about her twin, who her mother had miscarried; she lost one baby and kept the other.

"I was never meant to be alone," she murmured, totally engrossed in her thoughts of her lost twin. She added softly, "Sometimes I think I'm losing my mind. I can't sleep and rest from this terrible pain. If I only could sleep ..."

"Let me be your fisherman tonight," Dom Carlos said.

He straddled the bench and rested his back against the wall. She sighed deeply and leaned her head on his chest. In a few minutes, she was snoring.

He too fell asleep, and Angela woke up later with the roosters announcing the morning and with Dom Carlos drooling on her shoulder.

The winter was in full swing. It had been a terrible season, meaner and colder than usual. The sea was louder, hungrier, unforgiving and darker; it threw at the island salty mist that clung to the skin and burned the lips. The cold went deep into the bone, so deep that only a roaring fire in the shelter of home could dry it out. The sky was a blanket of gray and rain. The unrelenting wind fustigated the clouds, thin and fleeting across the sky.

Hawk Island, and especially Two Brooks, raw from loss, couldn't wait for spring, for the sun and for hope.

And life, resilient or indifferent, went on; Nascimento got married to her beloved Jaime just before Christmas, when the village was mourning Lazarus. Nascimento went up the road to the church with a group of friends and family as if she was going to a funeral. Everyone was quiet and denying themselves happiness for Angela's sake. And Nascimento had such joy in her heart to be marrying Jaime and such sadness for Angela and Madalena.

"I wish I could lock away half of myself for a while," Nascimento said to

Jaime, "that half of me that is sad for Angela and Madalena and guilty for being happy."

Ascendida was pregnant with another child on top of her two sets of twins. She was sullen and resentful for being pregnant again and directed her misery at Aldo. She froze him out with cold silences and snide remarks about love and responsibility, all the while aching for Mario as if he had just been torn from her heart.

Aldo kept on fighting between his two foes—the need for drink and for his redemption in Ascendida's eyes. There were times that he could shoulder everything that came his way, but other times, Ascendida's coldness hurt him so deeply that he left the house and walked down to the cliffs. Could the sea be colder than his heart during those dark moments? He knew that Ascendida was home thinking that he was getting drunk and swelling in her resentment of him. If he fell into the sea, he wouldn't be any colder than he was, and it would be so easy just to let go.

Madalena was hoping and waiting for a letter from Saul. She wrote to him every day and put away the letter. One day, she would find out where he was and send him a torrent of love, guilt, reproach, and hope.

Angela was slowly getting used to the idea that Lazarus was gone. Sometimes, this realization was so real that she broke down crying with such vivid pain, as if it had just happened. Although these episodes became fewer and shorter, when she was visited by that familiar but unannounced sorrow, she would be awake for days and nights, as if on a vigil, waiting for the fisherman by the gate, waiting for the sense of loss to abate.

And one night, when the fisherman did not go by the gate, she knocked on Dom Carlos's door. He was awake, reading. When she opened the door, she felt a tremendous sense of shame. She was a grown woman. What was she doing? But before she answered her own question, Dom Carlos got up and took her in by the hand to the bed.

"Can't sleep?" he asked.

Angela lay down, completely spent. "I'm so tired," she whispered, closing her eyes.

He pulled the covers up to her chin, grabbed a blanked from the armoire, and lay next to her, over the covers. Before he blew out the light, she was already snoring.

Dom Carlos was awake most of the night. He was hypersensitive to everything—to the perils of Angela's insomnia, to a gossiping village, to a promise to care for a heartbroken widow. He felt unsettled and weary. The menagerie was making noises downstairs, and the wind was howling around windows and doors, and he heard the pounding of hoofs on the road.

Someone was out and maybe for mischief.

Dom Carlos had kept from Angela the fact that Pedro was trying to take the carpentry shop and everything else away from her. In Pedro's head, everything belonged to his son, and his son belonged to him; since there were no children, everything that was Lazarus's should return to him.

Pedro was a bully, but he knew when to quit when Angela's attorney produced all the documentation necessary to nullify his claim. He could always find other ways to get to her, even if Dom Carlos thought he could protect her. He could always spread the rumors about that cunt; she was sleeping with Dom Carlos. She was sleeping with him even before Lazarus died; some would believe him, and some wouldn't.

Angela woke up to the sound of Narciso, the rooster, singing. She looked at Dom Carlos wrapped up in his blanket and still asleep. Quietly, she left the room.

Almost every night, Angela went to Dom Carlos's room and slept like a baby. She was no longer questioning the appropriateness of this action. If she could sleep and if Dom Carlos didn't mind, she would make use of that fisherman by the gate. This was their secret. No one had to know. No one needed to know. She was hurting no one.

The Sacristy met at Ascendida's for the first time since Lazarus died. The last time they'd met, Nascimento shared her belief that she had seen two men hauling a dead man up the pastures. No one believed her, because no one was dead. Saul and Manuel had left the island, and Lazarus had fallen into the sea. There was no body of evidence to sustain Nascimento's suspicions. And so they didn't talk about that anymore. It was probably a drunken man being helped by his friends.

Although they didn't talk about it, they remembered, once in a while, Nascimento's voice. "He was dead. I'm telling you!"

"Carlota received a letter from Maia," Madalena said. "She is going to have a baby."

Another baby, Ascendida thought. *Why do we keep putting children in this terrible world?*

"She also receives letters from some other part of the world. I know she does. She says that she has family in Brazil, but I …I think it is Saul writing to her," Madalena said.

"Have you had the chance to look at the envelope?" Angela asked.

"I got hold of one letter. It was from Luas Aroma, Carlota's cousin in Minas." Madalena was pensive. "Why doesn't he write to me? Is he that hurt?"

"Some of us have been wounded too many times," Ascendida said. "We only know that life is a bitch, and then we die."

"Aren't you a breath of hope?" Nascimento offered sarcastically. "I should stop hanging around with you creeps. Look at your sorry asses; you all lost the men you love. Bad luck may be looking for one of you again, and here I am, in the way … Something bad happens to me, or worse, to Jaime, I would never forgive you, never!" she concluded.

Spring that year came with such splendor that, if hearts were not broken, Hawk Island could be paradise. It was as if nature was apologizing for all the suffering. The brooks were running with clear water, the sun was out every day, the flowers were abundant and lasted longer than usual, the rain was measured, and the sky was full of bright stars and beautiful moonlight.

A new woman teacher would be coming in a few days to replace Maria Augusta, who had stepped in for André Moniz when he'd left after the Night Justice incident. Maria Augusta was going to marry her Canadian this summer, and she couldn't wait to live in a land that didn't know about the mean-hearted rumors, in a place where she wasn't known for having the whitest and fattest buttocks on the island. In the land of her Canadian, she would be only his bride.

The teacher was coming early, not to make the transition for the children easier but to appease the wagging tongues of the villagers. They were astounded that the monsignor had capitulated and allowed Dom Carlos to continue as a lodger after Lazarus's death. Everyone knew about the fight between Dom Carlos and the monsignor. And more perplexing yet was the fact that Dom Carlos had won.

The day Dom Carlos got home after his encounter with the monsignor, Angela already knew about the fight. Regina Sales had come by and told her that the monsignor and the engineer were screaming at each other, and all people heard was her name—Angela this and Angela that.

"What was that all about?" Angela asked Dom Carlos.

"He wants me to leave," he said.

Angela was holding a jug of water, and suddenly her hands lost grip, and the jar fell in the middle of the kitchen, spilling water and glass chards all over the floor. She let out a yelp and knelt immediately to pick up the chards, cutting her hand.

"Hey," he said, kneeling next to her on the wet floor. "Hey, give me your hand." He put his handkerchief around the cut and looked at her. "I'm not leaving. Not unless you want me to."

Angela took a long breath and looked at her hand and then at him. "Everybody is talking about us," she said quietly. "The monsignor was only thinking about me."

Dom Carlos held his breath for a few seconds. He asked again, "Would it be easier for you if I left?"

They stood up in the middle of the kitchen. Rosa came running with a mop and started to clean the kitchen. Dom Carlos was still waiting for Angela's answer. He would leave. He would do whatever she wanted him to do.

"He hired a teacher, a woman, to come here to my house as a permanent lodger," she said.

"I know. He told me," he said. "He does not believe that we are lovers, you know."

"He told me the same. He is only thinking about the inappropriateness of it all," she added. "And if he knew we sleep together …"

"Hawk, we don't sleep together," he said impatiently. "We don't make love, we are not intimate, and we don't even kiss … But he was worried about the rumors."

"I don't give a shit about what people think! They have no idea how I fight my battles," she snapped and left the room.

"You should have Ascendida patch up that hand," he called out after her.

For the last few days, she had been able to sleep alone, only occasionally waking up in the middle of the night. She was almost asleep when she heard a knock on her door, and she sat upright, surprised.

Dom Carlos came in with a lamp in hand. "When is this teacher coming?" he asked.

"In two days," she answered.

"Then come and sleep in my bed, because after she is here, you will not. Ever."

He was not sure if he was asking for her or his benefit. "I guess I miss you," he added.

"I'm trying to do it alone ..." she said. "I'm ashamed for not being able to conquer this weakness."

"I know," he said softly.

"I am also tempted ... I sleep so well when you are there," she said sheepishly.

"I know that too," he said gently.

He waited.

She was assessing. Somehow something had shifted. She frowned.

"This is a unique opportunity for you to have two blissful nights of sleep—no lodgers, no one to notice. And that will be it. We will never sleep together again," he said.

"How tragic!" she mocked. "I guess this was what the monsignor meant— us alone with no one to notice ..." She grinned briefly as if she had lost the ability to smile.

But she got up and followed him into his room. As soon as her head touched the pillow, she let out a long sigh and closed her eyes.

Dom Carlos was staring at her face, a few inches away from his, and he gently stroked her cheek. "Sleep well, Hawk," he murmured, wrapping himself in his blanket.

18

Dona Mafalda

The teacher arrived on a Sunday spring morning. Dona Mafalda was a pretty woman in her thirties. She had a bubbly personality and was full of self-importance and protocol. Dona Mafalda's hair was brown and shiny, full of natural bouncing curls; her eyes were warm brown, with long feathery lashes; and her mouth was pouty red with lipstick. When she smiled, she showed straight, small, pearly teeth. She was a little too plump to be elegant, but there was a way about her that spoke of money and of a cultured life. She was finely dressed and brought three trunks full of clothes and another three with books, records, and a gramophone.

When the new teacher met Angela, she shook Angela's hand with great enthusiasm, and in a glance, she took stock: Angela was not pretty; she was small, too thin, and a bit too tanned to be proper; she wore an apron and sabots. Sabots. Who in the world wore sabots anymore?

Dona Mafalda Maria de Lourdes Dias Santos Sampaio da Cruz. She would like to be addressed as Dona Mafalda.

Angela showed her the room and explained the rules of the house.

Dona Mafalda surveyed her surroundings with a critical eye and said after a while, "This will have to do, I guess." She smiled openly at Angela and shook her hand again. "I accept," she said, as if the room had been up for negotiation. "It is a pleasure to meet you, Angela. I am sure I will be very happy here in your village."

"I have two other rooms, but this one is larger," Angela said.

"I'm assuming that you gave me the best, my dear," she replied, sounding virtuous with the sacrifice of accepting the room.

"No, the best I have is occupied by Dom Carlos, the engineer across the hall," Angela said.

"Oh! You have other lodgers?" she asked with distaste.

"Yes, at full capacity, I can have four lodgers. I was in the process of getting one more room, but …" Her voice trailed off.

She was not going to talk about Lazarus and his drowning.

"Where is this engineer of ours?" Dona Mafalda asked.

"He is in the city. He will be coming home for supper," Angela said and left her new lodger organizing the room, giving orders to Lucas Pires, the mechanic, who was helping her with her trunks.

When Dom Carlos came home for supper he looked around. "She didn't come?" he asked, feeling hopeful.

"She is here," Angela said.

"How is she?" he asked.

"Pretty. She is a pretty woman. She has her own Victrola." Angela refrained from telling him her first impression of Dona Mafalda.

"Her name is Dona Mafalda Maria de Lourdes Dias Santos Sampaio da Cruz Calvario de Dores Pedrinha e Calhau."

Dom Carlos stopped in the middle of the kitchen and asked, perplexed, "You are joking, aren't you?"

Angela laughed. Dom Carlos hadn't heard her laugh since Lazarus died. He missed that throaty sound of her laughter, and he grinned. Just for Angela's laughter, he was grateful to the new teacher.

"I exaggerated but not by much. She is also from royalty," Angela added. "She made sure to let me know."

"What does she expect you to do, curtsy when you look at her?"

"Or genuflect at her feet," Angela added. And she laughed again.

Dom Carlos was basking in the sound of her laughter when Dona Mafalda came down the stairs, her hips gently bouncing with every step.

She had the demeanor of a queen.

He turned around and looked at Dona Mafalda and extended his hand, "Welcome Dona Mafalda," he said. "I am Dom Carlos."

Dona Mafalda looked as if she had been struck by lightning. She was rendered speechless. Dona Mafalda had never thought that she was going to live in the same house as this Adonis, here in front of her, with his hand extended to shake hers. Could it be possible that finally she had found someone at her level in this poor village? This was beyond her expectations.

Right there and then, Dona Mafalda fell in love. If love at first sight could have been illustrated, this was it.

As the weeks passed, Dom Carlos's impression of Dona Mafalda didn't falter. He detested Dona Mafalda, even before he met her. Now that he knew her, he was justified about the things he thought she was. She was an agent of the monsignor, she was an interloper, and she was upsetting the balance of the house with her bubbly personality, always full of glee in her pedantic manner, dismissing everyone and everything that didn't have to do with her wishes.

Dona Mafalda never missed the opportunity to talk about the mainland and her oligarchy family in the south of the country, her love of teaching and finding a job on her own, and her cultured and refined upbringing.

Angela had witnessed the love struck Dona Mafalda, and she took every possible chance to tease Dom Carlos. He would give her accusing stares, but the result was even more teasing.

"You have to come and see my collection of classic books and music. I have my own gramophone—my Victrola," Dona Mafalda said triumphantly one day after dinner when Dom Carlos was settling in to read his book.

There was only one other Victrola in the village; it belonged to Oldemira Soares, a sweet and lonely spinster who had no idea how to replace the needle and listened to scratching sounds more so than to music. Dom Carlos had replaced Oldemira's needle, and she too had fallen in love with him.

"Dom Carlos is an expert on gramophones," Angela said, remembering his kindness to Oldemira.

Dom Carlos looked at Angela sharply before accepting the invitation and going upstairs with Dona Mafalda.

"This is a marvelous machine," Dona Mafalda said, as soon as they entered the room and immediately started winding up the Victrola. Soon Beethoven was pounding throughout the house.

Dom Carlos was perusing the records and books, letting out small sounds of approval while Dona Mafalda beamed. She sat across from him and delicately sipped her tea while they enjoyed the music.

After Dona Mafalda met her students and Maria Augusta, she fell into a nice routine. She came home from school, prepared for the next day, and then she had dinner with the other lodgers. She spent the evenings reading, listening to her radio, and drinking tea. Very often, she invited Dom Carlos for a Victrola session in her room, and like a gentleman, he accepted. Angela would come in to refill their teacups. And when Dona Mafalda's plump back was turned to them, Angela would wink at Dom Carlos.

"Stop it!" he said after a session of Beethoven.

"Victrola night. How quaint," Angela said with a grin.

"This is terrible! I cannot be pursued 24-7. It is exhausting," he murmured.

"What's so bad about her Dom Carlos? She is handsome, cultured, rich … She owns a Victrola … She is in love with you."

But Dom Carlos was not even upset. He was laughing too because Angela was finding humor, as she used to do, and it had started with Dona Mafalda. For that reason alone, he couldn't dislike the woman; she gave Angela a reason to laugh.

"At least I'll have a reprieve for a week. I am going to England for the new machines we've talked about," he said.

Angela stopped her task of cleaning the table. Suddenly she became very serious. "I had forgotten about that," she said.

And that night, when Dona Mafalda heard about his trip to England, she looked deflated. He even declined Victrola night, and she went to her room utterly disappointed.

Angela was sitting quietly in the kitchen observing the exchange between Dom Carlos and Dona Mafalda.

"You are such a heartbreaker," Angela said.

"Don't mock me," he said. "One whole week without Dona Mafalda sounds heavenly. I'll take Thunder to the city and leave him with the chief of police; it is a beautiful night for a ride, and I miss that horse. I have my stuff in the apartment already."

"I don't trust you," Angela said. "Are you really going to England? Or are you playing Zorro?" she asked.

He took a plane ticket out of his pocket shirt and showed it to her. "You sound like a wife," he accused.

The night was indeed beautiful. A full moon turned everything dark blue and mysterious. Dom Carlos felt exhilarated with the idea of just galloping up the forest road all the way to the city. But like an enchantress, the cliffs and the sea called him for one small adventure that night. He had seen the ships come and go in the night, and he had seen the flickering lights on the cliffs.

He prepared Thunder, put on his hat and his cape, and went down the pastures, feeling the old excitement of running free and untamed. And there they were—the flickering lights on the cliffs. He stopped Thunder and listened for noise. A small boat was circling the water, and someone in diving gear was going into the water.

Suddenly, Thunder neighed and lifted his front legs up in the air. A flung object hit the flanks of the horse, and Dom Carlos was thrown down on the rocks. As he was flying toward the abyss, his first thought was of Lazarus. If he died, he could not keep his promise. Desperately he grabbed at the edge of the cliff. He was saved by the cape, which snagged on a rock and gave him a few precious seconds to secure his holding before the tie around his neck broke and the cape flew down into darkness. His feet were dangling, trying to find a hold. He heard voices coming in his direction, and he stopped struggling in order not be seen or heard. Thunder disappeared at a furious gallop up the pastures, almost trampling the men who were trying to catch him. Dom Carlos could feel blood run down his face and the rock biting into his hands.

He didn't know how long he could hang on.

A flash of light swept the cliffs and pointed down at the water. There was laughter and someone said, "Look, he left his hat behind." And when they ran to the hat, the wind picked it up and blew it down into the sea in an elegant dive while the men stayed at the edge of the cliffs throwing rocks at the ocean.

When the men left, Dom Carlos tried to pull himself up. But the effort was thwarted by a piece of rock that came apart from the face of the cliff, and he lost his grip and fell down to what he thought was his death. He landed on a small shelf of rock. He was dazed for a while, and then he realized that he was hurt. He stood very still, and finally he understood where he was. He had seen that shelf when he came down to the cliffs with Angela. If he climbed the shelf to the other side, he would be on the path out of the cliffs.

He was in pain, and he thought that he had broken an arm and ribs. He was not sure that he could climb that path and get home safely. He was not even sure that whoever attacked him was not going to do it again.

He felt faint with the pain and passed out.

Angela was unsettled. Something was not right. She couldn't sleep and was sure that Dom Carlos was into mischief. He was playing Zorro. Of course if he had to go to the city, he should have taken his car, not a horse.

Angela tried to find some thought that gave her respite. She came downstairs and sat with the menagerie. They too were alerted, as if looking for a special sound.

And then the special sound came—Thunder's hooves on the patio. She ran outside to a frightened horse. Thunder was covered with sweat, his eyes wide with fear and his coat rippling with shivers.

There were black sleeves hiding the white stripes on his legs. Angela took the sleeves off, gave him water, mounted the horse, and whispered in his ear, "Take me to him, Thunder."

The horse took off with Angela hanging on, lying low, and her face almost touching his neck. The horse flew down the pastures straight to the cliffs and then stopped. The moon was so bright that she could see the outline of the cliffs against a sky full of stars. Her heart started to beat wildly. Dom Carlos had fallen down the cliffs. Angela put a hand over her mouth in order to stop a scream forming in her heart. She dismounted and started going down the path as if guided only by intuition. Then she saw him, facedown on the path down the cliffs.

She touched him; he was cold but alive. She was afraid that he had gone into shock. She lowered her mouth to his ear and asked between fear and hope, "Dom Carlos, can you get up?"

He tried to get up and cried out in pain. Slowly, they moved up the path to meet Thunder, waiting for them like a faithful servant.

"Can you mount?" she asked.

She helped him mount the horse and mounted behind him with her arms around his waist for support. Slowly they went up the pastures until they reached home in the wee hours of the morning.

Angela put a finger on her lips, for silence. They didn't need Dona Mafalda to witness the undoing of Zorro. They went up the stairs, trying to be as quiet as possible, while Dom Carlos was biting his lip to stifle cries of pain.

Angela took him into her room. "No one will expect you to be hiding in my room. I'll lock the door. After all, everyone believes that you are in England," she whispered in his ear, afraid of waking up Dona Mafalda and thankful that the woman was a heavy sleeper.

He closed his eyes tightly as Angela helped him sit on the bed. Unceremoniously, she started palpating his limbs, looking for broken bones. When she touched his shoulder, he let out a cry. She squeezed his ribs, and he let out a louder grunt. They both stood still, waiting for Dona Mafalda to knock at the door.

But everything was silent on the other side of the hall.

Dom Carlos was shivering and cradling his arm. Angela started to remove his wet clothes, only vaguely aware that she was stripping him. She was worried, angry, cold, and afraid, and she didn't care that Dom Carlos was naked in front of her.

"Angela," he complained feebly.

"Don't you dare to *Angela* me," she hissed, grabbing a soft and warm blanket and placing it around him. "If I was not afraid of waking up Dona Mafalda, I would spank you until your buttocks bled."

"Maybe she would enjoy the show," he said with a clenched jaw, trying to contain the pain.

"Nothing is broken, I don't think, but your shoulder is out of place, and you have bruised ribs. You have a gash on your forehead and a broken lip. All in all, you were damned lucky! I must fix your shoulder before it settles permanently out of the socket."

Dom Carlos looked at her with some panic.

Angela said, "It will hurt—tremendously, much to my delight."

Dom Carlos cradled his arm against his stomach and closed his eyes again. The blanket was slowly sliding off his body.

"Put a pillow over your mouth," Angela said. "And try not to scream."

She turned on the radio. At least Dona Mafalda was used to her turning the radio on in the middle of the night when she couldn't sleep.

He bit his already bleeding lip. "Are you enjoying this?" he whispered.

"Yes, I am. I am going to enjoy inflicting pain on you because I am furious with you," she whispered back and handed him a pillow.

When he didn't take it, she shoved it on his face. "Hold it against your mouth, or Dona Mafalda will come to your rescue."

Angela positioned herself on the bed, kneeling in front of him and placing her hands strategically on the back and front of his shoulder. She adjusted the blanket again, tucking it around him. Her touch at first was gentle. Suddenly, she pulled and pushed all at once and the pain was so great that he let out a howl into the pillow and fell forward, losing consciousness.

She cradled him against her chest, both arms around his torso.

"Fool, you damn fool!" she whispered.

Dom Carlos came out of his faint to a torrent of insults whispered in his ear.

"I'm sorry," he said. "Worrying you was the last thing I wanted to do." He looked up at her, thinking of a million things and not able to say any of them.

"Promise me," she said with urgency, "promise me that Zorro is gone, that he died tonight."

He stared at her. There was a light in his eyes that she hadn't seen before.

"I promise," he whispered.

"What in the world draws you to the cliffs? Countless people perished there. My Lazarus died there!" Her voice had a ring of franticness.

"Please," he said, soothingly. "I promise you anything you want."

"You will?" she asked, gulping down the sobs that were threatening to erupt. "You promise me that you will kill Zorro tonight, and from now on, you'll be just a boring businessman?" she said.

"I promise," he said. "But do I have to be boring?" he quipped feebly.

"I'm serious!" she snapped.

The radio was playing a fado about a lying, cheating lover. It drowned his groan of pain when Angela shoved him against the pillow.

All of that pain could have been just a nightmare, and Lazarus was there, alive, wearing his favorite pair of pajamas. And she would tell him the horrible dream she had.

"Lazarus," she murmured. Immediately she bit her lip. She didn't think she had said it aloud.

Dom Carlos closed his eyes to avoid looking at her disappointment. "I can go to my room and lock the door," he said quietly.

Angela put a hand over her heart to steady herself and turned around to gather her composure.

"Angela, I really can be quiet in my room. I promise," Dom Carlos insisted.

"Don't be silly. It is easier for me to take care of you in here. I can go in and out without raising suspicion. But if I go into your room while you are away, Rosa may notice, or even Dona Mafalda."

Angela could see him vibrating with pain. She said, "Let's try to sleep a bit. Call me if you need anything. Tomorrow, I'll find you some painkillers." She touched him lightly on the shoulder and rested her head on the pillow.

In a few moments, Angela was sleeping and drooling on herself.

Pain in the ass, Zorro killer, little bully, I think you are going to be my undoing, he thought.

Throughout the night, the pain only got worse for Dom Carlos. His body throbbed as if a million hammers were at work. He was restless, getting up, going to the window, and returning to bed again. He opened the window and threw back the shudders. The full moon came in the room, illuminating Angela snoring softly. He sat in bed looking at her until he became drowsy and fell asleep.

The following day was Sunday, and the sun came through the window with undeniable brilliance. Angela was still sleeping peacefully, her mouth open and with her hand resting on his chest.

Downstairs, Dona Mafalda screamed.

Hercules.

Angela opened her eyes and sat up in bed with a start. She looked around and jumped out of bed and then looked back at Dom Carlos.

"What happened?" she asked.

"Nothing," he said. "Hercules is having Dona Mafalda for breakfast."

"How are you?" she asked.

"I wish I had something for the pain," he said.

"I will get it today from Ascendida." She touched his face, feeling the stubble on her fingers. "You don't have a fever. I will be in with your breakfast shortly. I'll tell Dona Mafalda that I am not feeling well, and I'll keep you company." She gave him an assessment look. "You have a fierce black eye ... You look like you've been in a terrible fight."

She gently leaned down and rested her cheek on his, feeling the chafing of his beard. "I'm so grateful that you are all right," she murmured.

Angela walked briskly down the road ignoring Dona Mafalda's call behind her. Angela was on a mission. She needed pain medication for Dom Carlos for two reasons—one was because he was in pain and was up all night, and the other reason was that, on meds, he would sleep most of the time, staying out of trouble, and not be tempted to venture outside the room. Those fools from the village would kill him for sure if they made the connection between the boogeyman and Dom Carlos. At least they all believed that Dom Carlos was in England.

On her way to Ascendida, the gossip was already fully grown. Elias Mendes and his father had killed the boogeyman; they had thrown him down the cliffs. Ivo Machado had even seen the boogeyman's shoes, down on a ledge, glowing as if they were lighted. But then the high tide had come, and the wind had taken everything down to the sea. They believed that he was the devil attacking people in the village. He'd attacked Pedro Matias and Ivo Machado. Maybe he was the one posing as the Night Justice and causing all that mayhem.

"At least we know that he is dead," José Eremita said from his wheelchair. "The Mendeses saw him tumble down the cliffs with a terrible howl, just like the devil when he sees the cross. It was terrible."

Angela was almost sick listening to the stories of the boogeyman and how close to the truth it could have been. She waited for Ascendida to give her the medication.

Ascendida gave her a slanted look.

"I cut myself, and it hurts like hell," Angela said, showing her the bandaged hand. "It throbs at night, and I can't sleep."

"Just take a little bit. Break it in four; they are strong," Ascendida said, giving her the medication.

Angela sat with Ascendida and her family talking about the boogeyman and the new teacher. Aldo was saying that Lucas Pires was in love with Dona Mafalda.

"As soon as he put his hands on her trunk, he was a goner," José Eremita said, delighted with his wit.

"And Regina is saying that she saw a ghost last night," Aldo said.

Angela loved to hear gossip from Aldo. He was such a good-natured man. He could talk about all the gossip in the world and never use malice. But this time, the gossip was about her—Regina saw Lazarus. She saw Lazarus in his pajamas at the window looking at the moon.

"It was Lazarus," Aldo said, imitating Regina. "Then he disappeared inside of the room. It was the ghostly hour of three or four in the morning." Aldo laughed, quite satisfied with the little bit of theater. "Regina couldn't sleep and went up to her terrace. From there, she can see inside your garden. And she looked at the window, and there he was, very pale and very sad, looking at the moon, his arms opened wide as if he was on a cross."

Angela felt her head spin. She sat up with a thump.

"Foolish woman!" Ascendida said. "She probably saw a shadow."

Angela couldn't wait to go home so she could drug Dom Carlos up.

Imagine if people started to say that Lazarus was a ghost?

When Angela got home, it was later than she thought. Dona Mafalda was in the garden reading and drinking tea. Angela's mother came to Dona Mafalda's rescue and prepared her breakfast. The morning was glorious, full of sun and soft breeze.

Dona Mafalda looked at Angela and said, "You don't look well, my dear. I hear you making noises and crying all through the night. Can't you sleep?"

"I have nightmares and wake up often in the night," Angela answered, somewhat truthfully. "I will be resting today. If you need anything, my mother will help you."

As soon as Dona Mafalda went to church, Angela locked the doors so Dom

Carlos could go to the bathroom. He took a shower and tried to shave, but he only accomplished cutting himself.

"Let me," Angela said, taking the shaving knife from his hand.

He looked at her suspiciously. "That thing is really sharp," he said.

But Angela didn't pay attention and made him sit facing the window and the morning sun. The sounds of the village came in diffused by the distance, the smell of soap permeated the house, and the silence was soothing and peaceful. She leathered his face as he closed his eyes, lifting his face to her. He sighed.

"I could get used to this," he said quietly.

"I loved to shave Lazarus," she said after a long silence.

It was so easy to think that she was shaving Lazarus. The knife rasping softly down Dom Carlos's neck that was so much like Lazarus's beautiful, strong, perfect neck.

"He was beautiful," she said dreamily. "I have never seen such a beautiful face as his."

She looked critically at Dom Carlos, assessing her work. "You too could be beautiful, if it weren't for your teeth," she said.

"What's wrong with my teeth?" he asked defensively.

"Your incisors overlap a little."

He ran his tongue over the offending incisors, and Angela grinned. She bent down and kissed his cheek. Her lips lingered on his smooth face.

"The kiss …is part of the job," she said, almost embarrassed. "It started with my father and then Lazarus …" She looked away.

It didn't escape Dom Carlos the sadness in her eyes.

She was not thinking about her father and the kiss after shaving; she was thinking about Lazarus—what she did with him.

"Thank you. You are an accomplished barber," he said.

"I'm your savior, your nurse, your barber … What else is there that I haven't been?" she said, putting away the shaving kit.

"I can think of hundreds of things," he offered quietly.

"Now you are going to take this for the pain," she said, ignoring the comment. "It will take you out of circulation for a few hours, and let's go up to your room before you're caught."

Angela told Dom Carlos about the ghost stories in the village. She gently touched his back and shoulder as she imitated Regina telling Aldo about the ghost.

"Bloody people!" he muttered.

His injuries had no sign of infection. His ribs were bruised but not cracked, and the arm would be completely fine after a few massages and rest. His face, however, was still bruised. The bruises were turning lighter but still quite visible. The hope was that, in a few days, he would be fine. And if he still showed signs of distress, he could always say that he'd had a car accident in England.

Dom Carlos was sitting on the edge of the bed, and Angela was kneeling behind him, dressing his cuts and bruises. She had seen Lazarus's back like that from beatings. She closed her eyes for a moment, lowered her head, and kissed Dom Carlos on his battered back.

He tensed.

"Go to sleep," he said quietly. "And I will not go to the window since the neighborhood is on the lookout for ghosts."

Angela stepped down from the bed and came around to look at him. Her eyes were bright, as if she had a fever. She knelt at his feet and looked up at him.

Dom Carlos felt disconcerted. "What is it?" he asked, searching her face.

"Do you remember your promise?" she asked, placing her hands on his knees.

"I do," he said.

They were staring at each other.

"I know that you are a secretive man," she said quietly. "You don't share your story. I don't know why, but you don't. You would have died if I didn't get to you that night, and there must be a very good reason why you've been around this island for quite some time."

"Is this why you are keeping me hostage in your room? To interrogate me?" he jested in a whisper, his mouth touching her ear for noise control.

"You can hardly breathe, but nevertheless you can't resist joking about everything," she whispered back. "I'm tempted to open my mouth real wide and bite your ear off."

He took a long breath and said, "I've been curious about your island for a very long time. Finally, I decided to do something about it and see if it was really true what they say about a sunken treasure on the coast of Two Brooks."

Angela was speechless. She even forgot to whisper.

"Are you serious? Do you know how many people died trying to find that miserable treasure? Do you know that Paulo Amora killed someone, supposedly because he was trying to get at that treasure? He went to jail and destroyed his family."

She waited for an answer, but her questions were rhetorical only.

"What makes you think that you are going to find anything?" She shook him, and he groaned in pain, placing a protective hand over his shoulder.

"I bought the rights to seek this treasure. I hired a crew. However, I know someone else is pirating my rights. These so-called rights are very tenuous."

Angela was perplexed. "You bought the rights to seek this treasure? How rich are you, Dom Carlos?" she asked, as if she had just discovered that he was a serial killer.

"I have money," he said impatiently. "You've always known that."

She got up and walked around the room, trying to collect her thoughts. "Is this why you are here?" she asked.

"No," he answered. "I came here for that, but I'm staying for something else."

"What are you staying for?"

"I found a place where I am happy," he said quietly.

"You are so secretive," she said, searching his face. "Such a worldly man cannot be happy on this island."

Angela looked at his mouth. She couldn't tear her eyes from him. If she closed her eyes and kissed him, would he feel just like Lazarus?

"I am not Lazarus," he said quietly, as if he had read her mind.

"I know!" she added in frustration.

Dom Carlos was hoping for the effects of the pill to knock him out, to rescue him from a conversation that could only end up badly. He lay back, closed his eyes, and waited for oblivion. Angela sat on the edge of the bed and stared at him until he fell asleep.

Angela woke up with someone knocking on the door. Her mother wanted to let her know that she was preparing supper and should be done in a little while. Angela turned around to face Dom Carlos. He was sleeping deeply.

She caressed his face, smoothed his eyebrows, and stroked his lips, but he didn't wake up. He moaned a little, sighed heavily and continued in his slumber. Slowly, she touched his lips with hers, just a touch, and he didn't wake up. She kissed him, brushing his broken lip with her tongue, and he moaned softly. She kissed his parted lips, small kisses, repeatedly. Her tongue gently ran over his teeth.

She stopped, horrified. Not for a second had she thought of Lazarus; she was so very aware that it was Dom Carlos who she was kissing.

She left the room in a hurry, as if she had committed a crime and needed to hide. She was trembling with the awareness that she had lost all sense of decency and measure. She needed to find her center and accept that Lazarus was gone before she did something foolish, before she destroyed a beautiful friendship.

Dom Carlos woke up and looked around the room. Angela was not there. He licked his lips, still wet, while he thought that he had had a sweet and crazy dream.

19

Killing Zorro

Dona Mafalda came back from church and surprised Maria Gomes, talking about the ghosts in the house. Dona Mafalda, intelligent and enlightened, was offended.

"There is no such thing!" she said righteously.

"You will find out that these people are very superstitious. I wish Lazarus was visiting me," Angela said.

"Don't say that, Angela," her mother interrupted. "Never wish to be visited by a soul. It means that he is not in peace. And you want him to be in peace."

"I want him to be here with me!" Angela said harshly.

Dona Mafalda was quietly observing.

Angela left the kitchen, taking the dinner to Dom Carlos as if it was for herself.

"She is getting worse," Maria Gomes said to Dona Mafalda. "She was doing well, but now I think that she is worse."

"Victims of trauma do regress sometimes," Dona Mafalda said in a compassionate tone.

Maria Gomes looked at her. Dona Mafalda was a fancy woman with fancy words, but she liked this pompous person.

"She will get better eventually," Dona Mafalda added, "with time."

Pedro Matias came around more than once during the week that Dom Carlos was supposed to be away. He first came around with the suspicion that Dom Carlos was not in England but at the bottom of the sea. But Angela's demeanor was so calm, everything so normal that he was convinced that the boogeyman was not Dom Carlos, and then Angela said that Dom Carlos had called, stating that he would be back soon. Then he came around because Angela's guardian angel was in England, and he wanted to annoy her.

"I want my carpentry shop back," he said, sitting without being invited.

Angela stopped her chores and said, "Get out of my house."

"Well," he said laughing. "Your knight in shining armor is not here to make me, and your father cannot punch a fly."

Angela turned around and walked into the chimney room, coming back with a frying pan full of boiling oil.

Pedro let out a scream and ran out the door with Hercules on his heels and Viriato barking after the cat. Nixon and Dalia were looking around, not able to decide on a safe place to hide.

It was dusk, and the sun was coming in, strained by trees and curtains that let it shine through only to create shadows.

With her hand on her chest, Rosa pointed up the stairs. "Lazarus!" she whispered, hardly being heard over the confusion. "I saw him at the top of the stairs looking down at us," she said louder, panic taking over.

Angela looked up at where Rosa was pointing, and she saw nothing.

"It was the shadows of the sun, darling," she said, hugging the girl, forgetting all about Pedro.

"No. He had on the pajamas you gave him last Christmas! How can the sun come up with pajamas? He went into your room." Tears streamed down her face.

Angela was exasperated with Pedro and with Dom Carlos. "When we are thinking about people we sometimes imagine things. Because Pedro was being difficult, you probably thought of Lazarus, didn't you?" Angela tried to convince a terrified Rosa.

Dona Mafalda came out of her room to check on the commotion. But Dona Mafalda didn't see Lazarus. She didn't know Lazarus. She fell asleep in her room while reading, and she woke up with everyone screaming.

"No, my dear, I didn't see anyone on the landing," she said to Rosa.

After Rosa was convinced that maybe she didn't see Lazarus, she went home in a hurry, as if the ghost she thought she saw was following her.

Dona Mafalda sat in the living room waiting for the house to calm down. She was pensive, massaging her temples. She was assessing her egregious error in thinking that she could fit in this place. This village killed people or made them disappear; they believed in werewolves and ghosts. They had a priest who was a madman and physically assaulted women. They had a band of reprobates taking justice into their own hands and terrorizing everyone. What was she doing here? She was a woman with tremendous mental acuity, she was handsome and rich, and she was well regarded by her peers and society. What in the world had she done?

But she knew what she had done; she had fallen in love with Dom Carlos. And short of being flogged in the public square, she would not leave. She would not lose her chances with him. She would wait, and he would fall in love with her. There was no one around who was his equal; he eventually would fall in love with her. She would wait and be tactful. There was nothing more despicable than a desperate woman.

Dona Mafalda had a younger sister and brother, both already married. Everyone expected her to have made a brilliant marriage by now, being the oldest. But somehow, one day she saw herself old, and the husband never materialized. She was always in love with someone, but she was so stuck on class and prestige that it was hard to find a partner she could love and be proud of at the same time. She was more focused on being relevant than on being in love. And when she found Rafael, wealthy, educated, good-looking, he lost interest in her and fell in love with her younger sister, Natalia.

Dona Mafalda was the matron of honor at their wedding. She smiled all the way through the ceremonies, and then she cried for hours alone in her room. Since then, she thought of love half-heartedly, always suspecting a disillusion around the corner.

It was her father who suggested that she should leave and try a different scenario. Her father, Count Tiago da Cruz, kind and thoughtful, loved all his children. But Mafalda was his favorite. And it broke his heart to see her being so courageous, so strong, putting her best foot forward and never showing defeat.

And she left because she was tired of being stoic, of suffering quietly; she had no more strength for courage. Would she now be courageous and fight for Dom Carlos's love? Had she been distracted with menial things, letting the important ones go by? Her pursuit for happiness waned. It was as if she was walking down the street wanting to get to one destination, and without explanation, she found herself in a totally different place, because she was distracted. How could she have lost her vigilance for meaning? She couldn't pinpoint that bend on the road that had taken her so off route.

After supper, Dona Mafalda went to her room to brood in the company of Beethoven. She was thinking of ways to let Dom Carlos know that she loved him without having to confess anything first. But what if he never said anything? Would she wait all her life? She had waited for Rafael to declare his love for her, and he hadn't. Women just sit and wait to be asked. That was a most impractical strategy!

When Angela entered her bedroom, Dom Carlos was pacing. "What did he do to you?" he asked breathlessly.

"Nothing, he did nothing," she said. "I chased him with boiling oil, and Hercules bit him." She sat at her desk and held her head between her hands.

"It was an immediate reaction—a visceral response to Pedro," he explained. "I heard his voice and heard you scream. I got into the room immediately when I realized the implications—"

"But not before Rosa saw you for a split second, and she thought it was Lazarus."

"Great," he mumbled, "more ghost stories."

"Why don't you go to your apartment in the city? After everyone is in bed, you can take your car and go."

"And how would you explain my car being gone? Isn't Pedro Matias sniffing around?"

"We could take Thunder. When night falls, I would go with you and bring him back," she said.

"No," he said vehemently. "I don't want you galloping about in the night."

They were quiet, thinking of viable strategies when he said, "You want to kick me out, and I'm hurt."

"You are going crazy stuck in here," she said impatiently.

They ate together, slept together. They had entire conversations whispering in each other's ear to avoid being heard. They fought and forgave each other in hisses and whispers. They listened to the radio and read in peaceful silence before going to sleep. At times, they laughed, stifling guffaws, drowning giggles on the pillow.

No, he was not going crazy. He would miss this strange and precious time.

She grinned. "You are almost cured." She peered at his face, touched his lip lightly with the tips of her fingers, and caressed his shoulder. "I guess I can stand you for a few more days."

Then she became very serious. The thought that he could have died assaulted her like a villain.

"Please don't break my heart," she said so softly that he strained to hear her. "Don't put yourself in harm's way. I don't think I can take it if anything happens to you."

His heart was pounding loudly, and he felt his eyes getting misty. And all he could say was, "I promise."

Suddenly, Beethoven was silent across the hall, and Dona Mafalda came out of her room and knocked at Angela's door.

"I'll be right out," Angela answered. She had forgotten that she'd promised Dona Mafalda to teach her how to prepare milk with honey and moonshine for insomnia. Poor Dona Mafalda; she used to sleep so soundly, and then love came along …

Angela closed the door behind her and followed Dona Mafalda, who was more interested in news from Dom Carlos than in how to fight insomnia.

It was so hard to look at Dona Mafalda's eager face.

"He will be back soon," Angela said, "only a few more days."

"He is very secretive about his private life, isn't he?" Dona Mafalda asked, hardly able to contain her curiosity.

"Very much," Angela said.

"So you don't know much about his life, do you?" Dona Mafalda leaned forward eager for information.

Angela felt a sharp pain of remorse. "I know that he has money, and he is a very astute business man, and that is all he allows us to know," Angela said.

That was the truth, at least.

"Is he married?"

Angela was surprised. It had never occurred to her that Dom Carlos could be married. "I don't think so," she said. "He has been here for three years, and no wife."

Angela became very quiet. Would Dom Carlos have a wife somewhere? He was not really generous with information about his life. The little that she knew was because she'd made him tell her. He never shared his life with her or anybody else for that matter.

Dom Carlos was quite a mystery.

"He could be homosexual," Dona Mafalda said, looking intently at Angela.

Angela started to laugh. "I don't think so … Neither does Regina."

"Regina?" Dona Mafalda shrieked. "That prostitute across the street?"

"Don't call her that," Angela warned. "She will hit you."

It was getting late, and Dona Mafalda was not showing signs of going to bed. Angela said, getting up, "I'm going to bed, I am tired."

"Angela …" Dona Mafalda said. "You will be all right. It takes a little time …"

Angela smiled. "I know."

When Angela went upstairs, Dom Carlos was already asleep. She went to the window and opened it, letting the night air into the room. She stayed there at the window, looking into the night. Sometimes she wondered if Nascimento was somewhere looking at her house, peering into the windows and looking for Lazarus's ghost. The last time Angela had leaned on the parapet of that window, Lazarus had been behind her, rubbing her back and whistling softly. How could she live without him? How could she fill that void? She lowered her head and cried.

"Lazarus," she said, knowing full well that it was Dom Carlos who brought her back into the room and away from the window.

"Will this ever stop hurting?" she asked.

But Dom Carlos, who knew so many things, didn't have the heart to tell her about the endless nature of pain.

Angela fell asleep with Dom Carlos gently rubbing her back while he thought about the trajectory of his life. How in the world had he ended up here in bed with a grieving young widow? Where was that bend on the road that had taken him to Angela? Why wasn't he able to prevent such a disaster?

He got up and went to the window. Hercules was there, sitting on the wall at the back of the garden; he could see his burning orbs. And then Hercules howled and ran away. Dom Carlos stepped back into the darkness of the room; Angela stirred and cried out.

There was a knock at the door.

"Angela, are you all right?" Dona Mafalda asked. She knocked again, and Angela woke up with a start.

"I was dreaming," she shouted. "I am fine. Go to sleep."

They heard Dona Mafalda's door close and the key turn in the keyhole.

"What were you dreaming about?" Dom Carlos asked, sitting next to her and trying to make out her face in the darkness.

"I …I don't remember," she said.

Angela closed her eyes again, resting her head on the cool pillow. She had dreamed that she was making love to Lazarus in the garden. He kissed her face and said, "Open your eyes, Angela." When she did, it was Dom Carlos making love to her and not Lazarus. She screamed and woke up Dona Mafalda.

They were both aware of the deep silence between them.

"Dona Mafalda asked me if you were gay. I was dreaming that you were coming down the street with high heels and a skirt," she said. "It was a frightening thing to witness."

"Gay? Why would she think that?" he asked, surprised and offended.

Angela was amused. "I don't know. What did she offer you that you declined?"

The moon was shyly looking in.

"What else does she think of me?"

"That if you are not gay, you must be married to be resisting her charms ..."

Dom Carlos stared at Angela in such a way that she frowned in surprise. "Are you?" she asked.

He placed his mouth in her ear and said, "Yes, I am. I am gay." And he did the same thing he had done the first time they'd met. He took her earlobe in his mouth and sucked at it gently.

Angela shivered and let out a yelp, and Dom Carlos laughed as he had that night.

Dom Carlos was coming back from England the next day. Dona Mafalda had flowers all over the house and was singing softly, hardly containing her joy. Not even the fight she'd had with the monsignor would obfuscate her happiness.

Rosa had also missed him, but she liked when he went away because he always brought her something.

But Angela was quiet. In Rosa's estimation, Angela was not happy with Dom Carlos's return. "It looks like you don't miss him," she said. "Dona Mafalda is bursting with happiness, and you are ..." She didn't finish. She didn't know what Angela was ... And happy she was not.

Dom Carlos was reading when Angela entered the room.

"Is the house ready for my return?" he asked without lifting his head from the book.

"Indeed," she answered and turned up the volume of the radio. She checked his shoulder, his back, and the other injuries. She traced lightly the cut on his forehead and lip. He sat obediently in front of her with his eyes closed, as if the inspection was too painful to endure. He was healing very well. He was ready to return from England, maybe claiming a minor car accident since he was still greenish around the eye.

"Does it hurt?" she asked, touching his face.

"Depends," he answered quietly.

"On what?" she asked, still tracing the cut on his lip and the area around his eye.

He opened his mouth and bit her finger, gently holding it between his teeth. Her finger was salty when he sucked at it.

She looked at him in surprise. "Are you upset?" she asked.

"No, I'm not upset!" he snapped letting her finger go. He moved his shoulder to gauge the pain, and he didn't feel any. "I will be coming in the middle of the night. A friend will give me a ride. And tomorrow morning, I will be in my room," he said. "If people ask about my injuries, which I think they will not because they are hardly noticeable, I will say that I had an accident."

"What kind of accident?"

"I don't know! An accident," he hissed.

"Okay. You fell off a bicycle, on your way to buy scones," she said.

"Very funny. You are full of mirth today," he said without humor.

"I bought you chocolates for Rosa. You always bring her something," Angela said. Then with a wicked grin she added, "Dona Mafalda is missing you to an inch of her life."

He ignored her.

"She is in love with you," she insisted in a whisper, trying to be heard over the fado on the radio. "You have to deal with it."

He stretched his legs and took off the arm sling, completely ignoring her.

"Tonight I will give you another shave," she said.

"I can do it myself," he answered.

"I know, but I want to do it. I enjoy having a knife to your throat." She grinned.

And that night, Angela snuck in the hot water and knelt in front of Dom Carlos while he sat cross-legged on the floor. She lathered his face and took in the smell of his soap. There was a sense of peace associated with his soap. She took her own sweet time, quietly listening to the radio while running the shaving knife expertly down his face.

"I love this smell," she said as if to herself. "It gives me the same feeling as the smell of boiled milk."

"What feeling is that?" he asked, opening his eyes and concentrating on her face.

She thought for a while trying to come up with something that could exemplify what she felt.

"It is peace … I feel so …content, so whole." She lowered the shaving knife and seemed to be looking into the distance. "All my anger dissipates," she added.

"It takes a trusting fool to let an angry woman put a sharp knife to his throat," he said quietly.

That evening, they ate supper quietly. The music from Dona Mafalda's room crossed the hall, soothing and peaceful, so they didn't need to turn the radio on.

"I must say that Dona Mafalda has excellent taste in music," he said.

"She has excellent taste in men also."

"I warned you, Angela," he said.

"Sure you did. I'm terrified of you. I can dislocate both of your arms in a second, if you annoy me."

He smiled.

They ate quietly. They were almost finished when she said, "I will miss you. I never had a hostage before. I like it."

"I will miss you too," he answered. "You were just as much my hostage as I was yours."

This was the confession that was hanging in the air and was finally out. Being so close for so many days felt like a blessing, not an inconvenience.

"We are not parting to different continents," he said.

"Then why are we saying good-bye?" she asked, looking at him intently.

"You started it," he accused.

"Did not."

"Yes, you said that you will miss me," he said.

"I'm sorry that I was mean to you," she said without looking at him.

"How sorry are you?" he asked.

They were sitting on the floor opposite each other with the food between them. Angela looked up to assess if he was joking. But he was serious and waiting for an answer.

She opened her mouth to answer but didn't say anything. Her eyes were fixed on his.

Dom Carlos kissed his fingertips and then reached across and rested his fingers on her mouth. His fingers were cool on her lips, and she closed her eyes for a second. She felt so vulnerable, so strange, so blessed for having Dom Carlos in her life.

"I'm so grateful for you, Dom Carlos. When I think that I was punished for losing Lazarus, I think that God repented and gave me you."

He held her gaze and said nothing for a while. He wished he could say what was in his heart. "I think your God is a temperamental fool," he said instead. "There is no reason why you couldn't have us both."

"There must be some reason that I can't grasp. Otherwise, I can't accept that Lazarus is gone," she said as if talking to herself.

That night, they left the window open to let the cold breeze in. The moon was so close to the earth, one could almost reach up and touch it.

Angela said, "Good night, my fisherman. With the moon as my witness I will never sleep with you again."

"Never say never, Hawk," he answered.

In the morning, Dom Carlos came down from his room and gave the chocolates to Rosa.

She smiled broadly, looking at the chocolates and looking back at him. "They have the same chocolates in England that we have here?" she asked.

Dom Carlos gave Angela a slanted look, and she stepped in. "Shame on you, Dom Carlos. You didn't buy these chocolates in England, did you?"

He started to mumble an excuse and blushed like a maiden.

"It's okay!" Rosa stepped in, feeling sorry for Dom Carlos's scolding.

Angela turned around, hardly containing her mirth.

"We had pretty strange things happening while you were away," Rosa said hurriedly to distract him from the chocolate fiasco. "The Mendeses killed the boogeyman, and Lazarus has been visiting the house—not Angela, just the house. I saw him, Regina saw him, and even Nascimento …" She lowered her voice and said, "He must be angry with Angela because he is not visiting her."

Dom Carlos looked at Angela's back.

Rosa stopped her narrative and looked at Angela with concern. "She knows," she whispered to Dom Carlos. "I think she is sad because she didn't see him, and she misses him very much."

Dom Carlos got up from the table and walked toward Angela. He touched her shoulder and asked, "Are you okay?"

She had tears in her eyes, and he gave her an accusing look. She had been silently laughing at him.

"I'm going to the city," he said. "I think I need respite."

"Can't you buy that here?" Rosa asked with disappointment.

Dom Carlos smiled and said, "No, there is no respite in Two Brooks."

Dona Mafalda is going to be sad," Rosa said. "She almost didn't go to school to wait for you."

That afternoon, when Dona Mafalda came home from work, she almost cried with disappointment when Rosa told her that Dom Carlos had gone to the city to get something that he couldn't find in Two Brooks.

In the city, Dom Carlos met with his friend, the chief of police, Gaspar Grima, who was a man of few words. He sat across from Dom Carlos and narrowed his eyes at him—woman trouble. He always recognized the signs.

Gaspar Grima, with his expensive and salacious appetites, had the uncanny habit of making Dom Carlos feel like a virgin schoolboy.

"One of these days, your 'friends' will bring you to a deleterious and shameful end," Dom Carlos said, referring to the women Gaspar Grima associated with. Dom Carlos got up and left the chief laughing behind his back.

Dom Carlos walked slowly to his apartment. When he opened the street door, he knew that his neighbor, Dona Gloria Montes, also a widow, would be looking for him. He knew that Dona Gloria was smitten with him, and most of the time, he was amused. Today, he was frustrated, knowing that she was going to regale him with attentions as soon as he put the key to his door.

And she showed up, smiling, assiduous as ever.

Dom Carlos invited her for a drink. He always did, as a courtesy. She sat across from him, crossing and uncrossing her legs as she spoke. She talked in a quiet voice, trying to draw him out of his glumness. He didn't even compliment her on her new dress.

Then she got up, walked to him, knelt at his feet, and said, "We are adults, and we could."

He didn't realize how imprudent, not to mention indecorous it was not to pay attention to one's visitor. But he was thinking about something else while Dona Gloria was talking. "Of course we could," he said, not knowing what he was agreeing to.

Dona Gloria smiled and said, "Nothing wrong with now is there?"

"Now?" he asked, trying to find out what part of her monologue he had missed.

Soon he found out when she put her perfectly manicured hand on his crotch. He held his breath, and much to his chagrin, he was having an erection. He vaguely thought that his penis had a mind of its own. He mentally ordered it to lie down. But like a cat, it didn't take orders.

Right before his eyes, Dona Gloria took off her panties, unbuckled his belt, and opened his fly. She took out his penis, licked it, and straddled him.

Everything seemed to happen in slow motion. He moaned and closed his eyes, grabbed the arms of the chair until his fingers hurt. He threw his head back and thrust his pelvis forward. He didn't want this to happen. He wanted to stop her, but what he did was to hold her down on him until he groaned with pleasure and release. The rocking chair moved back and forth slowly, as if to assist Dona Gloria mounting her steed.

There was nothing like the body of a woman to make a man feel good, Dom Carlos thought as he sunk into Dona Gloria. When she tried to get up, he held her down.

"No. Not yet," he whispered. And he climaxed again with a cry, "Oh God!"

For someone who claimed to be agnostic, he had a strange way of thinking about God; it was impious to say the least. When it was over, Dona Gloria rearranged her clothes and waited for him to do the same.

"We can't do this," he said, meeting her eyes. "I am in love with someone else; I don't want to mislead you."

"I know," she said, smiling sadly. "I am a big girl. And who knows, things can change, can't they?"

So much for respite, he thought as soon as she left. Now he had a brand-new complication—a rogue penis and an overly attentive neighbor.

In the morning, Dom Carlos woke up with someone knocking. Before he had a chance to put something on and go to the door, Dona Gloria let herself in with the key he had given her to take care of the plants. She came in, dropped her robe, walked to the bed, and got in with Dom Carlos.

She said, "Why can't we pleasure ourselves? We are not hurting anyone."

Dom Carlos couldn't believe his lack of self-control, but given the antecedents he knew he would not be able to resist. He feebly ordered his penis to lie down again, but to no avail.

"Relax," she said. "I'm not asking you for love or marriage, just comfort."

She straddled him with measured slowness. He held the bedpost above his head, and let Dona Gloria ride him again. He closed his eyes and bit his lip, promising himself not to call God this time.

When he climaxed, he imagined someone else gazing at his face. What a scoundrel he was. "Oh God!" he murmured.

"I didn't know you were a religious man," she said with a smile. "I'll come back later, and you can praise God again," she said, putting on her robe.

Dom Carlos had no strength or desire to say no, but he made a decision to end this craziness and emotional deceit. So when she came back for more, he said, "One last time, and that will be it."

"I could be good to you, if you let me," she said. "But I'll take what I can. Let's do it on the kitchen table. Do it for fifteen minutes, and don't come before that."

"What?" he asked, stupefied.

"Hold it for fifteen minutes," she repeated, walking to the kitchen.

She bent over the table, grasped the edges, and spread her legs apart.

Dom Carlos was behind her, mesmerized, thinking of the unlikelihood of ever being confused in front of a naked woman. He was awestruck with Dona Gloria's perfect buttocks inviting his perfidy. His pulse raced and he asked out of breath, "Fifteen minutes? Why fifteen minutes?"

"Long story," she said, looking at her wristwatch.

With a moan, he rammed into her, sending the table screeching across the floor until it stopped against the wall. "Oh God!" he cried.

"Start all over again," she said sweetly, looking back at him over her creamy shoulder. "I'm timing you. Fifteen minutes, not five."

With an increment of five minutes every time he tried, he finally fell back on a chair, panting, while a satiated Dona Gloria smiled at her wristwatch.

How gullible men were, she thought. And they couldn't even tell time.

"Why fifteen minutes?" he asked again.

"I just wanted to make sure that, indeed, time is a relative thing," she answered with a pinch of sadness.

It was late in the afternoon when he showered. He felt oddly relaxed without that pressure in his groin threatening to explode at any minute. On the other hand, he felt dirty and weak. The only woman he wanted was the only one he resisted. His school days of Latin came to mind: *Reductio ad absurdum.* His story with Angela was being taken to absurd lengths. Living like this was ridiculous, not to mention impractical.

He went up to Two Brooks, in time for supper.

"You are home," Angela said, delighted, as he came into the kitchen.

Home. How he loved that word.

Dona Mafalda had a sour expression. She felt unimportant, irrelevant, sitting there witnessing Dom Carlos beam as he talked to Angela.

As if on cue he said, "You look well, Dona Mafalda."

She gave him a tight smile and asked about his trip.

"It was apocryphal," he said.

Angela asked with a grin. "Really? What happened?"

Dom Carlos stumbled over words, mumbled a few hum ...hum ... and stared at her. "I ... the trip took a few unexpected turns," Dom Carlos said giving Angela a warning look.

Dona Mafalda was peering into his face. "Did you get hurt? Your eye seems a bit—"

"I ...I've been riding a bike—a bike that I wasn't used to," he interrupted.

"What were you doing on a bike?" Dona Mafalda asked in a recriminating tone. "Didn't you go to England on business?"

Dom Carlos looked at Angela's amused face; just like Dona Mafalda, she was waiting for an explanation as to why a business trip would include a silly thing like riding a bike.

Dona Mafalda's heart skipped a beat with the realization that he had gone to England to meet a woman, not on business. She turned away so he couldn't see her sadness.

20

The Wrong Bend in the Road

As soon as Carlota left the house, Madalena started looking in Carlota's room, making sure that nothing would show any signs of having been searched. Finally she found a bundle of letters inside a pillowcase on Carlota's bed. She took one from the bottom and hid it in her clothes and left the room. She walked out of the house and went to church.

Madalena's heart was beating so wildly that she thought her chest was going to burst. She sat on a pew, in the back of the church, near a window. Everything was quiet, and once in a while the sounds from the village entered the church—a dog barking, the mooing of cattle, children laughing, women singing, and some radio far away playing a fado. Madalena read:

> Dear Carlota,
>
> I've arrived in Angra. I am fine. The voyage from Africa to Brazil was arduous, but it was indeed worth it. I was able to claim our land from my family. I found old documents that strengthen our assumptions about the gold. We were on the right track. I will let you know the steps we must take next.
>
> Much love,
> Paulo

Madalena felt faint. She massaged her temples.

Saul's father was alive. He hadn't died in Africa. He had gone to Brazil to pursue some scheme, and Saul had joined him. She was shaking, not sure if it was anger or confusion. She hid the letter again and went home.

Carlota was already at home sitting at the window embroidering. She smiled at Madalena and said, "Come and sit with me. Let's have some hot chocolate."

Madalena had to find a way to put this letter back and get to the others. Or she could confront Carlota right now.

"I know your husband is alive." And Madalena showed her the letter.

Carlota stared at the letter. Then she said in a quietly disturbed tone, "Please, Madalena, let it be. You don't know where you are stepping in. The police are sniffing around, Saul is gone, and we are here alone. You know nothing, nothing! Do you hear me?"

"Where is Saul?" Madalena asked resolutely.

"That I don't know. But he left because of something else, and I don't know what. At first I thought it had to do with his father, but I don't think so. All he said was that he had to leave and would be back."

"He is writing to you as Luas Aroma, is he not?" Madalena insisted.

Carlota took her hands in hers and said in a hushed tone, "Madalena, please. If you don't want to do this for Saul, do it for me. You know nothing. Please, promise me. It is for your own protection."

After this exchange with Carlota, and after Madalena promised not to tell anyone about Paulo and Saul, Carlota set up a post office box in the city.

"But he could be dead, and we wouldn't know," Madalena answered every time Carlota promised that Saul would return.

Madalena was thinking about leaving. If she didn't leave she would die of loneliness. When she mentioned it to her mother-in-law, Carlota panicked. Madalena could not leave. People would wonder and think that they were running away, just like Saul. Probably the police would stop them, being as suspicious as they were. And where to? No, they should stay put and wait.

The letter from Paulo Amora had been written before Saul left. Madalena wondered if Saul knew about his father being alive, claiming his inheritance. Maybe Saul had found out like she did, reading Carlota's letters, and had gone looking for his father. She wished she could convince Carlota to tell her everything she knew.

Madalena often thought of a dream she used to have when she was young. It was a road full of light, the bright light of the afternoon sun before dusk, and two people were going in the direction of the light, walking away from her. She sat fascinated, at the attic window, not able to move. The pair called her, laughing, waving, but she was rooted in her fascination. They disappeared at the bend of the road into the light, and she stayed behind, wondering about that journey. The feeling that she had missed the opportunity to go into something new and bright never left her. It was a feeling that was hard to describe; it was her first taste of failure.

The Sacristy gathered in Ascendida's kitchen. The children were in bed, and the men were out. The women cherished this time to be alone with each other. But when Ascendida pulled out the moonshine, instead of the tea, they knew the conversation was going to get heavy.

"I have something to tell you," Madalena said.

The other women looked at her expectantly.

Madalena lowered her eyes. She wished she had been quiet about that. Wasn't she betraying Carlota?

"What?" Nascimento said, slapping Madalena on the arm.

"You have to keep a secret," Madalena said.

The others waited.

"You saw Lazarus's ghost also?" Nascimento asked.

"No, I didn't see Lazarus's ghost, and neither did you," Madalena countered, irritated.

"I did! I saw him with his arms open wide, at the window of his room, looking up at the moon," Nascimento answered heatedly.

Angela hugged herself and closed her eyes. The rumor about Lazarus's ghost roaming the village was gaining momentum. Even the monsignor had talked to her about it. But she didn't believe in ghosts and much less in this one.

"Paulo Amora is alive and living in Brazil," Madalena said. "He didn't die in jail as we all believed."

They put down the moonshine and stared at Madalena. After a long silence, Madalena told them about the letter she'd read and all the other letters in the pillowcase and about some scheme that he was plotting or had been plotting for a very long time.

"I think he was the one who sent the news of his death," Madalena said.

"But why?" Ascendida asked.

"For people to leave him alone, I suppose …" Madalena said. "I confronted Carlota, and she asked me not to say anything. She insisted that she too didn't know much and that the police are sniffing around …"

"The Amoras have been always mysterious," Angela said. "And the authorities always have been interested in them, for one thing or another."

"The monsignor is bringing a detective from the mainland," Ascendida said, "to get to the bottom of these disappearances and crimes."

"What crimes?" the women asked in unison.

"He believes that Lazarus's, Manuel's, and Saul's disappearances have to do with a crime. And he called the chief of police to look at the Night Justice … and if whether there was a connection between the disappearances and Night Justice," Ascendida said.

Angela put a hand up to her neck. "Who would want to hurt Lazarus?" she asked feebly. And she thought of Pedro.

"That's the question," Ascendida said, pouring more moonshine.

Now they understood the reason for the moonshine.

"He is also stumped by Saul's disappearance. Manuel left; this was Saul's dream. Why would he leave now that Manuel was gone, leaving the two of you alone? He is afraid that something happened to Saul," Ascendida said looking at Madalena. "The monsignor believes that a crime has been committed for Saul to take off."

"At first I thought he left because he felt betrayed," Madalena said sadly. "But now I am not so sure … I may be thinking that he left, but what if something happened to him? What if he is dead …like Lazarus, at the bottom of the sea?"

"The monsignor is mightily concerned," Ascendida said.

"And how do you know all of this?" Angela asked.

"Because I talked to the monsignor. I said that I was concerned for your sanity." She pointed at Angela and Madalena. "You have to move on, Angela. Lazarus is dead. He is gone. You have to accept it. You still think he didn't die …and you, Madalena, you wouldn't be the first woman in the world to be abandoned. Get used to it."

"I don't feel it. I don't feel that he is dead," Angela said softly.

"I know, and that's why I am concerned," Ascendida concluded.

Ascendida told them that this detective would be coming from the mainland because all the other detectives who came into Two Brooks had been seduced, duped, or co-opted, therefore yielding no results.

The women smiled because they knew it was true.

You could fence off land but not people; this was the Two Brooks motto. The government fenced off land to keep the villagers from using that land to fatten their livestock. During the night, the villagers would destroy the walls, and no witnesses. Many investigators came to Two Brooks for various reasons, especially because of Night Justice, but they failed. The chief of police thought that maybe an outsider would have more success.

One detective failed his assignment because he fell in love with Luciana, a wild-looking girl with black, curly hair and soft, tanned skin. She was an accomplished weaver, and she wove beautiful blankets and throws while she sang love songs. She still wove and sang mournful songs, maybe regretting not giving herself to that sweet, forbidden love. But of course no one knew for sure if she had, because Luciana was silent and the detective left, throwing away his promising career because he had fallen in love.

Then it was Detective Jorge Lourenço, who fell in love with Maia, forgetting the reason he was in Two Brooks. And there were others before, some falling in love, some falling into greed, but falling all the same.

Now they were going to send another poor devil to fail again.

The women were smirking at the thought of having an outsider come face-to-face with Luciana's love songs and magic weaving hands or Madalena's beauty or simply face-to-face with Regina.

"Who is this man?" Angela asked.

"He is from the mainland, and he is here already. He will be coming to interview us about the disappearing men," Ascendida said.

"Why Manuel? He left; he immigrated to Brazil. Nothing happened to him," Nascimento, said surprised.

"Well, his family is saying that, if he had gone to Brazil he would have written already and he hasn't," Ascendida said. "And they are afraid because Saul disappeared at the same time … And he didn't go and visit the monsignor on the day he left."

"Manuel was easily distracted," Madalena said pensively.

The women were very quiet.

Madalena got up to leave. "The monsignor had money for Manuel, and that money was from Saul. Maybe Manuel found out and refused to get it," Madalena said.

"I can see Saul offering him poison, not money," Nascimento said.

Angela was very quiet. At times, she only wanted to look at Madalena because she looked so much like Lazarus, and other times, she couldn't look at her for the same reason. She did the same thing with Dom Carlos; he had Lazarus's height and body shape, his hair and skin color. But everything else was so different: Dom Carlos was worldly, and Lazarus was afraid of everything; Dom Carlos was confident, and Lazarus was always in doubt; Dom Carlos was shrewd and tough, and Lazarus was easily manipulated.

Where was God? Why would Lazarus suffer so much and die when he was finally happy? She felt resentful and shook her head to chase away those demons.

If she lost God now, when she felt so alone, she would be completely lost.

The new detective arrived. He was a tall, thin man in his forties; he had a sullen expression, as if the world owed him an explanation. He didn't want to be in Two Brooks, in this small village without electricity and no indoor plumbing, looking into the lives of insignificant people doing significant damage to each other. He resented everything about this assignment, including the monsignor, who was looking at him with distaste.

"Detective, I have only concerns. I cannot do the job for you," the monsignor snapped at the new detective.

"But you know a lot more than you are telling me," the detective answered belligerently.

"I cannot share with you what I know, Detective. I learned through confession."

The detective put the pen and pad in his pocket and said, "I don't believe in that hocus-pocus, Monsignor. If you know what is going on, tell me; otherwise, don't call the law to help you when you don't want to help yourself."

The monsignor gave the detective a list of people who should be interrogated. At the top were Pedro Matias and the Sacristy, and right below their names were those of everybody else, including Dom Carlos.

Angus Pomba had the reputation of hitting his suspects. It was not by chance that the chief of police had requested him from the mainland. The chief was simply tired of Two Brooks, and he didn't mind if the villagers felt a little pain. If the monsignor could slap people around, so could Detective Pomba.

Angus's first visit was to Pedro Matias. He would squeeze this man to the size of a pea. When Angus entered the gate, Ferocious, the dog, came running snarling and showing horribly yellow, long teeth. The detective ran out and closed the gate. Disheveled and out of breath, he stared at the dog, still barking on the other side. In his haste, his jacket had caught a nail on the gate and was ripped from the pocket down.

This was not what Angus had in mind. He wanted to come into the village like a dark cloud announcing pain, but here he was in the middle of the street, ripped and with people gawking and smirking.

Pedro Matias was laughing inside of the house. He knew that a detective was coming, and he'd let Ferocious do the welcome.

Angus Pomba tried to compose himself by placing a hand over the ripped jacket and covering most of the white lining showing like a light in the dark.

"Mr. Matias!" he yelled from the street. "Contain your dog, or I will come back with a pistol and shoot it."

Pedro didn't expect that. Other detectives had come and gone. They took people to jail, but they never said anything about pistols.

Pedro came out to the gate, showing no vestiges of mirth.

"I am giving you notice," Angus said to Pedro. "I want to see you tomorrow in the city at ten in the morning. I am investigating the death of your son and the disappearance of two other men. If you don't show up, you will be arrested." He turned around and left down the road, leaving Pedro speechless.

Angus Pomba went to Carlota's house. When he knocked, he was expecting to find an incredibly beautiful woman. But the woman in front of him had eyes as big as the eyes of a cow and a look of sadness that lengthened her face. This could not be the woman that the chief talked about, or the chief had just decided to have a laugh at his expense. This woman was ugly, and he knew ugly.

"Madalena Amora?" he asked again.

"I'm Carlota Amora," she said, "her mother-in-law. Madalena is not home."

"I will come back to talk to her. Meanwhile, I need to talk to you regarding the disappearance of your son and the other two men, Manuel Barcos and Lazarus Matias."

Carlota paled and put a hand on her chest.

"I want you to go to the city tomorrow at ten o'clock. I will talk to you then."

Angus Pomba was not going to be sucked in like the others—by going in, drinking tea, eating soup, and falling for these deceitful people. He was going to interrogate them in his own environment and on his own terms. Maybe he would slap them around a bit. His strategy was going to be different, and he was going to succeed. If there was something to be found out, he would discover it. He had never investigated a case that he hadn't solved.

Angus Pomba went up and down the village, giving intimations to his list of suspects. When he got to Angela's house, he knew immediately that he was looking at Madalena Amora. Angus was prepared to see a beautiful woman, but not that beautiful. He was as much taken aback by Madalena as he had been by Carlota.

"I'm Detective Angus Pomba, and I need to talk to you about your husband's and your lover's disappearance, as well as your brother's death."

Madalena paled. She stared at him for a few seconds. "I never had a lover, Detective. Manuel was my boyfriend before I got married to Saul."

The detective stared and smiled briefly. Angus Pomba was enjoying her discomfort.

He smiled again, and Madalena thought that he had an offensive way about him. He was another arrogant mainlander.

"I will need to talk to you tomorrow, in the city, at ten."

"I will be there," she turned around and closed the door in his face.

Angus was surprised again. He didn't like the fact that, at every junction, these people had surprised him.

He knocked again, and this time, Angela answered.

"Angela Matias I presume?" he asked, slightly raising his eyebrows.

"Anus Pomba I assume?" Angela said.

"Angus!" He corrected.

"Sorry, I misunderstood. I though Madalena said Anus."

Angus was a humorless man because life could be that way—humorless. But he could appreciate a good laugh if it came his way, and this village, with damaging people, was funny. He let out a laugh that sounded like a bark. Dalia got scared and flew around the kitchen, disquieted by that sound. Viriato was whining softly. Angela stepped back, also surprised by that disturbing noise and by the coldness of the detective's presence.

"I need to talk to you too," he said. "In the city, tomorrow at ten."

He had a low, rumbling voice. He nodded his head and left with sure, wide steps. There was elegance in the man in spite of the ripped jacket and dusty shoes. But there was a glimpse of cruelty in his dark eyes that worried Angela.

Angus walked to his car under the gaze of the neighbors.

He let out a moan of frustration when he saw his car with all four tires slashed. He looked around, and everybody disappeared, not a soul to be seen. Angus Pomba walked back to the garage that he had seen on his way up. The door was closed. No one was there. The last bus to the city was gone; it had left one hour ago. He knocked at the garage door, but Lucas Pires was nowhere to be seen. There was the telephone post; he could call a taxi. But even there, the service that should have been opened twenty-four hours had no one responding to his knock.

Angus Pomba went to the monsignor, and the monsignor told him that he could walk to the city via the Forest Road, about three hours, or he could try to rent a room for the night with Angela Matias. She probably would say no, and he had to be nice.

"Do you know how to be nice?" the monsignor asked.

When he knocked at Angela's door, he was really upset and tired. "I need a room for the night," he said.

Angela smiled and said. "No." And she shut the door in his face.

He pounded on the door.

She opened it again and crossed her arms over her chest.

Angus had never been treated like that. People were resentful of him most of the time, but they hadn't dared to be disrespectful. This village was something else. But the villagers were going to learn a lesson about respecting authority. They were a bunch of thugs, in need of a lesson, and he was the man to deliver it. For now, though, he needed to be nice, like the monsignor had suggested.

"Please, I need a place to stay," he said in his most neutral voice.

Angela stepped aside for him to enter. He felt naked in the middle of the kitchen with animals looking at him and a cat hissing …or laughing under the table.

Madalena stared at him.

"Are you hungry?" Angela asked.

"Yes, I am," he said, almost convinced that she was going to say that there was no food for him.

"Sit then," Angela said.

Angus sat opposite Madalena. This wasn't good. He felt vulnerable with this physical proximity threatening to compromise his authority.

"Give me your jacket, Detective," Madalena said. "I can try to patch it up."

Angus was surprised, but he took the jacket off and handed it to Madalena.

"I will warm up the water for you to wash," Angela said in a businesslike tone.

"Thank you. You are very kind," he said to Angela as she set the food in front of him and poured wine.

"Remember that. Tomorrow when you talk to us, you must remember that we have suffered and lost much lately. You must be kind also. As for Pedro Matias, that man has been our living hell. I want you to remember that as well."

Angus didn't say anything. He ate quietly and drank the wine. When

Madalena finished mending the jacket, he looked at it, and he couldn't tell where the rip was.

"It wasn't ripped. The stitching was undone. And I was able to fix it," Madalena explained.

They were quiet.

Angela came in and said, "Your bath is prepared. There is a towel, soap, and a pair of pajamas in the bathroom."

Angus Pomba got up and went to the bathroom, understanding perfectly why his colleagues had failed miserably. He was about to fall under the spell, if he was not careful and if he didn't stick to his plan.

When Dom Carlos got home from the city, the house was silent. But Angela was sitting at the kitchen table, her head in her hands.

He frowned when he saw her.

"Why are you still up?" he asked.

"I was waiting for you," she said.

He frowned.

"There is a detective in the house. The monsignor asked for a detective to look into the disappearances—Manuel, Saul, and Lazarus, as you know. This detective, Angus Pomba, is here tonight because his car was vandalized, and he couldn't get to the city."

"Oh, that's not good … That man is lethal," he murmured.

"Tomorrow he wants me to go to the city and be interrogated at the police station."

"What?" Dom Carlos asked, between irritation and surprise.

"He was very clear that he is not interested in talking to or interviewing people. He will interrogate. I got the feeling that he will use violence if he sees fit.

Dom Carlos knew that. It was the trappings of living in a dictatorship; those in power could do anything.

"Don't worry, Hawk. He will not mistreat you," he said, lightly touching her hand.

"Maybe not, but he will mistreat the others," Angela said.

"What others?" he asked.

"Madalena, Carlota, Nascimento, and Regina Sales. They are going to be interrogated also. And Pedro Matias, but I don't care about him. We are to be there at ten, all of us."

Dom Carlos frowned. "I will go with you to the city," he said. "And I will talk to the chief. Let's say that you and I can only see him at the same time, around two in the afternoon."

Angela heard what she had been hoping to hear. She felt a wave of peace again take hold of her heart.

The next morning, Angus Pomba woke up early to the smell of fresh coffee. He came down and found Angela setting breakfast on the table.

Dona Mafalda was speechless to find a good-looking man in the kitchen with Angela. Introductions were made, and Angus Pomba gave Dona Mafalda a critical look and then dismissed her.

Angela told Angus Pomba that Rosa had gone to the garage, and his car was being fixed at that very moment. "You will be able to be there for your first appointment of the day," Angela said.

Dom Carlos came down and introduced himself to Angus Pomba, who took a list out of his pocket and said, "Who are you again?"

"A lodger, Antonio Nogueira."

Angela smiled.

"I need to interrogate Dom Carlos. Where can I find him?"

Dom Carlos smiled back at Angela and introduced himself again to the detective. "Antonio Nogueira, aka Dom Carlos."

Angus Pomba didn't find it amusing. He pressed his lips into a line and then said, "Interesting."

"I think so too," Dom Carlos said, winking at Angela.

"Tomorrow you have to see me at the station," Angus Pomba said.

"No. Not tomorrow. I am busy tomorrow. I am free today if you wish, but not tomorrow ... Tomorrow, Angela and I have a business meeting in the city, but we can see you today at two, or a little earlier."

Angus Pomba gave him a sideways smirk. "I'm not asking you, Mr. Nogueira. I'm telling you."

"I'm sorry to disappoint you, Detective," Dom Carlos answered matter-of-factly, "because we are not available tomorrow, but we can see you today."

The detective was thinking about whether it was worth creating a conflict with this self-assured man. "Today at two then," the detective said.

Dom Carlos bowed his head and smiled graciously.

When the detective left, Dom Carlos said, "Don't you provoke him or call him Anus as you did yesterday. Don't look at me with that innocent face; I know you called him Anus. Today, you and I are going to talk to that man, and we are going to be very polite. Can you promise me that?" He stared at Angela, waiting for a promise.

"Yes, I promise," Angela answered quietly.

"I promised Lazarus I would look after you, and I'm not doing a very good job," he said. Dom Carlos looked at her for a while before adding, "We will take care of each other."

Angela felt something shift inside of her. She couldn't say what it was, but it was something good. For a fleeting second, she felt complete peace; she knew that everything was going to be all right.

Everybody was talking about the detective from the mainland. This man had come to Hawk Island to crush them like bugs, to pulverize them into oblivion.

The detective had dished justice like a Viking in a plundering mission: Pedro had been grabbed by the testicles and hurled around the interrogating room. He had come home with a black eye, a dislocated shoulder, and a swollen lip. Ascendida was slapped so hard that she fell against the wall and had a bruised cheek. Nascimento had a broken finger. And Carlota was slapped across the face repeatedly until she lost her balance, fell, and rolled under the table. Madalena was sexually assaulted. But the worse treatment had been to Regina Sales: She was raped, beaten, and raped again. The only two people who had a civil conversation with Angus were Dom Carlos and Angela, both at the same time, drinking tea.

The monsignor was beside himself with disgust and fear. The villagers were more than terrified and not really sure if the monsignor could protect them this time.

When the monsignor talked to the chief of police, he got the same refrain. "Your village has been my scourge for years. My friend, they were getting worse, and you are not able to control them any longer."

As much as the monsignor didn't want to hear this, he knew that his friend was right.

Madalena sat by the window looking at her beautiful garden. Tomorrow would be the procession of Jesus Crucified. The village streets were covered with flower carpets, the radios were turned off, and the church was draped in black and purple. There was sadness all around. Not even the promise of spring could erase the veil of sorrow.

She was thinking about her interrogation with Detective Angus Pomba, and she felt dizzy with revolt. He had preyed on her fear, on her loneliness; he knew she was forsaken. She still felt his hand going up her skirt, looking at her, and saying, "I'll stop if you tell me the truth."

"I told you the truth," she said in a whisper, remembering Carlota's warning about the police.

"You know where your husband is, don't you?" his hand stopped and squeezed the inside of her thigh.

"I don't!" she said in horror as she walked backward until her back was against the wall

"Yes you do." His voice was soft and calm.

"Help!" she cried out.

"No one can hear you," he said.

With one hand, he held her wrists above her head and slid the other hand into her pants. She screamed and pushed a knee into his groin. He doubled over in pain, and she ran to the door. She pounded the thick wood and screamed. He came after her and grabbed a handful of hair and turned her around. She spit on him, and he slapped her across the face. He let her go for a second, but Madalena realized in horror that he let her go only to unbuckle his belt and zip down his fly.

There was a knock on the door.

"Detective!" a voice called. "The chief wants to talk to you."

He zipped up his pants; licked his fingers; and said, looking at her, "We are not done."

Madalena ran out of the room, bumping into the officer who had knocked at the door. She went up the stairs and down the corridors, frantically looking for light. Finally, she saw one door open, and she ran there, across the room and into the street.

She was vaguely aware that the secretary at the police station called after her while other people stared, but she just ran.

21

Angus Pomba Must Die

Hours later, Angela and Dom Carlos found Madalena walking home, by the forest road.

"Where is Carlota?" Madalena asked in panic.

"We thought she was with you," Dom Carlos started to explain.

And then they realized that their experience with the detective had been different from Madalena's. They turned around in a hurry and headed for the police station. When they got to Carlota, she was sitting in the waiting room, her hat askew, her face red and swollen, a bleeding lip. A poised secretary offered her a hot drink.

Angus didn't bother to interrogate Carlota; he simply asked where Saul was, and when she said she didn't know, he hit her.

Carlota didn't even cry as he slapped her. She could only think of Madalena, who had been separated from the rest, as soon as they had reached the police station. What had he done to her? And she prayed for Madalena while being beaten.

Angus was so furious with those rats from Two Brooks that, when he faced Pedro, he grabbed him by the testicles and said, "Kneel, you fucker! You are mine!"

And Pedro knelt and cried and promised to tell everything he knew—to inform on Angela, on Dom Carlos, on Madalena, or anyone Detective Pomba needed information on.

Angela and Dom Carlos learned the full extent of the assaults from Regina, who sat in her kitchen, recounting every detail, as if to memorize everything, every slap and kick, every injury, one by one, including her own.

"He had a hard time with Nascimento," Regina said, referring to Angus. "When he went for her, she ran around the room gyrating like a top and the man couldn't grab her; the most he got was one of her fingers, and she bit him. She was flying around the room like a blind bat …until she blundered into the door, opened it, and ran out. After that, he locked the door and started on us."

Regina took a long breath and continued, "He slapped Ascendida so hard that her ears are still ringing." Regina cleared her throat, forcing her voice to be steady. "He had us all together to witness each other's humiliation ... Except for Madalena; he had her in a separate room. We were in awe looking at Pedro being assaulted ... It was like a catastrophe ...something so horrendous that we couldn't stop looking ... I can still hear his groveling and begging ... promising to help the police." She took a deep breath. "Carlota fell with a punch in the face. She didn't make a sound. I knew she was thinking about Madalena; what had he done to her?"

In a very calm voice, Regina concluded, "Angus Pomba must die!"

Angela and Dom Carlos sat quietly listening to Regina's voice, as if she had hypnotized them. And then, as if propelled by a motor, Angela threw her arms around Dom Carlos's neck and started to sob. He took her in his arms and swayed her in a comforting rhythm. He pressed her head against his chest, and Angela heard his heartbeat gently drum in her ear, like a blessing.

That evening, Dom Carlos went to the monsignor's house. As soon as he entered the front door, Catarina made a face because there was going to be a fight. But much to Catarina's surprise, the monsignor motioned Dom Carlos into the study and closed the door. And they talked without yelling at each other.

The monsignor looked out the window. The afternoon sun was elongating the shadows on the street. The men were coming home from their fields, walking slowly, enjoying the quiet late afternoon, oblivious to the monsignor's shattered peace.

"I am here because of Angus Pomba," Dom Carlos said. "I talked with the chief of police, and he basically said that you asked him to bring someone tough, one who could not be seduced. I want you to call him off. He sexually assaulted Madalena, and he told her that he was not done with her. She is terrified. He also assaulted Regina and hurt the others to a lesser degree ... He is coming back ... I'm sure, and so is the chief."

"I know," the monsignor said in a subdued voice. "I can't call him off. He established that a crime has been committed, and now I cannot call him off."

The two men were quiet. They both knew that the police could do anything they wanted. They were only accountable to themselves.

"The chief of police will not support me," the monsignor said. "He told me that Two Brooks has been laughing at the law, the villagers doing whatever they see fit, for a long time. At first, he believed that I could keep them in line, but now he thinks that I lost control."

On his way back home, Dom Carlos stopped by Regina's house. She was brooding, sitting by the fire in her kitchen. She seemed almost like a different person from the Regina he knew—always ready for her games of seduction.

He touched her shoulder lightly and said, "I'm so sorry I was not able to help you."

She lowered her head and let out long, deep sobs that had been stuck in her chest for years. It was a sound that made Dom Carlos's hair stand up; it was visceral and wounded. He took her in his arms and rocked her gently to appease her pain. It took a long time before she stepped away and turned her back to him, as if embarrassed of her outburst.

"I've been mistreated before, and worse," she said quietly. "But this man is bent on hurting us all—Two Brooks. He said it while he …you know …that we didn't know …how he was going to fuck us all."

Dom Carlos frowned.

"He said that he had unfinished business with Madalena and Angela," Regina continued. "He said that he has surprises for them—that Angela is not a sacred cow. She's going to get it when she least expects it."

He let out a deep sigh. He could protect Angela, but to what degree? And furthermore, would she allow him to take the necessary measures? She was the most stubborn, and the most mulish person he knew.

"As long as you know that he is not done with Madalena and Angela …or any of us for that matter," Regina concluded.

Angela was setting the table for dinner when Carlota came through the door covered with sweat and tears and her nose dripping blood.

"They took Madalena," she said, out of breath. "The police took Madalena to the city."

Carlota briefly told them that a police officer had come to the door and arrested Madalena for obstructing justice. And when Carlota had stepped between the police officer and Madalena, he'd pushed her. She had fallen, hitting her head and losing her senses for a while. When she woke up, Madalena was gone.

Dom Carlos got in his car and flew down the village. He stopped at the monsignor's house, shoving him into the car as he explained the events.

When the police officer took Madalena to the interrogation room she was no longer crying. She walked in and stood still in the middle of the room, looking around with frightened eyes. The room had no windows; the walls were made of thick stone like the floor. A bright electric light hung high up on the ceiling; a chair and a table in the middle of it were the only furnishings.

It had been less than two weeks since Angus Pomba had molested her, and here she was again.

As if conjured up by her thoughts, the door opened and Angus Pomba came in.

"We meet again," Angus said with a mean smirk.

"Please," Madalena said. "I know nothing more than what I've told you."

"So …you are going to insist on lying, are you?"

Madalena was even thinking about telling him about that dark letter she had read from Paulo Amora. But she would be betraying Saul and Carlota. And this man didn't want the truth; he wanted to hurt her, even if she told him everything she knew.

He walked up to her and started to unbuckle his belt and undo his fly.

Madalena screamed and ran toward the door and started to pound it in a replay of a terrible nightmare.

"You have no one to hear you, Mrs. Amora. Your husband is gone, your lover is gone, your father is a douchebag, and you have no one."

Madalena had nothing to fight him with. She took off her shoes and threw them at him. He ducked and laughed.

Swiftly, he grabbed her and pulled her arms behind her back, pushing her toward the table and forcing her facedown. She hit the surface of the table hard while Angus Pomba lifted her dress up.

She screamed and struggled as she felt his hands pulling her clothes off.

Suddenly she was let go.

Madalena was dazed for a few seconds, and then she straightened up. Behind her, the young officer who had arrested her was looking at Angus Pomba, unconscious on the floor.

His police stick was still up in the air from hitting Angus Pomba on the back of the head, and he looked terrified, thinking that he had killed his boss.

But Angus was not dead. Slowly Angus started to moan, struggled to get up, and glared at the officer, realizing what had happened.

"Angus Pomba you are under arrest for assaulting a defenseless citizen of Hawk Island," the young officer said and placed the handcuffs on Angus.

The chief of police, the monsignor, and Dom Carlos came running into the room to see Angus handcuffed and with his pants and underwear at his feet.

Angus started to demand that the handcuffs be removed. The chief of police motioned for the keys to the handcuffs from the young officer.

Angus Pomba rubbed his wrists and pulled his pants up as soon as the handcuffs were off. Then he said, "This little prick is interfering with police procedure and with the interrogation of a suspect." He pointed to the young police officer.

The monsignor, Dom Carlos, and Madalena hugged each other like a strange trinity. Then Madalena started to cry. She sounded like an animal that had been trapped and was in terrible physical pain.

The chief said to the young officer, "Officer Balthazar, tomorrow we will debrief; until then, not a word to anyone. You may go."

The chief looked at his two friends comforting the poor woman.

"Angus," the chief said, "I recommend that you leave tonight if you can. I'll find you a flight leaving from the American base."

Angus, still tucking his shirt into his pants, addressed the chief. "You know very well that I get results; don't interfere if you want results!"

The monsignor walked up to the chief and said, trembling with rage, "Are you going to allow this rapist to get away scot-free?"

"My friend, one thing at a time!" the chief said, full of frustration. "I want this man to leave the island before someone kills him. I don't need any more problems."

Angus Pomba frowned and showed his teeth like a mad dog. He said to the chief, "I'm not going anywhere! I'm going to finish this case!"

The monsignor, Madalena, and Dom Carlos were walking to the door when Madalena stopped and turned to Angus. Her face was blotchy, and her lip bled from hitting the table.

Angus looked at her and said, "I'm not done with you!"

The room became completely silent as she turned slowly to Angus and fell on her knees at his feet. Like a flash, she grabbed him by the crotch with both hands and squeezed with all her might as a terrible scream ripped the air. Angus hit Madalena on the head, trying to get her off him, but she was not letting go.

She screamed even louder, and not even when he fell unconscious in front of her did she let go.

It took three men to take her away from Angus, now a heap of feces and blood.

When they took Madalena to the chief's office, an ambulance came in haste to take Angus to the hospital, with ruptured testicles.

The whole village seemed to be at Angela's house waiting for news. When Dom Carlos and the monsignor got there, they gave the neighbors a brief account and assured them that Madalena was now safe at home. Everyone left, looking back as if trying to catch some nuance that they'd missed.

Dona Mafalda, Angela, Regina Sales, and Dom Carlos sat silently at the table.

"Is it over?" Regina asked.

"No, not over," Dom Carlos answered.

The women looked at him.

"Angus may be in the hospital for a while. But he will be back, I'm sure. And even if we convince the chief to send him away, someone else will be coming; the investigation will continue. They will send someone else, hopefully someone who is ethical," Dom Carlos said morosely.

"At least that man is gone for a while," Dona Mafalda said. "What a menace!"

Regina licked her broken lip and got up. "Good night, all," she said. "I pity the fool who messes with us." She looked back at Dom Carlos and then asked, "She literally busted his balls …eh?"

They smiled at Regina, who was vindicated for being raped. Regina could never forgive those who forced her to have sex. If there was one thing that she had control over, it was sex. And to take that away from her was to take almost everything.

"Angus is a pig, and pigs should be slaughtered," Regina said as she left.

Nixon screeched under the table and ran to Dom Carlos, who appeased his panic with soothing sounds.

For a while, they were rooted in the kitchen without a word and with the clear feeling that something else was going to happen.

Slowly, Dona Mafalda got up and said, "I'm going to bed; I'm mentally and physically exhausted … Every day on this island I feel like a survivor of an apocalypse."

Dom Carlos raked his hair with his fingers, the sign of worry.

"What is it?" Angela asked.

"Nothing," he murmured.

"Don't lie to me, Zorro. I know you are worried."

"This island is a terrible place," he said.

"Made even worse by cruel mainlanders," she quipped.

He kept her at arms' length, squeezing her shoulders gently. "I'm offended," he said.

"Except for you. You are the token man; there is no one like you."

Dom Carlos gasped. "I'm a token?"

"Yes. There is no man like you, and I don't know if it is good or bad. There is no one I can compare you to, and at times, it is quite disconcerting. It is like a new taste, a new food, and one doesn't know if one likes it or not … because there is nothing to compare it with. Oh …yes …it tastes like chicken, or it tastes like cilantro … And then one can make a decision …but nothing compares to you."

This was said in measured tones, as if Angela was merely thinking it.

Dom Carlos laughed, waking the menagerie that had been nervous and sleeping with one eye open.

"Spring is here, and things have to be better. They simply have to," Angela said, looking up at his laughing face. She was not laughing; she desperately prayed for peace.

The Sacristy met again, at the end of the day, in the beginning of summer to talk about the happenings in the village. The Americans were coming again, Maria Augusta was going to marry her Canadian, and everyone was hoping for Lucia or Samuel Barcos to work up the nerve and declare their love to each other. But they didn't, and poor Olivia Dores was the one who paid the price.

"It was a terrible thing," Nascimento said. "Poor Olivia. Full of hope that her man was coming to marry her, and he proposes to Lucia."

The other women were silent, thinking that not even love was willing to be kind.

"I have something to tell you," Angela said. "And it is far worse than poor Olivia's broken heart."

Angela felt her stomach flip before saying, "Angus Pomba didn't leave the island. After he was treated, the chief wanted him to leave, but he refused." She put up a hand to stop the questions. Then she added, "The chief has the authority to take him off the case, but he doesn't have the authority to send him away. He could arrest him. However, the chief is trying to hide the miserable fiasco of Angus's interventions, and his arrest would only call attention to the issue. Angus Pomba asked to be transferred to Hawk Island, and he says that he has unfinished business with some people."

"Who told you that?" Madalena asked, perplexed.

"Dom Carlos. He said that the chief wanted to warn Two Brooks." Angela made a sound of frustration. "Actually, what the chief of police told Dom Carlos was that Angus was out for blood and pussy."

"Dom Carlos said pussy?" Nascimento asked, incredulously.

The other women jumped on her as if she had blasphemed because of the irreverent remark during this very serious conversation. But with fascination, Nascimento was imagining Dom Carlos's mouth saying pussy—his beautiful lips forming the word …*pussy*.

"So … Angus has the chief by the balls because the chief denies the attacks," Ascendida said.

"Yes, in a nutshell," Angela concluded. "Officer Balthazar didn't see anything; the chief didn't do anything. Angus Pomba denies any allegations against him, and he asked to be taken off the case for health reasons."

"I bet Officer Balthazar was promoted for being an outstanding public servant …and for being quiet about this fiasco," Ascendida said.

"And then they act surprised if there is such a thing as Night Justice," Madalena murmured.

They were silent for a long time. The night was beautiful and seemed more quiet than usual. They heard Luciana sing.

You think that love is in your head,
You plot around to make it gone …

Angus Pomba should have left when he had a chance. The chief of police was green around the gills when he made a statement to the media about the death of Detective Angus Pomba:

It appears that Detective Angus Pomba was mauled to death by a bull in the village of Two Brooks. Although he was no longer investigating a case there, he was working to tight up loose ends so he could transfer the case to a new inspector coming soon. Angus Pomba was a proud investigator and had a near perfect record of solved cases.

Detective Angus Pomba was found in the pastures of the Amora family in Two Brooks. It can be deduced that Detective Angus Pomba went to look for some of his former suspects, and he came face-to-face with a bull. He was gored to death. Witnesses say that they could not distract the bull from attacking the detective, although they tried.

Angela and her neighbors sat around the radio. They were quiet and pale. Regina Sales looked down at her hands, and Madalena looked at Regina Sales. Maria Gomes made a keening sound as if she was crying, and Carlota looked at her sharply.

It is over, they thought. *It is over at last.*

They heard Luciana sing:

> How many secrets can your heart hold?
> Tell me, beloved; tell me lies instead
> How many secrets waiting to be told?
> And cries of denial when all is done and said?

When the neighbors went home, Dom Carlos stayed in the same spot, as if rooted.

"Strange thing, is it not?" he asked. "This world is so big, and Detective Pomba dies in Two Brooks. Was he lured to the pastures, Angela?" The tone of his voice was low and steady.

"How would I know?' she snapped.

Dom Carlos was looking at her as if he saw her for the first time.

"What have you done?" he asked in a whisper.

"Nothing. At the time he was gored, I was with you," she said defiantly.

The monsignor waited for a confession that never came. The person or persons who took Detective Pomba to the pastures to meet his fate were not confessing anything. The monsignor had a feeling that his peace of mind was slowly slipping away again.

His friend the chief of police was not making demands on anyone. He made his statement to the public, and that was that. But the monsignor could not reconcile with the immorality of the whole thing. This people who he loved dearly had murdered a man. His thoughts went straight to Dona Lidia's murder.

The monsignor was kneeling in front of Jesus Crucified. The cross had lost a peace on top because the men who were carrying the float were in such haste to get from under it that they didn't lower the float and almost decapitated Jesus at the church door.

It was because of that procession that he had slapped Dona Mafalda. The monsignor groaned at the memory of Dona Mafalda spinning around with the impact and falling at his feet. He didn't want to think about Dona Mafalda now. He had bigger problems.

"Help me, Jesus!" he said. "When I asked you to protect Madalena, I didn't have murder in mind." The monsignor looked intently at Jesus as if waiting for an answer.

"Let it go!" a voice said from the back of the church.

The monsignor knew who it was. "You are not my friend," the monsignor said to Jesus before turning back to Dom Carlos.

"Angela engineered all of this. It has Angela written all over," the monsignor said, sitting next to Dom Carlos and letting out a long, tired sigh.

"Maybe, but it was not Angela who took him up to the pastures," Dom Carlos answered. "She was with me."

"It took more than one person to bring him up to the pastures and then let a raging bull loose on the man … And he was not a stupid man … This was a plot that involved more than one person," the monsignor said.

"Let it go," Dom Carlos said again. "The chief made his statement, and it's done."

"You know who did this, don't you?" the monsignor accused.

"No, not this time …" Dom Carlos said pensively.

Dona Mafalda felt her heart swell when she looked at Dom Carlos coming into the garden. He made her feel as if the world had no fault. His beauty stunned her, and his kindness left her weak. She was irrefutably lost for him, and there was no other way but to confess. She had been trying to summon up the courage to tell him, but every time she wanted to invite him for a session of Beethoven, something terrible happened. It was as if God was trying to derail her intentions. This time, she was going to tell him. This time, she would not allow anything to get in her way, not even if the chief of police came in to arrest Angela for killing Angus Pomba.

Dom Carlos smiled and sat next to her on the garden bench. He squeezed her hand, resting on her lap. "And how are you holding up? I've …heard that the monsignor slapped you … I'm sorry," he said.

"Well …in the scheme of things, that was nothing. But I was perplexed by the monsignor's audacity. You know … I've traveled to many places before," she said, turning a bit to face him. "I can say with all honesty that I haven't ever found a place like this village. Do you think it is something in the water?"

He chuckled. "I don't know, but one thing is for sure: If you are not vigilant, you'll turn into one of them. It is contagious, to say the least."

"Please! That in itself is a very frightening thought," she said, laughing and imagining punching the monsignor on the nose.

Dona Mafalda was trying to remember the opening lines she'd rehearsed to confess her love for Dom Carlos. She couldn't remember it, or it simply didn't make sense now.

"I've been trying to tell you something, Dom Carlos," she said in a quiet tone, her voice shaking a little.

He turned to her and waited. His beautiful green eyes searched her face.

"I'm in love with you," she said. "I'm sorry if I make you uncomfortable, but I had to let you know … Even if you don't love me, I've been honest with myself."

"Oh Dona Mafalda!" he murmured. He took a long, deep breath. "I'm honored and …ashamed. I'm honored because you love me and ashamed because I am in love with someone else and don't have your courage to tell her. I am afraid she will say no."

Dona Mafalda smiled, hiding her lacerated heart. She had known that this would be the result of her love offering. A woman always knows these things.

"How could she say no?" she murmured.

Dom Carlos didn't answer. He closed his eyes and lifted his face to the dark sky.

"Do I know her?" Dona Mafalda asked.

"No," he lied. "Could this be our secret?" he asked, holding her hand in his.

"Yes," she said, and her heart was breaking.

It was summer.

Two Brooks was preparing to receive their emigrants. They started to arrive, smelling like America and looking like movie stars. The girls and the boys put on their best clothes and went out, hoping that, next year, they would be the ones visiting and looking like brand-new people, shining like precious jewels.

At Angela's, everything fell into a sweet pattern of peace.

At the end of the day, Dona Mafalda, Dom Carlos, and Angela had dinner like a family and talked about their days. They read aloud in the evening, taking turns, while the others relaxed, closing their eyes and savoring the peace. Dona Mafalda brought down her Victrola to the living room, and they had Victrola nights with Beethoven and Mozart and sometimes Wagner, although only Dom Carlos liked Wagner and his thunderous musical statements. At times, Dom Carlos and Dona Mafalda would conspire about sending lodgers away, so there would be only the three of them. They would conspire on ways to get rid of Hercules, but it was always a halfhearted plan because the cat, although incorrigible, was Angela's second love—the first being Lazarus.

And when it came to Lazarus, Angela looked for him in everything she did, everything she remembered. There were days that she felt such naked sorrow that she would lose hope of ever moving forward. On other days, she thought of him in the light, in peace, with God …but never gone. She talked to him and closed herself up in the woodshop just to be surrounded by the smell of cedar. But there were also times of hope, and those times were far more frequent than despair.

Dom Carlos continued growing his business in the island and having fantastic fights with the monsignor. No one knew why those two hated each other so much but couldn't stay away either. Dom Carlos was as mysterious as ever, and the romantic tales abounded, making him even more desired by women of all ages. His life of Zorro was dormant but not gone. Once in a while, he would mount his horse and go out in the night with the speed of lightning, as if he was exorcizing a demon, and then lie to Angela so she wouldn't worry about the boogeyman or the werewolf being caught.

Dona Mafalda continued to wait for love to be kind, preferably with Dom Carlos. However, in her fastidious way of looking at the world, she couldn't hope. Her love offering to Dom Carlos was never spoken of again; it was as if it didn't happen, except for that dull pain lodged in her heart, like a chronic condition.

The monsignor was suspicious of peace in Two Brooks.

No one was fighting or being defiant, even Pedro was subdued, afraid of Night Justice and afraid of those who'd killed Angus. Oh yes, he had no doubt that someone had killed Angus. But since Angus, there were no murders, no misdeeds, and even the chief of police was breathing a sigh of relief that Two Brooks was like a sleepy place, an enchanted forest of fiends.

Madalena patiently waited for Saul, imagining him under the same sun that touched her or the same moon that came through her window. She wrote letters of love and recrimination, and then she vowed to fall in love with an immigrant and leave Hawk Island. At times, she wanted to hurt him. Most of the time she wanted to love him …wherever he was. Once in a while, she would have a good cry with Carlota, remembering the days when they were so happy.

Carlota continued to receive dark letters from afar. There was a pursuit of gold and magic in Paulo's letters that left Carlota quietly worried. If there were gold to be found, would Carlota think that she'd paid a too heavy price for it?

While embroidering tablecloths and cotton sheets, she was thinking about the value of gold. Her Paulo and Saul were more than precious. There was no gold on this earth that could pay for a day without them. And with a sorrow so deep that she could hardly breathe, she would get up and seek the company of her two new best friends—Maria Gomes and Regina Sales.

How did she live so long without the friendship of other women?

Nascimento married her beautiful Jaime Nobre. Every day, she promised to resist the hunger to look into other people's lives, but almost every night, she failed and went out like a prowling cat, especially on nights of full moon.

Ascendida's family mourned the death of José Eremita. They'd never thought that they were going to miss that old man as much as they did. He was always ready for a laugh and a glass of wine. Aldo missed him more than anyone; if José Eremita was a penance for Ascendida, for Aldo he was a friend and companion on his nights of card games and drinking. And now without José, Aldo drank for both of them. "One for me and one for José." And he would look sadly at the two glasses, side by side, on top of the bar.

Rosa, now totally convinced that Angela could not live without her, was happy and ready to work and gossip, just like her birth mother, who she vaguely remembered. Rosa was better than the radio for news. And even Dom Carlos and Dona Mafalda, who read the newspaper, could not live without Rosa's broadcasts. Rosa loved her adoptive parents and siblings with the blindness of a fanatic. Aldo was under her protection. She prayed for her dead family, for Lazarus not to haunt her, and for Aldo—for his lost peace of mind, for the joy that should be his, and for the sadness in his eyes.

Regina Sales slowly returned to her old self, administering her attentions to unsuspecting men, especially Angela's lodgers, who came to the village to sell their wares and left knowing a lot more about pleasure.

Regina had a few secrets to nurse that not even confession could appease. Furthermore, she didn't believe in confession. If there was a person who knew how treacherous confession could be, she was the one; she had known that since she was a child. Had she ever been a child? It was so long ago that it was no longer true. Some women were never children, ever. But she was happy now. Everything was back to normal, and only once in a while did she wake up with a nightmare about Angus.

Maria Gomes, much to her husband's chagrin, became close friends with Regina Sales and Carlota Amora. No one could explain the closeness of these three so very different women; but they were close—tea drinking close, and at times, moonshine drinking close. They relished their time together to embroider tablecloths with mystical themes and horned beasts. The village waited for an explanation about such strange friendship, but none came.

And so Two Brooks seemed to be in a perpetual state of waiting, albeit like Damocles gazing at the sword. They almost could touch hope, if they dared.

Printed in the United States
By Bookmasters